The Covenant
A Tale of the Antichrist
Tom Lewis

This book contains material protected under international and Federal Copyright laws and treaties. Any unauthorized reprint or use of this material, other than excerpts or quotes contained in blogs or reviews, is prohibited. No part of this book may be reproduced or transmitted in any form or by any means, electronic or otherwise, without the express permission of the author/publisher.

This book is a work of fiction. Any resemblance to actual persons, places, or entities, is purely coincidental.

Copyright © 2023 by Tom Lewis
All rights reserved.

In loving memory of the best man I've ever known. I miss you, Dad. Enjoy Heaven!

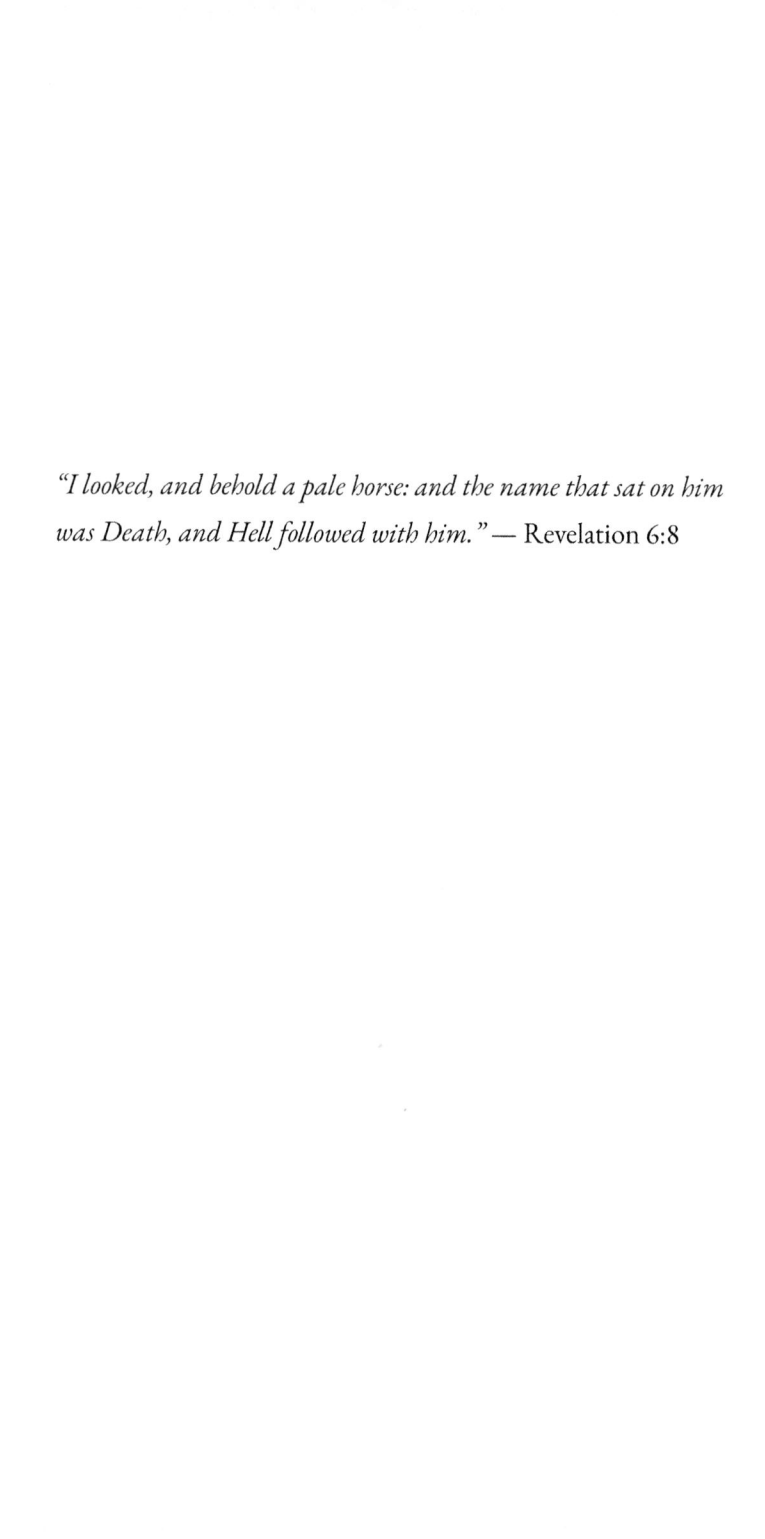

"I looked, and behold a pale horse: and the name that sat on him was Death, and Hell followed with him." — Revelation 6:8

Contents

Prologue	1
Part One: The Acheron Files	13
1. Kenzie	14
2. Life in Hell	20
3. The Whispers	32
4. The Disappearance	38
5. The Creek	46
6. The Long Road Out of Hell	54
7. An Exorcist's Tale	67
8. Acheron the Accursed	73
9. The Shunned City	86
10. The Thing in the Moonlight	90
11. Question Everything	102
12. The Cave	110
Part Two: The Prophecy	124
13. A Child Shall be born	125

14.	Stigmata	139
15.	Lilith	144
16.	In Aeternum Regnabit	150
17.	A Subtle Stirring	159
18.	Something Awaking	162
19.	Secret Things	169
20.	What the Storm Brought	175
21.	Something in the Room	193
22.	The Morgue	206
23.	The City in the Mist	214
24.	Destiny	220
25.	The People of the Covenant	225
26.	Prophecy	234
27.	Sanguine	241
28.	Acheron's Son	253
29.	The Message	270
30.	Best Laid Plans	280
31.	Thieves in the Night	286
32.	The Thing in the Window	299
33.	Wolves in the Night	306
34.	The Map	321
35.	Allies	325

Part Three: When Gods Walk the Earth	332
36. Final Farewells	333
37. The Dogs	340
38. Legacy	345
39. The Lost Voyage	351
40. They Came in the Fog	354
41. The Screaming Starts	360
42. Acheron	367
43. Prophets	376
44. When Gods Walk the Earth	383
The Author	393
The Necromancer	394
Hell: The Possession and Exorcism of Cassie Stevens	395
Aftermath	396

Prologue

Capetown, Maine, June 21, 1692

The blood moon loomed ominously in the night sky. Beneath its crimson eye lay the shores of Hallows Pointe, a narrow stretch of rocky coast, lined by towering cliffs on one side and the Atlantic's crashing waves on the other.

High above the icy waters, thirteen-year-old Jimmy Crawford and his eleven-year-old sister Sarah picked their way down the cliff's face to the shore. When they reached the bottom, he pointed to a large outcrop bulging from the cliff's face towards the ocean.

"'Tis over there that I saw it," he said.

Sarah brushed the dirt from her skirt and looked over at it. "Are ye sure 'tis a cave?"

"I think so," he said. "The opening is out by the water."

Sarah looked up at the blood moon, brooding high above them. She shivered as a chill brushed her.

"Did ye see the moon, Jimmy?" she said. "'Tis a blood moon. They say 'tis a bad omen."

Jimmy felt his skin prickle as he looked at it. The village elders taught them to fear such moons, for beneath their faint glow, unspeakable horrors crawled from forgotten graves to prey on the living. He took a nervous look around to make sure nothing was creeping up on them from the darkness, then turned back to her.

"We shan't be long. I promise."

He took her hand and led her across the slick stones to the end of the outcrop where it faced out to sea. A large orifice opened at its end, tall and wide enough for a grown man to walk through. He slid two sticks from his belt, both with their ends dipped in tar and wrapped in cloth, then lit them with a flint. He handed one to her, then waved his through the opening, watching its flickering light disappear down a long tunnel into the cliff.

"'Tis a tunnel," he said. "Come, let us see where it goes."

Sarah took one more look at the moon before following him down the tunnel. It continued for about twenty feet before opening into a large cavern deep inside the cliff. Jimmy swept his torch around, watching its warm glow flicker across the walls and high ceiling, before fading into the gloom at the back of the cave.

"Jimmy, look," said Sarah, sweeping her torch across a table-sized block in the chamber's center. A crimson cloth lay across it, with four golden candelabra on each side.

The kids slowly approached it until they were close enough to see an array of cryptic symbols woven into the cloth. The symbol in the center showed a serpent wrapped around a sun-like image, and to the left and right of it were eight-pointed stars, with eyes in the center.

Sarah swallowed and took a nervous step back. "Those are the symbols father spoke of. They are devil's sign."

Jimmy took a step back beside her. "Are ye sure?"

She nodded. "'Tis a bad place we are in, Jimmy. We must go and tell father of what we have found."

"I told him of the cave and the strange men I saw enter, but knew not of what was inside. Come, let us hurry."

They turned to leave when they saw the dancing yellow glow of torches coming down the tunnel.

"Someone comes," he whispered, looking around for a place to hide. "We can hide behind those rocks."

Taking her hand, they hurried over to a boulder near the entrance and crawled into the narrow space behind it. He quickly snuffed out their torches, plunging the chamber into darkness.

Seconds later, the chamber warmed in the eerie glow of torchlight. Twenty men, dressed in the dark hooded robes of monks, walked solemnly in and over to the stone block. Two men carried a large ornamental chest and set it down beside the block. Others lit the candelabra and placed their torches in nooks along the walls.

Jimmy took a quick peek around the side of the boulder, then pulled his head back. "'Tis the witches of Acheron," he whispered, giving her hand a comforting squeeze.

On the shore outside, four long ropes uncoiled down the cliff's face. Ten men climbed down them to the shore, then waited while the men up top lowered three wooden casks of gunpowder before climbing down and joining them.

"Where is this cave of which your son spoke, Nathanial?" said Joshua, brushing the dirt from a crimson sash slung across his shoulder.

"'Tis over beyond the outcrop," said Nathanial Crawford in his deep, gruff voice. At well over six feet tall, with the build of a blacksmith, Crawford was a bear of a man, looked upon by the nearby settlement of Capetown as their patriarch. Like Joshua and the rest of this brigand, he wore the crimson sash of the Brotherhood of Zion, a fraternity of men sworn to purge the region of the scourges of witchcraft and devilry.

Crawford led the men over to the outcrop, where he crept up to the opening and looked inside. Torchlight flickered at the far end.

"They be inside doing their witchery," he said, easing back to the men. He turned to the ones with the casks. "You men, place the casks inside the entrance. The rest of you, be ready with your rifles."

The men sprang to their tasks. Three of them rolled the casks to the opening, while the others loaded their muskets. Crawford joined the men at the opening and helped them insert fuses into the casks. When they finished, he removed a flint from his pocket.

"Get back to the others and find cover," he said and watched them hurry off. When everyone was clear, he struck the flint against a stone, spraying the fuses with sparks. He raced back to his men as thin flames trailed up the fuses to the casks.

Within seconds, the casks exploded in three massive concussions. Stones, dirt, and debris exploded from the entrance as the outcrop crashed down in a dense cloud of dust.

As the dust settled, the men came out from behind their cover to stare in awe at the mound of rubble. Crawford spat in contempt at the demolished stones, but years of experience dampened his optimism at this ending the scourge.

"God, grant they lie still," he muttered.

Capetown, Maine, Present Day

A fierce storm pounded the coast that night, sending waves crashing high against the jagged rocks of a long stone jetty. At its far end stood an aging lighthouse, its powerful beam scattered in the storm's gusts.

Floyd Monroe watched from the kitchen window of a small, weathered cottage beside the lighthouse tower. Despite living in New England for seventy years, he never got used to these Nor'easters; and now, as the lighthouse keeper, he had a front-row seat to their fury. They scared him, but not just from the torrents. This was Capetown, which had a reputation for the eerie and unexplained, and he'd heard talk on the docks of the strange things fishermen saw in the squalls. Things best unmentioned on nights like this.

He headed into the living room, where a TV against the far wall crackled with static. The reception came from a pair of rabbit ear antennas that belonged in a museum. On a good day, they picked up a few leftover UHF and VHF channels, letting him watch 'Andy Griffith' and 'I Love Lucy' reruns. The rest of the time, it was static.

His German Shepherd 'Zeus' anxiously paced the floor. Like most dogs, Zeus sensed the thunder ahead of the lightning; and from his rolled back ears and lowered head, Floyd could see there was about to be a big one.

When the lightning flashed, it lit the room like a spotlight. A second later, thunder exploded like an artillery shell outside. It rattled the walls; and as usually happened, the power went out.

"Oh, for Pete's sake," Floyd groaned in the darkness. He walked back through the opening into the kitchen and looked out the window. Power in the tower was also out. It meant he would need to go out into the storm to start its generator.

And in all likelihood, *She* would be there, waiting in the darkness for him.

A low whine came from his side. He looked down at Zeus, staring nervously at the door.

"Yeah. I ain't that thrilled about goin' out there either," he said to the dog. "Any chance of you comin' in the tower with me this time?" He said this knowing full well the dog wouldn't go anywhere near the tower at night.

Night was when *she* came.

"Didn't think so."

Floyd threw on his slicker, then, grabbing a flashlight from a kitchen drawer, he and Zeus trudged off through the storm.

Like clockwork, Zeus stopped when they were halfway down the path to the tower.

"Okay, chicken. You wait here."

Floyd ran the rest of the way to the tower. Opening its heavy wooden door, he shined his flashlight around the cylindrical room before going inside. Shadows from workbenches and equipment danced across the walls; but luckily, no sign of *her*. He hurried over to the generator and saw there was enough fuel to run it till morning. He turned the key and pulled down on a long lever. With a groan and wheeze, it sputtered on.

From outside came sudden barks. Floyd froze. The barks meant *she* was there, drifting somewhere in the dark tower, and he had to get out fast. He dashed across the room and out the door, slamming it shut behind them, then raced up the path to Zeus. To his surprise, he found the dog barking at the distant shore, and not at the tower.

"Whatcha see, boy?" Floyd said, cupping his hand above his eyes to shield out the rain as he stared into the distance. He could barely make out the faint outlines of the tall cliffs bordering the shore's inland side. They ran the length of the peninsula, from the southern tip where he stood, to the rugged region far to the north; and having lived in Capetown his entire life, Floyd knew every inch of them. Which was what caused him to pause when he saw something on the cliff's face he hadn't seen before. It was a dark splotch that stood out from the cliff's faint gray outline. He blinked several times just to be sure, but it was still there.

"Is that what you're lookin' at?" he said, looking down at the dog, who continued staring at the shore. "How about we go have a look and see what it is.

Floyd trudged off across the jetty to the shore, with Zeus following several feet behind. This southern section of shore, known as Hallows Pointe, was narrow and rocky, with cliffs towering high on its western side, and the Atlantic's icy waves pounding the stones on its eastern side. As they neared the area where he saw the dark splotch, his flashlight swept across large chunks of rock and debris, like someone emptied a dump truck of rubble on the shore. He shined his flashlight over to the cliff, where he saw the source of the rubble.

The lightning strike had blown an opening in an outcrop along the cliff's face.

"Well, I'll be damned," Floyd muttered as he walked over to the opening and shined his flashlight inside. "You seein' this, Zeus?"

From behind him came a pitiful whine. He looked back and saw his dog anxiously pacing ten yards away.

"It's just a cave, dummy. It ain't gonna hurt ya."

But no amount of coaxing would get the dog to come any closer. Floyd finally let out a groan.

"Okay. You wait here and I'll be right back."

Floyd stepped through the opening into a dark, narrow tunnel, shining his flashlight ahead of him as he went. It continued for a dozen yards before opening into a large cavern.

"You're kiddin' me," he muttered, shining his light across the walls and high ceiling, then towards the back, where it disappeared in the gloom. He shined it back across the floor and over to a stone block in the chamber's center. A crimson cloth lay across it, molded and mildewed with age, but he could make out what looked like cryptic symbols stitched into it. On the ground around the block lay several golden candelabra, along with clumps of dark brown cloth, half buried beneath years of sediment.

Floyd walked over to a clump and nudged it with his foot. Something rattled inside it like sticks. He knelt beside it and slowly pulled the cloth back before recoiling in shock.

Inside it lay a corpse, its brown decayed skin clinging like dried, crinkled paper to its skeleton.

San Gabriel, Honduras

Twelve-year-old Anna Lucia Ramirez awoke to a loud crash of thunder outside. She had dreamed deeply that night, and in her dream, the *Lady* came to her again with a dire message. A time of great sorrows and strife would soon befall the world.

These dreams of the Lady were nothing new for the young girl. She had dreamed of her for several months now, ever since the fever that nearly killed her; and Anna Lucia knew it was the Lady who made the fever go away when the doctors couldn't help her.

Anna Lucia hopped from bed, threw on a woolen poncho, and raced from the small adobe house she shared with her parents and younger brother and sister.

Rain battered the small mountain village of San Gabriel, turning its dirt roads into deep mud puddles. Anna Lucia splashed through them as she hurried across the village to the small church on the far side. The storm had knocked out the power, making it hard to see the dark houses and shops lining the narrow road; but up ahead, she saw the flickering candlelight in the church's stained-glass windows, and used that to guide her.

Anna Lucia reached the church and went inside. It was empty and quiet, except for the patter of rain on the roof and windows. At the far end, candles flickered on either side of the tabernacle behind the altar. Along the walls were statues of saints, with rows of small candles flickering in front of them, but it was the statue of the Virgin Mary that she focused on. The one that resembled the Lady in her dreams.

Anna Lucia went over to the statue, lit one of the small candles on the tray in front of it, and knelt down. She made the Sign of the Cross and looked up at the statue.

It was bleeding.

Anna Lucia rose to her feet and leaned in closer to the statue. From its eyes and palms came thin trickles of blood. Fear seized her for a moment, but a deep sorrow soon replaced it. The Lady was crying tears of blood.

Anna Lucia knelt down and made the Sign of the Cross again.

"Dios te salve, María, llena eres de gracia," she began in a whispered prayer, when she felt sudden sharp pains in the palms of her hands. She looked at them and saw deep wounds, the width of a thumb, form in the center of her palms, piercing completely through them. They broke the surface on the front and back of her hands and thin trickles of blood oozed from them.

They were the wounds of Christ. A Stigmata.

She looked up at the statue again, which now appeared rimmed in a faint halo of light. Its eyes seemed to watch her.

And then the Lady spoke to her.

Pontevedra, Spain

Kristof Stanzos stood on the balcony of his cliffside Spanish villa. Far below him, the marina's lights spread out in a sweeping panorama; and beyond them, the open sea. But his gaze was on the night sky, where a comet glowed brightly on the horizon beneath a blood-red moon.

While the blood moon was forecast weeks earlier, the comet's sudden appearance caught astronomers by surprise.

But it came as no surprise to Kristof. It was exactly as foretold long ago in the prophecy.

And exactly as it appeared thirty-three years ago on the night the *child* was born.

Two men, Jeremy Belkin and Hareen Nazarah, joined Kristof on the balcony. Like him, they stared at the anomaly in the sky with the same wonderment and awe as they had thirty-three years ago — the night they journeyed to America to witness the *child's* birth. They, too, knew of the prophecy these signs portended, as did countless others around the world.

Jeremy finally broke the silence. "The jet's ready."

"Very well, then," said Kristof, taking another moment to bask in the splendor of this omen. "I suppose we should be on our way."

PART ONE

The Acheron Files

Chapter One
Kenzie

Buzz... buzz...

Eighteen-year-old Kenzie Walsh's phone vibrated on her nightstand with an incoming text. With an annoyed groan, she reached out from beneath her blanket and swatted her hand across the nightstand until it found the offending phone. She held it to her face and read the brief text:

'You awake?'

She looked at the sender's name — *'Zac.'* Of course, it was from Zac. No one else got up this early on a Saturday. Even the sun was barely up.

'No,' she texted back and put the phone back on her nightstand. She wanted to kick herself for not turning it off before going to bed.

A second later, it buzzed again with another incoming text. She groaned and picked it up.

'Too bad. Something's going on down at Hallows Pointe.'

Her interest piqued. *'What is it?'* she texted.

'Madelyn has her excavation team out there working on something. Could be a story.'

Kenzie considered this for a moment. Madelyn Hayes wasn't someone known for getting up early on weekends, or anytime, for that matter. This could be something. *'I'll check it out,'* she texted back. *'Thx!'*

She set the phone back on the nightstand. Few things could get her out of bed early on a Saturday morning, but a lead on a possible story for her newsletter and website was one of them. And Zac's leads were generally reliable, as was Zac himself. Even if his timing sucked.

Kenzie called her website and newsletter *'The Acheron Files,'* taking its name from the legend of a city rumored to have once existed in her upper New England region. The legend told of a city so steeped in evil, and whose people were so wicked, that God cursed it, causing it to sink beneath the ground. But for one night each century, on the anniversary of its demise, it would rise from the mist-laden marshes of its unhallowed grave to spread its evil throughout the world.

While most people thought of it only as a legend, Kenzie believed it was real. But she didn't think its evil perished with the city's demise; she believed it had infested the land with a stain so vile, it could never be cleansed. She believed this because she saw evidence of its evil manifested everywhere. That belief led her to start *The Acheron Files*.

Kenzie climbed from bed in her T-shirt and gym shorts, stepping around piles of clothes and magazines as she walked over to the bathroom on the far side of her small studio apartment. On her walls hung posters of horror movies and TV shows, one of her favorites being the iconic *'X-Files'* poster of the UFO with the caption below it: *'The Truth is Out There.'* She lived by that motto.

She reached the bathroom and stared at the half-asleep teenager in the mirror's reflection. Her long red hair, matted to the side with bed head, was beyond hope. It was going to be another baseball cap day. The hair, along with her blue eyes and sprinkle of freckles, came from her Irish heritage, along with her sarcasm and penchant for mischief and stubbornness.

After brushing her teeth and hair, she threw on a flannel shirt and jeans from a 'clean' pile on the floor, pulled on a baseball cap, then headed down the narrow wooden stairs outside her door.

The stairs came down in the rear of the lobby of Rose's Coffee Shoppe, a cozy inn-styled cafe just off Capetown's Main Street. Several early morning customers were already there, dining on breakfasts of warm scones and fresh-brewed coffee.

Even before moving in upstairs, Kenzie was a fan of the cafe for its Old-World warmth and charm. It reminded her of pictures she had seen of rural pubs in Ireland and England, with walls of dark walnut and a stone fireplace where guests warmed themselves on frosty nights. Photos of the town and its residents, dating back decades, hung from the walls; and tucked away in a front corner near the windows, was a small platform that hosted local musicians and poetry readings.

Kenzie ducked into a storage space behind the stairs, where she tugged at a mountain bike buried beneath cleaning equipment.

"You're up early," a woman called over from behind the pastry counter across the lobby. She was Rose Larson, the widowed owner of the cafe and upstairs apartment where she let Kenzie live rent-free. A kind-faced woman with a graying head of hair, she was one of Kenzie's favorite people in the world. She had let Kenzie move in two years earlier when things became intolerable for Kenzie at the place where she and her younger brother, Chad, lived.

That last place wasn't her 'home,' as Kenzie always made clear. She and Chad lost their home on the night their parents died.

"I need to get Zac a watch," Kenzie said as she pulled her bike out from beneath the pile of mops, brooms, and cleaning supplies.

"Oh. Did he call?" Rose said.

"He texted," Kenzie said as she wheeled her bike across the lobby to the front door. "And like a dummy, I forgot to turn off my phone."

Rose smiled. "What on earth did he want so early?"

"He said something's going on down at Hallows Pointe that I should check out."

"What is it?"

"He didn't know," Kenzie said as she nudged the door open with her front wheel. "He just said that Madelyn's got her crew down there working on something."

"On a Saturday?"

Kenzie nodded. "That's what I was thinking. If she's down there this early, it's because she's doing something she doesn't want people to know about. Which means it's probably good."

"Well, stay warm. I heard there's a storm coming."

A chill, overcast sky and damp ocean air greeted Kenzie as she wheeled her bike out the door and climbed on. Capetown was quintessential New England, with Colonial-style wood-paneled houses, welcoming shops, and shady streets lined with elms. It sat on a peninsula that faced the mainland on its western side across a narrow sound. To its north lay thickly wooded hills; and just south of it, at the tip of the peninsula, was Hallows Pointe and the town's historic lighthouse. That's where she was headed.

Kenzie pedaled off down the town's Main Street. On her right was a row of small shops and cafes, where patrons sat outside enjoying their coffees and reading their morning papers. On her left was Crawford Park, a long, broad stretch of grass and trees with picnic tables, a small playground, and a gazebo. Named after Nathanial Crawford, one of the town's storied founders, the park was a popular spot for picnics, concerts, parades, and the town's annual Libertas Festival. A life-size bronze statue of Nathanial, seated on a horse, stood prominently near the gazebo.

Coming up on her right was the Mayflower theater, one of the big attractions along the Main Street. It was a historic old bijou with a single screen that regularly played classic films.

A block past the Mayflower was Sally's Diner, a cool 50s themed diner featuring black-and-white floor tiles, chrome trim, soda fountains, and framed movie star photos on the walls. It was like stepping into a James Dean movie, and Kenzie knew its features and layout by heart. It was once a favorite dining spot for her and her family before her parents' deaths.

She hadn't gone in there since.

Continuing down Main Street, she passed the town's seaport village, a tourist hub of souvenir shops and seafood restaurants along a street sloping down to the water. At the far end lay the pier and moorings, where boats rocked gently in the tide, their bells tinkling from tall masts. A flock of seagulls squawked noisily as they prowled the pier for discarded food, and the tart, fresh smell of salt water and fish hung heavy in the air. Kenzie used to come there a lot as a kid, but now it held too many memories. She rarely came there anymore.

It had been like this ever since her parents were killed, and she and Chad became orphans. The day Kenzie got her first glimpse of the supernatural horrors underlying Capetown.

Chapter Two
Life in Hell

Kenzie was eleven, and Chad was three when they lost their parents. She awoke that morning to find her parents dead in their bed, their bodies burned beyond recognition and their spines and necks twisted grotesquely. But the fire, or whatever did it, left their clothes and bed untouched. The police and coroner were at a complete loss for a cause. One investigator remarked it was like something just came through the wall and did it; but he was quickly admonished. As Kenzie would soon learn, you can't talk that way around Capetown.

Capetown's local newspaper, *'The Capetown Daily,'* wrote that they died in a fire resulting from a gas leak. This became the accepted cause of death around town. But Kenzie didn't buy it; fires didn't leave the area around the victims unburned; and it didn't twist the victims into gruesome contortions. For whatever reason, the *Daily* lied; and this planted the seeds for Kenzie's later skepticism at the news media.

With no relatives to live with, the state placed Kenzie and Chad in foster care with Bob and Carol Mahoney. They shared the Mahoney's three-bedroom cottage, built in the woods three miles outside of town, with two other foster children. Those children, both boys, were several years older than Kenzie, and wards of the state for juvenile delinquency. They made life hell, and Kenzie often had to defend herself and Chad from their bullying, which conveniently went ignored by the foster parents. It toughened her up quickly for the horrors she would face later in life.

The house was loveless. Kenzie came to see Bob and Carol as rent-a-parents, who took in kids for the paychecks the state sent them, and not out of kindness. They provided the bare minimum — a roof over the kids' heads, a room Kenzie and Chad shared with each other, meals that could barely feed a rabbit, and clothes that could have come from homeless people.

They also meted out what they called 'discipline' whenever Kenzie or Chad 'misbehaved,' and their definition of 'misbehaved' varied depending on how many drinks Bob had that day. It left bruises and the occasional bloody nose, and one time left Kenzie's ear ringing from a smack to the head after she accidentally left the tool shed's door open overnight.

On a typical night, Bob came home from work at around eight or nine, reeking of beers from the pub he stopped by on his way home. Kenzie and Chad always made sure they were in bed before then. They would listen as he lumbered in the front door, loud, ill-tempered, and slurring his words. On the worst of those nights, Kenzie let her terrified young brother sleep in her bed.

"Here, take this," Kenzie whispered to Chad, as they cowered in bed on a particularly bad night. She slipped the small St.

Christopher medal on a thin chain from around her neck and placed it around his. "It'll protect you when I'm not around."

Chad fingered the small medal. "This is the one mom gave you."

She nodded. "And now I'm giving it to you."

"Thanks."

At only eleven years of age, Kenzie was the closest thing her three-year-old brother had to a mom.

The breaking point came a year into their foster care. Bob came home in a particularly sour mood that night, which was made worse when he saw Chad had left his crayons near the stove, where they melted into colored wax stains. Bob stormed into their bedroom, dragged Chad out of bed by the arm, and hauled him into the kitchen, where he rubbed Chad's cheek on the wax until Chad's skin was raw.

Kenzie raced in after them, and seeing her brother being brutalized, grabbed a beer bottle from the table and heaved it at Bob's head. It hit with a sharp thud. Bob released Chad's arm and staggered back several steps, then unleashed his fury on Kenzie.

"You bitch!" he growled, grabbing Kenzie by the throat and hurling her across a chair. Both she and the chair tumbled hard onto the floor, leaving her with a bruised rib.

"What's going on in here?" Carol said as she rushed in with the two foster boys, all of them smelling of marijuana. Oddly enough, the boys never got disciplined for anything.

"That bitch threw a bottle at me," Bob shouted, rubbing his head where the bottle hit him. Kenzie hoped he had a concussion.

"He was hurting Chad," Kenzie said, climbing from the floor and holding her sore rib.

"Well, I'm sure Chad deserved it," Carol said, then turned to her husband. "Let me have a look at your head, honey."

"It's fine," he growled, pushing her away.

"I don't like it here," Chad whispered to Kenzie as they lay in bed later that night.

"Me neither, buddy."

"Can we leave?"

"Where would we go?"

"I don't know. Anywhere. How about Zac's?"

Kenzie thought about it for a moment. Zac Taylor had been her best friend since third grade, and one of the few friends who stuck with her when things went to hell. It didn't bother him that she looked like a homeless girl from the secondhand clothes Carol bought her and Chad, or that she often smelled of dirt and sweat from only being allowed to shower twice a week. Beneath the grime, she was still Kenzie.

Zac was that kid you found at every school, the skinny boy who sucked at sports but knew every line from 'Star Wars' and could write computer code in his sleep. They had hit it off over their love of old horror movies and used to get together at her home to binge on Universal's old black-and-white classics.

That was back when Kenzie had a home.

"Let's do it," she whispered to Chad.

The walk from the cottage to town was long and took them down a dark forest road. Kenzie hated that forest, and especially at night. Ever since her parents' mysterious deaths, she had grown increasingly convinced that things were out there that defied explanation. Things beyond our normal experiences. Things that prowled the dark corners of our reality. And what better place for them to hide than the forest.

But that night, nothing in that dark forest was as scary as the nightmare they just left.

The night felt unnaturally quiet and still, making the hard crunch of their feet on the gravel louder than she would have liked. She had only the flashlight on her cell phone to see by and kept it trained on the road ahead of them. She feared to shine it into the forest in case it reflected the glow of red eyes watching them from the darkness.

She looked down at Chad, walking close beside her and holding her free hand. "How's your cheek doing, buddy?" she said.

He shrugged. "Better. I think."

"Let's have a look." She shined her light on his cheek and was relieved to see that most of the raw pink color had faded. "Yeah. It's looking better. No more zombie face."

"What's a zombie?"

Kenzie paused. She couldn't believe she used that word. Her eyes made a quick scan of the nearly impenetrable darkness around them.

"Something we shouldn't be thinking about out here."

Twelve-year-old Zac Taylor had just started to doze off when three rapid knocks came at his bedroom window. He opened his eyes and looked over at the window.

Tap, tap, tap. The knocks came again. He walked over to the window and drew aside the curtains. Kenzie stood outside, leaning across a hedge so she could reach the window.

"Kenz?" he said, sliding open the window.

"Yeah. I have Chad with me. Can we come in?"

Zac helped them crawl through the window. "What's going on?"

"I can't take that house anymore, Zac." She looked down at Chad. "Show him your cheek, Chad."

Chad did, and enough pink remained to cause Zac to wince.

"And Bob did this to me," Kenzie said, pulling up the side of her shirt high enough to show him the deep black and purple bruise.

Zac cringed. "Can't you call the cops?"

She shook her head. "There's no other foster homes that'll take us both. They'll split us up."

"So, you're running away?"

"I don't know," she said, sinking down on the edge of the bed and brushing her long hair back from her face. "But we need somewhere to crash tonight. Can we stay here?"

"Sure. Let me grab a blanket and pillow and you guys can take the bed."

"Are you sure?" she said. "We can take the floor."

"I'm not making a chick and her kid brother sleep on the floor."

A small lump built in her throat as she watched him head for his closet and pull out a spare blanket and pillow. "Thank you."

Kenzie soaked for almost twenty minutes in the shower the next morning, closing her eyes and letting the warm water wash over her. It felt like heaven.

She and Chad climbed back out the window before Zac's parents woke up.

"Zac," she said, leaning back in over the windowsill.

"Yeah?"

"Come closer."

He did, and she planted a soft kiss on his cheek. "I'll see you at school."

Walking along the town's quiet Main Street that morning, Kenzie and Chad still had two hours until school started. Most of the shops and cafes were still closed, and having nowhere to go, they went inside Rose's Coffee Shoppe. Kenzie had come there a lot with her family over the years, and she hoped the cafe's owner, Rose Larson, wouldn't mind if she and Chad waited there till school started.

Rose had just finished unloading pastries on the counter when she saw Kenzie and Chad in the doorway across the lobby. Rose's face lit up with a smile. She'd known Kenzie since the girl was two and used to come there with her parents all the time. It had broken Rose's heart when she learned about their deaths. Like the rest of the town, she only knew what the paper reported, and not the grisly details.

"Well, hello, you two," Rose said with a warm smile. "Come in, come in." She tossed her apron on the counter and rushed over to wrap them in a motherly hug. "It's been ages since I've seen you."

"I'm sorry we didn't come before now," Kenzie said, feeling a guilty knot in her stomach for having avoided the cafe since her parents' deaths. Rose had always been kind to her, but like so many other places in town, the memories were just too painful.

"Oh no, hon, don't be," Rose said, gently brushing back Kenzie's hair. "I completely understand. All those places you used to go with your parents, those memories can be painful. It was like that for me for the longest time with all the places I used to go with my late husband. But you know what? Those memories are going to get easier."

Kenzie swallowed. "They will?"

"I promise you," Rose said. "Now let's get you kids something to eat."

"I don't have any money," Kenzie said.

"Don't you worry about that, hon, it's on me." Rose led them over to a table and sat them down. She had a better chance to look at them now. "The two of you must be starving. You're as thin as rails."

"Carol doesn't feed us much," said Chad.

"Carol's your foster mother?" said Rose.

"Yeah," said Kenzie.

Rose's eyes went from Kenzie to Chad and back to Kenzie, and she could see that there was a lot more to this story. But now wasn't the time.

"Well, you're welcome to come here and eat anytime you want, and it's on me. I'll let the staff know in case I'm not around."

"Really?" said Chad.

"Really," said Rose, patting him on the head.

"Cool."

"Thanks, Mrs. Larson," said Kenzie.

"It's Rose, hon. Let me go whip you up something to eat."

Rose returned a short time later with two plates of her famous breakfast of eggs, hash browns, sausage, and biscuits and gravy. Kenzie and Chad wolfed them down like famished dogs.

"So how was it?" said Rose when she returned to collect their dishes.

"It was like the breakfasts mom used to make," said Kenzie, and Chad gave a big nod in agreement.

Rose smiled warmly and gave her shoulder a gentle squeeze. "Nothing's like the breakfasts moms make, hon, but I don't mind being in second."

Kenzie smiled. "It was really great, Rose. Thanks."

"Yeah. Thanks," said Chad.

"Well, I meant what I said about you coming here anytime you want. I'll always have a warm meal for you and there's plenty of tables if you just want to sit back and relax in the mornings or after school."

With the long hot shower and warm reception from Rose that morning, Kenzie could almost have believed that things were on the upswing for her and Chad. But shortly after the start of her first period math class, reality reared its ugly head.

A knock came at the classroom door. The teacher answered it, then went outside into the hallway to talk to whoever it was. She returned a minute later and looked to the back of the room where Kenzie sat.

"Kenzie," the teacher said, "Carol's waiting for you in the principal's office. Go ahead and bring your books with you."

Kenzie knew this was going to be bad. Letting out a sigh, she packed her books into her backpack and headed out the door, knowing every eye in the classroom was on her.

"Where the hell'd you two go last night?" Carol growled as they pulled out of the school parking lot. She'd waited until they were in the car and away from the faculty before unloading on them.

Kenzie ignored her and just stared out the backseat window at the passing shops. Chad sat beside her, staring nervously at his feet.

"I'm talking to you, bitch," said Carol, her voice growing angrier and louder. But Kenzie didn't care.

"I heard you," Kenzie said, continuing to stare out the window and ignore Carol's question. That morning reminded her how good life once was, and she hated Carol for destroying that feeling.

"So, where the hell'd you two go?"

"To a friend's," Kenzie finally said, just to shut the woman up.

"What friend? You ain't got no friends."

"She has Zac," Chad said.

Kenzie quickly reached over and touched his arm. She shook her head. She didn't want Carol to know anything about Zac.

"Who the hell's Zac?"

"Nobody you know," said Kenzie.

"Don't get smart with me, girl. I said who the hell's Zac."

"And I said he's nobody you know."

"Well, you ain't gonna see Zac or nobody else no more."

"You can't stop us," Kenzie shot back.

"The hell I can't. When we get home, you two are gonna learn some manners."

"You touch me or Chad, and I'll call the cops."

"Like hell you will. Ain't nobody else gonna take the two of you."

"But you and Bob will be in jail."

Carol snorted. "They ain't gonna believe no twelve-year-old."

"They'll believe the photos I took."

Carol eyed her in the rear-view mirror, and Kenzie stared right back at her. Unflinching.

"I'm serious," Kenzie said. "If you guys ever touch me or Chad again, you're going to jail."

The rest of the drive home was tense and quiet, with nobody saying a word. Kenzie had thrown down the gauntlet, and Carol could see she was serious. And for the most part, Kenzie's threat worked.

For the next four years, Kenzie and Chad enjoyed a respite from the physical abuse, and Kenzie thought things might finally turn around for her and her brother. But as with everything in their lives, fate had other plans for the young orphans. They began on the day she and Chad heard the *'whispers.'*

Chapter Three
The Whispers

Kenzie was sixteen and Chad was eight on the day they heard the *'whispers.'* She had a part-time job working for Rose at the cafe now, and although she was old enough to get emancipated, she wouldn't be able to petition for guardianship of Chad until she turned eighteen, so emancipation was never an option for her. She would have walked barefoot over broken glass before leaving her younger brother behind with the foster monsters.

She had a car to drive now, which was a small victory. It was a badly neglected old clunker she found rusting on the lawn behind the tool shed she convinced Carol to let her use. Carol agreed, not out of kindness, but to avoid having to drive Kenzie and Chad into town for school.

For Kenzie, the car meant freedom, and a way for her and Chad to escape if the 'discipline' ever got physical again.

It also meant never having to walk along that lonely forest road again. The one where things watched; and waited.

Not until that day. The day of the *whispers*.

As she left the school building and headed for the parking lot that afternoon, Zac caught up to her from behind.

"Hey, Walsh," he said as he raced up. "What are you doing right now?"

"Same thing as usual. Picking up Chad and heading back to the hell house. Why? What's up?"

"Change of plans. You're coming over to check out my new app."

"It's done?"

"Yup."

"This is the one that can tell if people are lying?"

"Yeah. It detects voice inflections and variations from a common baseline I programmed into it. I'm calling it 'Truth Talk.'"

"Does it work?"

"Come over and see for yourself."

"I will. Let me drop off Chad, and I'll be right over."

"Why's Carol's car here?" Chad said as Kenzie pulled her old clunker onto the gravel drive outside the cottage. He fidgeted nervously with the St. Christopher medal around his neck, the one she gave him five years earlier, which he never took off.

"I'm not sure," she said, staring uneasily at the house. "Why don't you wait here while I check inside."

"But I gotta pee."

"Can't you do it on the side of the house?"

Chad shook his head. "Carol yells at me."

"Okay. We'll both go. But be ready to run if it's bad."

As soon as they stepped in the door, they saw it was way beyond bad. Carol lay passed out on the sofa, an empty bottle of whiskey lying on the floor near her outstretched hand, the TV tuned to some trashy tabloid show, and the smell of weed in the air. It had been a long time since they'd seen it this bad, and it would only get worse when she awoke to a screeching hangover.

"Let's go," Kenzie whispered in his ear. "I'm taking you with me to Zac's."

"He likes you, you know," Chad said from the passenger seat as they drove down the forest road into town.

"Who likes me?" Kenzie said.

"Zac."

"Why do you say that?"

Chad shrugged. "I can just tell. Do you like him?"

"Of course, I like him. He's my spirit animal," she said with a grin.

"What's that?"

"It means he's my buddy."

"Oh. But do you like him?"

"How about we change the subject?"

"You're dodging the question, aren't you?"

"Yup."

Kenzie turned the knob on the old AM radio, but the reception was spotty from the surrounding trees.

"I miss mom and dad's car," Chad said, settling into his seat. "Their radio played real music."

Kenzie nodded in agreement. "I know. This thing barely even gets static."

"Do you ever think about them?" he said.

"All the time."

"Me too. But sometimes it's hard to remember what they looked like."

"That's because you were only three when they died. I have a picture of them in my wallet. Remind me to show it to you when we get to Zac's house."

"Okay." He took a deep breath. "I really wish they hadn't died."

"Me too, buddy. Me too."

At that moment, the engine light clicked on and the car came to an abrupt stop, jerking both of them in their seats.

"You okay?" Kenzie said when she recovered from the shock.

Chad nodded. "Yeah. What happened?"

"I don't know. It's this piece of crap car. It just stopped."

She climbed from the car and held up her phone, frowning when she saw it had no reception.

"Crap." She angled it around, hoping to get at least one bar, but none popped up.

"Does it work?" Chad said as he climbed from the car.

She shook her head. "Nope. Nothing."

"Does that mean we have to walk?"

She looked up and down the deserted stretch of road. At this time of day, the chances of anyone driving by anytime soon were slim.

"Looks like it."

Her eyes drifted to the surrounding forest, looming deep and ominous around them. She swallowed a nervous lump in her throat.

"Are you afraid they're out there?" Chad said.

The words caught Kenzie off guard. She had never mentioned her fear of the forest, worried that it might spook him. But apparently, he had picked up on it.

"That who's out there?" she said.

"The bad things."

"What bad things?"

He shrugged. "I don't know. But sometimes I hear them at night."

She looked nervously around at the forest again, feeling a growing sense of oppression and danger. "We should get going."

He gave a hasty nod in agreement.

They set off for town. She figured they had driven about halfway there, so it wouldn't take long to walk the rest of the way. There was a gas station at the edge of town where she could have a tow truck sent to pick up the car.

They had walked for about five minutes when Chad suddenly stopped and looked nervously at the forest.

"What is it?" she said.

He stood frozen for a moment before whispering quietly. "They're here."

"The bad things?"

He nodded. "They're watching us."

Kenzie's heart skipped a beat. She felt it too in the sudden stir of hairs on the back of her neck.

"We need to hurry," she whispered back.

They picked up their pace as they hurried down the road, still about fifteen minutes away from town.

Then she heard it.

Sounds arose from the forest on either side of them, beginning in hushed whispers and rising in volume to a crescendo of inarticulate horror. It was as if the sounds came from the trees and plants or the air itself, filling the forest in a dense cacophony of eerie, unintelligible utterances. The sounds rushed at them, filling the surrounding air in disembodied voices that carried words but no meaning. They circled and swarmed in a dizzying array of disturbing, guttural sounds, each one overlapping with the others like the roar of a sports stadium.

Kenzie had stopped beside Chad when she first heard the sounds, but now she knew they need to move. And fast.

It was coming for them. Whatever *It* was.

She squeezed his hand. "We need to run," she said, no longer worried about keeping her voice hushed.

They took off in a sprint down the road... and moments later, the darkness swallowed them.

Chapter Four
The Disappearance

Six Weeks After the Disappearance

A pickup truck rumbled down a country road just north of Capetown, with several bundles of hay sliding around in back. A sign on its doors read: *'Dawson's Farm.'*

Terry Dawson drove while his brother Doug rode shotgun. They had seen a lot in their thirty-plus years in Capetown, but nothing like what they saw up ahead.

"Well, I'll be dammed," said Terry, staring out the windshield. A hundred yards ahead of them was a naked girl walking along the side of the road. She swayed unsteadily, as if drunk or stoned.

The truck slowed as it pulled alongside her, and Doug rolled down the passenger window. "Howdy, there," he said, trying not to spook the girl. "Everything okay?"

The girl stopped and looked at them through dazed, distant eyes. She was young and pretty and seemed completely lost.

Terry did a double-take on her from the driver's seat. "Holy, jeez, girl. Are you Kenzie Walsh?"

She stared at him for a moment as recognition seemed to flicker in her eyes. It was like someone splashed cold water on her. She nodded.

"Yeah," she said.

Doug turned to Terry. "You know her?"

"She's the girl in them missing person posters they had up around town. Give her your shirt to cover up."

Doug climbed from the truck and slipped out of his long flannel overshirt. He handed it to her and helped her slide her arms into it and button it up.

"Where you been, girl?" Doug said, helping her with the last buttons. "Had a whole lota folks looking for you."

She stared at him for a moment with the same dazed look as before, then around at the surrounding pastures. It was like she was waking from a dream.

"I don't know," she said.

Doug looked at his brother sitting in the cab, and the two exchanged a concerned look.

"I'm Terry and this here's my brother, Doug," Terry said from across the cab. "Why don't you let us take you into town and get you over to see Doc Weathers. You ain't looking so good."

"Now I want you to follow this pencil with your eyes only, Kenzie," said Dr. Alvin Weathers, one of Capetown's two practicing physicians. "Try not to move your head."

Doc Weathers, or just 'Doc', as he was known around town, was the kind of friendly small-town doctor you would expect to find in a place like Capetown, the kind who took care of everything from cradle to the grave, and every cut, scrape and illness in between. In his early seventies now, past the age when most doctors would have retired, Doc continued to chug along like a well-kept machine. He had been the Walsh family's physician since before Kenzie was born and delivered both her and her brother.

Kenzie sat on the examination table in one room of his four-room office. Like most of the professional offices in town, Doc's office used to be just another house on its oak-lined residential street. Only a wooden sign out front reading 'Alvin Weathers, MD' differentiated it from the neighboring houses. His staff consisted of him, a nurse practitioner, and a receptionist, who manned the phones in the reception area that was once a living room.

Doc held a pencil in front of Kenzie's face while shining a small flashlight in her eyes. He moved the pencil from left to right while watching her eyes follow it.

"Good, Kenzie," he said, setting the flashlight down and writing some quick notes in her file. The only other person in the room was Rose, who Kenzie had asked the receptionist to call when Terry and Doug dropped her off.

"Do you know what's wrong with me?" Kenzie said.

Doc shook his head. "Not yet, but there doesn't appear to be a concussion."

"Then why can't I remember anything from the past six weeks?"

"That's what we intend to find out. Now turn your head to the right," he said, picking up an otoscope and poking its tip in her left ear. "And now to the left." He repeated the process on her right ear, then set down the otoscope and wrote some more notes.

"Now comes the fun part. We need to take some blood."

"How's that fun?"

"It's not," he said, unwrapping a syringe and attaching a vial to the back of it, "but I thought I'd try to lighten the mood."

"It didn't work."

"It never does," he smiled. "Now I need you to make a fist."

She did and clenched her teeth as he poked the needle into her arm and waited several seconds — feeling like years to Kenzie — for the vial to fill with blood. He then removed the syringe and vial, pasted a label on it and placed it in a refrigerator.

"That wasn't so bad, was it?"

"For you, maybe."

"You want a lollipop? It's what I always give the little kids."

"Yes, please."

He laughed.

"So why did you take her blood?" Rose asked.

"We need to test it for drugs. Which certainly would explain the amnesia."

"You think she was drugged?"

He shook his head. "I honestly don't know. But we do need to explore the possibility."

"What about down there?" said Kenzie, pointing to her crotch. "Do you think they… you know, did something to me while I was out?"

"I certainly hope not, Kenzie," he said, all the humor gone from his voice. "But we need to run one last test to be certain."

"A rape test?" said Rose.

He nodded. "Yes. That's what they're commonly called. And Kenzie, I hope to God it comes back negative."

"Me too," Kenzie said.

When the tests were finally finished, Kenzie breathed a deep sigh of relief as she changed from the white hospital gown into the clothes Rose brought her. That was when a sudden ruckus of shouts erupted in the reception area outside.

"Where's Kenzie Walsh?" came Carol's shout, followed by the receptionist's frantic plea.

"Ma'am, you can't go back there. The doctor is seeing a patient."

"That patient is my ward."

A second later, the door burst open and Carol stormed in, smelling of liquor and cigarette smoke. She spun around to Kenzie.

"Where the hell have you been?" Carol growled. "The State's been up my ass ever since you ran off."

"I didn't run off," Kenzie said.

"The hell you didn't. You and that Zac kid, the two of you ran off and now the State's threating to revoke my license."

"I said I didn't run off," Kenzie said, more assertively this time.

"Then where the hell were you?"

"I don't know."

"What the hell's that supposed to mean?"

"It means she has amnesia," said Doc, rising to his feet. "Kenzie has no memory of the past six weeks. Now I ask you to kindly leave. You're upsetting my patient and interrupting her examination."

"Your patient is my ward and I'm not leaving without her." She spun around to Kenzie. "Where the hell's your brother? The State's been up my ass about him too."

"I don't know."

"How in the hell could you not know? He was with you, wasn't he?"

"I said I don't know," Kenzie shouted. "The last time I remember seeing him was six weeks ago. That's why I need to get out of here so I can go find him."

"Oh, no," Carol said, furiously shaking her head. "You ain't goin' nowhere except school and work till your ass turns eighteen."

"You can't stop me."

"The hell I can't. The law says you're mine till you're eighteen."

"You need to leave," said Doc, taking another step towards Carol. Normally, he found it prudent to not intervene in family matters unless there were signs of abuse, but he was making an exception now with this woman. She had already crossed too many lines.

"Says who?" snarled Carol.

"Says me," said Doc, taking another step toward her.

"And who's gonna make me? You?"

"If I have to."

"It's okay, Doctor," said Kenzie, hopping to her feet and stepping between them. She appreciated the intervention, but she knew how vindictive Carol could be. And the last thing she wanted was for him to risk his license. "I'll go with her."

"Are you sure, Kenzie," he said. "I can call the police and get you a protective order."

"I'd like to see you try," snarled Carol.

"I would be happy to," he said. "Just say the word, Kenzie."

Kenzie took a deep breath and shook her head. "I'd better not. Not till I find Chad and make sure he's safe." She then turned to Carol. "And you're not gonna stop me."

"We'll see about that."

"Very well, then, it's your choice, Kenzie," said Doc. "But if she so much as lays a hand on you, you call me. I promise you I won't rest until she's behind bars."

"Me neither," said Rose, rising from her chair and walking over to Carol. "You touch her, bitch, and I swear you'll be sipping soup through a straw the rest of your life. And I know some boys who'll do the same thing to your husband. Are we clear?"

"Kiss off," Carol snarled. "Come on, Kenzie, we're leaving."

Kenzie turned to Doc and Rose. "Thanks, you guys."

"I'll be in touch," he said.

"Me too," said Rose. "And don't you worry about your brother, hon. We'll find him. I'm heading over to Rick's right now to join the search."

"You'll let me know?"

"The minute we find him."

Rose wrapped her in a warm hug, and as she did, Kenzie felt her slip something small and rectangular into her pocket. She would find out later it was a cell phone to replace the one Kenzie lost when she went missing.

Chapter Five
The Creek

Kenzie dozed off sometime after midnight, exhausted and deflated after sneaking out her window to search for Chad late that afternoon and into the night. She kept a baseball bat beneath her blanket in case Bob and Carol decided she needed 'discipline.'

Her sleep came in restless fits of half-waking deliriums and stuttered dreams. In one instant, she and Chad would be in their bedroom hiding from Bob's drunken rage; and in the next instant, she and Chad were in the safety and comfort of Zac's bedroom, with the previous part having been a dream. And then they were in the dark forest, where unseen things whispered and moved stealthily through the surrounding trees...

'Kenzie. You need to wake up...'

It was Chad's voice, coming from somewhere beside her. It sounded so real that she couldn't tell if it was part of the dream's delirium, or...

'Kenzie...'

The voice came again, and Kenzie's eyes drifted open, her hands reflexively reaching for the bat before relaxing.

In the darkness beside her bed stood Chad, little more than a dim shape in the moonless night.

"I need you to come with me," he said urgently.

"What? Chad?" She sat up.

"Yeah. We need to hurry."

"Wait. What?" She wiped her eyes, trying to shake off the delirium and suddenness of this.

"It's me, Kenzie. We need to go right now."

"Go where?"

"To the place they took us."

"So, why did she ground you?" Chad said, staring out the passenger window at the darkness. They had been driving for almost thirty minutes and were now on a lonely road deep in the forests on the north side of the peninsula.

"Because she's a psycho and thinks you and I ran away."

"But we didn't. We were going to Zac's."

"But psycho bitch didn't believe me when I told her that."

Chad frowned and shook his head. "I don't like her."

"Me neither, buddy."

"You stay there because of me, don't you? That's why you don't get emancipated."

"Who told you that?"

He shrugged. "I just heard it."

"Well, it's you and me, buddy. That's how it's always been and how it's always going to be."

He nodded. "I'm glad I got to have you as my sister, Kenzie."

"Hey. Don't make it sound like it's over. You and I are just getting started." She looked out the windshield at the dark outlines of trees lining the road. "So can you tell me why we had to come out here in the middle of the night and not wait till morning?"

"'Cause it might not be there in the morning. You can stop right over here."

She pulled the car over to the side of the dirt road and parked. As soon as she clicked off the headlights, the forest plunged into almost complete darkness.

"So where is it?" she said.

He pointed out his window. "It's over there beside the creek."

"Are we going out there?"

"We have to if you want to see it."

"It would be a lot easier to see it in the daytime."

"But it might not be there then."

"Okay," she said, taking a deep breath. "Let's do this."

The night felt strangely still as they climbed from the car. The treetops hid most of the moonless sky, making it nearly impossible to see around them. She clicked on her cell phone's flashlight and shined it into the forest where Chad had pointed, but its narrow beam faded quickly in the darkness.

"Over there?" she said.

"Yeah."

"Okay. Lead the way, kid."

Chad led her off through the woods, seeming to have no trouble finding his way through the tangle of brush and trees in the near darkness. The ground sloped gently upwards for what must have been a hundred yards before reaching a crest, then dropped steeply down an embankment. Standing on the crest, she could see the starlight reflected in the creek's black waters flowing at the bottom of the steep incline.

"Is that the creek?" she asked.

"Yeah."

He started down with her following behind, grabbing onto rocks and tree roots to keep from slipping.

They reached the bottom, and Kenzie shined her flashlight around. They were in a small narrow ravine, bordered on both sides by dirt and rock embankments. Dark trees stood like sentries along the top edges of the embankments.

"So where is it?" she said.

"It's over here."

She turned and saw him standing about ten yards away, staring at something behind a rock outcrop.

"This is where they took us?" she asked as she walked over.

He nodded while continuing to stare at the ground behind the outcrop.

"It's where I died."

Kenzie stopped, the breath freezing momentarily in her lungs.

"That's not funny."

He nodded to the area behind the outcrop. "My body's still here."

Kenzie rushed over and looked behind it. The charred, twisted remains of a young boy lay there, half buried in the sediment. She threw her hands to her face and cowered back.

"Oh, God, no," she pleaded. She slowly knelt beside the remains and gently touched the muddy shirt. The body was charred and broken like those of her parents, but a small thin chain with a St. Christopher medal on it hung from the neck. Chad's medal. She swallowed hard, brushing away some of the mud from the shirt. It was the same one Chad wore on the day they disappeared and the same one he was wearing now... *standing right behind her*. She sprang to her feet and scrambled several steps back.

"If that's really your body, then how come I can see you?" she said.

"Because you saw *them*, Kenzie, and it's awaking something in your mind. You're going to see things other people can't."

"I don't remember any of it?"

He shook his head. "They won't let you. Nobody is supposed to see them, but you did. And they can't let you remember it."

"Why?"

"'Cause they're not supposed to exist. But they do."

"What are they?"

"I call them the shadow people, 'cause that's how they look. They're what killed mom and dad. And me."

"Why didn't they kill me?"

"The men saved you. They came, and the shadow people fled."

"What men?"

"The prophets. It won't make sense to you now," Chad said, seeing the confusion in his sister's face, "but it will."

"Why didn't they save you, too?"

"They couldn't. I was already dead."

Kenzie's heart sank at the reminder, and a painful lump filled her throat. This would probably be the last time she ever saw her brother.

"I don't have much time," Chad said, "but we were right about the bad things out there. And there's things even worse than the ones that killed me."

"What kind of things?"

"Evil things. Things that haunt the darkness and come for us in our sleep. Things that steal our souls." He stared out into the night at the trees and starlit sky, seeming to sense the movement of things through the surrounding darkness. He turned to her.

"Close your eyes, Kenzie, and you'll feel it. The desecration that's all around us. It's in the trees, the soil, the water, the air. Everything's defiled by something completely unholy."

She took a deep breath and closed her eyes, allowing her ears to probe the slowly expanding silence around her. Even the creek's burbling waters became little more than a whisper before fading into nothingness.

And then, in that utter stillness, she felt it. A strange malevolence hung all around her like an invisible film. It came from the ground and rocks and trees, surrounding her in a terrible, watchful sentience that chilled her blood. She opened her eyes and nervously scanned the surrounding area.

"What is that?" she said.

"The sin of Acheron. It permeates everything."

She looked at him. Acheron was a name she had heard before, as had most people in the region, but only as a legend. A creepy story told around campfires.

"Isn't that just a legend?" she said.

He shook his head. "It's not a legend, Kenzie, it's real. It was a city so vile that God banished it beneath the ground to rot. But its evil never dies. It waits in the ground for the night of its rising. And it'll bring the darkest horror the world has ever known. You need to warn people about these things before it's too late."

She swallowed nervously. "What do I tell them?"

"That Acheron is real. And its evil is real."

Kenzie followed Chad through the tangle of woods back to the car, her mind reeling in fear from Chad's warning, and the crushing numbness of grief. She opened her car door and looked over at his side.

He was gone. Around her, a lonely night breeze whispered through the pines.

The last of her family was gone, and she was alone in the world now. A lump filled her throat as she stared at that empty spot on the road.

'I'm glad I got to have you as my sister, Kenzie.'

She swallowed hard as the first tears misted her eyes.

She drove to the bluff overlooking Hallows Pointe and parked. She sat there for the rest of the night, staring out the windshield at the Atlantic, its black waters rippling to an infinite horizon in the cold starlight.

I'm glad I got to be your sister, Chad.

The tears broke free now, and she began crying. And didn't stop till long after the sun crested the horizon.

Chapter Six
The Long Road Out of Hell

"It's over here," Kenzie called back to the sheriff and his deputy as she led them down the dirt embankment to the creek.

It was the morning after she went there with Chad and she hadn't slept or gone back to Carol's house that night. She spent the night parked on the bluff at Hallows Pointe, crying until her eyes and cheeks felt hollow.

She met Rose at the cafe earlier that morning and told her Chad was dead. She said nothing about seeing his ghost; instead, she said her memory was coming back, and that was how she found his body. She hated lying to Rose, but the truth was just too crazy for now.

Kenzie also told Rose that she was moving out of Carol's and wanted to get emancipated. She asked Rose if she knew of anyone with a place where she could stay until she saved up enough money for an apartment. Rose offered her the small studio apartment upstairs from the cafe and said she could live there rent-free for as long as she wanted.

Kenzie sat with Rose in the cafe's lobby until the sheriff arrived for work a few hours later. She then drove to his office and told him the same story she told Rose.

The sheriff was Rick Channing, who had been re-elected every four years for as long as Kenzie could remember. He had been good friends with her parents, especially her dad, and every election cycle her dad helped Rick with his campaign and posted a sign in their front yard. The two of them even taught Kenzie how to shoot a pistol, much to her mom's annoyance.

With Rick was his deputy, Drew Collins, who looked barely out of high school, but was apparently a college graduate.

They followed Kenzie's car to the spot on the forest road where she and Chad parked that night. She then led them through the forest and down the embankment to the creek.

"Have any more of your memories returned since last night?" said Rick.

She shook her head. "That was the only one."

"Still no idea of who kidnapped you and your brother?"

Again, she shook her head. "I keep trying to remember anything, but there's just nothing."

They reached the creek's bank, and she led them over to the outcrop where Chad showed her his body. It was still there, partially submerged in mud. She felt her heart sink all over again and tears press beneath her cheeks.

"Oh, man..." Rick muttered, removing his hat and wiping his brow. "You're sure it's him?"

She nodded. "He's even wearing the St. Christopher medal I gave him."

"These are your footprints beside the body?" Deputy Drew asked.

"Yeah. I made them when I came here last night," said Kenzie.

"We'll make a note of that for the forensics team when they get here," said the sheriff. He walked over and stood beside Kenzie. "I'm so sorry for your loss, Kenzie. I know you and Chad were really close."

She swallowed hard and nodded. Her lip quivered.

He gave her shoulder a friendly squeeze. "You should go home and try to get some sleep. We can take it from here."

She nodded. "Will you call me if you find out anything?"

"You have my word."

Kenzie pulled up to Carol's house in the forest, timing it so she arrived after Carol left for the unemployment office. Carol still had no idea that Chad was found, and that Kenzie was moving out that day, so Kenzie planned to be long gone by the time Carol arrived home and exploded in rage. Not that she cared about Kenzie and Chad, but she cared a lot about the checks the State paid her to foster them.

Kenzie went inside and packed the few things she owned into a backpack, the most cherished of them being the laptop Zac loaned her. She kept it hidden under her mattress so Carol wouldn't find it. Carol could keep the clothes.

Before leaving, she wrote a brief note on a sheet of notebook paper and left it on the kitchen table along with the car keys. The note read:

'I found Chad last night. You'll never be able to make him cry again. I'm leaving.'

Kenzie went to the tool shed out back and pulled out her mountain bike, one of the few things she bought with her paychecks before Carol took the rest. She climbed on it and pedaled off.

The sun had set by the time Kenzie arrived at Rose's Cafe. Rose led her upstairs to the apartment and showed her the new furnishings she had delivered that afternoon. They consisted of a bed, desk, dresser, and TV, and Kenzie wouldn't have traded any of them for the world. In a day of crushing devastation, Rose had pushed the storm clouds back a little.

"Thank you," Kenzie barely squeaked out through quivering lips.

"You should try to get some rest," Rose said, gently stroking Kenzie's hair. "You've had a rough day."

Kenzie nodded.

After Rose left, Kenzie lay down in bed and stared at the ceiling, trying to quiet her mind enough to get to sleep. It apparently worked, because she awoke sometime later that night to shouts coming from downstairs. She eased over to her door and cracked it open just enough to see down the stairs to the lobby below.

Carol was there with two cops.

"Where the hell is Kenzie Walsh?" Carol barked.

"Get out of my cafe!" Rose yelled back at her. "Now!"

"Not until you turn her over!" Carol screamed.

One cop stepped forward to intervene, handing Rose a sheet of paper. "Ma'am, Mrs. Mahoney is listed as the girl's legal guardian."

"A legal guardian who abused Kenzie and her brother," said Rose.

"Like hell, I did!" screamed Carol. "Prove it!"

Kenzie had seen enough. There was no way in hell she was going back to Carol's. She'd rather sleep in the forest. She eased the door closed, threw on some jeans and a jacket, then hurried over to the window facing the back alley. She tugged it open and climbed out it onto the eave. She crawled over to the drainpipe on the side of the building and slid down it to the alley, then ran off into the night.

‘Tap, tap, tap.’

Zac looked over from his desk to his bedroom window. Only one person tapped on it late at night. He walked over and drew aside the curtains, and sure enough, it was Kenzie. He slid it open.

"Hey," he said, but before he could say anything else, she cut in.

"Chad's dead, Zac. And Carol's after me with two cops. Can I come in?"

"What? Yeah. Sure," he said, barely spitting out his words at the sudden shock of what she just said. He helped her climb in, then quickly slid the window shut. He checked both ways down the sidewalk outside to make sure she wasn't followed, then closed the curtains.

"Chad's dead?" he said.

She nodded, pressing her hands against her knees while catching her breath. She had sprinted the entire way from Rose's.

"I'll tell you about it in a second," she said, "but I moved out of Carol's place into an apartment Rose owns above her cafe."

"And you ran here from there?"

Kenzie nodded. "Carol showed up with the cops to take me back. She's out of her freaking mind. Rose is gonna help me get emancipated so I never have to go back, but until then, Carol's still got me."

"So, how'd they find Chad?"

"They didn't. I did."

"How?"

She took a deep breath. "I'm gonna tell you the craziest story you ever heard, and I really need you to believe me."

"Okay."

"Chad showed me."

He did a double take. "But he's dead?"

"He is."

"Oh, crap." He swallowed.

She looked over to his desk, where his phone sat beside a portable police scanner. "Do you have that app loaded on your phone? The one that lets you know if someone's telling the truth."

"Yeah. Truth Talk. It's on there."

"I need you to use it on me."

"What for?"

"Because I need you to know I'm telling the truth."

"I don't need an app for that, Kenz."

"Just, please, Zac. I don't want you to have any doubts."

"Okay," he said, and they walked over to his desk and sat down. She waited while the app loaded, watching the cool graphics load on the screen.

"Did you do those graphics too?"

"Yeah. You like them?"

"I love them. They look amazing."

"Thanks. They took a while."

"I can tell. So how do we do this?"

"I just need to ask you a couple questions so we can establish a baseline for you. I already have a ton of samples programmed into it to draw an average from, but having your own voice will improve the results."

"Okay."

For the next several minutes, Zac went through a series of questions, asking her to provide both truthful answers and lies, while he calibrated the baseline. Once he was satisfied he had a wide enough sample range, he settled back in his chair.

"It's ready," he said.

Kenzie took a deep breath, and for the next fifteen minutes she told him everything that happened the previous night, including the things Chad told her about Acheron and the evil that flowed from it. She left nothing out, being as completely honest as she had ever been. When she finished, she leaned forward and stared at the phone.

"What's it say?" she said.

"Can I be funny?"

"I hope you will. I need a laugh right now."

He looked at the app's display, then back at her. "It says you're full of crap."

A smile broke on her face. And it felt really good. "What's it really say?"

He looked at the app again. "It says that everything you said falls within the baseline parameters for truth. You weren't lying."

"Thanks for doing that, Zac."

"I didn't need the app, Kenz."

"I know. But I did. You see what I mean about how crazy it sounds?"

"It's definitely up there. Have you told Fr. Sean about it?"

"I'm going to after the funeral. Right now, my head's still spinning at like a million miles a second and I can't stop crying."

Zac watched her for a moment and gave her hand a gentle squeeze. "I'm sorry, Kenz. I'll take the floor tonight and you can take the bed."

"You took the floor last time when Chad and I were here. I can take it tonight."

"But then they'll take away my man card for making a grieving girl sleep on the floor. I'll take it."

Kenzie felt a lump fill her throat as she watched Zac walk over to his closet and pull out a spare blanket and pillow.

"Zac?" she said.

"Yeah?"

"I'll hit anyone who tries to take your man card."

Kenzie met Rose at the cafe the next morning, and together they drove to the courthouse where they met with Doc Weathers. He'd already spoken to the judge, a long-time friend of his, and stressed the need for a quick hearing on Kenzie's emancipation and a protective order until then. They filed the application, and the judge scheduled the hearing for the next day.

Bob and Carol showed up at the hearing to contest the emancipation, but it was a lost cause. Both Rose and Doc testified to seeing Carol's erratic behavior, but it was Kenzie who produced the bombshell — the photos she'd downloaded from her phone to her laptop, showing the deep bruising, scars, and cuts from years of abuse.

The judge not only granted Kenzie her emancipation, he also ordered that Bob and Carol's foster license be suspended until the State could conduct a thorough investigation.

It had been a long road out of hell, but Kenzie finally had her freedom. She only wished that Chad could be there to share in his big sister's victory. It was a victory for both of them.

And now it was time to plan for his funeral.

A soft rain misted down on the mourners gathered at the Faulkner Cemetery for Chad's funeral. Kenzie sat beside Rose and Doc in the front row of fold-out chairs at the graveside, the two women holding hands for comfort. Zac and three of his computer club buddies sat in the row behind her, and behind them were two more rows of Chad's friends from school and their families.

The cemetery sat atop Pioneer Hill, just outside the northern boundaries of town. It was the county's oldest cemetery, with graves on its eastern side dating back to the town's founding centuries ago. That part of it, often just called the 'old cemetery,' was steep and rugged, with monuments and gravestones of granite and marble tilted at odd angles from years of erosion beneath them. Dry grass grew long and unkempt, and leafless trees, their branches gnarled and roots exposed, stood like grim sentries. A centuries-old wrought-iron fence barred it from trespassers, but that didn't stop the local kids from sneaking in late at night to scare each other with ghost stories.

The cemetery's western half, usually just called the 'new cemetery,' stood in stark contrast to the eastern half. It was graded flat into the hillside, and its manicured lawn kept watered and green. It was a calm, restful place and gave her brother a good view of the town below.

Kenzie's cheeks felt swollen again as tears pressed to come out. But she fought to hold them back until she was alone.

Fr. Sean McCready, or Fr. Sean, as Kenzie had come to know him, presided over the funeral. She had met the young priest, who looked more like a baseball player than a typical priest, during her freshman year of high school at St. Matthews, which she attended on a scholarship the parish provided. He had seen her sitting alone on a fountain in the school's courtyard while the other students played, and walked over to join her. They talked for the rest of the lunch break, and she learned that in addition to his priestly duties as the parish's pastor, he also taught religious education at the school and coached their baseball team. He invited her to stop by his office anytime she needed someone to talk to or hang out with during lunch.

Kenzie took him up on the offer, and before long, a close friendship was born. Over the coming years, he would become like a brother to her; and along with Chad, Zac, and Rose, she considered him one of her favorite people.

Like Kenzie, Fr. Sean had suffered tragedy in his life. Following the attacks on 9-11, he and his brother Conor had enlisted in the Marines, and Conor's death to a suicide bomber left him emotionally shattered and in search of meaning. It would be a reading at Mass that finally banished his darkness and despair, and opened Sean's eyes to a new vibrancy in life.

When Sean later asked the priest about this reaction he had to the reading, the priest, an elderly Irish friar named Fr. Ian, gave him a knowing nod.

"'Tis God sendin' yeh one of His love letters," Fr. Ian said in his thick Irish brogue. "He's tellin' yeh yer brother's in Heaven wit Him and doin' jest fine."

It would be this revelation that set Sean on a path that eventually led him to the priesthood.

This idea of God sending us 'love letters' piqued Kenzie's interest. "He really does that?" she asked.

"He does. You just need to be open to it when it happens."

"How will I know when that is?"

"Your heart will tell you."

For three years now, she had done her best to keep an open mind about these 'love letters' from God. But on days like today, it wasn't easy.

Kenzie stuck around the cemetery after the mourners left. Rose gave Kenzie her car keys and caught a ride home with Doc. It was obvious that Kenzie needed some time alone with her brother.

Kenzie sat down beside Chad's headstone and re-read the inscription she had engraved beneath his name and the dates of his birth and death.

'And He shall wipe away every tear, and there shall be no more death, sorrow, crying or pain.'

"Hey, buddy," she whispered, her voice threatening to break at any moment. She sniffed back the first of many tears.

"You know when you said in the car that you were glad you got to have me as your sister, and how it sounded like it was over? Well, it's not, because I still get to be your sister, Chad, even if you're not here with me anymore." She took a deep breath and wiped at a tear that had formed in the corner of her eye. "Death doesn't get to take that away from me." She took another breath, not ready yet for the flow of tears that were bursting to come out. "I've been thinking about the stuff you told me about Acheron and the things that are out there, and I'm gonna do everything I can to warn people about it. I'm not sure how yet, but I'll figure it out. I'm gonna talk to Fr. Sean next week and maybe he'll have some ideas. I heard he performed an Exorcism once, so if anyone knows about this stuff, it's gonna be him." She took one deep, final breath. "Anyway, I just want you to know that your big sister's thinking about you and misses you like crazy." She kissed the tips of her fingers and touched them to the gravestone. "Enjoy Heaven, little brother."

No longer able to hold back the tears, she pressed her hands against her lap and wept.

Chapter Seven
An Exorcist's Tale

Kenzie poked her head in the office door and saw Fr. Sean going through a stack of papers at his desk across the room. She tapped lightly on the door to get his attention.

"Hey. Do you have time to talk?" she said as he looked up from his papers.

"Of course. Come on in, Kenzie."

He set aside the tests he was grading while she walked over and sat down across the desk from him. She always liked his office. It had a comfortable living room feel. Against one wall stood a bookcase where he kept his books and a shelf of trophies he'd won as an athlete himself and as coach of the school's baseball team. On the walls hung paintings of Jesus and various saints, along with photos of his family. One of them showed him and his brother Conor in their Marine uniforms, taken several years before Conor was killed in Afghanistan.

"How are you doing?" he said.

"Still crappy. But I'm crying less than I was last week, so I guess that's a start."

"I'm sorry, Kenzie. You and Chad deserved a happy ending."

"Can you tell that to your buddy God."

"You can tell Him."

"I tried, but He's ignoring my calls."

He smiled. "I'll put in a call for you."

"Thanks. Tell Him this grief stuff really sucks."

"He knows. But the alternative is not having someone you care enough about to grieve for. And to me, that's far worse."

"Maybe there's a happy middle ground somewhere."

"If you find it, let me know."

"I'll patent it."

He smiled at this.

"Can I talk to you about something really weird that happened?" she said. "It's kind of related to Chad, but in a really weird way. It's also totally out of left field."

"What is it?"

"Do you believe in ghosts?"

From his expression, she could see the question caught him off guard; but a moment later, he nodded. "I do. Why do you ask?"

"Because I saw one. It was Chad's."

"When was this?"

"The night he showed me where his body was."

"It wasn't your memory returning?"

She shook her head. "My memory's still gone. And Chad said it's not coming back. Want to hear the rest of it?"

"Whatever you want to share."

"Okay. But it's pretty wild."

For the next ten minutes, she told him everything about that night and the things Chad said. She left nothing out, including the strange sentience she felt in the forest. She concluded with Chad's warning about the coming of Acheron and her need to warn people about these things. To her relief, he remained attentive through the entire bizarre tale.

"Do you have any idea who these men were that saved you?" he said.

She shook her head. "Chad just said they were prophets. He said it wouldn't make sense now, but it will."

"So, he meant prophets in the literal sense?"

"I think so. Especially since they made those things go away."

"Have you seen any of the other things he warned you about? The ones he said are worse than the shadow people."

"Not yet. But I did see something weird this morning on my way to school. There was this woman standing outside Sally's diner. I've never seen her before, but I recognized her. She was even wearing the same clothes I knew she'd be in."

"Like a déjà vu?"

"Kind of. Except she was dead."

"How do you know that?"

"Because people were walking through her and nobody else saw her. But what creeped me out was the way she looked at me. She had this dead blank stare and could tell that I saw her. And I don't think she liked that. So, what do you think about all of this?"

"It sounds scary."

"You don't think I'm crazy?"

He shook his head. "Believe it or not, this isn't the craziest thing I've heard."

"What was the craziest?"

"When one of my students told me his friend was possessed by a demon. I found out the hard way she really was. That has a way of making you a believer, fast."

"It would me. Was that the Exorcism I heard you performed?"

"It was." He rose from his chair and walked over to his bookcase. He browsed through several titles before removing a book and taking it back to his desk.

"This is a book about the case," he said, handing her the book.

She looked at the title, 'Into the Periphery,' and then at the author's name. 'Reverend Sean McCready.'

"You wrote this?" she said.

He nodded. "Shortly after the Exorcism. It's based on the notes I kept and interviews with the girl and several students who knew her."

"Where'd you get the title, 'Into the Periphery'?"

"It's from an old saying, 'evil hides in the periphery.' Mystics believe we're able to see subtleties in our peripheral vision that don't appear in our direct sight. This girl saw the demon as a shadow from the corner of her eye, so I used that theme in the title."

"Can I borrow this?"

"It's yours. It'll give you some insight into these unseen worlds, and how they interact with our own."

She studied the book for another moment. "Was it as scary as it is in the movies?"

He shook his head. "It's scarier. A demonic encounter is a terror that touches deep inside your soul. There's no human experience to compare it to."

"But you beat the demon?"

Again, he shook his head. "That was all God. It's His fight. I was just there as His proxy."

She looked down at the book and the eerie image of the shadow-like spirit on the cover. "Am I being crazy if I do this?"

"What are you thinking about doing?"

"Writing a story about Acheron. And how its evil still affects us."

He paused for a moment as he appeared to think about this. "It's really going to depend on how you approach this. If it's an academic essay, you'll probably be okay. But if it goes beyond that, you need to be careful."

"What'll happen?"

"They'll come after you. And you don't want to be on the receiving end of a demon's attack."

Kenzie read Fr. Sean's book when she got home that day and it shed some terrifying light on the world of the demonic. The girl in the Exorcism, who he called 'Becky' to protect the real girl's privacy, had inadvertently fallen prey to a demon during her search for answers and meaning after her father's death. She fell in with a group of teens steeped heavily in the occult and began a downward spiral into ever darker places and practices. It culminated with her participation in a Black Mass, and from there, she was left vulnerable to the demon's assault. And when that assault came, it was brutal and merciless.

The girl, Fr. Sean, and the girl's friend barely survived the Exorcism, and the parish's former pastor, Fr. Dennis Jenkins, was killed in a dark, sinister way. Fr. Sean always suspected that his killing was linked to the girl's case, and his encounter with a possessed girl in the early seventies named Natalie Stark.

Kenzie closed the book and set it on the nightstand beside her bed. It was well after midnight by then, and every creak and rustle in the apartment caused her arms to break out in gooseflesh. She would sleep with the lights on that night, assuming she could quiet her mind long enough to fall asleep.

Fr. Sean was right about the book giving insight into the unseen horrors lurking in the dark corners of our reality; and of the many snares it set for the careless and unprepared. If she went through with this story on Acheron, she needed to be careful and as prepared as possible.

Chapter Eight
Acheron the Accursed

Kenzie began her research at the town's library the next day. The library, formally called the Crawford Memorial Library, was housed in an old colonial mansion, dedicated to the town a century earlier by two descendants of one of the town's founding families, Ethan and Elinor Crawford. It consisted of three floors above ground and a large reference section in the basement where the historical records, journals, and ancient manuscripts were kept. Many of its aged volumes dated back to the town's founding centuries earlier, with several having been brought over from Europe with the first settlers.

It had been a while since Kenzie visited the library, and her research skills were rusty, at best. Her dad used to take her there as a kid, hoping to impart to her his fascination with the town's rich history. It mostly bored her at the time, and she wished now that she'd paid better attention.

She began her research by reading all she could about Acheron's legends and planned to compare those to the historical Acheron. Assuming any records of it existed. It didn't surprise her to find that modern day historians dismissed the possibility of Acheron's existence. Pure folly and legend seemed to be the consensus. They all scoffed at the idea of an entire city disappearing without a trace. Things like that just didn't happen in a world governed by the laws of physics.

But this sentiment wasn't shared in the oldest journals, those written around the time of Acheron's demise. In those browned, aged pages, Acheron's contemporaries wrote of Acheron as just another coastal city, located a day's ride north of Capetown. Its merchants traded in fish, furs, and rare metals with their neighboring communities, and several of the journals' authors had even ventured within Acheron's dark walls.

One of the more prolific writers of that time was Nathanial Crawford, considered by many to have been the leader of Capetown's founding fathers. Many of the town's roads, bridges, and buildings bore his name, and a life-size bronze statue of him on a horse stood in Crawford Park in the center of town.

Crawford was renowned among his contemporaries as a witch hunter and Exorcist, and together with a group of Capetown's elders and clergy, founded the Brotherhood of Zion. The Brotherhood's mission was to purge the region of the scourges of witchcraft and devilry.

Crawford kept meticulous journals and wrote extensively of Acheron. His earlier writings described it as a dank fishing community along the Maine Coast, much older and larger than Capetown. It lay about fifty miles north of Capetown, close enough that a man on horseback or wagon could reach it in a day and then leave before night fell. Nobody wanted to remain in Acheron after dark. Even in those early days before the *event*, something was unsettling about the city.

Crawford had traveled there as a young boy with his father, a wealthy merchant who traded with the people of Acheron from time to time. It wasn't his father's preferred stop along his trade route for reasons the boy would soon discover, and that visit left deep and lasting impressions on the boy.

"Now hear me this, boy," the elder Crawford told his son as the town's spires slowly came into view above the mist, "this Acheron, she's a damnable place. Don't ye take none of it wit' ye when we leave."

It didn't take long after their arrival for Crawford to understand the reason for his father's caution.

'It was diseased,' Crawford wrote in his journal of the dreary mist-shrouded city that lay beneath a perpetually cold gray sky. *'To see Acheron, was to see a settlement shunned by the sun and void all light and warmth.'*

Acheron's inhabitants were as dreary and bleak as the town, and while not openly hostile, they made no effort at the pleasantries Crawford received from the other towns his father traded with. Acheron's inhabitants stayed mostly indoors behind shuttered windows, and the streets were nearly void of people and animals.

This gloom was reflected in the artwork that adorned Acheron's buildings, walls, and grand temples, and seeing it alarmed the young boy. These paintings and carvings showed scenes of horror and the macabre; images of torture, mutilation and decadence. Winged bat-like creatures descended from the sky to tear at people with taloned claws, and unspeakable monstrosities rose from the ocean to devour sacrificial victims. A long mural painted on a wall showed naked women strapped to posts along the waterfront, while from deep beneath the bay's murky waters came ghostly lights and glowing red eyes.

"Ye see what I meant now, son?" the elder Crawford said as he and his son departed from the city shortly before sundown. In any other town, they would have stayed the night in one of the town's inns, but Crawford's father had no desire to spend the night in Acheron, or to stay any longer than needed to conclude business.

"Ye never know what might be walkin' its streets after dark," the elder Crawford said, "or what might be watchin' ye in yer room while ye slept." The younger Crawford couldn't agree more and was as anxious as his dad to put as much distance as possible between them and the disquieting city before the moon rose. Like his dad, he suspected things moved through Acheron's dark streets in the moon's light that no sane mind should ever see.

And Acheron wasn't sane.

Kenzie opened one of Crawford's later journals, kept around the time he founded the Brotherhood of Zion. The situation had turned dire in Capetown by then, and Crawford noted with alarm the rise in unsettling occurrences. Its residents frequently reported seeing strange misshapen creatures along dark forest paths, and animal carcasses were found slaughtered in grisly ways. A blight infected much of their crops and fish catches became sparse and unreliable. All agreed that something dark had fallen over the land.

Then Capetown's children began to go missing. The ones who returned told of encounters with strange men in the forests and of seeing dark unholy rituals performed in moonlit clearings. Two boys recounted how they had wandered for days, lost in the depths of a seemingly endless forest they had explored in the past without ever getting lost. They knew every inch of that forest, and yet somehow, they had gone in circles, returning to the same areas time after time.

They also described the feeling of being watched the entire time; not by people or animals, but by an unseen presence that whispered silently in their thoughts.

The tipping point came when a young boy was found near starvation along the banks of a remote creek. He described seeing a clearing where strange, cryptic symbols were painted on the rocks and trees, and ornaments of those symbols hung from branches. He drew pictures of those symbols for Crawford and the elders, which Crawford then sketched in his journal.

The first image showed a serpent coiled around the sun. The second showed an eight-pointed star within a circle, with an eye in the star's center. Kenzie used her cell phone's camera to take photos of the symbols.

Crawford was alarmed when he saw the drawings. He had seen those symbols years earlier during the trip to Acheron with his father, where they adorned many of its walls and buildings.

They seemed strangely sinister to him at the time, and seeing them now, he didn't doubt their diabolical nature. He assembled the most pious members of Capetown's elders and clergy, men who shared his belief that Capetown's afflictions were of occult origin, and together they formed the Brotherhood of Zion. Its stated mission was to purge the region of witchcraft and occult activity, and they approached this task with the zeal of crusaders.

The Brotherhood made its first foray to the black streets of Acheron shortly after a hunting party found the mutilated remains of a young boy. Their dogs were drawn to the banks of a creek just north of Capetown, where they found the boy's remains buried in a shallow grave. The rains had washed away much of the sediment covering the young boy, and a putrid stench struck the men as they approached.

The boy's head and limbs had been violently torn from his body, then placed alongside his torso and covered in dirt. Nearby, painted on a rock along the creek's bank, was the image of the serpent coiled around the sun. The symbol of the great ancient demi-god, Set. The Morningstar.

Twenty members of the Brotherhood galloped north on horseback to Acheron, making camp in the woods of a hill overlooking the mist-shrouded city. But even at that distance, their skin crawled at the intangible aura of evil the city gave off. It encircled them, filling their minds with foul blasphemies and torturous thoughts.

It feels alive, one man noted, and the others nodded in agreement. Those black streets and spires felt somehow imbued in a hideous semblance of life. Even the clergy couldn't explain the queer feeling, but the reality of it was unmistakable. The city itself was sentient. And it was watching them.

Fearing to stay in the area any longer than was necessary, the men stole into the city that night and seized nine of its inhabitants. They took them back to Capetown, where they were tried and convicted of witchcraft.

None of Capetown's residents had any doubt over the men's guilt. They felt a dark aura surrounding these men, and following their arrival, domestic animals turned wild and fled into the forests. And the phenomena only worsened after the men's execution by fire.

Something stalked Capetown's streets and alleys in the dead of night, some unseen force unleashed by the men's arrival. The residents hid behind shuttered windows and barred doors, and the few who dared to look out were driven into fits of madness.

This force targeted the Brotherhood's members with particular savagery, leading them to grisly fates. One member, who told Crawford and the others of hearing 'voices,' later killed his family and himself. Another lit his own house on fire, killing himself and his young son. Two more were found burned beyond recognition, their bodies twisted and snapped like twigs, but their clothes oddly left untouched. Another dragged his son to the cliffs at Hallows Pointe where the two leaped to their deaths.

'I fear for the community and our descendants,' Crawford wrote in his journal. *'A fiend has loosed itself upon our people, against which our weapons are powerless.'* He later wrote of hearing a familiar voice call to him from outside his shuttered window at night. The voice was that of a Brotherhood member who had killed himself and his son a week earlier.

'The clergy tell that this curse shall follow into the first-born sons of our descendants,' Crawford wrote in a subsequent entry. By that time, of the twenty Brotherhood members who had raided Acheron, only thirteen remained.

As the night of the solstice approached, Crawford learned it would coincide with a lunar eclipse. This one would be the dreaded blood moon, feared by the settlers for the doom it portended. Beneath such moons, all manner of evil roamed freely, and its appearance on the solstice combined for a powerful, black magick.

Crawford's son, Jimmy, the oldest of four boys and two girls, told him earlier that week of a cave he found on Hallows Pointe, and of strange robed men he saw enter it. Crawford took alarm at this. The high priests of Acheron wore hooded robes, and if they intended to work their magick on the solstice, then Crawford and the surviving members of the Brotherhood needed to stop them. He gathered the members together, and procuring three casks of gunpowder, they went to Hallows Pointe and detonated the casks, sealing off the cave's entrance.

Jimmy and Crawford's daughter, Sarah, went missing that night and were never found.

Shortly after the cave's destruction, Crawford decreed that the night be forever commemorated as 'Libertas Night,' the night on which the community liberated itself from the scourge of witchcraft.

Kenzie made a mental note of this. This had to be the origin of the town's annual festival, the 'Libertas Festival,' which also fell on the summer solstice.

In his final journal entry, recorded around the time of the cave's destruction and his decree, Crawford wrote: *'It be'eth my prayer, O Lord, that this cave ne'er be opened, lest the evil we rid the world of this night be loosed again upon men.'*

Acheron vanished the same night as the cave's destruction.

Kenzie opened a new journal, this one kept by one of Crawford's contemporaries, the Reverend Elijah Forester. Forester wrote:

'Acheron's sin was so grave, and its people so depraved, that it cried to Heaven for vengeance. And Heaven answered.'

In the blink of an eye, the accursed city had vanished. Forester surmised that Acheron was swallowed by the ground on which it stood, and this became the consensus which later bled into the legend.

As to the nature of Acheron's sins and deeds, there remained much speculation. Forester was the first to suggest that its inhabitants were members of the Esoteric Order of Set, an ancient cult dedicated to the worship of their demi-god, Set, an entity known in Christian teaching as the fallen archangel, Lucifer. He drew the connection from the cult's use of the symbol of the serpent encircling the sun, an ancient symbol for the morning star, which the prophet Isaiah gave as one of the names for Lucifer.

'How you have fallen from heaven, O Lucifer, morning star, son of the dawn! You have been cut down to the ground, O destroyer of nations.'

Forester believed the cult had made a covenant with Lucifer, basing this belief on the first-hand account of a sailor he had spoken with. The sailor had been among the crew of a merchant vessel, the Alighieri, bound from Europe to Boston when it blew off course in a storm and wrecked off the coast of Acheron.

Prior to the wreck, the crew had discovered a crate on board which didn't appear on the manifest. When they opened it, they found a large ornamental chest inside. On its gold-plated sides were etched cryptic symbols of an occult nature, and the men reported feeling a queer sense of dread and distress whenever they came near it.

Aboard the ship were two Franciscan missionaries, Brother Elijah and Brother Enoch, who expressed particular alarm when shown the chest. At their request, it was thrown overboard, and the crew watched as it sank beneath the waves.

Two days later, it was found again in the cargo hold.

Following the chest's discovery this second time, sinister events began to occur. The ship's watch reported seeing a man prowling the deck at night, a man who they swore had no face. Or at least none they could see in the moonlight. A search of the entire ship during the day found no such man, but that didn't stop the sightings from persisting at night.

Crew members began to disappear and were feared to have leaped overboard into the Atlantic's icy waters. Others went mad and became mutinous, insisting that the ship be set ablaze and the crew escape in lifeboats. Even to the most rational crew members, it was clear that something diabolical had befallen the ship. The captain himself wrote in his log of seeing eyes burning from the darkness of his cabin's closet.

Then the storm came, more ferocious and violent than any the crew had ever encountered, and for days it blew them off course. It ran aground on a reef off the dark coasts of Acheron, and all but one of the crew perished. The surviving sailor was found clinging to a driftwood plank by two of Capetown's fishermen. They brought him back to Capetown, where he lived long enough to tell Forester and his attending physician the bizarre story, and drew pictures for them of the strange etchings on the chest's side. The etchings were of the eight-pointed star and the serpent encircling the sun, images later recounted by the young boy who had gone missing outside of Capetown, whose tale prompted the raid on Acheron by Crawford and the Brotherhood.

The sailor's other sketch was of a chalice he had seen etched onto the chest's side, and upon seeing this, Forester's blood ran cold. He believed the chalice to be the legendary Calicem Noctis, or Cup of the Night, in its English translation, the most coveted talisman in occult lore. To occult practitioners, it was the equivalent of the Holy Grail, the mythical cup sought by Christian explorers as the cup from which Christ celebrated His Last Supper with His apostles.

The chest and its contents were presumed to have perished in the Atlantic's icy waters along with the ship's wreckage, but Forester had his doubts. He believed it was no coincidence that the ship blew off course to Acheron, and that Acheron's residents salvaged the chest from the wreckage. He drew this belief from the sinister changes that befell Acheron shortly thereafter.

Kenzie next moved on to later journals, written a century after Acheron's disappearance. It didn't surprise her to find that doubts had arisen over Acheron's existence, as eyewitnesses would have been long dead by then. There was one writer from this period, however, who broke ranks with his contemporaries. His name was Thomas Stockdale. Stockdale had met with two travelers on a trip through Maine, who both swore they saw Acheron arise from the mist. They were sleeping atop a hill at the time, when a violent jolt from the ground shook them awake. As they looked down on the mist-shrouded valley beneath the faint, blood-red moon, they saw Acheron's black temples and streets arise from the cold damp earth.

Stockdale noted that this happened on the night of a lunar eclipse on the centennial of Acheron's disappearance. Soon afterwards, it became part of the legend that Acheron would arise from its unhallowed grave for one night each century during a lunar eclipse.

Kenzie spent three days at the library that week, going there after school and staying until it was time for her shift at Rose's. She took pages of notes and photos of the illustrations sketched in the volumes. She then went to work writing her essay, titling it 'The Shunned City,' a reference to Forester's belief that, even before its demise, God had removed His benevolence from the city on account of its sacrilege.

She concluded her essay with her belief that Acheron's legacy of evil continued to the present day. To some degree, most people in Capetown had experienced encounters with the inexplicable, and Kenzie sought to tie it all back to Acheron. The land itself was festering in its growing evil. And it would only grow worse as the night of Acheron's rising approached.

Kenzie finished her essay two days later, and now it was time to share it.

Chapter Nine
The Shunned City

Fr. Sean was out for a run around the track that morning, when he spotted Kenzie over by the dugout. He slowed down and headed over.

"You wanna read something really cool and scary, and way less sweaty than running?" she said as he walked up.

He smiled as he grabbed a towel off the fence and wiped the sweat from his face. "You finished your essay?"

"Yup. Just last night." She held up several sheets of paper. "Everything you never wanted to know about Acheron and didn't know you didn't want to ask."

"That's a long list."

"It's about to get longer. Do you have time to read it?"

"Sure."

She handed him the papers, then followed him over to the bleachers where he sat down and began reading. For the next ten minutes, she fidgeted anxiously while waiting for him to finish. When he finally did, he looked up and nodded approvingly.

"This is really good, Kenzie. How much of it's historical?"

"Every last typo and run-on sentence. Most of it's stuff from the journals those guys kept."

"What're you gonna do with it?"

"Hopefully get people to read it. I uploaded it to a website Zac helped me make, and I was thinking about submitting it to the school paper to see if they'll run it as an op-ed."

"This could go well with their Halloween issue."

"That's what I'm hoping. I was gonna drop it off over there before class."

"Do you have an extra copy? I can give it to their faculty adviser."

"That would be huge if you'd do that, father. Thanks. Yeah, you can give them that copy."

"What's the name of your website, and I'll have him check that out, too?"

"It's called 'The Acheron Files.'"

By the time Kenzie arrived home, the paper had emailed to let her know her story would run in their upcoming Halloween issue.

The issue came out later that week. As one of the local shops that carried copies of the paper, a stack of them was waiting in Rose's lobby by the time Kenzie came downstairs that morning. She snatched up a copy and quickly flipped to her article. And there it was, in glorious black and white:

'The Shunned City,' by Kenzie Walsh. It included her website address at the end.

Kenzie looked across the lobby at Rose, who smiled at her from behind the counter.

"Did you read it?" Kenzie said.

"First thing this morning," Rose said, waving a copy of the paper. "I loved it."

"We all did," said a patron named Marty, one of the cafe's early morning regulars. He nodded to the copy on his table. "Nice work, Kenzie."

"Rose passed them out as we came in," said Chip, another one of the cafe's regulars. "It's really good."

Two other patrons at a nearby table nodded in agreement.

"So, what's your next story about?" said Marty.

Kenzie had already bounced around several ideas for her next story with Rose, and they both agreed that a story on the town's supposedly haunted lighthouse would make a great one. Especially if Kenzie found proof of the hauntings.

Built in 1902, the lighthouse was considered to be ill-omened even before its completion. One of its construction workers plunged to his death when the scaffolding beneath him collapsed, and another drowned when a rogue wave crashed over the breakwater and swept him out to sea.

The lighthouse's first keeper was a man named Jonathan Collins, who lived with his family in the small cottage next to the lighthouse tower. Collins' daughters, Amy and Michelle, died of pneumonia during an ice storm their first winter in the cottage, and his distraught wife leaped to her death from the tower a week later.

The hauntings began shortly after that.

Rumors circulated of a 'wailing woman,' dressed in white, appearing at night on the narrow catwalk around the tower's lantern room. Even Collins himself claimed to have seen the specter, who he believed to be the ghost of his dead wife. He quit his job as keeper and moved from the cottage shortly after that.

The next keeper was a man named Clyde Williams, who moved with his family into the cottage shortly after Collins' departure. But their stay didn't last long either. He first noticed the strange phenomena during a warm summer night when he suddenly encountered a pocket of cold air in the balmy weather. It was something his wife had also noticed. But it wasn't until his daughter began talking to a 'woman in white' that Williams decided it was time to move out.

Over the coming decades, other keepers reported similar experiences, most of whom lasted in the job less than a year, with the longest lasting five years. There were several other deaths as well.

The current keeper, whose name Kenzie found in the lighthouse registry, was a man named Floyd Monroe. He had been there for a year, and if the pattern continued, wouldn't be there much longer.

She planned to pay him a visit after school the next day.

Chapter Ten
The Thing in the Moonlight

"Can I help you?" said the grisly gray-haired man as he opened the door of the cottage next to the lighthouse tower.

"Hi," said Kenzie, picking nervously at her thumbnail. "Are you Floyd Monroe?"

"Who's askin'?" said the man.

"I'm Kenzie Walsh. I'm a student at St. Matthews High School. I wanted to talk to Mr. Monroe about a story I'm writing."

"What kind of story?"

"It's about the lighthouse, and... you know... how it's supposed to be haunted. Are you Mr. Monroe?"

"Call me Floyd. So, you've heard the stories about this place, Kenzie?"

"Just the ones I found in some old newspapers. I couldn't find anything recent."

"Don't surprise me none. Them folks over there at the town's paper ain't all that keen on this sorta stuff."

"You talked to them?" she said.

"Them and the sheriff. Ain't none of them ever come out here to check it out."

"So, the stories are true?"

"True as me and you standin' here."

"Did you see the ghost?"

He shook his head. "Ain't never seen it, but me and my dog, Zeus, we sure as hell felt it. And I'm pretty sure Zeus seen it."

"What'd it feel like?"

"Like eyes watchin' me when there weren't no one around. You ever felt that?"

She gave a slow nod, remembering that time on the road with Chad when their car broke down. "Yeah. It's not fun."

"Ain't that the truth. And that goes on a whole lot around here. You wanna take a walk with me over to the lighthouse while we do our talkin'?"

"Okay."

She followed him down a narrow stone path to the tall lighthouse tower, standing like an obelisk against the gray sky. He unlocked the heavy wooden door at its base and led her inside.

The smell of damp timber and mildew hung heavy in the air as they stepped inside the cylindrical room. Its walls were of grey concrete with narrow windows cut up the sides and long water stains trailing down them. The windows gave just enough gloomy light to see by. Against the walls stood an old generator, a wooden workbench, and some equipment. Wooden stairs coiled along walls to the ceiling high above.

It looked exactly the way a haunted lighthouse was supposed to.

"Is it okay if I take some pictures?" she said.

"Be my guest."

Using her cell phone's camera, Kenzie snapped several shots of the room, making note of how the light filtered through the windows in narrow beams.

"Started noticin' somethin' weren't right about a week after me and Zeus moved in," Floyd said as he led Kenzie up the wooden stairs to the top. "Kept havin' this feelin' I was being watched and hearing sounds like some woman cryin'. But there ain't been no woman around this place since I've been here."

They reached a trap door on the ceiling and Floyd shoved it open. They climbed through it and into the lantern room that housed the large light. "Been feelin' these areas of cold too," Floyd continued. "Could be the warmest day out, but then you step into a room and the damned place feels like ice."

Kenzie remembered reading about that in the library, about how unexplained pockets of cold air often accompanied hauntings, and about how sudden drops in temperature signaled the arrival of an unseen presence.

Her eyes ran a quick sweep of the cylindrical room. In its center sat the powerful light on a motorized swivel, and surrounding them were walls made entirely of glass. The panes to her front overlooked the Atlantic, while those behind her gave views of the cliffs and shore.

"Zeus could tell somethin' weren't right in them rooms too," Floyd said as he led her through a glass door onto a narrow catwalk circling the outside of the lantern room. A chill ocean breeze tossed her hair as she stepped over to the rail and looked down at the jagged breakwater eighty feet below.

"I read that animals can see things we can't," she said while still looking down over the rail.

"That sure sounds like Zeus," Floyd said as he joined her at the rail. "Does the same thing with this here tower. One day, just outta the blue, he stopped coming near this place. Just stands back there on the path and growls at it."

"He sees something," she said.

"Was thinkin' the same thing."

"Did you ever hear the story about the first keeper's wife?"

"Heard she killed herself or somethin'."

Kenzie nodded. "She jumped over this rail after her kids died."

Floyd followed her gaze, looking down at the rocks far below. "Not the way I'd choose to go. Ain't nothin' but air between you and them rocks."

Kenzie stepped back from the rail as the height finally got to her. "It's supposed to be her ghost that haunts this place. At least that's what I read."

"Wouldn't surprise me none."

She turned to him. "Would it be okay if I came back here tonight?"

Floyd wasn't sure he heard correctly. "You wanna come in this place at night?"

"Not really. But I think I should for my story."

"You know, that's when the ghost comes, don't you?"

"That's what I read."

"So, you're hoping you see it?"

"Yeah. And no. But mostly, yeah."

"You got some balls on ya. I'll tell ya that much. You know me and Zeus don't go anywhere near this place at night."

"I'll be okay."

"Sure hope so."

"So can I?"

He took a deep breath and gave a reluctant nod. "Long as you're okay being out here alone, I guess it's okay."

Kenzie returned to the lighthouse that evening just as the sun was setting over the hills to the west of them. She found Floyd and his six-month-old German Shepard pup, Zeus, waiting outside the cottage door.

"Was kinda hopin' you'd change your mind about doin' this," he said, looking at her somberly.

"I was kinda hoping I would too," she said, casting a wary glance at the lighthouse tower, looming even more ominously now against the darkening sky. Its powerful beam swept across the horizon in long, lazy arcs.

"Gotta admire your guts, though," he said. He reached down and pat his dog, who nudged nervously against his leg. "Zeus, this here's Kenzie. She's gonna be staying in the tower tonight."

The dog looked up at him with the confused expression dogs often give. "Yeah, I know. Don't make no sense to me either. But you know how them women are."

The dog padded over to Kenzie and sniffed her leg. At six months, he was about a third of his full-grown size and had yet to grow into his ears and paws. She cast him an amused look. "He's not gonna eat me, is he?"

Floyd chuckled. "Naw. He only eats bad folks, don't ya, Zeus."

"Hey, boy," she said, reaching down and patting his head. "You'll let me know if anything bad goes in there tonight?"

"Oh, you can count on that," Floyd said. "Dang thing won't stop barking once it shows up."

"Does he ever bark for no reason?"

Floyd shook his head. "Not that I know of. Most of the time, he's quiet as a kitten. So you hear him barkin' tonight, it means you got somethin' in there with ya."

Kenzie swallowed. She looked again at the lighthouse tower. The moon had risen behind it, casting it in silhouette, and making it resemble a dark obelisk to some ancient god.

"S'pose we oughta get a move on before we lose the light," he said.

For the second time that day, she followed him down the stone path to the lighthouse tower, while Zeus trotted along beside them. Halfway there, the dog abruptly stopped and refused to go any further.

"That's as near as he comes to the place," Floyd said as he unlocked the heavy door and led her inside the dark chamber.

"Is there a light?" she said, trying her best to see around the nearly pitch-black chamber. A few shafts of moonlight came in through the narrow windows, but that was it.

"Just them windows," he said, "but they ain't gonna do you much good down here. You'll have moonlight upstairs in the lantern room."

She slid her cell phone from her pocket and clicked on its flashlight. It wasn't ideal, but it would help her see up the stairs.

"You bring a cross or anything like that?" Floyd said.

"What for?"

"In case you run into something tonight that ain't on good terms with the Big Guy upstairs."

Kenzie swallowed. She hadn't even considered that. She slid a small cross on a slim silver chain from beneath her collar and showed it to him. It was a Confirmation gift from her parents. "Will this work?"

He shrugged. "Guess you'll be findin' out tonight."

A dog's low whine came from outside. Floyd looked back at Zeus, and then again at Kenzie. "Better get back to him before he goes all nuts. But you be careful in here tonight, girl, and don't go doin' nothin' crazy. You see somethin' you think ain't right, you get your butt outta here."

She nodded. "I will." She turned and shined her light up the wooden steps to where they faded into darkness. "Would it be okay if I left this door open?"

"Probably be a good idea," he said. "Never know when you might need to get outta there in a hurry. And doors have a funny way of lockin' themselves around here."

The possibility of getting locked inside hadn't occurred to her, but she shook off the nervous chill that brushed across her. "Thanks for letting me do this, Floyd."

"Let's hope yer still thankin' me tomorrow. Good luck tonight, Kenzie."

Again, she had to brush off a nervous chill. "Thanks."

With that, he turned and walked up the path to Zeus, who paced anxiously. "Sorry, boy," he said, leaning over to pat the dog, "but gonna need you to stay out here tonight and keep an eye out for that girl."

Zeus looked up at him.

"Gotta stay here, boy. Stay."

'Stay' was one of the few voice commands Zeus understood. With a pitiful whimper, he slumped back onto the path, his head resting on his forepaws.

Kenzie watched Floyd head on up the path and disappear around the cottage corner, while Zeus remained on watch twenty yards away. That was when the reality of it all sank in. She would be alone that night in a lighthouse that was supposed to be haunted. It was the craziest thing she had ever done. Taking a deep breath, she turned and headed up the stairs.

Kenzie climbed through the trapdoor and into the lantern room, bathed in the moonlight's ghostly pall. Long shadows from the windows' joints and the light's globe crept across the floor. No longer needing her flashlight to see by, she shut it off to conserve its battery. She planned to use its audio recorder that night to see if it picked up any sounds. She saw that on a TV show once, where they left a tape recorder overnight in a cemetery. When they returned the next day, it had recorded eerie sounds she preferred not to think about at the moment.

She walked outside onto the narrow walkway circling the lantern room, feeling chill wind billow her hair and ruffle her jacket. She stepped over to the rail and looked down at the breakwater, barely visible in the moonlight. White crests of foam shot up from waves as they crashed against the rocks.

She walked around to the side facing the shore and felt a bit of relief at seeing Zeus still on the path. She would prefer for him to be in there with her, but apparently the dog had more sense than she did.

Kenzie went back inside the lantern room and sat against the glass wall with the moon to her back. She pulled a small notepad and pen from her pocket, planning to start on her story while waiting for the ghost to make its appearance. Fortunately, the moonlight coming in from over her shoulder provided enough light to see by. She turned on the phone's audio recorder and set it on the floor beside her, then started on her story.

Kenzie wasn't aware of falling asleep, but she awoke with a startle sometime later that night. The pen and notepad had fallen from her hands onto her lap and her neck ached with a painful crick from having slept while sitting up.

The first thing she noticed was the cold.

The room was considerably colder than she remembered. She zipped up her jacket and rubbed her hands to warm them.

Then she heard the barking.

From outside came a ruckus of barks. Kenzie tensed as the reality sank in.

She was there.

Kenzie slowly reached for the phone on the floor beside her. The time showed 12:17am, which meant she had slept for three hours. She opened the phone's camera app and left its audio recorder running.

Holding the phone close to her face, she slowly scanned the room through its camera. She noticed the shadows had shifted since she last looked, but other than that, everything seemed the same.

Outside, the barking continued.

Kenzie crawled on her hands and knees around the room's perimeter, afraid that standing might draw attention to herself. She had nearly completed a full circle of the room, when she felt *her*.

Kenzie froze, as a sudden realization struck her. The ghost wasn't inside the lantern room; it was outside on the catwalk. She slowly turned and looked out the window to her right.

The ghostly figure of a woman stood against the rail outside, her long white nightgown flowing in the moonlight. The figure was pale and white, with stark patches of gray and black where skin tones should have been. It faintly resembled the harsh, inverted negative of a black-and-white photo.

Kenzie barely breathed as she slowly raised her cell phone and snapped several quick shots. The camera's flash reflected from the window in blinding strobes, lighting the area around her and catching the ghost's attention.

The apparition spun around to face Kenzie, its empty black eyes filled with hate and fury. The deep black chasm of its mouth opened grotesquely wide, and from it came a hideous shriek.

Kenzie sprang to her feet and nearly tripped as she raced for the trapdoor. She threw it open and nearly tripped several more times as she scrambled through it and down the stairs.

From behind her came hideous shrieks and maniacal laughter as the specter drifted down through the open trapdoor.

Kenzie reached the bottom of the long circular stairs and raced across the chamber to the door. As she neared it, it suddenly slammed shut with a heavy crash.

"No!" Kenzie threw her weight against the door and pounded on it with her fists, but the heavy door refused to budge.

A low moan came from above her, like the whisper of wind through barren marshes, followed by shrieks and hideous screams. She looked back, and in the eerie streaks of moonlight from the narrow window slits, she saw the phantom floating down from the rooftop hatch.

"Floyd!" Kenzie screamed, spinning back to the door and pounding on it. "Floyd!"

A breath of a cold air brushed her from behind. She screamed louder and threw her weight against the door.

"Floyd!"

With a groan of rusted hinges, the door slowly opened, and Kenzie saw Floyd outside tugging on it. She sprang out the door past him and raced up the path to where she finally collapsed beside Zeus. He watched her pant for a moment before licking her face with his long tongue.

Further back behind her came a heavy crash, as Floyd slammed the tower's door shut. A moment later, a hand touched her shoulder from behind and she nearly jumped.

"Easy, there, girl. It's only me," Floyd said calmly. "Whatever you seen in there, it ain't followed ya out."

Kenzie looked past Floyd to the tower and was relieved to see he was right. She took a slow, deep breath to steady her nerves.

"I'm takin' it you saw what you's lookin' for?" he said.

She could only manage a nod.

Chapter Eleven
Question Everything

The reaction to Kenzie's second story on the lighthouse was even better than for her first. At Rose's suggestion, Kenzie published it as a newsletter this time to go along with her website, and dropped off copies at several dozen shops, diners, and cafes where Rose knew the owners. A local printer where Zac worked part time covered the printing costs, in exchange for an ad Kenzie placed on the inside of the back cover.

Within the first day, all one hundred copies were gone, and Kenzie found a dozen more outlets willing to carry future issues. She also tripled the number of subscribers to her website, which now numbered over a hundred, and would continue to grow from there.

Over the coming months, Kenzie's stories dug ever deeper into the undercurrent of evil flowing beneath Capetown and the region, and disturbing patterns emerged. Kenzie discovered Capetown suffered more unsolved murders, assaults, and disappearances than cities three time its size, many of which hinted at supernatural elements, but these cases were all swept aside. One particular case involved a father who reported his teenage daughter being attacked by something 'dark and mist-like' that floated in through her window at night. An examination of the girl revealed deep bruising and penetration, but when her father and other family members were cleared of suspicion, the case was set aside with no investigation into the girl's and her father's claims. Like so many other cases that hinted at supernatural antagonists, it was filed away as 'unsolved' and no further action was taken. And when other similar attacks were reported, they too were filed away as 'unsolved.'

The sheer volume of 'unsolved' cases, dating back for decades, was staggering. The sheriff's department stored their case files on an online database that could only be accessed through a password-protected portal. Fortunately for Kenzie, Zac and several of his hacker buddies had previously cracked the password in order to delete the 'minor in possession of alcohol' charges they were busted on. He gave Kenzie the password so she could do her own sleuthing through the case files.

Kenzie spent many hours browsing through the database's files, taking a particular interest in those marked as 'unsolved.' It was in there that she found hundreds of files, dating back decades, where transcripts of eyewitness interviews often described encounters with strange supernatural beings and phenomena.

What she found especially troubling was the large number of 'missing person' reports on file. Kenzie had seen 'missing person' fliers posted around town occasionally, but she had no idea how pervasive the problem was. And even more alarming was the large number of cases involving missing children. It reminded her of the entry in Nathanial Crawford's journal, where he wrote of all the children who went missing in historic Capetown. She did some quick math and discovered that the incidence of missing children per capita in Capetown far exceeded the national average. But as with so many other cases, these too were marked 'unsolved' and buried in the volume of 'unsolved' case files.

Shortly after publishing her fourth issue, which by then was carried in forty-three outlets around town and kiosks at school, Zac introduced Kenzie to three of his hacker buddies, Trey, Dillon, and Brett. Zac and these guys had a hacker club they called 'The Lone Gunmen,' taking the name from a group of conspiracy theorists in their favorite TV series, *'The X-Files.'* The name fit them to a T.

As it turned out, the boys had their own paranormal encounter to share. It happened during a camping trip they took in the remote forests on the north side of the peninsula. They awoke that night to a strange disturbance in the air. A disquieting stillness surrounded them, with a complete cessation of all sounds that accompany a forest at night. Even the whisper of wind through the pines was gone. It felt like the night was holding its breath, was how Trey described it.

That eerie stillness broke suddenly with the hard crunch of pine needles and stones as something moved swiftly through the brush. Within seconds, an enormous wolf burst from the foliage into a small moonlit clearing. Its thick, coarse fur was black as the night, and its eyes reflected hungrily in the ghostly moonlight. Beneath its fur, powerful muscles rippled as it shifted from side to side, searching its surroundings.

The boys lay completely still in their sleeping bags, fearing to even breathe. Had they not been downwind from the creature, they would have been torn apart in seconds.

Then, as they watched in horror, the creature rose on its hind legs to stand upright like a man. It titled its head back on thick neck muscles and howled the most bloodcurdling sound the boys ever heard.

A sudden rustle came from the far side of the clearing, and seconds later, a deer bounded from the brush. It stopped abruptly as it spotted the creature, then spun and bounded back through the foliage. With a ferocious growl, the creature dropped onto four legs and plowed through the brush after the deer.

The boys waited until the sounds of the chase faded in the distance, then they tore off on their bikes as fast as they could go, leaving behind their sleeping bags and camping gear.

They returned the next day to retrieve their camping gear and found it torn to shreds, along with large bear-sized prints in the shape of a wolf's. They left and returned an hour later with plaster they used to make casts of the paw prints. They gave Kenzie photos of the torn sleeping bags and paw prints which she uploaded to her website and included in her newsletter on the boys' story.

Based on the comments she received from her readers, other people had seen this creature too.

Later that week, Kenzie had a local gunsmith make her five silver bullets from a silver spoon she bought at a pawnshop. He did it free of charge when he learned what she needed them for. It turned out that he had also seen things he couldn't explain, and it pissed him off when the authorities ignored it.

Kenzie kept one bullet for herself and gave the other four to the boys. A fast friendship was born after that, and the boys made her an honorary member of their Lone Gunmen club. They thought it was cool that a chick believed in the same things they did, and even cooler that she had platforms to share these stories on. Plus, it didn't hurt that she was cute, and probably the only girl who talked to them.

The boys hung out in the basement of Brett's parents' house, which they had converted into their own bat cave. It had computers, video games, DVDs, computer servers, junk food, and more supernatural and conspiracy themed posters than even Kenzie had.

She remembered with amusement the first time she ventured into their den, a place where literally no girl had gone before. As she came down the stairs, she heard the boys deep in discussion over something, but the talk stopped abruptly as she came in the door. Four guilty faces all turned to look at her.

"What?" she said, looking at the boys one by one.

"Nothing," Brett said, and Dillon, Trey, and Zac all nodded in agreement.

"Now, I know it was something."

It turned out she had walked in during a discussion over who had better legs, Kenzie or Maggie Dawson.

"You weirdos were talking about my legs?"

Four guilty grins provided all the answer she needed.

"But it wasn't in a bad way," Trey assured her, and the other three nodded in agreement.

"And you won," said Zac, which was also met with three other nods.

"I did?" She stared down at her legs wrapped in jeans. She guessed they were okay.

"Yup," said Brett. "Wasn't even close."

"We think you should wear miniskirts more often," said Trey.

Kenzie tried not to laugh, but it was too funny not to. Hormones aside, these four misfits were her tribe, and they never failed to come through for her in a jam. Other than Rose and Fr. Sean, Kenzie had no one she could fall back on like she could with the Lone Gunmen.

By the one-year anniversary of The Acheron Files' launch, Kenzie's readership had expanded beyond Capetown to include neighboring cities and communities. Even people as far away as California, Oregon, and Canada had subscribed to her website, having found it while searching the web for true ghost stories and hauntings.

The topics she covered had expanded as well. While the focus remained primarily on the unseen horrors lurking in shadowed crevasses of our reality, she now included 'conspiracy theories' whenever she saw ties between them and her underlying theme of evil. She had the Lone Gunmen to thank for this new obsession. The boys saw conspiracies in things most people took for granted, and it didn't take long for them to connect the dots for her. And once she saw the connections, she couldn't unsee them.

Kenzie's conspiracies covered the usual range of suspects, from international cabals and organizations, to secret societies, esoteric cults, and everything in between. Any time an unelected global elite met behind closed doors to plot the world's fate, they landed on her radar. She had her own way of fact-checking the conspiracies, that worked something like this — the harder the mainstream news and social media worked to discredit a story or censor it, the more likely she was to believe it. Yes, it was admittedly cynical — Kenzie blamed her Irish heritage for that — but given her experiences with Capetown's local newspaper, she had zero confidence in the news media's integrity.

A frequent target of her conspiracy theories was a tech billionaire named Calvin Hawkins. Hawkins came from old money, and Kenzie saw ties in him to that granddaddy of conspiracy theories, 'The New World Order.' He was the founder, chairman, and majority shareholder of a bio-tech giant called Anubis Biosystems, and landed on Kenzie's radar with his company's foray into 'transhumanism.' Calvin described the science as a merger of biological systems with technology in what he promised would usher in the next stage in human evolution.

Kenzie thought it sounded too much like 'Frankenstein,' and mailed a copy of that book, anonymously, to Calvin at the company's new headquarters in Arkham. She then wrote a story for her newsletter on the subject, titling it *'Hackable Humanity.'*

In helping Kenzie research her story, the Lone Gunmen dug deep into Anubis' finances, and discovered that much of its research funding came from the Defense Advanced Research Projects Agency, or 'DARPA' for short. DARPA was already well known in conspiracy circles as the agency where the Defense Department housed its mad scientists, so anything funded by them raised an immediate red flag.

As troubling as Calvin's association with DARPA was, along with the other horrors plaguing Capetown, they came nowhere near the terrifying discovery Kenzie was about to make as she pedaled her bike across town that morning to follow up on Zac's text. Without realizing it, she was beginning a journey that would lead to her encounter with a demon, and an ancient prophecy portending doom for the world.

Chapter Twelve
The Cave

Kenzie arrived at the bluff at Hallows Pointe a half hour after receiving Zac's text that morning. As she pedaled up, she found the dead-end street lined with cars and work trucks, something unusual for this early on a Saturday morning. So, apparently Zac was right about something going on.

She chained her bike to the guardrail and walked over to the cliff's edge. It overlooked the shore some thirty feet below, and ahead of her in the distance, she could just make out the lighthouse tower poking its head through the mist.

Looking down through mist's dense layers, she saw dozens of workers in bright green vests and hard hats hauling crates over from down the shore and stacking them against the cliff's base.

Kenzie walked back to the trucks parked along the street, and after searching their backs, found one with several hard hats and vests in it. She put them on, then headed down a creaky flight of wooden stairs to the shore.

The mist folded in around her as she reached the bottom. Looking to her left, she saw several workers emerge like ghosts further down the shore. They stacked their crates against the cliff, then turned and headed back. Kenzie hurried over and fell in behind them.

She followed them for nearly eighty yards until they came to an area sealed off with yellow 'caution' tape. To her left was the cliff, towering high above her in the gray mist, and just ahead of her, a short distance beyond the yellow tape, was a large opening in the cliff's face.

Kenzie knew the area well, having gone there hundreds of times over the years, and this opening was something new. At nearly seven feet tall, and wide enough for a man to easily pass through, it wasn't something she would have missed.

A man in a black jacket, with the word 'security' stenciled across it in white letters, stood behind the yellow tape. He paid little attention to the workers as they ducked beneath the tape and headed for the opening. Kenzie followed them as they passed through the opening and into a narrow tunnel. It continued for about ten yards before opening into the chamber of a large cave.

Kenzie stopped at the mouth of the chamber and took it all in. Three work lights, mounted on stands, cast the room in a harsh, uneven light. It appeared to be roughly oval shaped, as wide as a basketball court, and at least twenty feet in height. Deep shadows from stalactites traced across the ceiling, and the walls were marred in shadows from uneven indents and outcrops. Far across the chamber, the back wall disappeared into the gloom beyond the light's reach, so she assumed the cave extended deep inside the cliff.

A dozen workers toiled throughout the chamber, brushing dirt from half-buried artifacts, and carefully removing them from the ground. They handed them off to other workers, who wrapped them in protective bubble wrap and loaded them into crates like the ones stacked against the cliff.

Kenzie spotted Floyd, the lighthouse keeper, standing near the wall on her far right. Like her, he seemed to be just watching all of this, and not actually a part of the excavation. She hesitated about going over to say 'hi' and seeing if he knew anything about this, but decided to wait till later. She couldn't risk blowing her cover. She doubted that any of the workers would mind her being there, but whoever was sponsoring the excavation definitely would. And Kenzie had a good idea who that person was.

When no one was looking, Kenzie hurried over to the far wall on her left, then crept along it to the back of the cave. As her eyes adjusted to the dim light, she saw long tapestries hung from the back wall, with strange, cryptic symbols woven into their cloth. One showed a serpent coiled around the sun, and the other an eight-pointed star within a circle with an eye in the star's center, and seeing them caused her skin to prickle with unease. They were the same symbols she had seen sketched in Nathanial Crawford's journal, the ones he saw as a young boy on a trip to Acheron with his dad, and which were later drawn by the boy they found missing in the woods.

Just to be sure, Kenzie opened the photo app on her phone to the photos she took of the journal's sketches, and they perfectly matched the symbols on the tapestries. So, this had to be the cave that Crawford wrote about, the one that he and the Brotherhood of Zion blew up centuries ago on the night of the solstice.

The night Acheron vanished from the earth.

Goosebumps broke out along her arms. This cave was never meant to be reopened. Sealing it had lifted the dark hex that Capetown fell under centuries ago, and she didn't see how anything good could come from its unsealing. Her hands shook ever so slightly as she snapped several photos of the tapestries, zooming in close enough to see the details in the symbols.

"Careful now," a woman's husky voice echoed from across the chamber. Kenzie looked over and saw a heavy-set, middle-aged woman waddling in the entrance. With her were three men, looking completely out of place in their expensive business suits. The men were Kristof Stanzos, Jeremy Belkin, and Hareen Nazarah, who managed the world's largest asset management fund, 'The Stanzos Group.' Kenzie couldn't think of any reason they would be there in person. Even if Stanzos was funding the excavation, it made no sense for the bosses to come all the way there, when they could just delegate the supervision to one of their employees. She made a mental note to email Jason Talbot about it. Jason was one of the independent journalists she followed, who, like her, covered stories no other news sources would touch.

Kenzie watched the heavy-set woman waddle over to two men as they carried a heavy ornamental chest over to a large stone block in the chamber's center. Then Kenzie paused, doing a double-take on the stone block. It was the size of a table, with its top chiseled flat to resemble one.

It also resembled the altar in a church.

Kenzie tensed at the unsettling thought. She looked around again at the cave, at the tapestries in back, and candelabra on the ground. This cold, dank, forsaken cavern was a church, and she chilled at the thought of what god it might have been used to worship.

She looked back at the men carrying the chest, each holding it by a handle affixed to its sides. She zoomed in on the chest with her phone's camera and saw that its sides were plated in gold and etched with intricate carvings. In addition to the symbols from the tapestries, these carvings also depicted grisly scenes of horror and the macabre. They showed monstrous beasts rising from the sea and winged creatures descending from the sky. They showed scenes of naked women splayed across altars in sacrifice to some unholy deity.

And they showed a chalice, like the ones used in Mass. Kenzie's hands shook slightly as the realization dawned on her. This had to be the chest that Forester wrote about in his journal, the chest brought over from Europe on the ill-fated voyage. The chest that he believed found its way to Acheron.

Kenzie swallowed uneasily. She lowered the camera and looked around again at the cave's dank walls and ceiling, then to the tapestries hung from the back wall, and to the altar seated so ominously in the chamber's center. It all felt suddenly wrong, as if an unseen veil was lifted and its true nature exposed.

It felt defiled.

"That's it. Easy does it," said the heavy-set woman, drawing Kenzie away from her thoughts. Kenzie eased several steps further back into the darkness to avoid being seen. It wouldn't go well if that woman saw her.

The woman was Madelyn Hayes, and for as long as Kenzie could remember, she had been the local museum's curator and head of the Greater New England Historical Society. She was as close to a walking encyclopedia of historic New England as you could find.

Kenzie got along fine with Madelyn whenever the topic was the region's history. Madelyn would happily talk Kenzie's ears off all afternoon about mundane things like the town's founding, early trade, and even its involvement in the Revolutionary War. But any time Kenzie asked about the town's haunted legacy, Madelyn's demeanor turned hostile and cold.

"Why can't you ever just let things be, Ms. Walsh," Madelyn would snap. "Those beliefs of the past are best left in the past, and I care not to further indulge in our ancestors' silly superstitions."

Kenzie received the same reaction from the town's leaders. Those legends of the past were behind them now, they insisted, and had no bearing on modern-day Capetown. Let the past stay buried in the graveyards of history.

The problem was, as Kenzie saw it, nothing stayed buried in Capetown. Literally and figuratively. Things crawled from Capetown's unhallowed graves in the dead of night, posing the same threat now as they did centuries ago.

But the town's leaders, law enforcement, and the so-called 'establishment' refused to entertain the possibility of supernatural phenomena. The local newspaper, *'The Capetown Daily,'* or 'Capetown *Dreary*' as Kenzie called it, went after anyone who even brought up the subject, which made Kenzie a constant target of their scathing editorials. In their words, she was a *'deranged conspiracy theorist in search of social media clicks.'*

Kenzie's Irish nature couldn't resist a fight, and she threw it back in their faces. She had custom T-shirts made for her and the Lone Gunmen boys, with the caption *'deranged conspiracy theorist'* printed on the front. She sold several hundred of them from her website and sent one to Jason Talbot. He wore it in several of his investigative videos and tagged her on them.

Kenzie also added the caption *'What the Capetown Dreary Didn't Show You This Week'* to her weekly stories.

The irony was, every time the Dreary mentioned her, her readership and subscriber base grew, and she now had almost double their number of subscribers. Without realizing it, they had inadvertently provided her with free publicity. She thought at one point about sending them a 'thank you' note in jest, but was afraid they would stop printing stories about her.

Kenzie finally got the chance to call out one of the town council members on this attempted censorship when she cornered him outside a restaurant. She streamed the entire confrontation live on her cell phone so he couldn't duck away and run off as others had.

Predictably, he denied any attempts at censorship, calling it another one of her kooky conspiracies. He and the town's leaders had more important things to do than monitor some high school girl's website. But Kenzie came prepared. She presented him with dozens of examples, none of which he could refute, so he came up with a new excuse. He and the town's leaders were protecting the town's reputation from the superstitious nuttiness consuming it. He said it was chasing away businesses, and as an example, he pointed to the recent move by the bio-tech giant, Anubis Biosystems, from its old home in Santa Clara, California, to its new facilities in Arkham, a city on the mainland, thirty miles west of Capetown. The company's chairman, a billionaire philanthropist named Calvin Hawkins, had deep ties to Capetown and the peninsula. His family was among the earliest settlers, and he continued to live in the family's estate on the peninsula when he wasn't traveling the world in his fleet of jets. So it stood to reason, argued the man, that had it not been for all the superstitious nonsense surrounding Capetown, and Kenzie's outrageous conspiracies about him, Calvin would have moved the company to Capetown instead of Arkham.

Kenzie called him out on this. First, she doubted Calvin ever read her newsletter; he had his hands full creating his master race with DARPA's money, and attending meetings with his fellow elite in Switzerland. Besides that, Capetown's population of fishermen, loggers, and shopkeepers lacked the advanced degrees needed to work at Calvin's company, so it wouldn't have made sense to move the company there.

As expected, Kenzie's argument fell on deaf ears. She began to suspect the town's leadership didn't want to believe in the supernatural threat facing them; or they believed and were doing everything they could to cover it up. She and her Lone Gunmen buddies suspected it was the latter, and another conspiracy theory was born.

Easing slowly from the back of the cave, Kenzie zoomed her cell phone's camera in on the chest. She prepared to take another shot, when the handle on one side of the chest snapped off, causing it to swing down like a pendulum. The startled man on the other side released his handle and leaped back, letting the chest crash down. It toppled onto its side, knocking open the lid, and a silver chalice rolled out. An inky black liquid flowed from it onto the ground.

"Quick. Pick it up. Pick it up!" shrieked Madelyn.

Before the men could react, Kristof Stanzos dashed past her and picked it up. He carried it to the stone altar, then removed a handkerchief from his pocket and wiped the dirt from it. Jeremy and Hareen joined him, while Madelyn scowled at the two men who dropped the chest.

Kristof pocketed the handkerchief, then held up the chalice for Jeremy and Hareen to see. "Exquisite," he marveled, and his partners nodded in agreement.

"Yes. Quite so," added Hareen. "And such fine detail."

Kenzie saw the reverence in their eyes as they beheld the chalice. It was like they were looking at a priceless heirloom. She zoomed in her cell phone's camera on it and saw that its sides were also etched in those same cryptic symbols as the tapestries and chest. She snapped several shots.

"Whatever is that on the ground?" said Madelyn, staring down at the dark liquid that spilled from the chalice. She leaned down for a closer look.

"Do not touch it," boomed a man's voice from near the cave's entrance. It resonated in a deep, commanding tone.

A strange familiarity stirred in Kenzie at the sound of his voice. She looked over and saw two men standing in the cave's entrance. They wore the brown woolen habits of monks, frayed from years of wear, and long, grisly beards of gray hair masked most of their faces. But in their eyes, Kenzie saw wisdom and a keen intelligence at work; and a distant, vague recognition stirred in her memory. But she couldn't quite place it.

They approached the liquid for a closer look, then recoiled quickly, as if from a snake. They crossed themselves, then turned back to the others.

"You must not touch it," said the monk who had first spoken. He watched the puzzled expressions on the faces of Madelyn and the Stanzos partners, then his eyes fell on the chalice in Kristof's hands.

"The item you hold," said the monk, "it is very evil. And very dangerous."

"This?" said Kristof, taking a curious look at the chalice. "Why, it's just a chalice."

"It is much more than that. It bears the sign of Lucifer, who is called the Morning Star."

"Nonsense," said Madelyn, appearing to have tired of this interruption. "Did Father McCready send you?"

He shook his head. "The good father knows nothing of us or our being here."

"Then who are you?"

"We are mere travelers, Miss Hayes," said the second monk, "who have long prayed that the day of this cave's opening might never come."

"It is cursed ground upon which we stand," said the first monk. "The relics of this cave, they are very powerful. And very evil."

"They should be returned to the cave and its entrance sealed," said the second monk.

"I insist you stop this talk right now," snorted Madelyn. She turned to Kristof and his partners. "Gentlemen, I do apologize for this intrusion. I'll have these men escorted away."

"It's quite alright," said Kristof, appearing amused as he set the chalice down on the altar. "I'm curious to hear what these gentlemen have to say." Looking past her to the two monks, he said, "Please. Do go on."

"I ask only that you listen to this," said the first monk. "These items which you take, they are not like the other artifacts at the museum. They will cause great harm."

"Do you not feel the evil of this place?" said the second monk, casting his eyes warily around the chamber's walls and ceiling. "The very walls whisper of things ancient and unholy. Of an evil as old as time. You would wish now to unleash this evil upon the world?"

"That's enough," Madelyn snapped. "I must ask that the two of you leave, or I shall be forced to call security."

"Very well," said the first monk, breathing a deep sigh. "We shall go, but I leave you with this warning. If you continue with this excavation, you will not escape God's wrath for the evil you will have unleashed."

Kenzie watched the monks leave, still convinced she somehow knew them or had seen them before. But where?

She looked back at the altar, where Kristof and the others' attention was again on the chalice, seeming amused at what the two men said. But Kenzie wasn't amused. She felt the unease from earlier returning, and with it came a suffocating sense of dread. She looked around again at the dank walls and ceiling, sensing something stirring deep within them. A sentience seemed to be awaking after centuries of dormancy.

Every instinct told her to get out of there. She could return later once she better understood it, but for now, she had to get out before it fully awoke.

Before it saw her.

Keeping close to the cave wall to stay in the shadows, Kenzie hurried across the chamber and out the entrance.

A slight drizzle met her as she raced from the cave. Dark storm clouds had rolled in, and thin trails of mist shrouded the shore. She looked up the shore toward the stairs, hoping to spot the two men. She wanted to ask them about the liquid, since everything in the cave seemed to change after it spilled from the chalice. She also saw the way they looked at it and backed away. They were terrified of it.

The shore was completely empty, with all the workers having gone inside the cave.

She looked in the other direction, but it, too, was empty. She brushed the wet hair back from her face and turned to the security guard, who had been watching her curiously this whole time.

"Did you see which way those monks went?" she said.

"What monks?"

"The two who were just here. Kind of older, dark habits."

He shook his head. "No one's come past here."

She looked at him oddly for a moment, but maybe he just wasn't paying attention. She ducked beneath the tape and headed up the shore toward the stairs, being careful not to slip on the slick rocks.

She stopped when she was halfway to the stairs. From there, she could see the entire staircase banking up the cliff's face. It was empty.

She looked out across the jetty, where the lighthouse tower rose high above the mist. It was also empty. She blinked away the rain while taking a moment to think this through. Even if the monks had run the entire way — which was doubtful in their habits — she didn't see how they could have gotten up the stairs or across the jetty before she got there.

It was then that she felt the hairs twitch on her neck with the sensation of being watched. She spun around to face the cliff, but found the shore behind her empty. Her eyes then drifted up the cliff's face, and in the gray misty layers at the top, she saw the two monks, quietly watching her from the cliff's edge. And again, that vague recognition stirred in her memory. She knew them; but from where?

They continued quietly watching Kenzie as the mist folded around them, hiding them from view. A few seconds later, as the mist slowly drifted past, they were gone.

Far up the coast, in the vast salt marshes of a valley blanketed in fog, where the black spires and streets of Acheron once stood in gloom beneath a perpetually gray sky, a foul wind whispered and moaned as it blew south.

Acheron's time was coming. And an ancient prophecy would soon awake.

PART TWO

The Prophecy

Chapter Thirteen
A Child Shall be born

Applause rang out through the crowded banquet hall. Guests rose from tables draped in fine linen and enthusiastically applauded their support for the speaker behind the podium at the far end of the room.

The event was the annual shareholders' meeting of the bio-tech giant, Anubis Biosystems, and the speaker was the company's CEO, Matt Weaver. His broad smile showed he shared their excitement at the meteoric rise of the company's stock over the past year.

During his tenure as chief executive, Matt had been a frequent guest on news and business talk shows and was often hailed as a visionary for having steered the company to success in an industry often known for its hardships. But it was the next speaker, who Matt was preparing to introduce, that was the true genius and mastermind behind everything Anubis did. That man was Calvin Hawkins, who, at thirty-three years of age, was listed among the richest people in the world by Forbes magazine. But despite the plethora of companies in his portfolio, Anubis was his baby, and the shareholders in attendance knew this. And they loved him for it.

"Now as much as I'm sure you've enjoyed hearing me speak about balance sheets and earnings projections," Matt continued to some polite chuckles from the audience, "we all know that it's our next guest who you've been waiting for. He's a man whose name adorns the buildings of many of our great universities and research institutions, and who's become synonymous with leadership, finance, innovation, and, of course, philanthropy. A man who I've had the great pleasure of working with for the past five years, and who, incidentally, celebrated his thirty-third birthday yesterday. Ladies and gentlemen, it's my honor to introduce to you Mr. Calvin Hawkins."

The audience rose from their tables again in thundering applause. From a door on the right side of the hall stepped a man who looked every bit the part of a relaxed, youthful billionaire. Casually combed hair, unbuttoned suit jacket, and two days of beard growth, he walked purposefully to the podium where he and Matt shook hands and exchanged a few words off mic. Matt then returned to his chair behind the podium while the newcomer approached the microphone and adjusted it.

This was Calvin Hawkins, Wall Street's latest darling, but to this roomful of passionate shareholders, he was their messiah. He waited a moment for the applause to simmer down and the audience to return to their seats. After thanking them for their warm reception, he held up his cell phone and flashed its screen in their direction. Although far too small for any of them to see, the screen showed a stock ticker with the company's stock price displayed.

"In case you're wondering why I'm holding up my phone," he said, "I have the company's current stock price displayed on its screen. You'll be pleased to know that during the time you were listening to Matt, its share price has increased by one percent."

More applause erupted, including from Calvin himself, who gave Matt a grateful nod of acknowledgment before turning back to the microphone. He waited another moment for the applause to die out before beginning.

"I get asked quite often during interviews about why I do this, why I continue to focus so much time and energy on Anubis and our projects. Why not spend my time seeing the world and having fun while I'm still young enough to enjoy it? We've all heard the saying that no one on their deathbed wishes they'd spent more time at the office, so why not relax and enjoy some leisure time? And I tell them the same thing that I'm about to tell you. Because the world needs what we make here. The future of our species demands it."

More applause broke out and Calvin took a moment to scan the faces in the crowd to see who else was on board with this sentiment. He was happy to see they all were.

The three partners from The Stanzos Group joined the others in applause. Their table was near the back, after the drive from Hallows Pointe to this banquet hall in Arkham took longer than expected.

Nothing in their appearance betrayed the importance and power of these men. To those seated around them, they seemed like every other shareholder in the room. But to those in the know, they were far from ordinary shareholders.

Kristof and his partners managed an asset management fund, known simply as the 'Stanzos Fund,' whose combined value exceeded the economies of all but the largest nations. Kristof started the fund shortly after leaving his job at a Wall Street investment banking firm. He was joined a year later by Jeremy Belkin, who brought in a large number of institutional investors, public and private pensions, and banks from North America and Latin America. Hareen Nazarah joined them that same year, bringing with him accounts from across Europe, Asia, and the Middle East. Together, these men built a leviathan that defined the meaning of 'too big to fail,' since its failure would cause the collapse of economies and markets worldwide. They had access to central banks around the world, owned controlling interests in a majority of Fortune 500 companies, media conglomerates, and news outlets, and could dictate corporate policies and procedures on a whim. They bought up housing developments and large swaths of real estate, pricing many would-be buyers out of the market, then turned around and rented those properties at greatly inflated prices. Without realizing it, many tenants across the country paid their monthly rent to a Stanzos-owned company.

Despite all of this, they kept a low profile with the public. Few people outside of financial circles even knew of them. They were the men behind the curtain, and they preferred to keep it that way. They took their seats as Calvin resumed his speech.

"I'd like to share a story with you," Calvin began, "about what drove me to found Anubis and continues to drive me to this day. For those of you who've heard this story before, I'd ask that you indulge me for a few minutes while I share it with the others. It's important that you understand why I do what I do, and why I'm so committed to the company's success. It's the story of two boys who grew up not far from here. Those boys were my younger brother, Billy, and myself. We enjoyed the same childhood adventures as most boys, whether it was climbing trees, fishing, camping, sailing, and, of course, playing sports. And that's what we were doing on the day it happened. It was a sunny day that afternoon, which for those of you unfamiliar with the peninsula on which we lived, was quite a rarity. I was the pitcher for our team and Billy was playing first base. I remember looking over at him before throwing the pitch and thinking that something looked wrong. He was swaying like the heat was getting to him and I thought about calling for a time out, but before I could, he collapsed."

Calvin took a moment to clear his throat and compose himself. "It was the last game Billy ever played."

This time, he had to take several deep breaths before continuing. "We took him to the hospital, and they diagnosed him with ALS. Amyotrophic lateral sclerosis, or Lou Gehrig's disease, as it's more commonly known. For those of you who aren't familiar with it, it's a neurological disease that advances rapidly after the onslaught of symptoms. For those of us who've witnessed it, it's hell. It's not something a young boy, or anyone for that matter, should ever have to go through. First, it robbed him of his motor skills, and two years later, it robbed him of his life. He was ten when he died."

He took a moment to step away from the podium and recompose himself before continuing. "So, when people ask me why I do what I do, it's to ensure a future where no one ever has to experience that kind of suffering. Or watch a family member die from cancer. Or see children born with unspeakable deformities. That, my friends, is why I do what I do."

Another round of applause broke out and Calvin nodded in acknowledgment while waiting for it to die down. "It's said by the extremists, and I hope that term doesn't apply to any of you in this room, but it's said that God doesn't make mistakes. That He made us exactly the way He intended us to be, flaws and all. But that's not the God I know. The God I know gave us a brain, and He intends for us to use it. He gave us the ability to learn the sciences and to explore what it is that makes us uniquely human. Our ancestors once looked out from their cave openings and saw omens in the sky. Today we travel through that same sky at the speed of sound. And those aeronautical sciences that enable flight are no different than the genetic sciences that enable us to journey inside the human genome and unleash its vast untapped potential. Now there's those outside this hotel right now who'll say that's blasphemy, but I tell you, friends, that to not use the minds God gave us to perfect His creation is blasphemy. It's an affront to these incredible minds He gave us and the sciences He endowed us with. Why wither away in misery, death, and disease, when we have the ability to go beyond it? To bring humanity to a level of perfection undreamed of by our forebears. To move evolution forward at exponential speed. I tell you that today we stand on the threshold of a new dawn for humanity, and all of you gathered here today will be a part of ushering that in. And that, ladies and gentlemen, is my vision and desire for the future of Anubis. And the future of mankind."

The audience rose to its feet in resounding applause, and for the next hour, Calvin and Matt fielded questions from the enthusiastic crowd. Calvin hadn't disappointed.

The Stanzos partners stuck around till the very end. They had heard Calvin's speech before, but it never grew tiring. They shared his desires and visions for the future, but not necessarily the ones he professed publicly.

They shared the other ones. The unspoken ones. The ones that called to them in their dreams.

The ones that brought them across the Atlantic thirty-three years ago to witness his birth.

Kristof and his partners remembered vividly the night Calvin was born. They had watched from the balcony of Kristof's seaside villa as a comet trailed the distant horizon beneath a blood-red moon. The anomaly, which caught astronomers completely by surprise, appeared much as it would again thirty-three years later on the night the cave opened.

These three men, who had recently come together as partners in Kristof's new asset management fund, knew the prophecy to which the sign portended. *'A Child Shall be Born.'* They also knew the family into which the child would be born, having determined that only one family remained in whose blood flowed the promises bestowed upon a once great people.

The night, patiently awaited for generations by followers of the prophecy, was now upon them.

Kristof and his partners wasted no time in flying to Capetown, Maine. As the Star of Bethlehem once led the Magi to the stable where Christ was born, these three new 'wise' men followed the comet to the site of another birth, until its tail came to rest high above the massive Gothic estate of the Hawkins family.

They arrived just moments before the child's birth. From the hallway outside the master bedroom, where a fire glowed warmly from a fireplace inside, they heard his mother's agonized labor screams, followed by moments of tense silence. And then came strong cries, as the child's healthy lungs breathed air for the first time.

The men entered the room, carrying with them a small chest of gold, and vials of frankincense oil and myrrh as tribute. They set them at the foot of the bed where the child lay wrapped in swaddling clothes in his mother's arms.

Their appearance that night came as a complete surprise to the child's mother, Candace. But it was no surprise to the child's father, Malcolm. For the past nine months, he had known they would be here when this night came. It was all part of the agreement.

Malcolm knew nothing of the prophecy, nor did he have any interest in religious or spiritual matters. He was a pragmatic man, who had inherited the sizable fortune passed down through generations of his ancestors. But all of that had teetered on the brink of collapse at one point not too long ago.

Malcolm had bet heavily on a pharmaceutical company, which was on the verge of bankruptcy at the time he met Kristof and his partners. When the banks refused to extend further credit to his struggling company, and threatened to call in his overdue loans, Kristof came to him with an offer of financial assistance. Kristof's asset management fund, The Stanzos Group, would provide a sizable investment in Malcolm's company, and all they required of Malcolm were two things: that Kristof and his partners be allowed to witness the birth of Malcolm's first-born son; and that the child could never be Baptized.

Malcolm found these terms extremely odd. His wife was infertile, having lost her ovaries three years earlier to cancer; and as for Baptism, Malcolm considered it to be an archaic ritual. He accepted their offer, and within twenty-four hours, they wired the investment to his bank account. He used a portion of it to meet payroll and pay off his loans, and set the rest aside for research and development. To his astonishment, he learned that day that several of his company's long-gestating products received FDA approval and would be ready to launch in the coming months.

When he arrived home from work that night, Candace told him she was pregnant. And for the next nine months, he had expected this night.

"Might I hold him?" Kristof asked Candace, who still had no idea who these men were or why they were in her bedroom.

Candace shot Malcolm a surprised look. "Honey?"

"It's okay," Malcolm assured her. "They're friends."

Candace nervously handed the swaddled child to Kristof, who took him gently in his hands while his partners gathered around. Holding the child with one hand, Kristof gently brushed aside the thin wisps of dark hair from the child's forehead and stared in wonderment at what he saw.

A small, thin birthmark, the size of a pea and in the shape of a coiled snake, marked the child's forehead just beneath the hairline.

Jeremy and Hareen leaned in for closer looks before exchanging approving nods with each other.

Everything was going according to the prophecy.

"My dear Candace," Kristof said as he handed the child back to his mother, "you and your husband are truly blessed. This child shall be destined for the rise and fall of many nations and his name will be proclaimed from mountaintops to all the earth."

As he said this, something caught his attention in the open doorway across the room. A woman in a red dress watched them from the dark hallway outside, seeming to go unnoticed by the others in the room. But Kristof noticed, as did Jeremy and Hareen when they followed his gaze out the door. It didn't surprise them to see her there.

She was the woman who came to them in their dreams and told them of the prophecy.

Protesters swarmed the street outside the hotel where the shareholder conference had just concluded. In stark contrast to the adoring shareholders inside, the protesters waved angry signs, reading: *'Stop Eugenics Now'*; *'On the Sixth Day, God Created Man, On the Eighth Day, Anubis Destroyed Man'*; *'Anubis Makes Monsters'*; and various reminders of the Nuremberg Code's ban on human experimentation.

In the years since founding Anubis, Calvin had become the subject of considerable controversy and distrust. While the vast majority viewed him as a great humanitarian, a small but vocal minority saw him as a powerful elitist. An even smaller minority saw him as the Antichrist and spun wild conspiracy theories to that effect. He'd already had to explain to his girlfriend, Emma, that he wasn't making monsters, when she read an article about him and his research in some high school girl's newsletter, The Acheron Files.

Calvin looked out the window from the backseat of his limo as he and his entourage of black SUVs pulled out of the gated parking garage and onto the street. The police cleared an opening in the protesters for the cars to pass through.

Seeing the protesters massed outside his speeches rarely phased Calvin. He'd grown used to controversy over the years, likening himself to Galileo and so many other pioneers of the sciences who were branded as heretics in the past. They would erect statues to him one day.

Calvin's long-time chauffeur and bodyguard was a former NFL lineman named Marcus Williams. He glanced back at Calvin in the rear-view mirror.

"Looks like your fan club followed you again, Mr. Hawkins," Marcus said in jest, and Calvin let out a chuckle.

"They'd be doing the same thing if I was Galileo telling them that the Earth revolved around the sun," Calvin said. "You know what fuels me, Marcus? Proving them wrong."

"Nothing like a good 'I told you so,' ey boss," said Marcus.

"Nothing sweeter, Marcus," said Calvin. "And this time it's going to be a big one."

Something hard thudded off the limo's roof, and Calvin flinched before remembering that the limo was bullet proof. Nothing short of a rocket-propelled grenade could get through its armored sides.

The phone in Calvin's coat pocket vibrated. He slipped it out and looked at the caller ID — *'Rebeka.'*

"What's the word, Rebeka?" he said, taking the call.

"How'd the shareholder meeting go?" came a woman's voice from the other end.

"It went great. The shareholders loved it. The mob outside wants to burn me as a heretic."

"I saw it on the news. You doing okay?"

"They don't bother me. All their noise just makes victory that much sweeter. So, what's up?"

"It looks like your birthday party's a go for tonight. The guests have been checking in all afternoon, and I have the caterers already setting up at your estate. What time should I have the limos pick up the guests?"

Calvin checked his watch. It was a little after noon. "Have them arrive at around seven. I don't want to start too early."

"Will do."

"You're a gift, Rebeka." He turned off the phone and sat back in the plush seat. It was a half hour drive back to his estate on the peninsula, so he settled in for the ride. But as he did, he noticed that something felt somehow off. It was subtle, like an unspoken whisper.

Someone was watching him.

He shifted uneasily in his seat and looked out the window. The protesters had swarmed the police barricades, trying to push past them and chase after the limo. They waved angry signs, shouted, and hurled objects at the procession of cars. But they weren't who he was looking for. It was a woman. And he had the vague understanding that he would know her when he saw her.

And he did.

Moving through the crowd, as quiet and undisturbed as a whisper, was a woman in a red dress whose hair was as dark as night. His eyes met hers, and despite the dark tint in the windows, he knew she saw him, and something stirred uneasily in his soul.

As the limousine moved on down the street, he lost sight of her in the crowd. He craned his neck to look out the back window, but all he saw was the crowd swarming around the barricades and back onto the street behind him.

He took a deep breath and settled back in his seat, trying to put thoughts of that woman behind him. She couldn't have seen him.

Then how did he know to look for her out the window?

Calvin brushed that thought aside as well. He had a party to prepare for. A party that, without him knowing it yet, would bring him one step closer to achieving his desires.

The unspoken ones.

Chapter Fourteen
Stigmata

San Gabriel, Honduras

Fr. Jacob Kessler stood on the front patio of the friary just outside the small village. Despite the warmth and humidity from last night's storm, he still wore the heavy woolen habit the Franciscan friars had worn since their founding, and wouldn't have it any other way.

In his late sixties now, with a heavy paunch and coarse gray beard that made him look like Santa Claus, Kessler had a deep mirth that made him a favorite with the children at the village school where he taught religious education and English. It was a far cry from the life he once envisioned for himself while studying archeology at Oxford, but one that brought him peace and contentment.

Looking off in the distance, he saw a young boy racing down the muddy road and up the path to the friary.

"Come, father," said the young boy, Elan, panting for breath after his sprint across the village, "you must come quickly. She asks for you."

Fr. Kessler wasted no time in joining the boy as they hurried off down the muddy road. While the boy could have easily raced off like a rabbit, Fr. Kessler needed to go a bit slower, since his sandals tended to get stuck in the mud and pulled from his clumsy feet. But he still felt the urgency to get to the church as quickly as possible.

He had found the young girl, Anna Lucia, inside the church when he arrived to say Mass that morning. As far as he could tell, she had been there all night praying in front of the statue of the Virgin Mary. She didn't appear to be moving, and as he approached her, he saw she wasn't blinking either. Her gaze was fixed entirely on the statue's face. He turned to look at the statue and instantly recoiled several steps back.

Thin trails of blood trickled from the statue's eyes and hands.

"Anna Lucia?" he said gently, not wanting to startle the girl, but when she didn't respond, he stepped closer to see if he could get her attention. It was then that he noticed the serene expression on the girl's face. It was a look he could only describe as sheer bliss. The girl was in the midst of an ecstasy, a heightened state of prayer he had read about in books on the lives of the saints.

His eyes then fell to her hands, clasped together in front of her. They bore the Stigmata of Christ.

Without deliberation, he dropped to his knees and watched the girl in awe. He had read of miracles, but never thought he would be a witness to one. His eyes went from the motionless girl to the statue, then back to the girl. Something truly profound and unprecedented was happening, and he couldn't imagine anyone more worthy of it than Anna Lucia.

He had known Anna Lucia her whole life, having Baptized her as an infant, taught her the catechism and introductory English, and presented her with her first Communion. In a lifetime of travels before professing his vows to the Franciscan Order, both as an archaeologist and as a graduate student at Oxford, he had met many bishops and cardinals, and even three popes, and none of them left more than a passing impression on him. But this twelve-year-old girl, who had little education and no aspirations to greatness, was the first person he considered to be truly holy. And that wasn't a word he took lightly. Anna Lucia had a humility of spirit and simplicity of faith that put him and the other friars in his community to shame. While they could recite Bible verses from memory, and knew the catechism inside and out, the Faith was imprinted on the girl's soul in a way only God could have done. And it humbled him to admit that.

Anna Lucia came from a poor family of sheepherders, and every day after school, he would see her in the field tending to the family's sheep. But she did it with an ease he never saw before. She never needed to call them, they simply came to her when she arrived, and followed her into the pen as evening approached.

The heavy clang of the door opening had snapped him from his meditations that morning. When he looked back, he saw several people enter and sit down in the rear pews. He hurried over to them and politely ushered them outside, taking care to make as little noise as possible. He didn't want to interrupt whatever conversation the girl was having with the Virgin Mary.

Fr. Kessler held Mass outside that morning, being careful to keep everyone out of the church so they didn't disturb the girl.

By the time Mass was over, he saw that the road was lined with dozens of people. He noticed that many of them came from other villages, arriving in horse-drawn carts and carrying statues of Christ and the Virgin Mary and other religious objects. He had never seen anything like this before. It occurred to him they might have come because of Anna Lucia, but with the phones knocked out by the storm, there was no way word could have spread so quickly.

He left Elan and his brother, David, to guard the church and Anna Lucia while he hurried back to the friary to tell the other friars about the girl. There were almost a hundred people outside when he left. And now, as he and Elan approached the church on their way back, he saw the entire road flooded with people outside the door.

"David will not let them in," Elan assured him, seeing the bewilderment in the priest's eyes, "but they still try."

"Where did they all come from?" said Fr. Kessler.

"They come from all over," said the boy. "Many come from far away."

"They came to see Anna Lucia?"

Elan nodded. "Yes. They come to see the miracle."

"How did they know about it?"

"I ask them this, and they say they dream of it."

"They dreamed of Anna Lucia?" said Fr. Kessler.

Elan nodded. "Yes. And of the statue that bleeds."

Fr. Kessler and Elan squeezed through the throng and got inside the church. Elan's older brother, David, quickly closed the door behind them and bolted it shut.

Fr. Kessler looked over to the front pew, where Anna Lucia sat with her family.

"She wishes to speak to you," said Elan.

Fr. Kessler walked over and sat down with the family. He saw that Anna Lucia's hands were wrapped in gauze bandages, with dark stains where they covered the wounds.

"What's happening to her, father?" said Anna Lucia's mother, Maria, her face fraught with concern and fear.

"Why don't we let Anna Lucia tell us," said Fr. Kessler.

"I tell mama not to worry," said Anna Lucia. "It is only the Lady. She wishes that I come to the church every morning for seven days."

Fr. Kessler nodded. "I'll arrange to have someone bring you here. Did she say anything to you?"

"Yes. She has much for me to tell you. She says to tell the priest that the hour approaches when the seven seals will be broken and the man of perdition will arise."

Chapter Fifteen
Lilith

By seven o'clock that night, Calvin's birthday party was in full swing. Like every party he had thrown over the years, he held it in the backyard of the sprawling estate his family had owned on the peninsula for generations.

The estate's main house was a massive Gothic Tudor. Built from large gray stones, with towering gables, it stood two-stories tall and spanned thirty thousand square feet. It boasted thirty rooms, seven fireplaces, and a guest house larger than most homes on the peninsula. It sat atop a cliff overlooking the Atlantic, with a large, manicured lawn that rolled out to the cliff's edge.

A fleet of limos had shuttled guests in from their hotels all evening, and by the time the sun set over the hills to the west, the yard was packed with society's elites. They consisted of Hollywood celebrities and studio executives, tech billionaires, Wall Street bankers, and politicians. Calvin's parties were featured in society magazines as places to see and be seen, so guests cleared slots in their calendars to attend.

Calvin worked the crowd with an easy confidence and charm, shaking hands with guests, engaging in a few minutes of conversation, then moving on to the next. Accompanying him was his live-in girlfriend, Emma Kalchik, who, like every woman Calvin dated, was stunning. At thirty now, she was once a renowned fashion model, gracing the covers of magazines across Europe and America. Several years earlier, the swimsuit issue of Sports International, featuring her on the cover in a string bikini, sold out within hours of publication, and her posters adorned the walls of high school boys and college dorms across America.

A native Hungarian, Emma met Calvin two years earlier while he was in Europe attending a summit of the world's elites. Using his contacts in the State Department, Calvin arranged a visa for her to come to America, and the two had been together ever since. But even Emma's beauty and charm weren't enough to keep Calvin's eyes from wandering, especially when so many women willingly threw themselves at him. He often boasted to his friends that he had yet to meet the woman who could completely captivate him and satiate his lust.

That was before this night.

Before he met the *Woman*.

Calvin was on his third glass of champaign, going from guest to guest, when he felt the peculiar stir of being watched. It was subtle, a prickle in the hairs on his neck. He turned to scan the crowd, and that's when he saw *her*, moving as quietly as a ghost through the throng of guests.

His eyes met with those of a goddess.

Tall and lithe, with hair the color of night and eyes like the sea, she moved with the subtle ease of a cat, each step opening wide the high slit in her long red dress.

A strange hush fell across him at that moment, muting the party's background chatter into a dull hum; and in that eerie silence, he heard her voice whispered in his mind's ear.

'Come to me, Calvin...'

It came so softly and subtly, it could have been his imagination, but his racing pulse told him otherwise. He continued watching her until she disappeared behind the crowd.

The hush fell away, and he was aware again of being surrounded by guests vying for his attention. But any conversation was impossible at this point. He had to find that woman.

'Come, Calvin. Come to me...'

Excusing himself from Emma and his guest, he flagged down a waitress, and taking two champagne glasses from her tray, he squeezed through the crowd in search of the woman.

He emerged on the far side of the throng to find the lawn ahead of him empty, with only the untouched grass leading to the cliff.

'Come to the shore, Calvin...'

Moving with the pull of someone in a trance, he walked over to the cliff's edge near a flight of stairs and looked down at the shore far below.

In the light of the crescent moon, he saw her crossing the shore toward the water, allowing her dress to slide from her body onto the sand. She reached the water and waded in, her naked body silhouetted against the moonlit sparkles.

Balancing the champaign glasses, Calvin descended the stairs to the shore and walked over to where her dress lay on the sand. He had lost sight of her when she disappeared beneath the waves, so he sat down beside the dress and waited.

After several minutes, her head broke the surface like a siren from the deep, followed by her shoulders and breasts. Moonlight glistened from the soft curves of her silhouette as she stepped from the water onto the sand, her hips swaying with a delicate, seductive ease.

Calvin climbed clumsily to his feet as she approached him. He held out the champagne glasses, and to his horror, uttered the most awkward opening line of his storied playboy life.

"I brought you some champaign," he said, feeling a cringe as the words left his mouth.

She eyed the two glasses. "Who's the other one for?"

"Me?"

"That's presumptuous."

"Can it be wishful?"

Although she stood in silhouette against the moonlit sky, he detected a slight grin. "You should be careful what you wish for, Calvin."

"How about hopeful?"

"Is there a difference?"

"I'm not sure," he said nervously. She had him completely off balance. "What's your name?"

"I go by lots of names."

"Which one should I use?"

"Lilith."

"So, you're an actress?"

"When I want to be."

"I know people in Hollywood I can introduce you to."

Her lips curled in a coy smile. "They're already mine, Calvin," she said, reaching over and ripping open his shirt. "Hollywood's been my playground for a long time."

With the precision grace of a cat, she traced her finger down his chest and along his arms, circling around to his side and then his back. He let the champaign glasses fall from his hands as she slid off his shirt, never breaking her smooth feline flow as she circled around to his other side and back to his front.

"Now, I'm going to make you my playground, Calvin."

For a brief moment, something inside Calvin alerted to danger. It was something deep and primal, a primitive instinct that alerted to unseen dangers. But it faded quickly into lust.

With a strength he never would have expected from her lithe size, she lowered him to the sand and ripped off his pants. Flinging them aside, she crawled onto him and straddled his waist, letting him enter her as she gently swayed her hips in a smooth circular motion around his.

"Madelyn Hayes is going to call you tomorrow, Calvin," she said without breaking her rhythm. "You need to meet with her and see what she has to show you."

Calvin grimaced. The last thing he wanted to think about now was Madelyn, and what would undoubtedly be her plea for a donation to the museum.

"Why do I need to meet with her?"

"Because she holds the key to your deepest desires."

"What are those?"

She leaned into his ear and whispered, "Immortality. And dominion."

At that moment, he climaxed in an explosion of excruciating bliss, more powerful than anything he had ever felt.

In his last conscious thought before sinking into a dark oblivion, he noted how her eyes seemed to reflect the moonlight like a predator's.

And then he fell into darkness.

Chapter Sixteen
In Aeternum Regnabit

The moon loomed high above, as Kenzie pedaled her bike down the dark streets to Zac's house. She needed to go back to the cave that night when Madelyn's crew wasn't around, and hoped to talk Zac into coming with her. Even with all the hauntings she had explored over the past two years, it still scared her to go to spooky places alone at night. And in a life of disappointments, Zac was one of the few constants who never failed her.

Arriving at his house, she lay her bike on the front lawn and hurried over to his bedroom window. She was relieved to see the light still on inside, which meant he was probably awake and working on his computer. That increased the odds of him coming with her. She leaned across the hedge beneath his window and tapped lightly.

A moment later, the curtains drew aside, and Zac peered out.

"We're closed for the night," he said.

"The sign out front says open 24-hours."

He chuckled as he slid open the window and stepped aside. "You know, we do have a front door."

"I thought this was the front door," she said as she climbed through.

"Only for booty calls."

She rolled her eyes. "I need to show you something," she said, sliding her phone from her pocket and opening its photo app.

"Does it involve cheerleaders?"

"Maybe some dead ones. But I heard they're less bitchy that way. You know the text you sent me about Hallows Pointe?"

"Yeah. How'd it turn out?"

"I think we hit the jackpot, Zac. Check these out." She handed him the phone and let him scroll through the photos she took of the cave.

"Is that a cave?" he said.

"Yeah. It's in the side of the cliff. Check out the rest of the photos."

He did, scrolling through them until she stopped him at the ones of the tapestries.

"There. You see that symbol?" she said.

"The creepy, demonic looking one?"

"Yup. Now check this out." She took the phone from him and pulled up a photo of the sketch in Nathanial Crawford's journal showing the symbol. She opened it on the screen side-by-side with the image from the tapestry. They were identical. She handed him back the phone.

"It's the same symbol that was in Nathanial Crawford's journal," she said. "He saw it when he went to Acheron as a kid, and then that boy who went missing drew it when they found him. He said he saw it painted on the rocks in the forest."

Zac's eyes went back and forth between the two images. They were clearly the same symbol.

"So, you think this cave has something to do with Acheron?" he said.

"I think their priests used it as a church. Keep scrolling, 'cause there's more."

He scrolled through more photos until she stopped him again on the photos of the chest.

"There. You see that chest?" she said. "I think it's the one Elijah Forester wrote about in his journal."

"The one that was on the ship that wrecked?"

She nodded. "It was heading to Boston when a storm blew it off course. It wrecked off the coast of Acheron. Forester thought it contained something called the Calicem Noctis. Go to the next photos."

He did, and she stopped him on a photo of the chalice lying on the ground near the chest.

"I think that's what he was talking about," she said.

"It looks like a chalice they use at Mass."

"Calicem Noctis means Cup of the Night in Latin. It's supposed to be like the Holy Grail for satanists."

Zac swallowed uneasily as he zoomed in closer for a better look at the dark liquid on the ground near the chalice.

"What's that stuff on the ground?" he said.

"That's what I need my best friend to help me find out."

Hallows Pointe lay shrouded in mist as Kenzie and Zac descended the stairs to the shore. She briefed him on the ride over about everything that happened that morning, including seeing the three Stanzos partners, which Zac found as curious as she did.

"Does this mean they stopped trying to make us eat crickets?" Zac said.

"I doubt it. I think they're just adding spooky relics to the menu."

"As long as they lay off my hamburgers. So, I'm your bodyguard for the night?"

Kenzie grinned and shook her head. "Nope. You're dinner."

"I don't get it."

"You know the joke about being chased by a bear?"

"Do I want to know it?"

"Probably not. The joke is that you don't have to be faster than the bear. You just have to be faster than your friends." She shot him a grin, but Zac failed to see the humor in it.

"Next time we bring Dillon with us," he said.

She laughed. "Deal. We can trip him if he starts to catch up."

He laughed too, but they both fell silent as they descended the last steps and were swallowed in the mist. It was a sober reminder of where they were going.

With visibility down to about twenty feet in every direction, they used the cliff to guide them as they worked their way down the shore. From far to their right came the splash of waves against the shore.

As they neared the cave, they saw the warm glow of a fire burning in the mist and heard the chatter of at least two voices.

"Someone's over there," Zac said.

Kenzie frowned. "Freaking, Madelyn. It figures she'd have security there overnight."

"Should we go back?"

Kenzie shook her head. "Let's see who it is."

They crept in closer, keeping tight to the cliff to avoid being seen, until they were near enough to make out the two figures. Kenzie immediately recognized one of them as Floyd, the lighthouse keeper, and the other one was a handyman named Daryl, who she had seen around town working odds and ends jobs. They warmed their hands over a fire burning in an oil drum near the cave's entrance.

Floyd's dog, Zeus, was also with them, pacing nervously nearby. Kenzie was grateful for the breeze blowing in from the ocean, which kept the dog from detecting their scent.

While Floyd probably wouldn't have a problem with her going inside to investigate the cave, she wasn't sure about Daryl. She tapped Zac on the shoulder and motioned him closer to the cliff so they could listen in on the two men.

Zeus let out a sudden bark and retreated several steps from the cave. His lips curled back in a snarl.

Daryl watched the dog with growing concern. "The hell's wrong with your dog, Floyd? He ain't gonna bite us, is he?"

Floyd watched the dog for a moment, then shook his head. "It ain't us he's barkin' at. It's this place. I think he's seen somethin' he don't like."

"Like what?"

"Like somethin' that ain't good."

Daryl shifted uneasily. He took a nervous look behind him at the cave. "You think he's seeing it now?"

"Could be," Floyd said. "You know them animals, they see things us humans can't."

"I seen something like that happen when I was a kid," said Daryl. "After my grandma died, my dog used to stand in the hallway outside her bedroom door and growl like there was a cat inside there or something. But there weren't nothing in there."

Another sudden bark caused them both to nearly jump. Floyd looked again at Zeus, who continued to pace nervously and had retreated several steps back.

"Suppose I oughta get him back to the lighthouse before he gives us both a heart attack."

"You do that," said Daryl. "You gonna be here tomorrow?"

"Bright and early."

Kenzie and Zac watched Floyd take Zeus and head off down the shore toward the lighthouse, disappearing soon in the mist. She looked back at Daryl, who was warming his hands above the fire. At that moment, a sudden loud screech, like the squeal of a giant bat, echoed from the cave. Kenzie and Zac looked over and saw a faint, pulsing red glow coming from the entrance.

"What is that?" Zac whispered.

Kenzie just shook her head. "I don't know."

She looked at Daryl, who had turned to stare into the cave. From where he stood, he would have a clear view through the opening, while Kenzie and Zac could only see it from the side.

"Hello?" Daryl hollered into the cave, his face colored in that faint, pulsing light. "Is someone in there?"

When no answer came, Daryl slowly approached the cave. He reached for the walkie talkie hung from his belt and keyed it. "Hey, Floyd. You there?"

He listened as static crackled across it. "Hey, Floyd, need you back here, man. Something weird's going on in that place." He released the key, and again, only static crackled across it. Frustrated, he slid the walkie talkie back in the holster on his belt and looked back at the cave. And gasped.

A woman stood a short distance back inside the narrow tunnel, appearing as little more than a silhouette against the red glow from the chamber. Her thin gossamer gown, backlit in the light, did little to conceal her lithe figure beneath it. She raised a slender finger and beckoned him to follow.

Daryl strode forward like someone in a dream, his eyes never straying from her haunting beauty. He followed her down the tunnel and into the chamber, where he stopped just a few feet short of the black liquid that had spilled from the chalice onto the ground. He never noticed how it simmered in small bubbles near his feet, radiating the faint red glow that painted the walls and ceiling in its hellish light.

Around the altar stood twelve ghostly shapes. Dark and misty, they appeared like shadows, each bearing the resemblance of a monk in a dark hooded robe.

On the ground near Daryl's feet, the simmering liquid began slithering toward him.

Kenzie stirred anxiously outside the cave. From where they stood, she and Zac hadn't seen the woman who lured Daryl into the cave. They had only seen the strange trance-like way in which he entered it.

"Wait here," she finally said to Zac, then eased over to the cave's entrance and crept inside. The tunnel pulsed faintly as she eased down it to the chamber's opening and peeked inside. She spotted Daryl standing near the altar, and close to his feet, the liquid from the chalice simmered a fiery red as it slithered across the ground like a tentacle. She wasn't sure if Daryl even noticed the liquid, as his head remained turned toward the altar while he murmured something too faintly for her to make out the words.

And then she saw them.

Around the altar stood twelve dark, spectral forms, so vague and intangible that she had mistaken them for shadows. They were the priests of Acheron, returned from black, nighted gulfs to consummate a dark, unholy sacrifice.

And tonight, Daryl would be that sacrifice.

Before Kenzie could shout a warning to Daryl, he raised his arms and cried out in a loud voice:

"In aeternum regnabit."

The entire cave rumbled and shook, sending small stones and dust falling from the ceiling. The glowing liquid touched Daryl's feet and rode up his ankles. It erupted suddenly in flames, lashing up his body and consuming it entirely in a fiery blaze. His body rose into the air until he hovered five feet above the ground, flames jetting from every inch of his body. He remained there for several seconds before crashing down to the cave floor in a crumpled heap. The flames extinguished from him and the liquid, quickly plunging the cave into pitch darkness.

The scream froze in Kenzie's throat as she spun around and raced from the cave. Zac stepped out from behind his rock as he saw her burst from the cave and race his way.

"What happened?" he said.

"Run!"

Chapter Seventeen
A Subtle Stirring

Calvin's eyes squinted open to a gray morning sky. Beneath him, the shore's coarse sand scratched at his bare back, legs, and arms.

With a painful groan, he sat up, giving it a moment for the nausea and dizziness to pass. Every cell in his body ached, and despite the chill in the morning air, he was beaded in sweat.

He looked up and down the deserted shore, veiled in a dreamlike mist. Waves washed gently onto the sand a short distance away, and from high above came the lonely cry of seagulls.

The woman was gone. He sat there for a moment, trying to remember what he could about her, but his memories were hazy. His clothes, which lay strewn on the sand, were the only evidence that the night had even happened.

Rising unsteadily to his feet, he shook the sand from his clothes and slid them on. He sat back down and rubbed his temples for a moment, trying to clear the fog from his mind. Everything felt strangely off, his thoughts, the woman, his memories of last night. It felt like chasing the fleeting memories of a dream as they merged with waking consciousness.

Maybe sleep might help.

Calvin shuffled upstairs to his bedroom, where he found Emma already awake and dressed. She looked over from across the room and appeared stunned at his disheveled appearance.

"Are you okay?" she said. "You disappeared from the party."

"I know," he said, offering a contrite nod. "And I apologize. I went for a walk on the shore and must have passed out."

"Have you eaten yet?"

He shook his head as he shuffled over to the bed and kicked off his shoes. "I'll eat later. Right now, I just need some rest."

She walked over and touched her hand to his forehead, beaded in sweat.

"You're burning up," she said.

He simply nodded and lay down on the covers, letting the sand trickle from his shirt onto the sheets.

"Do you want me to call the doctor?" she said.

He shook his head, covering his eyes with his forearm to block out the light. "Just rest."

Emma walked over and pulled the curtains closed.

"When you feel better, Rebeka needs you to call her at the office," Emma said.

Calvin groaned and gave a painful nod of acknowledgment.

"Oh, and Madelyn Hayes called," Emma added.

It was like a sudden jolt of electricity.

'Madelyn Hayes is going to call you tomorrow, Calvin,' Lilith's words echoed in his memory. *'You need to meet with her and see what she has to show you.'*

His breathing slowed, and his forearm fell from his face.

Why do I need to meet with her? The memory played on.

'Because she holds the key to your deepest desires.'

Emma watched the strange, flushed reaction cross his face. "Calvin?" she said.

At the sound of his name, Calvin snapped from his memories. "I'm sorry," he said, shaking off his thoughts. "You were saying?"

She continued to eye him curiously. "Just that Madelyn Hayes called. Are you okay?"

Calvin did his best to play it off. "Yes. Yes, of course. Did she leave a message?"

"Just to let you know she called. She said she needs to talk to you about something."

A chill brushed Calvin's arms as he lay back on his pillow and contemplated this. Hazy memories of the previous night fluttered through his mind like phantoms. Memories of Lilith and her transcendent beauty. Of the way her body felt when pressed against his. Of the way the moonlight traced the delicate curves of her naked body. And of her whispered words.

'Immortality. And dominion.'

Chapter Eighteen
Something Awaking

Kenzie paced the cave's floor, making several loops around the main chamber before settling on a spot.

"Here. This is where it happened," she said, pointing to the spot on the ground where she watched the glowing liquid crawl across Daryl's foot.

"You're sure?" said Rick, who watched from nearby along with his deputy, Drew, and the town's coroner.

"Yeah."

It was the morning after Daryl's death, and after a fitful night of restless sleep, Kenzie had called the sheriff's office to report it. She told him about everything that happened that night, leaving out only the parts about Daryl levitating in the air and the twelve ghostly shapes she saw standing around the altar. Rick would never believe those parts anyway, so why further complicate something that was already complicated enough?

She also left out the part about Zac being with her. It was bad enough that she was firmly planted on Rick's radar. She didn't need to drag Zac into it too.

Rick knelt and pinched a bit of dirt from the ground where Kenzie was pointing. He held it to his nose but smelled nothing out of the ordinary. He wiped it from his fingers.

"It's just dirt, Kenzie," he said. "There's no liquid here."

"Maybe it burned up," she said.

"Maybe." He rose to his feet and turned to Drew. "Get a sample of this over to the lab. Make sure they check for any accelerants."

"On it," Drew said, removing a Zip-Lock bag from his pocket and scooping a sample of dirt into it.

Rick turned to the coroner, Clyde Simpson, who was watching from near the cave's entrance. "He's all yours, Doc," Rick said with a nod to the corpse. "How soon can you get me an autopsy?"

"A day, maybe," said Clyde.

Rick nodded. "Be sure to check for accelerants too."

"Of course."

"Can you let me know what you find?" Kenzie asked him. "Especially around his feet and ankles where that stuff got on him."

Clyde looked at Rick for approval.

"Check with me first," Rick said. He then turned to Kenzie, and an annoyed frown crinkled his brow. The girl had a knack for being at the wrong place at the wrong time. Knowing the hell her life had been, and out of respect for her deceased father, who had been a good friend, he cut her more slack than he normally would have. But his patience at her amateur sleuthing was wearing thin.

"You want to tell me what you were doing here last night?" he said.

She shifted uneasily and looked down at her foot before looking back at him. "Snooping?"

"For what?"

"For whatever's going on in this place."

"Is this for your website and newsletter?"

"Yeah."

"Isn't a cave a bit outside your wheelhouse?"

"Not if the people of Acheron used that cave."

Rick groaned. Kenzie's obsession with Acheron was a constant annoyance, and something he hoped she would have moved on from by now, but apparently that wasn't the case.

"What would the people of Acheron, if it even existed, be doing in a cave outside of Capetown?"

"That's what I'm trying to find out," she said. "But I think they used it as a church."

Rick looked around the cave, at its dank walls and stalactites drooping from the ceiling like ice cycles. With the artifacts packed away now at the museum, there was nothing about it to even remotely suggest a church.

"Why would you think it was a church?" he said.

"It looked a lot different before Madelyn took all the stuff to her museum."

Rick took a deep breath and let it out. "Look, Kenzie. I'm not going to waste either of our time explaining to you again how Acheron is only a legend. I'm sure you could recite it all from memory. But right now, this is a crime scene, so I need you to keep away until I finish my investigation. Can you behave yourself until then?"

"I can try."

"I need you to do better than that."

She took a breath. "Okay. I'll keep away till you guys finish." She meant it too. Despite butting heads with him over Acheron and anything supernatural, she knew he cut her a lot of slack and appreciated that.

"Good girl," he said.

"Whatcha all doin' in here?" came a voice from the cave's entrance. Kenzie and Rick looked over to see Floyd and Zeus standing there. The dog paced nervously near his leg.

"Daryl died last night, Floyd," Rick said, nodding to the charred body being zipped into a body bag. "Do you know anything about it?"

"He died?" Floyd said, looking completely baffled at the news. "Me and him was just outside here last night. What happened?"

"He burned to death," said Rick. "That's all I've got to go on right now."

"It was that liquid that spilled on the ground from the chalice," Kenzie said, quickly jumping in. "It got on his foot and that's what caught him on fire."

"We're investigating Kenzie's claim about a possible accelerant causing it," Rick said, adding his own clarification.

"You mean that black stuff them men got all worked up about?" Floyd asked Kenzie.

"Yeah," she said. "It was right after you left. That stuff started glowing, and I guess Daryl came in here to check it out. That's when it happened."

"You seen it?" Floyd asked.

She nodded. "I was hiding outside, and followed him in. He looked like he was in a trance or something."

"You saw this liquid she's talking about?" said Rick.

Floyd nodded. "Sure did. Stuff was blacker than the ink ya used to dip pens into. Scared the bejeezus outta them two men."

"What men?" said Rick.

"Couple priests or something. They showed up and started going on about how the place was evil and cursed and all that. Maddie finally run them off." Floyd paused a moment to look around at the dark, clammy walls and ceiling, and an uneasy expression fell across his face. "Not so sure them men weren't wrong about this place."

"Do you know these men?" Rick asked.

"Nope. Never seen them before."

"They wore habits, like monks," Kenzie jumped in, "and had long, gray beards. If that helps."

"It might," said Rick. "I'll check around and see if anyone knows them."

"And here you thought I was just some annoying teen girl," Kenzie said, patting herself on the back for her contribution.

"You are an annoying teen girl," said Rick. He turned back to Floyd. "You gonna be around in case I have any more questions?"

"You know where to find me."

Kenzie caught up to Floyd and Zeus on the shore outside. "You felt it too in there, didn't you? I saw the way you looked around at the cave."

He gave a slow, hesitant nod. "Not sure what I felt, but somethin' sure as hell ain't right with that place."

She looked down at the dog. "You feel it too, don't you, boy?"

Floyd gave another nod. "That dog there's a smart one. Probably outta listen to him more often."

"Maybe both of us should," she said in agreement. She knelt beside the dog and held out her hand. "Hey. You remember me? I'm the crazy girl who spent the night in the lighthouse."

The dog walked over and sniffed her hand, then wagged his tail to signal his approval.

"Good luck gettin' rid of him now," Floyd said with an amused smile.

"Naw. He's a keeper. Aren't ya, Zeus?" His tail wagged even harder as she gave him a good scratch behind his ear.

"Could I talk to you about all this stuff sometime?" she said, rising to her feet while continuing to scratch Zeus.

"You doin' a story about the cave?"

"Yeah. And the stuff they found inside it."

He looked past her to the cave's entrance, where Rick, Drew, and the coroner were lugging out Daryl's body in a body bag. "S'pose it wouldn't hurt answerin' a few questions," he said, "but you best be careful on this one."

"Why's that?"

"'Cause I can't help thinkin' somethin's awaking in that place. And I ain't so sure it wants us talkin' about it."

Chapter Nineteen
Secret Things

A long banner proclaiming the town's upcoming 'Libertas Festival' stretched from telephone poles across the town's Main Street. It was the town's largest annual event, the day when they commemorated the town's founding, but Calvin barely took notice from the backseat of his limo as it passed beneath the banner and proceeded on down the main street. He needed no reminder of the celebration. As one of the two surviving descendants of the town's founders, Calvin was called on every year to give a speech at the festival; an honor which, for Calvin, had become a big annoyance.

The other surviving descendant of the town's founders was Christopher Crawford, a man whose family name was inscribed on schools, streets, and parks. Unlike Calvin, Christopher relished the opportunity each year to share stories about the town's heritage, and Calvin was happy to give him the spotlight.

Calvin awoke from his nap a short while earlier, feeling no better than when he awoke on the shore that morning. A queer pressure filled his mind, making it difficult to concentrate for long on anything. Memories of the previous night came clouded in a haze, feeling distant and foreign, as if he was reliving someone else's memories. But the one memory that remained clear was Lilith's insistence that he meet with Madelyn — that somehow, in some obscure way, this meeting was tied to his destiny.

He had already concluded that Lilith had to work for Madelyn, since he couldn't think of any other way for her to have known about the call. So he saw this meeting as not only a chance to hear what Madelyn had to say, but to also see Lilith again and hopefully get some answers to the myriad of questions that plagued him.

The limousine drove a little way further down the main street, then turned onto a side street and parked along the curb in front of the Museum of Antiquities. Two dark SUVs pulled in behind it and parked.

The museum was housed in an old colonial mansion, previously owned by one of the town's founding families, the Rutledge family. They donated it to the town in 1919, shortly after the First World War. Originally called the Veterans Memorial Museum, they dedicated it to the town's residents who fought in the war. The town later changed the name to the Museum of Antiquities as its prominence grew.

Calvin and his entourage of bodyguards passed through the ornamental wrought-iron gate and headed up the tree-lined cobblestone path to the museum's entrance. They climbed the short flight of steps between two matching marble columns and went inside.

While the exterior of the two-story mansion remained largely unchanged from its colonial days, its interior was carefully remodeled to accommodate the array of displays and exhibits it now housed, with entire rooms dedicated to particular themes.

"Mr. Hawkins," Madelyn greeted them excitedly as she joined them in the foyer. "Thank you so much for coming."

He gave her a cordial smile. "Please, Maddie. It's just Calvin. My dad was Mister Hawkins."

"Of course," she said, giving his hand an eager shake. "Calvin it is."

"By chance, is Lilith around?"

She gave him a puzzled look. "Lilith?"

"Yes. The young lady I met at my party. She was quite insistent that I meet with you."

Madelyn shook her head. "I'm not familiar with anyone by that name."

Calvin looked at her for a moment. "She doesn't work for you?"

Again, Madelyn shook her head. "There's no one by that name around here."

"Interesting," he thought aloud, with a slight nod of his head. This woman, Lilith, was becoming more of a mystery by the minute. "She told me last night that you would be calling."

"That's rather odd," said Madelyn. "I don't see how anyone could have possibly known."

"Neither do I," he said. "Well, I understand you have some things you'd like to show me."

"That I do," she brimmed. "If you'll follow me."

She led them through an arched opening into a new room, where rows of glass display cases were lit in track lighting. The narrow cone on each light focused only on the display beneath it, drawing the observer's attention to that display in the otherwise dark room.

"These were discovered only this week in a cave down at Hallows Pointe," she said.

"I wasn't aware of a cave at Hallows Pointe," he said.

"Nor was I. A lightning strike unsealed its entrance during the storm a few nights ago. Come, I'll show you what we've found so far."

She led him over to the first row of displays. "At some point, I plan to fashion the room to resemble the cave's interior, but for now, we're housing the artifacts in these temporary cases."

Calvin looked through the glass panels at the myriad of artifacts inside the cases and then above them at the long tapestries hung from the ceiling. He couldn't help noticing the strange, cryptic symbols found on most of the items.

"Those symbols seem to repeat across the items," he said. "Do you know what they mean?"

She shook her head. "I have my team researching them over at the university's library, but so far, they've found nothing. Apparently, they're a lot older than the library's records go back."

"Interesting," he commented. "Maybe to the town's founding?"

"Possibly even before that."

"Are they religious?"

"I believe so. Obviously not of any Christian sects."

"I wouldn't assume so."

She led him down the row to the glass case housing the chalice and stopped. "This one created quite a stir when we found it," she said. "It fell out of that chest," she added, nodding to the gold-plated chest in the next display over.

Calvin leaned in closer to the glass panel for a better look at the chalice. "It looks like a goblet of some sort. Perhaps a chalice for religious ceremonies."

"That would be my guess too," she said. "I have my team investigating it as well."

"It has the same markings on it as the tapestries," he said, leaning in even closer.

"Indeed, it does," she said. "As does the chest it was inside of."

Calvin angled above the chalice to look down on it through a glass panel on the display's top, and it was then that he noticed something inside it. It was a liquid, as black as night, that filled the bottom half of the cup.

As he stared at it, he felt something vague and subtle stir inside him, like an unspoken whisper of thoughts in the back of his mind. He took an uneasy step back.

"There's something inside it," he said.

Madelyn nodded. "Yes. And I have no way to account for that. When it fell from the chest, the liquid spilled onto the ground. And yet by the time we brought it here, the liquid had somehow replenished itself."

He brushed a slight chill from his arms and leaned in closer to the front panel for another look at those arcane etchings. As he did, he felt that sensation stir again in his mind. It was quiet and discreet, and seemed to suggest things; but as to what they were, he didn't know. They were secret things, things too dark and ancient to be holy. And he had the subtle understanding those secrets could be his, but something was required of him first.

'All will be revealed in time, Calvin.'

The voice was Lilith's, soft and unspoken, heard in his mind's ear. But the eeriness of that didn't scare him; it lured him as it did at the party. She was there, somewhere in this room.

Calvin leaned slightly past the display case, allowing his focus to shift to the dark, unlit displays several rows back. It was there that he saw Lilith, moving as quietly as a shadow amongst the displays before disappearing into the darkness. She was exactly as he remembered her, a siren beckoning to him with her ineffable beauty and haunting grace. And in the brief, faint gleam he caught in her eyes, he saw approval.

'Soon, Calvin, all will be yours.'

Chapter Twenty
What the Storm Brought

A fierce storm blew in that night, whipping gusts of rain across Capetown. It came down in thick sheets, swaying trees and sending loose branches skittering across streets and yards.

With the storm, came *something else*. Something dark and obscene. A blasphemy that moved silently through the night, and which no doors or storm shutters could keep out.

Deep in the basement morgue at the coroner's office, Clyde Simpson neared the completion of Daryl Corbet's autopsy. Despite the clock on the far wall showing a little past eight, Clyde was determined to conclude the autopsy before going home. He was as curious as Rick to learn the cause of death; and maybe even more so after reading the lab's preliminary findings.

Earlier that evening, Clyde received the lab's preliminary results on the tissue samples he sent them from Daryl's ankles. The results were something he had never seen before and raised questions he had no answers to. At least, not yet.

Turning back to Daryl's charred corpse, Clyde pinched the skin flaps on Daryl's open chest tightly together and used a postmortem stapler to staple it shut. He removed his latex gloves and tossed them in the trash, then washed his hands and headed upstairs to his office on the ground floor.

Clyde turned on his laptop and waited a moment for it to boot up. On the desk beside it sat a file with the lab's preliminary results. When the laptop booted, he opened Daryl's file and began entering the lab results.

A sudden pop came from somewhere in the hallway outside his door, and a moment later the lights flickered and died. His laptop, now on battery power, gave off the only light in the windowless office.

Simpson breathed an annoyed sigh. Hopefully, it was only the circuit breaker. He slid the small penlight from his pocket and used its narrow beam to find his way down the hallway to the breaker box on the wall. He opened the panel and frowned when he found all the switches turned on. It meant the power was out in town and he would need to wait for the utility company to get it turned back on.

A muted clang came from somewhere beyond the stairwell door behind him. It sounded like something heavy fell over on the morgue's floor. Using the penlight to see by, he headed down the stairs to the morgue.

A rush of cold air met him as he opened the morgue's door and stepped inside. He shined his light around the pitch-dark room, and its narrow beam fell across an autopsy table lying on its side on the floor. Beneath his lab coat, the hairs on his arms stirred. The table was far too heavy to have fallen over on its own. Something had to knock it over.

"Hello?" he said into the dark room, hoping that maybe the janitor or a worker had stayed late and accidentally knocked it over. But the dead silence that came in response confirmed that he was alone in the building.

He slowly brought his light around to the table where he performed Daryl's autopsy, and the table was empty. The body was gone.

Simpson breathed uneasily. He wasn't normally a man given over to superstition, but being alone in that dark basement in the empty building, and discovering a corpse was gone, filled him with a supernatural dread. Maybe there was a logical explanation for all of this, but he sure as hell wouldn't stick around that night to find out.

Simpson hurried back upstairs to his office and picked up the phone. The line was dead. He pulled his cell phone from his coat pocket and punched in the sheriff's number. After several long rings, it went to voice mail.

"Rick, it's Simpson. Call me when you get this message. We've got an issue over here." He slid the phone back in his pocket and headed outside.

Rain poured down in the thick sheets across the dark parking lot. Pulling his jacket snuggly around himself, he hurried across the lot to his car, taking care not to slip on the slick asphalt.

As he reached his car, in a brief flash of lightning, he saw the lone, dark figure of a man watching him from far across the lot. A dark, inexplicable dread filled Simpson at the sight of that figure. He quickly fumbled through his pocket and pulled out his keys. Sliding them into the lock on the driver's side door, he caught something in the window's reflection.

The dark, featureless shape stood right behind him.

With a startled yelp, Simpson spun around, but only the dark, empty parking lot was there. He scrambled inside the car and locked the door. He jammed his key in the ignition and turned it. The engine let out a pathetic wheeze, then went silent. He tried again, but this time heard only a dull click.

The phone in his pocket buzzed with an incoming call. Simpson pulled it out and looked at the caller ID. The word *'Unknown'* displayed on the screen. He swiped the 'X' to cancel the call and slid it back into his pocket. He tried the key again, and once more heard only a muted click.

His cell phone buzzed again, causing Simpson to nearly jump. He pulled it out, hoping it was Rick calling him back, but once again the caller ID said only 'Unknown.' Simpson swiped up this time to accept the call.

"Clyde Simpson," he said, then waited a moment for a response. None came.

"Hello?"

Only silence, and the steady thump of rain on the roof. He hung up and set the phone on the passenger seat. He pumped the gas pedal several times, then tried the ignition again. Once more, only a dull click came from the engine.

Simpson reached beneath the dash and pulled the hood release. He wasn't a mechanic by any means, but maybe only a cable had come loose. He climbed from the car and went around to the front, where he opened the hood. He looked around at the engine, then gave the battery cable a quick wiggle. It was loose. He twisted it several times on the battery post until it slid down far enough to grip firmly. Hopefully, that's all it was. He closed the hood and hurried back inside the car.

Closing the door against the rain, he immediately noticed how much colder it felt inside. Just like how it had in the morgue. On the passenger seat beside him, the phone's screen glowed from a missed call. He picked it up and read the caller ID:

'Daryl Corbet.'

Simpson tensed. He slowly willed his hand to dial the sheriff's number, then waited for the brief message to play out before going to voice mail.

"Rick, it's Simpson," he said nervously into the phone. "I need you to call me the minute you get this. Something's going on..."

His voice trailed off as his eyes drifted up to the rear-view mirror.

Something sat in the back seat behind him. Something in the dark shape of a man. Charred hands suddenly shot forward from the backseat and grabbed him on either side of his head. A second later, Simpson's head erupted in flames.

Simpson's dying scream was the last sound recorded to Rick's voice mail.

Far across town on the jetty, Floyd watched the storm batter the shore from the kitchen window of the lighthouse cottage. The storm had rolled in fast that night, knocking out power to most of the peninsula, including the tower and cottage. While the tower's generator had turned on automatically, he would need to manually start the cottage's generator down in the storm cellar on the side of the cottage.

Floyd was torn. While he dreaded the thought of going outside in the storm, he dreaded even more the loss of the fresh food in the refrigerator if the power remained out for long.

"Damn storm," he grumbled, resigning himself to just going outside and getting it over with. He grabbed a flashlight from a kitchen drawer, then, throwing on his slicker, he stepped outside.

Within seconds, the slicker was drenched, and Floyd's ears filled with the patter of rain on its hood. Cupping his hand above his eyes to shield off the rain, he looked out across the jetty at the ocean. A fog bank lay offshore, something rare, but not unheard of in storms. But what caught his attention was the way it rolled in against the wind, heading his way. He couldn't recall seeing that happen before.

Floyd trudged off through the mud to the storm cellar's low slanted door on the cottage's side wall. He tugged it open, then climbed down the wooden steps into the cellar, sweeping his flashlight ahead of him as he went. At the bottom, he shined the narrow beam across the dank cellar to the generator against the far wall. He walked over and checked the fuel gage on its front.

The dial showed it was half empty. Hopefully, that would be enough to last until the power came back on. He powered up the generator, then headed back inside the cottage.

Floyd grabbed a beer from the refrigerator as he passed through the kitchen into the living room. He sat down in his recliner chair and clicked on the TV. To his annoyance, it only ghosted with static. Floyd cursed and thought about throwing the damn thing into the ocean.

Thunder crackled and boomed outside. Zeus stirred uneasily on the floor, then sat up, his eyes fixed on the arched opening to the kitchen.

"It's okay, boy. Just the storm."

A low growl rumbled deep in Zeus's throat as he continued staring at the kitchen.

"Come on, boy. Yer damn near about to scare me, too."

Lightning flashed outside, followed seconds later by a thunder crash. It rattled windows and shelves and startled Floyd forward in his chair. He dropped the beer, which fell to the flood and spilled in a puddle.

An instant later, the power went out.

"Oh, for Pete's sake," Floyd groaned, staring into the dark room. It was probably a circuit breaker this time, which didn't make things any easier, since the breaker box was in the cellar with the generator. He breathed a deep sigh, wondering if it was worth it to go outside again, or just wait for the storm to pass, and hope the food didn't spoil by then.

A sudden knock came at the kitchen door, sounding loud even in the storm.

Zeus rose to his feet, every muscle tensed as he glared through the opening into the kitchen.

Two more knocks came, and Floyd felt his own stomach tense. Especially after seeing his dog's reaction.

"Who's there?" Floyd hollered across the room, then waited in silence for a reply. But none came.

A deep growl rumbled deep in Zeus' throat, followed suddenly by barks.

"Easy, boy. Easy," Floyd said, rising from his chair. "Let's see who it is before you go eating them up."

Floyd walked into the kitchen and over to the door. He opened it to find a dense wall of fog outside. He stared into it for a moment, looking around for whoever had knocked, then noticed something peculiar about the fog.

It glowed, with a faint, eerie light deep within it.

Floyd swallowed uneasily and took a nervous step back. "Hello?" he called out, but the only sounds were the storm and crash of waves on the nearby rocks. He started to close the door, hoping that maybe the knocks were noises from the storm, when suddenly Zeus bounded past him and out the door.

"Zeus!" Floyd hollered. "Get your butt back in here!"

He waited for a moment, as Zeus' barks faded in the distance.

"Oh, for crying out loud," he groaned, tempted to just leave the dog out there. But he couldn't do that. With a curse, he threw the drenched slicker back on, then grabbed the flashlight and went back outside.

Rain pattered down on the slicker's hood, making it hard to hear anything over the constant drum.

"Zeus!" he hollered again, walking deeper into the fog. "Get back here, dumbass!" He paused to look around, then proceeded even deeper into the fog, keeping track of his direction so he could find his way back.

"Last chance, dummy. And I mean that."

He waited a moment, and when Zeus never came, he turned back toward the cottage. To his horror, it was completely hidden in the fog. He began slowly walking in what he hoped was the right direction.

From somewhere behind him came a faint, distant sound. He spun back around and stared into the fog. From deep within its depths came that dim, glowing light.

"Zeus? You okay, boy?" he shouted, then paused for a moment to listen. "Keep barking, boy, and I'll come find ya."

There were no more barks.

As Floyd stared into the fog, he had the sudden, chilling sensation of things moving around him.

He swallowed nervously. "Is someone there?"

'Floyd...' The word breathed like a whisper, carried on the wind.

"Who's there?" he hollered.

'Floyd...' It came again, seeming to float past him on his left.

"Y'all ain't supposed to be out here," Floyd said, taking a nervous step back toward the cottage.

'Floyd...' He felt it drift past him on the left.

"I mean it. Y'all better go before I call the sheriff."

Staring into the fog, he saw faint figures drifting through it like shadows, visible for only an instant before fading.

"Who is that?"

'Floyd...' the ghostly voices whispered, floating past him in the air.

Floyd raced back into the cottage, slamming the door shut behind him and locking it. He caught his breath for a moment, then went into the living room and removed a pistol from the closet. He checked the cylinder and found six rounds inside.

He walked back into the kitchen, where he stopped as he noticed something on the floor. A row of muddy footprints trailed across the floor into the living room. He leaned down for a closer look at them and felt the hairs on his neck stir. The footprints weren't his — they came from bare feet.

Gripping the pistol tightly in one hand and flashlight in the other, he followed the footprints into the living room and across it to the hallway, where they disappeared inside the bathroom. He charged into the bathroom, sweeping his flashlight and pistol around, but found it empty.

He shined the flashlight at the floor, where he saw the footprints leading over to the shower. Raising his pistol, he eased over to the shower curtains and threw them aside.

The shower was empty.

Floyd backed away from the shower and turned to the mirror over the sink. Something was written on it in dark red liquid. He leaned in closer and read it.

'Sanguine.'

In the reflection, something moved in the hallway behind him.

Without thinking, Floyd spun around and fired a shot. The sudden, loud burst in the cramped bathroom caused his ears to momentarily ring.

Recovering from the jolt, Floyd shined his flashlight into the hallway, but found it empty. He eased back down it to the living room, where he paused for a moment to listen. The only sounds were those of the storm.

A sudden, loud bark from outside caused him to startle.

"Zeus?"

Frantic scratching came from the kitchen door. Floyd raced back into the kitchen and threw open the door, expecting Zeus to bound in past him. But all he saw outside was that strangely glowing fog.

"Zeus!" he hollered into the storm. "You okay, boy?"

A faint bark came in the distance.

"Keep barking, boy, and I'll come find ya."

Floyd trudged back out into the fog, gripping his pistol tightly.

"Zeus?"

Floyd had walked a short distance from the cottage, when again he felt that sensation of things moving around him through the fog. He stopped to look around and listen.

"Y'all, I got a gun this time. And I ain't afraid to use it."

'Floyd...' came a whispered voice from the mist, seeming to float past him.

"Who is that?"

'Floyd...' the voice drifted past him through the air.

Floyd spun to his left, and then his right, aiming his pistol into the dense cloud.

"Who said that?"

'Floyd...' it whispered past on his left.

"What do you want?" he shouted, spinning to his left, and for a brief instant, he saw a shadow drift past through the fog before fading.

'You, Floyd...' a voice whispered from his right.

'We want you...' it whispered from his left.

'The children need to feed...'

Over the patter of rain came a new sound — hissing, like the air leaking from a hundred tires. Floyd's eyes fell to the ground where the sound came from, and the breath caught in his throat.

Hundreds of snakes slithered across the stones toward him. He spun around to race back to the cottage and saw hundreds more coming from that direction. As they reached his feet, they coiled and sprang at him, with at least four sinking their fangs through his jeans into his calves.

Floyd cursed in pain. He kicked and thrashed, managing to shake them off, then bolted through them into the cottage. He slammed the door shut, then turned to face the kitchen. And his heart nearly stopped.

Snakes filled the entire room, looping down from ceiling lights and fixtures and slithering across the floor and counters. Floyd kicked at them as he dashed into the living room, where his foot came down on a mass of them. They squished beneath his boot, causing his feet to slip out from beneath him. He fell backwards to the floor, banging his head hard on the wood floor. And then it was over for him.

Floyd swiped and kicked at them the best he could, but the snakes came at him by the hundreds. He felt long fangs punch through his pants and slicker, and his body swell as venom flooded his veins.

From the kitchen came the low creak of the door opening, and the storm's sounds poured in. Despite the balmy temperature outside, an icy chill now filled the room, and Floyd knew *something* was in the kitchen. Something far more terrifying than the snakes. He craned his neck to look over at the kitchen opening, and what he saw chilled his blood.

The dark outline of a man stood ominously in the opening.

"Daryl?" Floyd uttered in recognition before the darkness engulfed him.

Farther north on the peninsula, as the storm continued to vent its fury, Calvin dreamed. In his dream, he felt the strange sensation of awaking on the dank streets of an ancient New England city, over which darkness hung like a shawl. The dark cobblestone streets lay deserted, lit in pale moonlight and the sickly yellow glow of gas lamps along the sides.

Despite the apparent absence of people, Calvin sensed he wasn't alone in this darkly haunted city. Something hung in the surrounding air, something ancient and terrible that permeated the city long ago, and from which all vestiges of light and goodness fled. He felt its cold hunger watching him and studying him; and then, in some obscure way, he understood he had met with its approval. And this awareness sent a strange thrill rushing through him.

He walked down to the deserted seaport, where empty fishing boats and merchant vessels bobbed in black waters beneath shimmers of moonlight. A long promenade stretched the seaport's length, with a waist-high stone wall bordering the ocean side, and the eerie glow of gas lamps lining the other side.

He approached the stone wall and looked over its side at the ocean twenty feet below. Deep beneath its murky depths, something monstrous stirred. Calvin stepped back from the wall, then approached it again. Large, luminous eyes stared up at him from the black depths, and in his thoughts, he heard its unspoken call beckon him like a siren.

It knew him.

Farther up the street away from the seaport, Calvin saw the bouncing movement of torches as a procession of people flowed onto the street and headed up the hill away from him. At the top of the hill stood a massive Gothic temple, its black walls and spire towering ominously in the moonlight.

As the last of the procession rounded the corner and headed up the hill toward the temple, Calvin caught up to them, keeping far enough back to avoid being seen. He could see now that these people, who numbered at least a hundred, all wore long hooded robes and murmured strange chants in a language that Calvin assumed was Latin. He watched as they streamed inside the temple through its high arched doors, and he waited back until the last of them entered. Then he crept up to the doors and sneaked in.

The temple's main sanctuary was massive, with a towering arched ceiling, stained glass windows along the walls, and statues which, upon closer inspection, bore no resemblance to the statues he had seen before in churches. These statues were hideous, depicting beings that no sane mind could have dreamed of. It was the same with the stained-glass windows and murals painted along the walls, showing creatures and abominations conjured from a nightmare.

The hooded figures sat in pews lining either side of a long center aisle, at the far end of which stood a marble altar. Calvin's attention was drawn to one of these figures, who took his position behind the altar and raised what looked like the chalice he saw in Madelyn's museum.

Calvin eased in closer to the sanctuary's entrance for a better look, then paused as the giant fresco painted on the wall behind the altar came into view.

On the fresco was a naked woman, strikingly realistic in her depiction and beauty. Beside her was an enormous serpent, which stretched far into the distant garden behind her. Its thickness was as wide as a couch, and its head was the size of a table. With her right hand, the woman reached up to caress the serpent's head.

The breath caught in Calvin's throat as he stared at the woman and her striking eyes. He had seen those eyes moments before fading into darkness on the night of the party.

The woman in the painting was Lilith.

To the left of the serpent stood a man, dressed in the same dark hooded robe as the people in the pews. But unlike them, the man's hood was pulled back, revealing his face. Like the woman, the detail in his painting was striking and realistic. His eyes, deep, piercing, and magnetic, seemed to stare out from the fresco at the congregants, following them no matter where they sat.

Calvin knew those eyes. They were the same eyes that stared at him every morning from the mirror. The man was him.

Back in Calvin's bedroom, Emma awoke to a loud crash of thunder from the storm. Rolling over in bed, her hand felt across the empty spot beside her where Calvin should have been.

She sat up and looked around, thinking that maybe he had gone to the bathroom. But its light on the far side of the room was off.

A cold rush of wind blew in from the open double-doors to the balcony. She looked over and saw the heavy drapes billowing inside the doors, and from outside came the harsh patter of rain on the balcony. This struck her as odd, since they locked those doors before going to bed.

Emma walked over to the doors to pull them shut, when a sudden flash of lightning lit the yard below. In its brief flash, she saw someone standing on the far side of the yard near the cliff. Although too dark and distant to be certain, the figure looked like Calvin.

Rain pounded her umbrella as Emma hurried across the yard to the figure, who stood in the same spot where she saw him from the balcony. Although he faced the cliff with his back to her, she was close enough now to see it was Calvin.

"Calvin?" Emma said, rushing over to his side. It was then that she noticed the trance-like gaze in his eyes. They were open and fixed on something in the distance, but it wasn't anything she could see. He was in the thralls of a dream.

She took a step back, unsure whether to wake him. She had heard it was dangerous to awaken a sleepwalker, but it could be equally dangerous to leave him outside in the storm.

As she watched him, she noticed his lips were moving, as if speaking to someone — or *something* — in his dream. She leaned in closer, but heard only the faint mutter of words, spoken too softly to make out over the patter of rain on her umbrella. She collapsed the umbrella and lowered it to her side, then pressed her ear closer to his mouth. She could just make out the words now, spoken evenly and almost mechanically. And those words, seemingly random and vague, sent a sudden rush of fear through her.

'Your will be done.'

Chapter Twenty-One
Something in the Room

Dark clouds hung low over Capetown that morning. Its streets, pocked in deep puddles, were slick with rain from the overnight storm.

Kenzie splashed through several puddles as she pedaled her bike to the coroner's office at the morgue. She hoped to convince Clyde to show her Daryl's autopsy results before Rick had a chance to tell him not to. It was a long shot, but she would try anyway.

She rode up to the parking lot's entrance and stopped at a strip of yellow 'crime scene' tape stretched across it. Looking past the tape, she saw Rick, Drew, and two other men inspecting a car. The two men wore jackets with 'Crime Scene Investigations' embroidered on the back, which meant Rick had called in a forensics team from the neighboring city of Arkham to help with whatever was going on. And whatever it was, it had to be bad.

Kenzie ducked beneath the tape and wheeled her bike over.

"What happened?" Kenzie said as she walked up.

At hearing her voice, Rick turned and shot her a frown. "What're you doing here?"

"I was seeing if Clyde finished Daryl's autopsy. What happened?"

He nodded to the crime scene tape. "You see the tape back there?"

She nodded. "Yeah?"

"It means keep out."

"I thought that was just for civilians."

"And what are you?"

"The press."

He smirked. "Nice try. Now, I need you to leave so I can get back to my job."

"Is that finding out who killed Clyde?" She took a wild guess on this, and for all she knew, Clyde was inside his office. But Rick's response would give her the answer she needed. And it did.

"Who told you that?" he said.

"You just did when you didn't say 'no.' Plus, you've got the CSI guys out here and Clyde's not around."

Rick frowned, but he reluctantly had to give her credit. She kept him on his toes. "Yes. That's what we're doing."

"How'd it happen?"

"I don't know yet. Which is why I need you to leave, so I can get back to my investigation."

"Just real quick. Did he find out what the stuff was that got on Daryl's feet?"

"I don't know."

"Can I go check his office?"

"You're kidding me, right?"

"It was worth a shot."

Rick groaned. "Bye, Kenzie. And don't come back until the yellow tape is gone. You got it?"

"Got it."

"Good girl."

Kenzie turned and wheeled her bike back across the parking lot. As she went, her eyes made a quick scan of the building's exterior, making a mental note of its doors, windows, and security system. If she couldn't get the answers about Daryl's death the easy way, she would get them the hard way. It wouldn't be the first time.

Thirty miles west of Capetown, in the corporate offices of Anubis Biosystems in downtown Arkham, Calvin sat with the board of directors for a briefing by the company's CEO, Matt Weaver, on the ongoing clinical trials of the company's new cognitive enhancement drug.

Despite the mostly positive news, Calvin couldn't keep his mind from wandering. Ever since the night on the shore with Lilith, his mind had been mired in a haze of vague, nondescript thoughts and ideas. They came unannounced and unprompted, and Calvin felt them increasingly competing with his own thoughts for dominance.

He was fairly certain now that they originated outside of himself; but if so, from where? And how had they invaded his mind?

And what did they mean? They seemed to suggest deep hidden secrets, but only teased at what they were.

Equally curious was the dream from last night, and Emma finding him sleepwalking in the rain on their back lawn. As far as he knew, he had never sleepwalked before in his life.

At least not before the night he met Lilith.

While the sleepwalking concerned him, the oddity of the dream didn't. In some queer way, he felt himself drawn to and seduced by the cold, radiant darkness of that city in the moonlight.

It knew him, and promised answers to the secrets hinted of at the museum. And whispered in his mind.

After Matt's presentation concluded, Calvin caught the elevator down to the first floor and went outside. The building's ground floor was occupied by high-end boutique clothing stores, upscale restaurants, and a lively tavern where he often met for drinks with his executive team. But Calvin barely noticed any of it as he walked past, his mind lost again in memories of that haunted city in the dream, and the words Lilith said on the night of the party.

'Immortality. And dominion.'

He had shared those desires with only a handful of people over the years, and none of them could have possibly known Lilith. So how then did she know that death, and the 'great nothingness' that followed it, was what he feared more than anything? Ever since he watched it take his brother when they were kids, and then his parents ten years ago, that fear drove everything he did. The only desire that came even close to defeating death was power. He craved it the way most men might crave a beautiful woman. It consumed him with a lust he could almost taste. He had sampled bites of it in corporate meetings and global summits, but that power was constrained and required approval from others. He wanted the kind of power that required no outside approval. He wanted to be the ultimate decision maker, and with that kind of power, he could fix the problems that plagued humanity. The world was dying, divided into warring factions, and needed a leader to bring it together. And Calvin saw himself as that leader. But talk like that scared people, and so he kept those thoughts to himself. But the whole while, every decision he made, and action he took, was aimed at achieving those two goals.

Lost in thought, Calvin startled suddenly as something caught his attention from the corner of his eye. It was something red he glimpsed briefly in the reflection from a large storefront window on his right. He stopped and turned to the window, and in its reflection, he saw Lilith watching him from the sidewalk across the street. She wore the same red dress as the night of the party, and its color was what caught his attention in the reflection.

He spun around to look across the street, but she was gone. He stared in confusion for a moment, as doubts crept in over whether he actually saw her. And if he didn't, what was it then? His imagination?

"Calvin, my friend," came a man's voice from behind, jarring him from his thoughts. He turned to see three men standing there, men he had met several times at his shareholder meetings and at the global summits. They ran the world's largest asset management fund, a behemoth called the Stanzos Fund, whose size rivaled the economies of most nations. They were both revered and feared by politicians and corporate executives alike.

"Gentlemen," Calvin said with a welcoming smile as he extended his hand. "It's good to see all of you."

"As it is with you, my friend," said Kristof Stanzos, the fund's original founder, as he reached out and shook Calvin's hand. "We were in town for your shareholder meeting and thought we might stick around and enjoy your lovely city."

"Well, it would be my pleasure to show you around," said Calvin, shaking hands with the other two men, Jeremy Belkin, and Hareen Nazarah.

"We would like that very much," said Jeremy.

"Consider it done," said Calvin.

"Might I ask what you were looking at as we approached?" said Kristof. "You seemed rather occupied."

Calvin stole a quick glance across the street at where Lilith had stood in the reflection, but there was no sign of her anywhere. He turned back to Kristof.

"It was nothing. I thought I saw someone."

The men exchanged curious, knowing looks with each other.

"This person, is she a woman?" said Hareen Nazarah.

"As a matter of fact, she is," said Calvin. "And a very attractive one, I might add."

Kristoff smiled. "Might her name be Lilith?"

Calvin's expression fell slack for a moment. "You know Lilith?"

All three of the men nodded. "Yes. We are quite familiar with her," Kristoff said. "Tell me, is it often that you see her?"

Calvin thought for a moment. "No. Not really. I met her at my party, and I thought I saw her at the museum in Capetown. And then again, just now. What do you know about her?"

"Quite a bit, my friend," said Kristof, "but it will be best if she tells you herself."

"How do I find her?"

Jeremy shook his head. "You don't, Calvin. She finds you."

"When will that happen?"

"When she feels the time is right, I suppose," said Hareen.

"Tell me, my friend," Kristof cut in, "have you dreamed of a city? One that's quite old."

Calvin swallowed. "Just last night. How do you know about that?"

"We've all had the dream," said Hareen.

"And you saw the fresco painted in the church?" said Jeremy.

Calvin gave a slow nod. "How do you know about these things?"

Kristof reached out and rested his hand on Calvin's shoulder. "That, my friend, is something Lilith will also need to explain to you. But I trust things will be much clearer for you after tonight."

Back on the peninsula at the Hawkins' estate, Emma sat on the back patio, watching the mist recede over the distant horizon. She still hadn't gotten over the shock of finding Calvin sleep walking in the rain the previous night, and shortly after Calvin left for work that morning, she told her friend, a young Guatemalan maid named Maya Ortega, all about it.

Like Emma, Maya had seen the subtle, peculiar changes in Calvin ever since the night of the party; but unlike Emma, Maya sensed these changes ran much deeper than just his distant, dreamlike stare.

"I fear Mister Calvin is not well," Maya said from the porch swing beside her.

"I was thinking the same thing," said Emma. "I should try to get him to go see a doctor."

"That will work only if what troubles him can be cured by a doctor."

"What do you mean?" Emma said, eying her curiously.

Maya shifted uneasily. "I am sorry. I have said too much. I should get to back to my work."

With that, Maya excused herself and headed off.

As Emma watched Maya hurry off, an unsettling thought occurred to her. She could see that Maya suspected what might be wrong with Calvin; and whatever it was, it had Maya scared.

Later that afternoon, Emma would understand why.

As Emma crossed the foyer late that day, she found Calvin's two dogs at the base of the grand staircase that swept up to the second floor. The dogs, which Calvin named 'Bear' and 'Beast,' were massive pit pulls, with heavily muscled legs and backs and fur as black as night. They feared nothing, and yet at that moment, Emma sensed fear in their eyes as they stared up the staircase. Low growls rumbled deep in their throats.

"What is it?" Emma said calmly to avoid startling the dogs. "Do you guys see something up there?"

The dogs barely paid her any attention, as their eyes remained focused on the top of the stairs.

Easing around them, Emma slowly crept up the stairs to the second floor, where she noticed a sudden chill in the air. Looking down the hallway to her right, she spotted Maya staring into Calvin's master bedroom through its open doorway.

Maya nearly jumped as Emma approached her from behind.

"Hey? You okay?" said Emma, surprised by Maya's startled reaction.

Maya gave a hesitant nod as she shook off the sudden fright. "I am okay," she said in her broken English, "but the room, it is not okay. It is not good."

"What do you mean it's not good?" Emma said. "It's mine and Calvin's bedroom."

"You should find another bedroom, Miss Emma," Maya said nervously. "There is something already in this one."

Peering in the doorway, Emma looked around the empty bedroom. No one was there.

"I don't see anyone in there," Emma said. "Are you sure?"

Maya nodded. "I am very sure, Miss Emma. It is very bad."

Emma stepped into the room and was met by an icy chill in the air, even colder than the hallway. Goosebumps broke out along her arms, as much from the cold as from a sudden unease. She looked back at Maya, who watched nervously from the doorway.

"You feel it too, do you not?" Maya said.

"I think it's just a draft from somewhere," said Emma.

"Is more than just a draft," Maya said. "Please. You should come out of there."

Ignoring Maya's concerns, Emma looked over at the window, where the curtains billowed softly in a breeze from outside. She walked over and pulled it shut.

"That's all it was," Emma said. "Just a draft from outside."

As Emma turned back to the doorway, she froze as a sudden awareness struck her. The room wasn't right.

It didn't feel empty.

Emma hurried from the room and joined Maya in the hallway outside the door.

"You felt it, as I did," said Maya, making a quick Sign of the Cross. "The room is not empty."

Emma could only manage a nod. The icy chill stopped at the doorway, somehow confined to the bedroom, but that gave her no comfort. Without thinking, her hand went instinctively to the small gold cross hung from a chain around her neck. It was a gift from her mom when she was twelve to celebrate her confirmation, and she wore it beside the gold, heart-shaped locket Calvin gave her when they started dating.

That was back when she and her mom still spoke to each other.

Emma's mom, a devout Catholic, had never approved of Emma's career in modeling, which often required her to pose in clothing her mom considered indecent, and sometimes in the nude. She never told her parents about the nude photo-shoots.

Her parents met Calvin only once, and his wealth didn't impress them the way it did Emma and her Hungarian friends. They lived in a small rural village in Hungary, where the days were long, the work hard, and the pleasures simple. To her parents, God was as real as the sun and crops, and the neighbors they gathered with for picnics and festivities. God and hard work provided for their needs, and vast wealth meant no more to them than an extra stein of lager.

Growing up, Emma shared in the robust faith that sustained her parents, but much of that was gone now, wilted in the decay that came with material pursuits. She never told her parents that she was moving to the U.S. to live with Calvin, only that she was moving there to model. She knew they wouldn't approve, and especially her mom. Her dad kept his opinions mostly to himself, with only an occasional disappointed sigh to let her know how he felt. But her mom had no problem letting Emma know when she had gone astray, and Emma couldn't bear the thought of seeing the disappointment on her mom's face if she told her she would be living with a man out of wedlock.

She hadn't talked to either of her parents since the move, and it was an ache that gnawed at her daily.

Despite having the world at her fingertips, Emma was lonely. Other than Maya, she had no close friends to share things with. The kinds of things that mattered. Sure, there were parties and the guests they had over for dinners, but she didn't know any of those people beyond what they did and their status in the world. They might as well have been two-dimensional cardboard cutouts seated around the table. At least with Maya, they could talk about deeper things, things that left them vulnerable and scared. Things that made them happy and hopeful. Emma didn't need to flash her smile and pretend that everything was perfect, when deep inside, she was hurting.

But their friendship had to remain a secret, since Calvin frowned on her fraternizing with the hired help.

As Emma fingered the small cross, staring warily into the room, she thought about calling her parents. Something bad was happening. She could feel it in the pit of her stomach. First, with Calvin's odd behavior ever since the party, and now with the room. And she sensed it was only beginning.

Chapter Twenty-Two
The Morgue

It was a little past nine that night and the streets lay quiet and deserted. Kenzie and Zac pedaled down a dark alley, coming to a stop behind the morgue. They leaned their bikes against the building, then crept down the narrow walkway along its side to the building's front. Kenzie peeked around the corner into the parking lot. A single streetlight stood in the center of the lot, but looking around, she saw no cars.

"We're clear," she whispered to Zac, and they quietly slipped back to the alley.

"You got the plans?" Kenzie said.

"Right here," Zac said, pulling up an image on his phone. It showed the building's blueprints, filed with the county recorders' office prior to construction, which he downloaded from their website that afternoon.

He also found the permit on file for the installation of a security system. Fortunately, it was one that Kenzie had circumvented before, so she was hopeful of being able to do it again. The plans showed the locations and wiring information for three cameras, two of which were in hallways and the third was in the basement morgue.

Kenzie fingered through the blueprints, committing to memory a general idea of the building's hallways, staircase, offices, doors, and windows.

"Do you know which office is his?" Zac asked.

"I think it's this one," Kenzie said, pointing to the largest of the offices. It was at the corner of adjoining hallways, with one of the security cameras installed at the far end. "It's the largest. Hopefully, they'll have names on the doors. You got our coms?"

"Yup," he said, pulling two walkie talkies from his jacket pockets and handing one to her. She slid it into her dark backpack, which already contained two ultra-bright LED flashlights and two bean bags, each about the size of a softball.

"Let's do this," she said.

They pulled dark ski masks down over their faces and went to work.

One of the clandestine skills Kenzie had learned since starting The Acheron Files was lock-picking. She bought the kit, consisting of a tension rod and several variations of 'rakes,' from a survivalist website that she and the Lone Gunmen shopped at more times than they cared to remember. After watching several hours of online training videos, she began practicing on every lock she could find, and within a few months, had a fairly good grasp of the skill. It had already come in handy several times over the past year.

Kenzie slid on a pair of latex surgical gloves to avoid leaving fingerprints, then went to work on the back door. She inserted the tension rod into the bottom of the lock, then gently eased the rake in and out, feeling for the subtle click as each tumbler fell into place. Within a few minutes, she had the door open.

Zac ducked behind a nearby dumpster, while Kenzie disappeared through the door and into a hallway. It was one of two hallways that didn't have cameras, at least according to the plans recorded at the time the permits were filed, so she felt safe using a small penlight to see by. She eased down the hallway to the corner, then, ducking to the floor, peeked around it into the adjourning hallway. The building's three offices were along the right side of this hallway, with an opening on the left leading to the front office.

At the far end of the hallway, the LED on a security camera mounted in the top corner glowed red. Kenzie fished one of the two flashlights and bean bags from her backpack. She set the beanbag on the floor and the flashlight on top of it, then angling the flashlight towards the camera, she turned it on.

The hallway lit up like daylight. The brightness deactivated the camera's infra-red censor and caused its aperture to completely close to protect its photo diodes. It was a gimmick she learned from a special operations manual she bought on eBay, which let her disable security cameras without damaging them.

With the camera disabled, she slid on her backpack and crept down the hallway to the first office, keeping quiet enough to not set off any motion sensors. The permit Zac found didn't mention the installation of any motion sensors, but Kenzie wasn't taking any chances.

She lucked out with the first office. Not only was the door open, but a small brass plate on it read 'Clyde Simpson, MD.' Apparently Clyde had been in a hurry to get out of there on the night he was killed, and left the door open. It would save her from having to pick another lock.

Kenzie eased in the door and over to a desk in the back of the small office. A laptop sat on it, along with stacks of files. One file lay open, apparently being the last one Clyde worked on before his death, and it turned out to be the one she needed.

At the top of the first page were the words 'Toxicology Report: Preliminary.' Beneath that, typed into one of the rectangular boxes, was the deceased's name, 'Daryl Corbet.' She scanned down the page, skimming past the overly technical parts she didn't understand, and finally slowed when she came to the section on tissue analysis.

Two of the samples were taken from Daryl's ankles, and skimming again past the description of the methods used by the lab for their analysis, she finally found what she was looking for. The results.

The tissue tested positive for blood. But not from the decedent.

The tests found trace elements of a blood-like substance on the tissue, but not of any known antigen. This meant it wasn't of any common blood types such as '-A,' 'B,' 'AB,' or 'O.'

It also didn't match any known animal type. The substance was completely unprecedented and bore only a structural resemblance to blood.

Beneath her sleeves, Kenzie felt her arms break out in goosebumps. Laying the pages from the lab results across the desk, Kenzie snapped photos of them with her phone's camera, then slid them back into the file folder.

Kenzie placed everything back the way she found it, then quietly eased from the office. She had one more thing to do that night, and the thought of it made her stomach churn. She needed to get her own tissue sample from Daryl's ankle, since evidence like this had a strange tendency of always disappearing. Especially once Rick read the lab results.

Kenzie eased down the hallway to the stairway door, then took the stairs down to the morgue itself. Opening the door just a crack, she quickly located the camera's red LED glowing in a top corner of the dark room. Using her second flashlight and bean bag, she disabled the morgue's camera the same way she did the hallway's camera, then went inside.

The room was in disarray, with a heavy autopsy table overturned on the floor, and the instruments from an examining tray scattered everywhere. She swallowed a nervous lump in her throat as she approached the table and knelt beside it.

Several charred flakes of skin clung to the table's top like scabs, which meant this was probably the table Clyde performed Daryl's autopsy on. It hadn't been cleaned, so Clyde definitely left in a hurry that night.

On the wall far to her right were the metal doors to the freezers where the bodies were stored. She walked over and checked the labels on the doors until she found one marked 'Daryl Corbet.' She pulled the handle and opened the door.

Inside was a long tray on runners, allowing a body to be slid in and out with relative ease.

The freezer was empty.

Kenzie closed the door and backed away. Every instinct told her to get out of there fast, that something bad had happened. Something that would soon find its way into Rick's 'unsolved' files and be forever lost. But first, she needed to check something.

Going on a hunch, she went back to the overturned table and knelt on the floor beside it. Leaning her head close to the floor, she looked for footprints of anyone, or anything, that might have taken the body.

She hoped she was wrong about what the hunch was telling her.

But she wasn't.

There on the floor, leading from the autopsy table to the door, were flakes of charred skin where bare feet had crossed the floor. Bare feet burned so badly that dead skin stuck to the tile like ash from a fire.

Kenzie pulled her phone from her pocket, and angling it just right, snapped photos of the footprints. They were the footprints of a dead person who had walked from the morgue. She started to rise when the walkie talkie in her backpack squawked. She ducked back down and fetched it out. She pressed the 'talk' key.

"What?" she said, then released the key and listened for whatever had caused Zac to break radio silence. But what came from the receiver wasn't Zac's voice.

The sound was faint, like breathing or a low croaking. She held it closer to her ear and listened. It was breathing, but there was something else too, a distant sound so disturbing it chilled her soul. A sound she heard once before.

The whispers.

All at once, the room grew cold. The flashlight in the doorway dimmed and went out, plunging the room into complete darkness.

Pocketing her cell phone, Kenzie crawled across the floor toward the door when she suddenly stopped.

Something was there with her. Something as cold and black as the surrounding darkness. She tensed, holding her breath as she listened in that dreadful silence.

It was moving, making no more noise than a thought as it glided through the darkness.

The walkie talkie screeched suddenly, causing her to nearly scream. She felt the unseen thing stop and turn towards her.

Kenzie sprang to her feet and rushed for the door, keeping her hands outstretched in the darkness to keep from colliding with it.

Her hands banged into the wall. Feeling across it to the door, she grabbed her flashlight and bean bag and fumbled down the hallway to the stairs. She scrambled up them in the darkness to the ground floor, then snatching up her other flashlight and bean bag, she bolted down the adjoining hallway and out the exit, never slowing until she felt the chilly night air against her face.

"Hey," Zac said, rushing out from behind the dumpster and nearly startling her again. "You get it?"

Kenzie looked nervously at the building as she backed into the alley. When she was finally sure it was safe, she waved her cell phone at Zac.

"We got it," she said. "Let's get the hell out of here."

Chapter Twenty-Three
The City in the Mist

Shortly after midnight, Calvin awoke from a restless and fitful sleep. An icy chill filled the air. He rolled over to see if Emma felt it too, before remembering that she was sleeping in one of his guest bedrooms.

They had gotten into an argument earlier that evening over some nonsense about his bedroom being haunted. He found the idea absurd, but she insisted on sleeping in one of the other bedrooms and pleaded with him to join her. He refused to indulge her hysteria, and so for the first time in two years, he slept alone.

He suspected it was his Guatemalan maid, Maya, who planted the idea in Emma's head. Maya was one of those religious fanatics he detested so much. While he tolerated organized religion to an extent, Maya took it to an extreme level with her talk of angels and demons, and now she had crossed the line by spooking Emma with her superstitious nonsense. He already found it offensive that the two women were friends, something he repeatedly scolded Emma for as being beneath her, but now that friendship had interfered with his own life, which was something he refused to tolerate.

To make matters even worse, he came home that day to find his bed unmade and his room uncleaned, and when he pressed Maya about this, she refused to enter the room. That insubordination was the final straw, and he planned to fire her as soon as Rebeka could find him a replacement.

Looking across the room to his window, he saw its curtains billowing softly in the moonlight. He found that a bit odd, since he was always particular about closing it at night to keep out the draft. But maybe he overlooked it in his annoyance with Maya and Emma.

Calvin climbed from bed and walked over to the window. He leaned his head out and was surprised to find the air outside balmy and much warmer than the air inside. Apparently, the chill came from somewhere inside the room.

Before turning, he already knew *She* was there.

With his back still to the room, he felt Lilith's cold eyes watching him from behind. He spun around to see her dark form standing in the hallway door across the room.

The breath caught in his throat at the strangeness of this. "Lilith..."

She gave no reply as she raised her hand and motioned with her finger for him to follow her.

Compelled like someone in a dream, Calvin crossed the room and followed her down the hallway to the grand staircase. She led him down the stairs to the main floor, then past the kitchen and across the massive banquet room. Through the large bay windows lining the far wall, he saw the backyard clouded in a dense fog that glowed faintly from within.

Lilith opened the large patio doors and slid through them into the fog, quickly disappearing inside its churning folds. Calvin followed her, instantly feeling the fog swallow him in its icy chill. He could no longer see Lilith through the dense veil, yet felt compelled on toward the cliffs. He continued, walking like someone in a dream, until his bare feet met with the edge of the cliff. He hesitated.

'Don't be afraid, Calvin,' her voice whispered from somewhere ahead of him, somewhere that would take him over the cliff's edge.

He took the step and felt himself fall forward into the fog, the air whooshing past his ears as he tumbled down. All around him, the fog peeled back like the tide rolling out to sea. He closed his eyes and braced himself for impact with the rocky shore.

But it never came.

Soft grass rose gently to meet his feet. Calvin's eyes opened. He was atop a remote moonlit hill, whose slopes plunged steeply to a vast mist-laden valley. Beneath the mist lay the dark, murky waters of a marsh which carpeted the entire basin. Distant mountains and forests bordered its northern and western sides, while the Atlantic's black waters spread out to its east.

Looking a short distance to his right, he saw Lilith staring out across the valley, her hair and dress tousled in the night's chill breeze. For a moment, he could only stare, his thoughts lost in her ineffable beauty.

Finally regaining himself, he walked over and stood beside her.

"Where are we?" he said.

She raised her finger to her lips, never taking her eyes off that moonlit bog. *Shh. 'Do you feel it, Calvin? How it stirs beneath the ground.'*

He looked around at the ground. He felt something, a deep rumble coming from somewhere beneath it.

"What is it?"

'Acheron,' she said. *'It stirs restlessly as its hour approaches.'*

A sudden violent jolt nearly knocked him off his feet. Beneath the mist-shrouded valley, something monstrous stirred, an abomination awaking from an infinite night.

The ground began to rumble and shake, and the wind rose in howling gusts. Calvin swayed unsteadily, like standing on the deck of a rocking boat, but Lilith appeared unfazed by the shifting ground and wind. She raised her hand and pointed across the windswept marsh.

'Behold, Calvin. The glory to come at its rising.'

Calvin steadied himself and looked out across the valley. From beneath the crumbling ground, something enormous was rising steadily through the surface. Great, dark bulks of different sizes and shapes emerged, scattered across hundreds of acres of marsh. Rising higher and higher, the entire valley soon filled with dark silhouettes of centuries-old buildings. Stone houses and shops broke from the surface along cobblestone streets, their dark walls glistening coldly in the moonlight. Hills pushed from the surface, atop whose peaks stood temples to unknown gods, their black spires and steeples towering darkly against the night sky.

Acheron was massive, dark, and brooding. Unloved and unloving, it loomed arrogant and hating in the night. Even at this distance, Calvin felt its icy chill sting his arms. He understood he was seeing only a vision of its imminent return, and yet it was enough for him to sense the immense power and sway it once held. The power it would soon hold again.

The wind died to a whisper, and the night grew cold. Calvin folded his arms against the sudden chill.

"Acheron..." he whispered in confirmation to himself. He stared in awe and trepidation at the colossus looming darkly in the mist. It was the city he dreamed of. The city that called to him from its grave beneath the earth. The city that knew him.

'The land of your people, Calvin,' Lilith said. *'Acheron's blood flows in your veins as it did for your ancestors of old.'*

He turned from the valley and shook his head in confusion. "My ancestors came from Capetown."

'Your ancestor came to Capetown to flee the cataclysm, but in his blood flowed the covenant.' Her eyes met his, and for a moment he caught something in them as cold and malevolent as that accursed city. *'You're a child of the covenant, Calvin, the last descendant of Acheron. And now, the covenant must be renewed through you.'*

"What covenant?"

'The one forged long ago by your people. From it flows everything you have. Before the covenant, you were nothing, and without it, you would return to nothing. But with its renewal, the world will be yours. Nations will bow at your feet and kingdoms will fall before you. And you will never know death.'

Calvin swallowed and looked back across the demon haunted city, somehow beautiful in its terrible darkness. He wanted what it promised.

"How do I do this?" he said.

'Heed the instructions of the men I've sent to guide you, Calvin. They've prepared a long time for your coming.'

Chapter Twenty-Four
Destiny

The quiet whisper of vague, nondescript thoughts flurried like ghosts through Calvin's mind that morning. He had felt their subtle suggestion for several days now, always teetering on the periphery of his consciousness, but this morning they seemed almost within his grasp.

They weren't his thoughts; they came from somewhere outside of him, invading his mind and drowning his own thoughts in an endless cacophony. This notion should have terrified him, but instead, it thrilled him, teasing his imagination with the promise of hidden mysteries. Of *secret things*. He had only to quiet his mind and listen.

He was ready.

At breakfast that morning, he grew increasingly irritated at Emma's attempts to draw him into a conversation. Each time she spoke, or a noise sounded, it disrupted the thoughts before they had time to fully coalesce and reveal their messages. He finally excused himself and took his coffee onto the back patio deck, where he could be alone. And there in the silence, while watching the morning mist fade out across the ocean, he listened to the thoughts.

They whispered quietly in his mind of things ancient and secret. Of unimaginable wealth and powers never before possessed by humans.

The powers of gods.

'Nations will bow at your feet and kingdoms will fall before you. And you will never know death.'

While a soft, small voice warned him of vague dangers, he pushed those fears aside. He was on the cusp of achieving his dreams — dreams he had spent his life pursuing through science. He saw now that there was a different path towards those dreams. A secret, hidden path. A path once tread by his ancestors. And he had only to open the door and step through it, and those dreams could be his.

And on the day you eat of the fruit, ye shall be as gods.

He sat in silence for another hour, listening to the thoughts as they whispered and tempted with their dark, forbidden secrets. And then it was time to find out more. To learn what he could about this covenant and the role his ancestors played in it. And if this information was to be found anywhere, it would be in the vast collection of ancient volumes housed in his family's library.

Calvin's library filled the walls of the third largest room in the estate after the grand ballroom and dining hall. It comprised hundreds of shelves lining the walls from waist level to the towering, frescoed ceiling, with two ladders on runners providing access to the top shelves. The shelves held a prized-collection of thousands of books, many of them first-run editions of classics, assembled over the generations since his ancestors built the mansion. Calvin sometimes wondered if anyone had read all the books, or if they were there for posterity, like so many of the paintings that adorned the estate's walls.

The oldest volumes and manuscripts were housed in a large walk-in dehumidified room that occupied the back third of the library. If any records of the artifacts existed in the collection, that's where they would be kept.

A slight pop and hiss of air met him as he opened the dehumidifier's door and went inside. Thirteen rows of bookcases ran parallel to each other from front to back, with the materials arranged by age. The oldest were shelved in the back. He slid on a pair of disposable latex gloves, then headed down the aisle to the back. He planned to start his research with the writings of the seventeenth century occultist, Eldin Muldridge, who wrote extensively about the esoteric practices and witchcraft in the early colonies. If the artifacts were used in occult practices, as their symbols suggested, they would have been, then Muldridge likely came across them at some point.

For the better part of the morning and early afternoon, Calvin sat at a table in the back corner of the room, diligently pouring through the aged documents, but finding little in the way of answers. He broke for a quick lunch, then picked back up with renewed vigor. He sensed he was close; he only needed that one kernel to point him in the right direction, and as the day wore on, he felt himself growing closer.

And then he found it.

The discovery came unexpectedly. He had just returned a volume to its shelf, when a dull thud came from the next row over. He walked to the end of his row and looked down the next one. Halfway down the row, a leather-bound volume lay on the floor, which explained the sound he heard, but not how it fell from the shelf.

"Dennis?" he said, looking around uneasily in the otherwise quiet room. Dennis Carlson was the estate's live-in butler, who had been with the estate ever since Calvin was a kid. Calvin kept Dennis and the rest of the staff on when he inherited the estate a decade earlier.

There was only silence, and the faint hum of the room's dehumidifier.

Calvin walked over and picked up the volume. Like so many of the older volumes, its cover was made of coarse dry leather with the pages bound on one side by thin leather strips. But it was the image burned into the cover, as if by a hot branding iron, that made him pause.

The eight-pointed star within the circle, with an eye in the star's center.

Calvin carefully opened the cover, and on the first page was an inscription:

'Our Life in the Covenant.'

Beneath this inscription was a sketch of the serpent encircling the sun. One of the two symbols etched onto the relics in the museum.

Calvin swallowed as his eyes scanned down the page to the author's name:

'Tobias Hawkins.'

Calvin's breath came slowly and unsteadily. Tobias was the oldest of Calvin's known ancestors, with nothing known about his parents or Tobias' own life prior to settling in Capetown. The family always presumed that he had immigrated over from Europe along with so many of the early settlers, but any records of that were long gone.

Calvin carried the volume back to the table, and for the rest of the afternoon and late into the evening, he poured through its browned, aged pages into the legacy of his family's past. And as he read, a growing tension built inside him.

His family's history didn't begin in Capetown, as they always presumed. It began in Acheron. Just as Lilith said.

Chapter Twenty-Five
The People of the Covenant

Tobias Hawkins' journal began with the annals of Acheron passed on to him by his father. Long before either of their births, Acheron had been a thriving city, considered to be among the jewels of the early colonies. It stood proudly along the rugged northeast coast of what was now Maine, with majestic temples of dark stone lining the sky. Cobblestone streets, flanked by gas lamps, shops, and houses built of the same dark stone, crisscrossed neatly as they sloped down to the seaport's promenade and rocky coast. The surrounding fields, once laden in marshes, were drained by canals and converted to farmland.

Daily life in Acheron found merchants plying their trade from storefronts, and farmers selling their produce from the lively promenade. The waters off its coast teamed with fish and catches rivaled those of its neighboring communities.

That first generation of settlers, the men and women who built Acheron one stone at a time, were God-fearing folks of robust faith. They praised God and recognized His providence in the prosperity of their community. But little of that zeal found its way into subsequent generations, who had never known the hardships faced by their forebears, and when the last of the founding generation died, Acheron's faith died with him. Acheron's once great temples stood vacant, and over the coming generations, fell into disrepair and rot.

But those temples weren't empty. Although void of congregates, something moved within their towering black halls. Something that had supplanted the God of their founders.

Tobias' parents immigrated from Europe during this time of spiritual desolation. Their surname was 'Metryus' at the time. They found much of the joy was gone from Acheron, but its prosperity remained, and Tobias' father, Malcolm Matryus, quickly built a thriving trade in rare gems and minerals with his buyers in Europe and along the coast.

Tobias was born two years after their arrival and two years before the *Blight* struck Acheron. Acheron was wealthy beyond belief by then, as was his family, whose fortune was considered among the greatest in New England. But all of that came crashing down with the Blight.

The Blight was the name given by the residents to a confluence of events that nearly decimated Acheron. Within a few months, a blight wiped out their crops, infections spread through the cattle, forcing their slaughter, a fungus infested the fish off their coast, and an outbreak of the plague killed much of the population. Many of the residents fled, and life for those who stayed behind grew grimmer by the day. Acheron might have perished entirely had it not been for the bizarre events that began in the wake of a storm that summer.

It was a storm that brought with it the *Order*.

The wind howled that night, hurling gusts of rain past the towers where the night watch stood guard. In the distance, amidst the rise and fall of the ocean's swell, they spotted the dark outline of a ship heaved about in the storm. They saw it for only a few moments before it disappeared behind the swell and never reappeared. A search of the waters off the coast the next morning found no signs of wreckage, so they presumed the ship had made it away safely.

That evening, the first sightings of the strangers were reported. Several residents reported seeing strange men in dark hooded robes roaming the dark alleyways and traversing outside the temples. When more reports came in, a search was made of the entire city, but they found no sign of these men.

It wasn't until a week later that the men finally revealed themselves to the residents. They introduced themselves as spiritual pilgrims, high priests of an ancient esoteric sect called the Hermetic Order of Set. They came from distant, far-away lands the residents never heard of, and told of how they were summoned by the great cry of Acheron's people and their plight. They assured the residents that they meant no harm and came only to offer help. They could show Acheron's residents a new way of life, a pathway to enlightenment and an end to their miseries. They would see an end to the Blight and a new era of prosperity that Acheron's forebears could only have dreamed of. As a demonstration of this power, they asked that several of the fishermen set out to sea and cast their nets. They would find the fish abundant and free from the fungus.

The fishermen did as instructed, and when they returned, their nets were near the bursting point with healthy fish.

The astonished residents embraced the newcomers, and by week's end, the Blight was gone. Fresh crops sprang from the soil, healthy cattle roamed out onto green pastures, and the coastal waters once again teemed with fish. But most startling of all, those suffering from the plague, many of whom had been on death's door just hours earlier, were suddenly and miraculously cured.

As their part of the bargain with the newcomers, Acheron's residents returned to the temples for worship, but found things radically different from the way they were before. While some aspects of the services felt familiar, such as carefully curated passages from the Bible, they were presented in new ways and given alternate meanings. Set, the god they worshiped, was presented in Genesis as the snake in the garden, and elsewhere as Lucifer, the light bearer. The Morningstar. One of the cryptic symbols that now adorned the church, supplanting the cross that had previously hung above the altar, depicted Set as a giant serpent coiled around the sun.

The other symbol that featured prominently was of an eight-pointed star within a circle, with an eye in the star's center. This was the all-seeing eye of Set.

The sermons preached of enlightenment, of the coming of a New Dawn and the age of a covenant to be made between Set and Acheron's people. They would be his chosen people and he their god. Acheron would be the seat upon which Set placed his crown and established his kingdom for all the world.

The residents, including their children, were baptized into this new church in preparation for the coming of the covenant. As part of their baptismal vows, they were required to renounce their Christian baptisms and embrace the great light bearer, Set, who promised them the world in exchange for their allegiance. He had once offered the same to the Nazorean when they stood on the mountain and beheld the great kingdoms of the world.

'All of this I will give you, if you will bow down and worship me.'

In the coming years, Acheron became more prosperous than ever, and the people ignored the changes that had come over themselves and the city. Tobias' father now owned a fleet of ships he used for trade, and by the time Tobias was in his early twenties, he assisted his father in running the company. None of them seemed to notice or mind the perpetually gray skies that now hung over Acheron, although Tobias wrote once in his journal of seeing the sunny skies in the cities he visited in Europe and pondering at the bright vibrancy of the surrounding colors. Acheron had grown bleak and gray by then.

His father dismissed such talk as nonsense and heretical. Acheron was wealthier than all of those other cities combined. It was the envy of the European aristocracy, who often visited its brothels and bathhouses to indulge in the lascivious activities for which Acheron had become known. Every vice and debauchery imaginable could be found in Acheron and the concepts of excess and sin no longer existed.

Over the years, Tobias grew into these beliefs, as was apparent from the later entries in his journal, where he fondly recounted many of his exploits. He now saw the only sin as being the denial of carnal pleasures and dismissed the beliefs of his youth as naivety.

Tobias was in his thirties when Acheron entered into the covenant, the next stage in its marriage with darkness.

A Man arrived during a storm, bringing with him a gold-plated chest which the high priests of the Order called the arc of the new covenant. The Man's ship had been dashed to splinters on the reef off Acheron's coast, but the Man himself remained strangely unscathed. Few of the residents saw the Man, who was known only as Logan, and none of them could describe his appearance, which always remained concealed in shadow. Only one resident, Henry Charles, claimed to have seen Logan outside the confines of the shadows as Logan emerged from the dark entrance of the temple at dusk. He swore that Logan had no face, that the front of his head was featureless and obscene, and yet somehow possessed of a keen intelligence and malignancy.

Tobias knew Henry and his family, and so Tobias felt the need to at least tell this much of Henry's story in Tobias' journal, no matter how scandalous it might sound. Henry fled Acheron with his family a day later and their whereabouts were unknown. It was supposed by some that they had run off to the settlement of Capetown, a day's ride down the coast.

Inside the chest, or the 'arc' as the high priests called it, was a silver chalice engraved with Set's signs of the Morningstar and the eight-pointed star. It was called the Calicem Noctis, or Cup of the Night. Within it was a black inky liquid which the residents were made to drink on the night the covenant was consummated. Despite the large number of residents who drank from the chalice, the cup never ran dry, as the liquid continued to replenish itself throughout the ceremony.

From that day, until the night of the cataclysm when Acheron was swallowed into the earth, neither Acheron nor its residents knew any touch of light. A darkness, blacker than night, fell across their souls and they descended into wickedness and depravities previously unknown and unthinkable. It became the Acheron of legend; the Acheron feared by the surrounding communities and only visited reluctantly by desperate merchants who fled its black walls before night fell and unspeakable horrors took shape in the shadows.

Tobias was overseas on trade missions throughout most of Acheron's final days, and was in England on the night of the cataclysm. He suspected it happened around the time of the solstice, the night on which the high priests of the Order were to travel to an area of the coast outside of Capetown called Hallows Pointe. It would be there, during the lunar eclipse, that they performed an ancient rite to consecrate Capetown to almighty Set.

Tobias returned from his travels to find Acheron completely gone, and the saltwater marshes having flowed in to reclaim the land where the city once stood. With nowhere left to go, he set sail for Capetown, where he purchased the estate on the eastern coast of the peninsula. With much of his wealth still intact from the shrewd deposits his father made in European banks, Tobias had no difficulty starting over in this new settlement.

After withdrawing the deposits from the European banks, Tobias changed his surname to Hawkins to avoid prosecution from zealots like the Brotherhood of Zion, and established a new trading company, selling Capetown's wares with his overseas buyers.

Shortly after his arrival in Capetown, Tobias met a young maiden named Bridget, who he married a year later. She knew nothing of his past, and assumed, like many others, that he had immigrated from Europe. They had ten children, seven of them boys and three of them girls.

In the last pages of his journal, Tobias wrote a strong admonishment to any of his descendants who discovered the journal.

'To whosoever should read these pages, know that they should never leave the walls of this house, nor their contents be revealed outside of the family. I have seen in these last years, hidden amongst the dark corners of the house, and in the moonlight cast upon the shore, things of which I dare not speak, lest my words draw them to me. But I know my time shall come. 'Tis a great

debt we owe Set, from whom our bounty has flowed, and 'tis a debt which in time must be repaid. I have tried repeatedly to find the arc in which the Cup of the Night resideth, but have failed at each attempt. I therefore admonish thee, that should the Cup be found, that it be used to renew the covenant in satiation of the debt, lest great ruin befall us all.'

And there the journal ended.

Calvin turned on his cell phone, which he had kept off while reading, and checked for messages. Dozens had come in since that morning. As he scrolled through them, looking for any marked as urgent, he stopped when he came to one. It was from Kristof Stanzos. He opened it, and the brief message read:

'I trust that things have become clearer for you, my friend. Would you be able to meet with myself, Jeremy, and Hareen at 10:00am tomorrow at Hallows Pointe?'

Calvin sat back and stared at the message for a moment, then texted back:

'Yes.'

Chapter Twenty-Six
Prophecy

Fr. Sean blew the whistle, and his sophomore physical education class raced off the baseball field into the locker room to shower up. As he headed past the dugout, he spotted Kenzie watching from the bleachers. She came down and met him at the fence.

"Hey," she said as he walked over. "Do you have time to help a sleep-deprived girl with something a little less sweaty?"

"Why's that girl sleep-deprived?"

"Because she's an idiot and stays up all night writing scary stories."

He smiled. "She needs to get some rest."

"I keep telling her that, but she never listens."

"I've heard that about her. So what's up?"

"Something really weird."

She pulled up the photo app on her phone and flipped to the photos of the chalice lying on the ground next to the spilled black liquid. She handed it to him.

"I'm pretty sure that thing right there is the Calicem Noctis," she said, pointing to the chalice. "They found it in the cave over at Hallows Pointe."

"The chalice you wrote about in your story?"

"Yup. I'm like ninety-nine percent certain that's it."

He used his fingers to zoom in on the image. "It has symbols etched on it."

She nodded. "Those are the same symbols Nathanial Crawford sketched in his journal. They're the ones he saw in Acheron as a kid."

He looked at her. "So, you think this chalice came from Acheron?"

Again, she nodded. "I'm like ninety-nine, point nine percent certain it did. What I need to find out, is what that black liquid on the ground is."

He zoomed in again for a closer look. "It looks like ink."

"Ink that kills people. After it spilled, the whole cave felt like it was... waking up, if that makes any sense. These two guys in monk habits were there, and that stuff scared the hell out of them."

"Who were they?"

"I don't know. I tried to find them after they left, but they were already gone."

"You said it killed people?"

Kenzie nodded. "Daryl Corbet. I went back that night and he was working security. This weird light came from the cave, so Daryl went in to check it out. I followed him, and that stuff was glowing and moving across the ground like a snake. Some of it got on Daryl's foot and he burst into flames. And right after that, he rose like five feet in the air."

"The paper left out most of that."

She frowned. "That's because they're idiots. And you really need to stop reading the fake news."

He smiled. Kenzie's ongoing feud with The Capetown Daily was hardly a secret. "Point taken."

"He said something right before he caught on fire. In aeternum regnabit. I looked it up, and it's Latin for 'forever he shall reign'."

"Forever who shall reign?"

"Probably someone we don't want reigning. Go to the next pictures."

He did, and she stopped him when he came to the pictures of the lab report.

"Those are the lab results for the tissue sample they took from Daryl's ankle where that liquid touched it. It tested positive for blood, but not for any known antigen."

"So, it's not human?"

"It's not anything. They don't know what it's from."

He looked back at the screen. "Do I want to know where you got this lab report?"

"Probably not. Just pretend Rick showed it to me."

He shook his head in amusement. Kenzie's antics weren't all that different from the mischief he and his brother Conor got into when they were her age.

"That takes a lot of pretending," he said.

"Okay. I might have broken into the lab. But I had a good reason to do it."

"You wanted to get arrested?"

"I wanted to get those lab results before they mysteriously disappear. And we know that's what's going to happen."

Fr. Sean nodded. Once again, point taken. "So it's blood, but not from any known species."

"Yeah. And I was hoping you might be able to help me find out what it's from."

"I know someone at the Vatican I can ask. It's a long shot, but maybe they have something in their repositories about that chalice. Can you send me those photos?"

"Doing it right now," she said, quickly typing out a text and pressing 'send.' "Sent. Thanks for doing this, father."

"Thank me by staying out of jail."

Calvin's limousine pulled up to the bluff at Hallows Pointe, where he found Kristof, Jeremy, and Hareen waiting for him. The men walked over and greeted him with warm, solemn smiles as he climbed from the back seat.

"Thank you for coming, my friend," Kristof said as they exchanged handshakes. "I trust you now have a better understanding of why we consider this to be such a pivotal moment in the world's history."

"I have some idea," said Calvin. "But I still have a lot of questions."

"No doubt you do, my friend," said Kristof. "And we shall do our best to answer them. But come, let us talk while we show you to the cave where so much of this has happened."

Calvin followed them down the steps to the shore, leaving their entourages behind with the cars. They led him across the damp stones to the cave and went inside.

"How did you find this place?" said Calvin, staring in awe as he stepped from the tunnel into the chamber.

"It was revealed to us in a dream," said Hareen, "much as you've had this week. We were told to look for a sign in the night sky, and the sign would lead us to it. That sign appeared on the night the cave opened."

"Many generations have searched for the Calicem Noctis," said Jeremy, "but it is to our generation that its blessings will now bestow."

"This is the chalice in the museum?" said Calvin, recalling the peculiar feeling he had when looking at it.

"That it is," said Kristof. "It is the chalice of which you have read in your ancestor's journal."

Calvin paused. "How did you know about that?"

"Lilith shares much with us, my friend, as she shall with you. This chalice, the Calicem Noctis, is the instrument of Set's covenant with the people of Acheron. With your people, Calvin."

"What is Set?"

Kristof smiled. "That, my friend, is part of an old story. A story which, you might say, is as old as creation." He paused for a moment as he walked over to the altar and traced his hand across it.

"Long before man took his first breath," Kristof resumed, "gods walked the Earth. These were the Old Ones, the Great Ones, whose names are written in the stars and in the minds of men. The greatest of these was Set, the Morning Star, who ruled the Heavens before being cast down to Earth. History depicts him in artwork as a great serpent, but Set has no material form. He exists, you might say, in the cosmos beyond all time and space. But at no place was his presence more concentrated than Acheron."

"We are of an ancient Order, Calvin," added Hareen, "who call ourselves the Hermetic Order of Set. It was our Order who long ago brought the worship and teachings of Set to the shores of Acheron, where it was embraced by the people. They entered into a covenant with Set, by which they became his people, and he became their god. In return, Set blessed them with many favors which passed on through their descendants."

"You, my friend," said Kristof, "as the last of those descendants, are a recipient of those favors. And now that the Calicem Noctis has been found, the covenant must be renewed so that even greater favors might be bestowed on all of us."

Calvin wandered over to the altar and ran his hand across its smooth, flat surface. When he looked up, his eyes met with Kristof's, and in them, Kristof saw the distant, contemplative sheen of thoughts stirring deep inside Calvin's mind.

Thoughts that came from outside of Calvin.

"You have heard them, Calvin," said Kristof, "the ancient gods of which we speak. They come to you as thoughts, which even now I see stir in your mind."

Calvin gave a slow nod. "I have."

"Your coming was foretold long ago, Calvin," said Hareen. "As the prophecy states: And you, Acheron, land of the north, are most blessed among the tribes of the Earth, for from your sons shall arise a ruler to lead all nations into the New Dawn."

"The time of Set's coming approaches, Calvin," said Jeremy. "The time when you, and we of the Order, will sit beside his throne in the New Dawn."

"What's the New Dawn?" said Calvin.

"A time of glorious rebirth, my friend," said Kristof. "A time when creation is returned to its rightful rule under Set, and all peoples and nations are subjugated to his will."

"Your arrival heralds its coming," said Hareen.

"Many generations have awaited this day, my friend," said Kristof. "Come, now, there is much we must do to prepare."

Chapter Twenty-Seven
Sanguine

It was in the early afternoon, as Kenzie rode her bike down the Main Street past Crawford Park, that she spotted a large German Shepherd near the gazebo. She stopped and watched him for a moment.

"Zeus?" she hollered, and the dog instantly looked over.

She lay her bike on the lawn and walked over to him.

"Hey. That is you, isn't it?" A slight wag of the dog's tail let her know it was. She knelt beside him and scratched behind his ear. "What are you doing out here by yourself?"

She looked around the park, but other than her and the dog, it was empty.

"Where's Floyd, Zeus?" she said. "Did you lose your dad?"

The dog let out a small, pitiful whimper. She looked at him.

"What is it, boy?" she said, but the dog only looked at her with his brown, soulful eyes. "Did you run away?"

A worried knot settled in her stomach as she watched Zeus hang his head. This was a far cry from the last time she saw him, and unless she read him completely wrong, he looked sad. And lonely.

Rising to her feet, she reached down and took hold of his collar. To her relief, he didn't seem to mind or react aggressively.

"Come on, boy. Let's go check on Floyd."

Maya stepped down from the ladder in the extensive library of Calvin's estate. All that remained to be cleaned was the dehumidifier room, which usually went quickly since barely any dust seeped through the filters. Tucking her feather duster in a front pocket of her apron, she slid on a pair of latex gloves from the dispenser outside the door and went inside.

The door closed behind her with a sharp hiss. Pulling out her feather duster, she began on the front row of shelves and worked her way to the back, where the older volumes were kept.

It didn't take her long to reach the back row, and to her surprise, she found one of the older volumes lying on a table. She walked over to it, then came to a sudden stop when she saw its cover. Seared into the leather hide was an eight-pointed star within a circle, a symbol she had seen long ago in her childhood.

It was in the remote mountain village of Guatemala where her family lived that she first saw the symbol. The village's small stone chapel was vandalized one weekend, and that symbol, along with several others, was painted in blood on the altar and walls. The head of a goat, whose blood was splayed across the chapel, was draped across Christ's head on the crucifix that hung from the back wall.

After the chapel's desecration, the village's priest, Fr. Gabriel, a very holy missionary who had traveled far and wide, gathered the village's children together and warned them to never venture out on their own or after dark. These symbols were of a very dark and ancient cult who worshiped the devil in the form of a serpent they called Set. Their followers were spread throughout the entire world, and he had seen their unholy symbols painted on the walls of Vatican City and the catacombs deep beneath Rome. And he had reason to believe they occupied seats of power in governments and institutions.

The desecration, he felt, was their way of leaving their mark on this small, quiet village, to let the villagers know that the cult's presence reached everywhere. He suspected they had already moved on from the village, but didn't want the children to take any chances.

Every nerve in Maya's body tensed. She quickly crossed herself and eased several steps back, never taking her eyes off the fiendish cover as if it might jump out and bite her.

For several seconds, she just stared at the book, taking in slow, deep breaths to steady her nerves. She couldn't think of any reason why something so diabolical would be in the library, much less here on the table. Other than her, and occasionally one of the other maids, Calvin was the only one who came into the library. And he forbid the staff from touching any of the volumes in this chamber, which meant he was the one who took it out and apparently read it.

Taking a deep breath, Maya slowly eased toward it again. She stared at the cover for a moment before flipping it open. On the first page was another symbol sketched in charcoal. It showed a serpent encircling the sun, another symbol that marred the small chapel in her village. Above that was the inscription: *'Our Life in the Covenant.'*

Maya swallowed as a sudden chill brushed across her. The word covenant had a particular meaning in her Catholic faith. It was the bond God first made with the Israelites in the Old Testament, which was later fulfilled and made new by Christ's blood in His sacrifice on the cross. The word's use, in connection with those symbols, was a profanation.

Maya hesitated for another moment, then sat down and read it.

Emma sat on the patio that afternoon, fingering the gold heart-shaped locket Calvin gave her early in their relationship. She read, and then re-read the inscription on the back. *'To the woman who stole my heart. Never give it back.'* Inside it was a small piece of a napkin from the restaurant where they had their first date.

He was like that back then, always making these small, thoughtful gestures. But he hadn't been that man in a long time. And now, she barely recognized him.

Emma startled as Maya rushed outside. "Miss Emma," Maya said frantically. "You must come quickly to the library."

"What is it?" Emma said, nearly spilling her coffee as she hopped to her feet. In the two years she had known Maya, she had never seen the young maid so anxious about something.

"It is something very bad," said Maya. "You must see it."

Emma's eyes traced down the journal's brown, aged page to the bottom, then she carefully turned to the next page.

Maya watched her from across the table, fidgeting nervously with her feather duster. She checked her watch and saw it was almost five. They had been in the dehumidifier room for over a half hour, and needed to get out of there soon before Calvin came home. She didn't think he would react well to them knowing about the journal.

Emma finally reached the end and closed the journal. She stared at the cover for a moment before looking at Maya.

"It is as I said, is it not?" said Maya.

Emma nodded, pushing the journal away to distance herself from it. "He read it?"

Maya nodded. "It was not here when I cleaned two days ago, but was here today."

"Why would he be interested in something so terrible?"

"Maybe he wishes the power that comes with the covenant," said Maya. "We have felt the evil in your room. Maybe it is Mister Calvin who invited it in."

"What do we do?"

"He must not know that we know," said Maya. "There is someone we should talk to."

"Who?"

"It is a girl who writes about things such as this."

"Do you mean the Acheron Files?"

"Yes. You have read what she writes?"

"I did a couple times. Calvin said it's all lies and conspiracy nonsense."

Maya watched her. "Do you believe what he says is true?"

Emma looked down at the journal. "I don't know what to believe."

"But you do, Miss Emma. You know what is truth. Your mind tells you what your heart does not want to. Let us go see the girl."

"What if we're wrong about all of this?"

"Then there is no harm in speaking with the girl. But you know we are not wrong. You have felt it in the room and read it now with your eyes." Maya reached across the table and held Emma's hand. "Trust what your mind tells you, Miss Emma. It is only way we can stop this."

Emma took a deep breath. "Okay. Let's meet with this girl."

The sun had set by the time Kenzie arrived at Hallows Pointe. She walked her bike with one hand, while guiding Zeus on a leash she picked up at the pet store with the other. So far, he hadn't given her any trouble, but as she chained her bike to the guardrail, she sensed his hesitancy in a slight tug on his leash.

She approached the edge, and looking down, saw a dense fog clouding the shore. Zeus let out a low whine. She looked at him and saw him staring at the lighthouse tower, its lantern room rising above the fog. She felt the same hesitancy as him. It never looked so ominous.

"It does look pretty spooky, doesn't it?" she said, bending down and scratching him behind his ear. "But we gotta get you home."

With a gentle tug on the leash, she coaxed him into following her down the stairs to the shore, but again felt his hesitancy as they descended into the fog.

"Come on, boy," she gently coaxed him, "we're almost there."

They followed the path across the jetty until the tower and cottage emerged as faint, ghostly shadows in fog. They were close enough for her to see that the kitchen door was open.

Zeus came to a sudden stop and began nervously backing away.

"Zeus?"

A low growl rumbled deep in his throat.

"What is it, boy?"

He let out a sudden loud bark, startling her back. She realized she wouldn't be able to coax him any further. He already saw something he didn't like. She turned back to the cottage.

"Floyd!" she hollered. "I found Zeus. I have him out here with me." Then she paused. In the gloom beyond the kitchen door, she could swear she saw something move.

"Floyd!" she yelled again, but the only sound was the splash of waves on the rocks. She looked down at Zeus. "You're gonna make me go in there by myself?"

It was obvious he was. She took a deep breath. "Okay. You wait here. Bark if anything scary comes."

The dog looked up at her and gave a low, pitiful whine. She gave him a quick pat on the head, then slowly approached the cottage, listening for any sounds that might alert her to danger.

She reached the kitchen door and poked her head inside. The kitchen looked as it always had, with no sign of the snakes having been there.

"Hey, Floyd, it's Kenzie," she called inside. "I found Zeus in the park and brought him home."

From the adjoining living room came a TV's low static hiss, and looking at the entrance, she saw flickering static play off the wall.

"Floyd?" She waited another moment. "I'm coming in. I hope that's okay."

She crossed the kitchen and entered the living room, where she found the TV against the far wall crackling with static. An empty beer bottle lay on the floor beside a recliner chair, its beer spread across the floor in a sticky puddle.

Like the kitchen, there was nothing to let her know that hundreds of snakes had been there.

"Floyd? It's Kenzie. Your door was open."

She listened for a moment, but the only sound came from the TV's static.

"I have Zeus outside."

Several barks came from outside, seeming to come from the side of the cottage. Kenzie hurried outside and around the side of the cottage, where she found Zeus barking at the storm cellar's open door.

"Hey. What is it, boy? You see something down there?"

She walked over to Zeus and stared down into the darkness through the open door. "Floyd? You down there?"

A sudden rush of cold air blew from the cellar, wafting her in the foul stench of rot and decay. Zeus backed away, letting out a low, squeaking whine. Any defiance she saw in him earlier was gone.

"You felt that too, didn't you?"

The dog just stood there, his head lowered and tail between his legs.

"I'm gonna check down there to see if Floyd's okay. You keep watch."

She ducked through the low opening and took the rickety wooden steps down into the dank, musty cellar. The stench of mold and mildew nearly overwhelmed her. She pulled her shirt collar over her nose and mouth and continued down.

Halfway down the steps, she passed beneath a long string dangling from the ceiling. She pulled on it, and the room lit in the harsh light of a single bulb mounted to the overhead rafter. Deep pockets of shadow darkened areas behind beams and partitions.

"Floyd?" she said again as she reached the cold, concrete floor at the bottom. Looking around, she saw rickety old workbenches, cabinets, and shelves propped against walls.

As she crossed the floor, passing a partition on her right, a dark back area of the cellar came into view. On the far wall, painted in blood-red letters, were the words: *'In Aeternum Regnabit,'* and beneath them, the words *'Libertas'* and *'Sanguine.'*

Beneath the words, in the same blood-red paint, were the cryptic symbols of the eight-pointed star and the serpent coiled around the sun.

Kenzie felt her blood go cold. She slid her cell phone from her pocket, frowning when she saw its 'low battery' indicator blinking red, and snapped several photos before the battery completely died.

Sudden barks came from outside, causing her to nearly jump. She looked back across the room at the stairs, in time to see the bulb above them flicker several times, then go out.

With a sudden, heavy crash, the cellar door slammed shut, plunging the basement into nearly complete darkness.

Kenzie stood frozen for a moment in the sudden darkness, unable to even see her hands held out in front of her. In the darkness and silence, every sound was amplified, along with her other senses. The ones that sensed things other people couldn't.

Extending out her hands, she eased across the floor toward the stairs, being careful not to trip over anything in the darkness.

Her hands met with the partition, and feeling her way around it, she saw thin slats of light between the door's planks at the top of the stairs.

Then she sensed something moving stealthily through the darkness behind her. Something her ordinary senses wouldn't have detected.

Something dead.

In a panic, she clambered up the stairs, nearly tripping several times on the rickety wooden steps. She reached the top and pushed against the door. To her horror, it budged only a few inches.

The thing in the darkness was coming up the stairs behind her.

Kenzie's pulse pounded as she threw her shoulder against the door with all her strength. It swung open on rusted hinges that time, and she dashed through it into the mist outside. She slammed the door shut behind her and staggered back several steps, never taking her eyes off the door.

Zeus's barks from the front of the cottage caused her to startle and look in that direction. She followed the barks through the dense gray haze until she found Zeus at the cottage's front corner, his gaze fixed on something a short distance away. Kenzie looked in that direction.

A man stood outside the cottage's front door, little more than a faint gray shadow in the mist. But Kenzie could tell from the general outline that it was Floyd.

And he was dead.

Kenzie swallowed nervously as she reached down for the dog, but her hand found only empty air. She looked down and saw Zeus slowly advancing toward the shadow, which continued to stand motionless outside the door. As she watched, the fog folded in around the figure and hid it from sight.

"Zeus," Kenzie said quietly. "Don't. Stay."

The dog didn't listen, continuing to pad slowly toward the spot outside the door where the faint, ghostly shadow had stood. The shadow that was once his owner.

"Zeus?" Kenzie called again, but to no avail, as the dog continuing padding forward until it disappeared in the fog. Taking a deep breath, Kenzie followed him, hearing the crash of waves grow louder as she neared the jetty's edge.

Kenzie found Zeus stopped on the jetty's edge, his lips curled back in a snarl as he stared out in the distance. Looking down, Kenzie saw the jetty's stone side disappear in the fog as it sloped steeply down to the water. Ahead of her, the fog blanketed the ocean and sky in a dense gray cloud. Deep within its depths, she saw Floyd's faint ghostly shadow turn to face her and Zeus. He floated high above the ocean, his arms outstretched like a preacher heralding his flock; or a grim mockery of Christ on the Cross.

Chapter Twenty-Eight
Acheron's Son

Kenzie sat on the steps of the gazebo in Crawford Park that morning, keeping one eye on the entrance to the sheriff's office across the street, and the other on Zeus. The dog lay at her feet, chewing on what was left of one of her shoes he found in her closet overnight.

She brought the dog home with her after leaving Floyd's cottage the previous night. With Floyd dead, and nobody to take care of Zeus, she couldn't bear the thought of him going to the pound. She wasn't sure how this would play out long term, but at least for now, Rose was letting Kenzie keep him in her apartment.

It was already proving to be interesting.

In the one night he had been there, Kenzie learned that full-grown German Shepherds and small studio apartments don't mix well. Especially not in Kenzie's case, with her habit of leaving her clothes and things lying around the floor. She learned the hard way that loose dog hairs stick to clothes like magnets, and shoes make great chew toys. She figured it was the universe's way of telling her to clean her room.

She also learned that Zeus had an annoying habit of waking up early — even earlier than Zac — and then licking her face until she woke up.

But looking at the positive side, she now had a bodyguard to bring with her on investigations, one who could see and sense the same otherworldly threats that she could. And one with sharp teeth, as her shredded shoe and flannel shirt could attest to.

She was staking out the sheriff's office that morning, hoping to catch Drew alone. The things she had to tell him were going to sound crazy, and she knew she wouldn't get anywhere with Rick, but she might have a shot with Drew if his boss wasn't around.

After waiting for nearly an hour, she finally saw her chance, as Drew strolled from the building and headed off down the block. Kenzie waited several seconds for him to get a little further down, then she and Zeus crossed the street and followed him, keeping far enough behind to avoid being seen.

On the next block, Drew headed inside Sally's Diner. Kenzie hurried over to the large front windows facing the sidewalk and watched the hostess escort Drew to a table in the back corner. Kenzie then took Zeus by the leash and went inside.

Drew looked up from his coffee to see Kenzie leading a large dog across the diner toward his table.

"Hey," she said as she walked up. "Okay if we join you?"

Drew's eyes went from her to the dog then back to her. He nodded to the dog. "He looks like he'll bite me if I say 'no.'"

"He'll probably just lick you too death," she said as she sat down in the chair across the table from him. Zeus curled up on the floor beside her feet.

"Isn't that Floyd's dog?"

"He used to be."

"What do you mean?"

"I'll circle back to that in a minute. But first, I need to ask you something."

"What is it?"

"What happened to the coroner and Daryl's body?"

He wiped his mouth with his napkin. "You know I can't discuss an ongoing investigation. Rick would have my ass."

"Then just tell me if they're about to be added to your guys' 'unsolved' case files." She made the quotation marks with her fingers.

Kenzie watched Drew shift uneasily in his chair and take a nervous look around at the other diners, apparently making sure none of them were listening.

"You look nervous, Drew," she said. "Was I not supposed to know about those files?"

"How do you know about them?"

"Everybody knows about them. It's like your worst kept secret. People come to you guys for help, and if their case hints at anything supernatural, you guys just file it away and do nothing about it. Tell me I'm wrong."

He took a deep breath and watched her for a moment before leaning across the table. He motioned for her to lean in closer.

"Do you promise this stays just between us?" he said, his voice barely above a whisper. "You can't write anything about it."

"Scout's honor."

"You're not wrong. And I'm not happy about the way they handle those cases."

"Then why do you do it?"

"It's not my call." He took a deep breath before going on. "Look, Kenzie, I've read your stories. Rick doesn't want us reading them, but I do anyway. And you're not wrong about these things."

"Then why do you guys pretend it's not happening?"

He shook his head. "I don't know. I've tried talking to Rick about it, but he won't go there. Between me and you, I think he's scared."

"Of what?"

"Of people who are a lot more powerful than a small-town sheriff."

"Any idea who?"

"Not that I'm comfortable sharing yet."

"Will you tell me when you are comfortable?"

"Assuming they haven't gotten to me by then."

Now it was Kenzie's turn to shift uneasily. These were all things that she, Zac, and the Lone Gunmen suspected, but seeing it played out in Drew's worried expression really hammered home the gravity of it.

"You're scared too, aren't you?" she said.

He gave a slow nod. "You should be too."

"I am. This brave face is just me pretending. So, will you tell me if the coroner's death and Daryl's disappearance are about to end up in the 'unsolved' files?"

He gave another slow nod. "They probably will."

"What happened to them?"

"We're still off the record?"

"I won't say a word."

He took another deep breath and gave the area one more scan to make sure they weren't being eavesdropped on. They weren't.

"Clyde's body was... burned."

"Like Daryl's?"

He nodded. "Exactly like Daryl's. Every inch of his body burned beyond recognition, but his clothes and the car untouched."

"What about Daryl's body?"

"It's missing. That's all we know at this point."

"Was it taken?"

He shook his head. "Clyde's footprints were the only clear ones we could find."

"What about unclear ones?"

He took an uneasy breath. "We found some."

She nodded knowingly. "They were barefoot, weren't they?"

He did a double-take, which was enough for her to know she was right.

"How'd you know that?" he said.

"Because Clyde would have removed Daryl's shoes when he performed the autopsy."

"You think Daryl walked out on his own?"

"Isn't that what you thought when you saw the bare footprints?"

It was. He took a deep breath. "You know how crazy all this sounds."

"No crazier than two men bursting into flames. Or any of the other things you guys keep covering up."

He gave a reluctant nod in agreement. "You know, I keep trying to think of rational explanations for these things, but there aren't any."

"That's because you can't rationalize the inexplicable. You're trying to fit these things into neat little boxes you know and understand, but they'll never fit. You have to accept that they are what they are."

He nodded at Zeus, watching them from the floor near her feet. "Is your being with Floyd's dog going to fit into a neat little box?"

"Only if that box has room for ghosts." She took a breath. "Floyd's dead. And I think when you find his body, it'll be another case for your 'unsolved' files."

"How do you know that?"

"Because I saw his ghost when I went to bring Zeus home."

"You see ghosts?"

She nodded. "I see lots of things nobody else can. It's why I'm so weird."

He smiled and waited for the punch line, but it soon became apparent there wasn't one.

"You're serious?" he said.

"Deadly serious. Pun partially intended."

"How long's this been happening?"

"Ever since I went missing. Chad said something happened to me, and it makes me see things other people can't."

"Your brother said that?"

She nodded. "He was the first ghost I saw. He showed me where his body was."

"You said it was your memory returning."

She shook her head. "That's because I knew you guys wouldn't believe the truth back then. But I think you're ready to now. And if you don't, people are going to keep dying. And it could be a lot of people."

She had his full attention now. He leaned forward on the table. "Tell me what you know."

"When I was in Floyd's cellar, there were two words written on his wall. I'm pretty sure it was in blood. They were libertas and sanguine. I'm assuming libertas means the festival, but I had to look up sanguine. It's Latin and literally means a bloodbath."

Drew sat back. "You think there's going to be a bloodbath at the festival?"

"I'm just telling you what I saw. But yeah. I believe that. And I'm hoping you can make Rick and the town council believe it too."

Kenzie arrived back at Rose's cafe a short while later. As she came in the door with Zeus, Rose looked over from behind the pastry counter.

"You have some visitors," Rose said, nodding to a table in the back corner. Two women sat there, watching them.

"Who are they?" Kenzie said, keeping her voice down.

Rose shrugged. "They just said they needed to talk to you."

The women rose from their chairs as Kenzie walked over. One was a young Hispanic woman who might be in her twenties, and the other a tall, statuesque blond, with the high cheekbones and slender figure of a fashion model.

"You guys wanted to see me?" Kenzie said.

"Are you Kenzie Walsh?" said the blond.

Kenzie nodded. "Yeah?"

"I'm Emma, and this is my friend, Maya. We were hoping we could talk to you about something."

"What is it?"

Emma looked nervously around to make sure none of the other patrons were listening. "We should probably sit so we don't draw any attention."

They all sat down, and Emma leaned across the table towards Kenzie and motioned for her to do the same.

"First, I should tell you I'm Calvin Hawkins' girlfriend," Emma said, and at the mention of his name, Kenzie noticeably tensed. "Don't worry," Emma quickly added, "he doesn't know we're here. We're doing this on our own."

"Mister Calvin would be very angry if he knew we were here," said Maya, and Emma nodded in agreement.

"He would be," said Emma. "So he can't ever know any of what I'm about to tell you."

"What is it?" said Kenzie, relaxing a bit and her curiosity now piqued.

"An Acheron File," said Emma. "A really big one. But it's something you'll need to see."

On the drive to Calvin's estate, Emma and Maya filled Kenzie in as much as possible on everything that happened since the night of the party. About Calvin's odd behavior and the unseen presence in the bedroom. But mostly, they focused on the journal.

The chauffeur was Emma's personal driver, Titus, who Calvin assigned exclusively to her. Over the years, they had become friends, and she came to trust him for complete discretion. The same trust applied to the rest of the staff, except for Calvin's personal driver and bodyguard, Marcus, whose loyalties lay with Calvin. But he was away in Arkham with Calvin that morning.

Upon arriving at the estate, the women gave Kenzie a brief tour of the mansion, and it was like nothing she could have imagined. The chandelier alone, which hung high above the foyer, would have cost more than Rose's entire cafe, and the kitchen could have fed an army.

In the backyard, Kenzie got to meet Calvin's two pit bulls. They were massive, layered in thick muscles with fur as black as night. They were friendly enough while she had Emma and Maya with her, but she pitied anyone stupid enough to sneak into the estate.

Back inside, Kenzie followed Emma and Maya up the sweeping staircase to the second floor. As they reached the top, Kenzie felt a sudden, stark change in the atmosphere. The air was heavy and cold, and as she stepped from the landing into the hallway, something subtle stirred in the surrounding air. Something sentient and awake; and watching them from the darkness with cold, malevolent eyes.

"You feel it, do you not?" said Maya, seeing the sudden alertness and worry in Kenzie's expression. "How it watches us."

Kenzie nodded. "Yeah."

"You will feel it more down there," Maya said, pointing to Calvin's master bedroom at the far end of the hallway.

They proceeded down the hallway, when Kenzie came to a sudden stop halfway down. The bedroom door was cracked slightly open now, but was closed when they started down the hallway.

It wanted them to come in.

"The door's open," said Kenzie.

Both Maya and Emma nodded, as if this was expected.

"What is inside waits for us," said Maya, "but only Mister Calvin ever goes in."

"Most of the staff won't even come up to this floor anymore," said Emma.

Kenzie couldn't blame them. Of all the investigations she had conducted, none had felt as ominous and threatening as whatever waited beyond that door. It was the kind of threat Fr. Sean warned her about from his experience in the Exorcism. A threat that reached the soul.

"You feel it in there, as we do," said Maya, seeing the cold fear in Kenzie's eyes.

"Yeah."

"Is very evil."

Kenzie nodded in agreement. Every instinct told her to get out of there as fast as she could and never come back. But she had one more thing to do first.

"Can I see that journal?" Kenzie said.

Emma and Maya sat across the table from Kenzie, waiting in silence while Kenzie read the journal. As she read each page, Kenzie snapped a photo of it with her phone's camera.

After nearly an hour of reading, Kenzie finally finished the journal and closed it. She slid it away from her, as if a few inches of distance could remove the vile stain she felt from touching it. She looked across the table at the women.

"Calvin's ancestor wrote this?" Kenzie said.

Emma nodded. "Tobias is Calvin's oldest known ancestor. But Calvin always assumed he came from Capetown."

"Did Calvin read this?"

Maya nodded. "He is only one who would remove it from the shelf. I find it here on the table yesterday."

"Did he mention it?"

Emma shook her head. "Not a word. But we haven't really talked since I moved into one of the guest bedrooms."

"Do you think he would do this?" Kenzie said. "Renew the covenant."

Emma shifted uneasily at the thought. Even with the growing tension between them and breakdown in their relationship, she was hesitant to think of him doing something so intrinsically evil. But Maya had no such qualms and quickly weighed in.

"There is no doubt he will do it," Maya said. "Mister Calvin cares only about money and power."

Emma gave a slow, hesitant nod in agreement. "He's changed from when I first met him. He's grown cold. And I hate to even say this, but I don't think there's anything he wouldn't do to keep his wealth and gain even more."

"Like make a covenant with the devil," said Kenzie.

"I think in many ways, he and the people he associates with have already done that. You see it in the way they manipulate people and control them and take away our freedoms. The covenant lets them take that to a whole new level."

"They will have the help of Satan," said Maya. "It is why we cannot allow this to happen."

Kenzie nodded in agreement. "They need the Cup of the Night to do it. So we can't let them get it."

"You know where it is?" said Emma.

"It's at the museum," said Kenzie. "They found it in a cave down at Hallows Pointe this week. And now that I think about it, the three partners of a global equity fund were at the excavation."

"Are you talking about the Stanzos Group?" said Emma.

"Yeah. And they showed a lot of interest in that cup."

"They're some of Calvin's associates I mentioned before. If they were at the excavation, it's because they knew what they would find."

"So, they're a part of this, too," said Kenzie.

"It wouldn't surprise me. For people like them, power's a drug, and they constantly crave more. And the covenant gives them absolute power."

"So what is it we do with this cup to keep them from getting it?" said Maya.

"We need to steal it from the museum and get rid of it," said Kenzie. "Throw it in the ocean or something, where they can never find it."

"I do not think the ocean is deep enough to hide an evil such as this," said Maya. "You see how it has freed itself from the cave."

"Then we destroy it," said Kenzie.

"You assume it would allow itself to be destroyed," said Maya. "I am not so sure of this."

Kenzie swallowed. Maya had a good point.

"There has to be a way," said Kenzie.

"Yes. I agree," said Maya. "But we must find someone first who can tell us the way."

"My friend might know someone," said Kenzie, reaching for her cell phone. She planned to call Fr. Sean, but as her screen lit up, she saw that a text already came in from him while she was reading the journal. She opened it and read the brief text.

'I heard from my contact at the Vatican. Can we meet this afternoon at the Hallows Pointe cave?'

Fr. Sean was already waiting outside the cave by the time Kenzie, Emma, and Maya arrived. After making quick introductions, Kenzie turned to look at the cave. Even in the daylight, it was menacing.

"Nice place, isn't it?" she said sarcastically.

Fr. Sean nodded. "Like a lion's den."

"You should see it at night. It's like this on steroids."

"I'll take your word for it."

"Is much evil," said Maya, cautiously approaching the entrance and looking inside. "I do not wish to go in."

"You can wait out here with me," said Emma.

Kenzie turned to Fr. Sean. "You wanna look inside?"

"I probably should," he said.

Kenzie led him down the short, narrow tunnel into the main chamber, then turned on her cell phone's flashlight and shined it around. Fr. Sean stepped up beside her.

"Not much to see without all the artifacts," she said, sweeping her light around, "but there's the stone I think they used as an altar."

Kenzie held her light on the stone block while Fr. Sean walked over to it. "I think you're probably right," he said, leaning in for a closer look. "You can see the chisel marks where the top was carved flat."

"Be careful where you step," said Kenzie, aiming her light at the ground as she walked over. She pointed to a spot on the ground. "This is where that stuff spilled."

Fr. Sean knelt and looked closer at the dirt.

"It's gone now," she said. "But I wouldn't take any chances. Not after what happened to Daryl."

He rose to his feet and took several steps back. "We should get back to the others."

"Your text said you heard from your friend at the Vatican," Kenzie said as she and Fr. Sean walked from the cave and joined Emma and Maya outside.

"I did. And he was helpful. He said there's a monk we should talk to named Father Kessler. He was an archaeologist and graduate student at Oxford before joining the Franciscans, and wrote his thesis on secret societies and their origins in the Crusades. His thesis mentioned the Calicem Noctis."

"Can we talk to him?"

"He's in a monastery outside a small Honduran village called San Gabriel. It's in a mountain range, and the only roads to get there are pretty bad."

"Can we call him?" Kenzie said.

Fr. Sean shook his head. "The village has been completely dark since last Friday. There's been no calls in or out of it."

At hearing the day, a sudden, troubling thought occurred to Kenzie. She looked behind her at the cave and then around at the shattered stones from the lightning strike that opened it.

On Friday night.

"Friday was the night that thing opened," said Kenzie, exchanging wary looks with the others. "In case anyone was wondering."

They were all wondering now, as each of them turned to look at that gaping maw in the cliff's face, which seemed to mock them now.

"It knows what it is we plan," said Maya, taking an uneasy step back.

Emma took a step back with her and turned to Fr. Sean. "What about airfields? Are there any near there?"

"I saw a small one on the map just outside the village," said Fr. Sean, "but it's way too small for a commercial jet."

"What about a small commuter plane?" said Emma.

"It's probably big enough for that," he said.

"We can use one of Calvin's planes," said Emma. "He has a small turboprop he keeps at an airport outside of Arkham."

"Won't he notice it missing?" said Kenzie.

"He hasn't used it ever since he bought the Gulfstream. He's had it for sale now for several months."

"Who'll fly it?" said Kenzie.

"My driver, Titus, can. He has a pilot's license. You can fuel it on the company's account. The accounting department will assume Calvin was flying on the Gulfstream."

"Can you translate for us, Maya?" said Kenzie.

"If is okay with Miss Emma."

"It's fine with me," said Emma. "I'll have the other staff cover for you."

"You're not coming?" Kenzie asked Emma.

"Calvin would get suspicious if I was gone that long."

Kenzie looked at Fr. Sean. "You're coming, right?"

"Wouldn't miss it."

She turned to Emma. "How soon can we leave?"

"It's going to be about a six-hour flight," said Emma, "with a stop in Tampa to refuel. So, if you leave tonight, you can be there first thing in the morning."

"I guess we leave tonight if that works for everybody," Kenzie said, wiping her hands on her jeans. Her palms were already feeling sweaty.

Maya and Fr. Sean both nodded.

"It works for me," said Maya.

"I'll let the rectory know I'll be gone tomorrow," said Fr. Sean.

Chapter Twenty-Nine
The Message

The turboprop touched down on a small dirt airstrip in the early morning hours. Kenzie and the others climbed from the plane and stretched their legs. It felt good to stand and walk around after being cramped in their seats for seven hours.

Kenzie looked around and took in their surroundings. According to Fr. Sean's map, they were less than a mile outside the small village of San Gabriel. It sat in the foothills of a rugged mountain range, rising high in the distance to the west of them. The vegetation was lush, with the airstrip cut through vast patches of grass, brush, and trees.

They headed off toward the village, with Titus staying behind to guard the plane. Kenzie turned on her cell phone along the way, and to no one's surprise, it had no reception. But she kept it on anyway to use its camera.

They were nearing the outskirts of the village when they came across the crowd. Hundreds, and possibly a thousand, religious pilgrims trudged along the dirt road in a steady procession into the village. There were families with small children, and horse-drawn wagons and carts, many with the infirm loaded in back, all parading in the same direction for as far as the eye could see. They sang prayers, and carried statues of the Virgin Mary, adorned with roses, above their heads.

"What's going on?" Kenzie said, eying the crowd. "Is there a festival?"

Maya shook her head. "They come to honor Mother Mary. I do not know why they choose this day."

"They're on a pilgrimage," said Fr. Sean, noting the statues and prayers resonating through the crowd. "We need to find another way around the village."

He unfolded his map and traced his finger along the dirt road running through the village and then over to a dense grove of trees.

"It looks like there's an orchard just south of us we can use," he said, folding up the map. "The friary is going to be on the west side of the village."

They headed off through a citrus grove on the southern side of the village, taking a path through it to the far side of town. It joined with the road, which they took up into the foothills. They soon came across a path, veering off the road to their left, which led up a gentle slope to the Spanish-style hacienda where the Franciscan missionaries lived.

They followed the path to the wall surrounding the property, where they found a gate propped open. They headed through the gate into the hacienda's front yard, where they found a friar tending to a small garden. He looked up as they entered, then dusting the dirt from his hands, walked over to greet them.

"Hi," Fr. Sean said, shaking hands with the friar, "we're looking for Fr. Jacob Kessler."

The friar noted the white Roman collar on Fr. Sean's black shirt, then looked over at Kenzie and Maya before turning back to Fr. Sean. He looked stunned.

"It is true then," the friar said, "that you are the ones who come to us from America."

"We're from America," Fr. Sean said, looking stunned himself, "but how did you know we were coming?"

"You are the ones who have seen the chalice, yes?" said the friar, making certain these were the right people.

"I've seen it," Kenzie said as she and Maya walked over and joined them.

"Is it true that it has engraved on it the sign of Lucifer?"

"Yeah," Kenzie said, then watched as the friar quickly crossed himself.

"It is you and your friends, then, that Fr. Kessler has been expecting," said the friar.

"How did he know we were coming?" asked Fr. Sean.

"This, it is best that Fr. Kessler explains, as he has much to tell you and your friends."

"Is he here?" said Kenzie, looking past the friar to the hacienda.

The friar shook his head. "He is at the village church, which you will find down the road. You will tell the young boy outside, Elan, that you are the Americans who Fr. Kessler awaits, and he will allow you inside."

Excusing themselves, Fr. Sean, Kenzie, and Maya took the road back into the village, where they soon came across a large crowd gathered outside the church. Looking over the crowd, Fr. Sean spotted two boys standing on the steps outside the church entrance, both of them struggling to keep the throng out.

"I see two boys out front," Fr. Sean said, then he, Kenzie, and Maya squeezed through the crowd until they reached the steps.

"Is one of you Elan?" Fr. Sean hollered up to the boys over the ruckus.

One boy looked down from the steps at him. "I'm Elan."

"I was told to tell you we're the Americans Father Kessler is expecting."

The boy's expression lit up in surprise. "Yes. Yes, he has said to let you in when you come. Here, follow me."

He and the other boy opened the heavy wooden door, allowing Fr. Sean, Kenzie, and Maya to slip past them into the church, then pulled the door closed again with a loud thud.

Inside, Fr. Sean and the others found two rows of pews, with an aisle between them, leading to an altar at the far end. A large crucifix hung from the wall behind the altar, and beneath that was the ornate tabernacle.

A friar, dressed in the brown woolen habit of a Franciscan monk, sat near the front. He looked back as they entered, and seeing them, rose from his pew and walked over to them.

"We're looking for Father Kessler," said Fr. Sean.

"I am Father Kessler," said the friar. "Might you be the Americans I was told would come?"

"I believe so," said Fr. Sean, "but I don't know how anyone could have known we were coming."

"Is it you who have seen the Cup of the Night?"

"I have," said Kenzie.

"Then it is you and your friends who I was told to expect. Come, let us sit."

Fr. Kessler led them over to a pew in the middle of the church where they sat down.

"For many years, since my studies at Oxford, I have wondered if the Cup was real or but a legend. But you have truly seen it?"

Kenzie nodded. "Yeah. They found it in a cave outside of our town."

"This news of its discovery is indeed quite troubling," said Fr. Kessler.

"We were hoping you could tell us more about it," said Fr. Sean. "But I'm curious about how you knew we were coming."

"It was told to the young girl over there by the Lady she sees in her visions," said Fr. Kessler. He pointed to the far end of the church near the altar, where they saw a young girl kneeling in front of a statue of the Virgin Mary. "Her name is Anna Lucia."

"She's a visionary?" said Fr. Sean.

"That she is, father. And she bears the wounds of Christ on her hands."

"A Stigmata?" said Fr. Sean.

Fr. Kessler nodded. "I have seen it with my own eyes."

"So, the people outside, they come to see her?" said Maya, angling around for a better look at the young girl.

"They come to see her and the statue that bleeds."

"How long's this been happening?" said Fr. Sean.

"It began Friday night during a storm," said Fr. Kessler. "I found her here on Saturday morning when I came to say Mass."

"The cave where they found the Cup also opened on Friday night," said Kenzie.

Fr. Kessler nodded. "It would seem that both Heaven and Hell were at work on that night."

"How do the people outside know of this if the phones do not work?" said Maya.

"I have asked several of them this very question," said Fr. Kessler, "and they said they dreamed of it."

"They all share the same dream?" said Maya.

Fr. Kessler nodded. "It would seem that God is calling to His people to share the Lady's message."

"What message is that?" said Kenzie.

"That humanity sits upon the precipice of its doom. And it is in many ways tied to this Cup which has now been found. But we should discuss these matters in the sacristy, so we do not disturb the girl."

Fr. Kessler led them into a back room that served as the church's sacristy, and for the next thirty minutes, recounted to them the history of the Calicem Noctis. The sinister relic known as the Cup of the Night.

While the Cup's origins were unknown, Fr. Kessler found numerous mentions of it throughout history during his research for his graduate thesis. The first records dated back to the year 1202, when the Knights Templar discovered it in the Holy Land during the fourth Crusades. It was found in the ruins of the mount where the Temple of Solomon once stood and brought by the Templars to the Vatican, where it was locked away in a sealed vault.

Three centuries later, it went missing during the early years of the Protestant Reformation, and was believed to have been stolen by a heretical order of monks. During that time, secret esoteric sects arose across Europe, and one of those was the Hermetic Order of Set. This highly secretive cult was believed to have been one of the earliest overtly Satanic cults, and witnesses claimed to have seen the Cup's use in dark ceremonies and rites performed by the order. One of those witnesses, the sixteenth century theologian Alger Helms, wrote of the mystical powers it seemed to convey on those in possession of it, and of the ghastly degradation and corruption that later befell those people.

The Cup demands sacrifice, Helms wrote, and many people — children, in particular — would go missing in areas where the Cup was purported to be kept.

There was no record of the Cup after the year 1602, although it was rumored to have been brought by members of the Order to a colony in America. That colony, Fr. Kessler believed, was the legendary city of Acheron. He knew the stories of Acheron's rapid descent into madness and depravity, and those stories were consistent with the Cup's corrosive influence in other areas where the Cup had been. But outside of the legends, he found little literature about Acheron.

"Acheron's real," said Kenzie, "and they had the Cup." She pulled up the photos on her phone of the pages from Tobias Hawkins' journal. "This was a journal kept by one of its inhabitants, Tobias Hawkins. His descendant, Calvin Hawkins, lives in our town. Maya works for him."

"Are we talking about the billionaire, Calvin Hawkins?" said Fr. Kessler.

Kenzie nodded. "It's the same guy."

"This is indeed troubling," said Fr. Kessler. "May I see those images?"

She handed him her phone, and for the next several minutes, they waited while he skimmed quickly through the images. Then he slowed as he reached the part on the covenant and began reading it in detail.

When he finished, he handed her back the phone. His face looked ashen. "Do you understand the significance of a covenant?" he said.

"Sort of," said Kenzie, turning a curious look to Fr. Sean.

"Why don't you explain it, father," said Fr. Sean.

Fr. Kessler nodded. "In a theological sense, a covenant is a sacred pact God makes with His people. The Bible describes five such covenants, one of those being with David, to whom God promised a Savior would arise from David's descendants. We, as Christians, see that promise fulfilled in Christ, and made new in

Christ's Blood on the Cross. Satan, in his undying war against God and creation, mimics and mocks that sacrifice in the Cup of the Night."

"What exactly is the Cup?" said Fr. Sean.

"It is a sacrilege, father. A blasphemy against the Holy Spirit. As we believe the chalice at Mass holds the Blood of Christ, the Cup of the Night holds the blood of Satan."

A hush fell over Kenzie and her friends. "I've seen it," Kenzie finally said, feeling her skin crawl at the memory of that black liquid oozing across the cave's floor. "It's black, like ink. Some of it got on this guy's foot and he burst into flames."

"This does not surprise me," said Fr. Kessler. "The Cup demands sacrifice. And many lives will be lost in consummating the covenant. But it is what comes after the covenant that chills my soul."

"What is that?" said Fr. Sean.

"The abomination of desolation, spoken of in the Bible. As God gave us His Son, Satan will anoint his own emissary with his powers, and the Lady has revealed to Anna Lucia that this man of perdition walks among us."

"You're talking about the Antichrist," said Fr. Sean.

"I am, father," said Fr. Kessler. "And I believe Calvin Hawkins may very well be that man."

"What makes you think that?" said Fr. Sean.

"His lineage, father, and ancestral ties to the covenant. It has always been Satan's pattern to mock God's plan for our salvation, so it reasons that if Christ came to us from the tree of David, then Satan's emissary will come from a tree whose roots are planted in the darkest bowels of Hell. That place is Acheron."

"And Calvin's a descendant of Acheron," said Kenzie.

Fr. Kessler nodded. "Precisely. I believe this covenant will be his anointing as an apostate of Hell, and the beginning of Satan's reign on Earth."

Kenzie took an uneasy breath. "How do we stop it?"

"I am afraid there is no way to destroy the Cup. Many have tried over the ages and met with ghastly fates. But I believe it can be quieted and contained as it once was upon the site of Solomon's Temple."

"So, we need to bring it back to the Temple Mount in the Holy Land?" said Fr. Sean.

"Yes, father. And there, it must be buried beneath the ruins from which it was long ago taken by the Templars. And it is imperative that it does not fall into Calvin Hawkins' hands. For if such were to happen, the Bible warns of unspeakable horrors to befall the world at the coming of the Antichrist. It is upon you to ensure that this does not happen."

Chapter Thirty
Best Laid Plans

The turboprop arrived at the airfield outside of Arkham shortly after nine that night. The flight home had been long and subdued, with Kenzie, Fr. Sean, and Maya overwhelmed by the gravity of the news Fr. Kessler gave them. Even Titus, who was normally talkative, was silenced by the weight of what lay ahead.

Kenzie volunteered to steal the chalice from the museum, which only made sense since she was the most adept of them at breaking into buildings and defeating alarm systems. Fr. Sean would arrange for them to stay with a group of missionaries once they reached the Holy Land, and Titus volunteered to fly them. He had no intention of ever returning to work for Calvin.

Kenzie wasted no time in getting started. After the short drive back to Capetown, she rode her bike over to Zac's, arriving just before ten. She was relieved to see the lights still on in his bedroom.

"I need your help with something, Zac," she said as he slid open his window.

"What is it?"

"Saving the world. And we're gonna need the guys' help on this."

"No way?" said Trey, as much in shock at Kenzie's news as he was in awe. "So Hawkins is the freaking Antichrist?"

"That's what this priest thinks," said Kenzie. "And he checks a lot of the boxes."

"So we're talking *The Omen* and all that stuff," said Brett.

"I guess," said Kenzie.

"Woah."

Kenzie, Zac, Trey, Dillon, and Brett sat in the basement of Brett's parents' house, the notorious 'bat cave,' as the boys called it. It was nearing midnight now, and for the past hour, Kenzie had filled them in on everything that happened over the past two days. Beginning with meeting Emma and Maya at Rose's, to reading the journal, which she downloaded from her phone to Brett's computer for them to read, and finally to her trip to Honduras, and Fr. Kessler's ominous warnings.

"I knew that guy was evil," said Dillon, "ever since we traced all of those grants from DARPA to Anubis."

"They're all evil," said Brett. "I'll bet you Stanzos is in on it too."

"Emma thinks they are," said Kenzie. "And I saw them at the cave that day."

"I can't believe you met Emma Kalchik and didn't invite us," Trey said from out of the blue.

Dillon nodded. "Yeah. I still have her Sports International swimsuit issue from freshman year."

"Me too," said Brett. "Is she as hot in person as she is in photos?"

Kenzie rolled her eyes. "Seriously? That's what you guys are thinking about?"

The boys exchanged looks with each other. It's what they were all thinking.

Kenzie groaned. If she lived to be a hundred, she would never understand teenage boys. "Yes. She's beautiful. Now focus. We need to get the Cup before Calvin does."

"So, what's the plan?" said Zac.

Kenzie took a breath. She had thought about this on the flight home, and breaking into the museum and getting past its security system was going to be a challenge. But there had to be a way, and if anyone could help her figure it out, it was these four misfits, assuming she could get their minds off girls long enough.

"Can you guys pull up the museum's blueprints," she said, "and also find out what security system they're using? Then we'll need to find the schematics for it."

"Gotcha," said Brett, as he and the others hopped from their chairs and headed for the array of computers. "We're on it."

It took the boys less than fifteen minutes to pull up the museum's blueprints from the county recorder's office, and while Kenzie studied them, the boys went to work identifying the security system from permits filed at the time of installation.

Once they had that, they could pull up schematics and general descriptions of the system from the US Patent and Trademark Office's website. It all took less than an hour, and when they finished, they printed out the documents and spread them across the floor.

"It looks like everything feeds into this control box in the basement," Zac said, tracing his finger along the blueprints. "The problem is, the only way to shut off the alarm without triggering a fail-safe is by entering the security code on this numeric box inside the front entrance. It's programmed to go off if the code isn't entered within forty-five seconds after the front door opens."

"Can we bypass it through the control box?" said Kenzie.

"I was just getting to that," said Zac. "And I'll now turn the floor over to Trey."

Trey cleared his throat. "It looks like we might be able to trick the system into thinking the code was entered by using an array of stents to bypass the circuitry." He looked over to a nearby desk, where Dillon was soldering wires together into what looked like a giant spider. "How are we coming on that, Dillon?"

"Almost done," Dillon said.

"So, we need to figure out how to get into the basement and to the control box without triggering the alarm," said Kenzie.

"I think we've got that figured out too," said Zac, moving on to another sheet of paper. "This shows the locations where the censors are installed, and it looks like there's a basement window right here that doesn't have one."

"So, we could break it and get inside that way," said Kenzie.

"We're not sure how big it is from the blueprints," said Brett, "but it should work."

"There also aren't any sensors along the wall surrounding the backyard," said Zac, "so we can access the yard that way."

"What about motion sensors?" said Kenzie.

"There's a ton of them," said Trey, "but they're all upstairs around the exhibits. There's also infra-red heat censors. But everything feeds to that control box, so once we get the stent inserted, they'll all shut off."

"We hope," said Dillon, walking over and setting the stent array on the floor in front of them. It was about the size of a hand, consisting of three crisscrossed wires taped together at the center, with small alligator clips soldered to the ends of each wire.

"It looks like that thing from Alien," said Kenzie, staring at the spider-like array.

Dillon grinned. "I know, right?"

"So how does this work?" said Kenzie.

Dillon slid over a diagram of the inside of the control box. The box was about two feet tall, by one foot wide, and six inches deep, with an array of wires and circuitry inside it. A series of conduits fed into it from both sides.

"This thing here in the center is the processor," Dillon said, pointing to the schematic. "What you need to do is clip one end of each wire to the connector on one side, and the other end of the wire to the connector on the other side. But you need to do them both simultaneously, or else it'll trigger the fail-safe. You do that for all three wires."

"How will we know if it worked?" said Kenzie.

"The alarm won't go off when you open the door at the top of the basement stairs," said Dillon.

Kenzie's frown let him know she didn't find the joke funny.

"There's a light on the numeric pad near the front door," he quickly added. "It'll turn from red to green when the alarm's disabled. I should be able to see it from this window." He pointed to a side window near the front on the blueprints.

"And if it doesn't turn green?" she said.

"We run like hell, 'cause we just tripped the fail-safe on the alarm."

Chapter Thirty-One
Thieves in the Night

A damp mist shrouded the sleeping town in its cold blanket. Kenzie and the boys pedaled their bikes down the dark, deserted streets until they reached the alley wall behind the museum's backyard. They hid their bikes behind a dumpster, then scrambled up and over the six-foot high wall.

They came down in the museum's backyard. Keeping close to the wall, they listened for any signs that they were spotted. A dog barking, or person yelling. But all they heard were the sounds of night, and the chill breath of wind through the trees.

Across the yard, thirty feet ahead of them, stood the museum's dark gray form, towering ghost-like in the mist. Kenzie's skin prickled at the sight of it looming so ominously against the night sky. A look at her friends' faces let her know they shared the same dread. All the bravado and thrill from the ride over was gone, and they were left with the harsh reality of what they came there to do. To break into that place and steal a chalice which was said to contain the blood of Satan.

"Anyone else feel like it's watching us?" said Trey in a hushed whisper. The others all nodded.

"You guys still with me on this?" said Kenzie. She wouldn't have blamed them if they weren't.

"We're in," said Zac, and the others slowly nodded in agreement.

"Yeah. We're cool," said Brett. He slid off his backpack and pulled out four walkie talkies. He handed one to Dillon, who would keep watch on the museum's left side. A window towards the front would let him keep an eye on the alarm's control panel and let them know when the indicator light turned from red to green.

Brett handed the next walkie talkie to Zac, who slid it into his backpack along with the spider-like array to disable the alarm. He would go inside with Kenzie.

Brett handed the third walkie talkie to Trey, who would keep watch on the museum's right side, and Brett kept the fourth one for himself. He would keep watch from the backyard.

Kenzie took a deep breath and looked at the others. "Let's do this."

Kenzie and Zac sprinted off across the yard to the museum's back wall, where they hoped to find the basement window, while Dillon and Trey rushed around to the museum's sides. Brett remained by the wall, watching as the others disappeared into the mist.

Kenzie found the basement window concealed behind a hedge. It was about three feet wide, eighteen inches tall, and built into the wall four inches above the ground. A single padlock secured it shut.

Using her lock pick, it took Kenzie only a few minutes to open the lock, then she and Zac squeezed through the window and into the basement. The room smelled of mildew and dust, with dusty old boxes and worn furniture piled along the walls. Brushing aside several loose-hanging cobwebs, they walked over to the control panel mounted to the far wall. Kenzie turned on her cell phone's flashlight and held it while Zac removed the front panel from the control box. To their relief, the inside matched the diagram Dillon downloaded from the patent office.

Zac slid off his backpack and removed the walkie talkie and spider-like array. He handed Kenzie the walkie talkie, while he placed the array over the control panel's central processor. Thankfully, its wire legs were long enough to reach the connectors on either side of the processor.

"Tell Dillon we're in," Zac said. "Ask him if he's able to see the alarm panel."

Kenzie keyed the walkie talkie's 'talk' button. "We're in. Can you see the alarm panel?"

"I've got eyes on it right now," came Dillon's voice. "The light's red."

"Copy that," Kenzie said, with the walkie talkie's speaker loud enough for Zac to hear it too.

Taking one of the alligator clips on opposite sides of the array in each hand, Zac carefully clipped them onto the connectors on opposite sides of the control panel's central processor. When they were in place, he let out a deep breath and gave Kenzie a nod.

"He's got the first two connectors clipped," Kenzie said into the walkie talkie. "Is the alarm panel still behaving itself?"

"So far, so good," came Dillon's voice.

Zac moved onto the next two wires, and when he had them clipped, he looked again at Kenzie.

"He's got the next two in place," said Kenzie. "We still good?"

"Yeah."

Zac then moved onto the final two wires, and when he had them clipped in place, he took a step back and looked again at Kenzie. Before she could key the mic, Dillon's voice came across the speaker.

"It just turned green."

"So, the alarm's disabled?" Kenzie said into the walkie talkie.

"It should be. But be ready to run, just in case."

"We are," she said.

Zac slipped his backpack on, then he and Kenzie crept up the staircase to a door at the top. She shined her cell phone's flashlight across the door's top edge, where the light fell across two alarm censors butted against each other.

"Hold this," she said, handing Zac her cell phone. He shined its light on the doorknob while Kenzie inserted her lock pick's rake and tension rod into the keyhole. She worked it in and out several times until she felt the clicks of the tumblers falling into place.

"It's open," she said as he handed her back her cell phone. "Cross your fingers that spider thing worked."

"They're crossed."

She turned the knob and slowly pushed open the door. To their relief, no alarm went off. She let out her breath.

"Tell Dillon it worked," she said.

Zac keyed the walkie talkie. "We're in the basement door. Kenzie said she won't have to beat you up."

"Tell her to get me Emma's autograph on my swimsuit issue," Dillon's voice came back, loud enough over the speaker for Kenzie to also hear it.

"Tell her to get mine signed too," Brett's voice cut in.

Kenzie rolled her eyes. "Tell them they both need help."

Zac keyed the walkie talkie again. "Kenzie said you're both degenerates and need to keep away from small animals."

"Roger that."

Kenzie just shook her head in dismay. She looked through the open door into the dark room beyond it, and sweeping her flashlight around, saw that it was used as another storage area cluttered in boxes and antiques.

"See any bad things?" Zac said.

"Not yet."

They slowly eased into the room, sweeping their flashlights ahead of them, before coming to an abrupt stop several steps inside. All humor from a moment ago fled them. The room was so cold, they could see their breaths, but something else was there as well. Something that hung in the air around them like a dark pall. It reminded Kenzie of the feeling she had in the hallway outside Calvin's bedroom. The feeling of unseen eyes watching them. And beckoning them to come further inside. She looked at Zac, whose eyes were wide in fear as he scanned the room. He felt it too.

"What is that?" he whispered.

"This place. It knows we're here."

"Oh, crap."

"You don't have to do this, Zac. I can take it from here."

"And have your ghost haunt me?" He shook his head. "Nope. But it's your turn to be dinner."

Despite the horror surrounding them, Kenzie couldn't suppress a slight smile. Zac was risking his life for her, and her heart warmed at the gesture.

"We forgot to bring Dillon in here with us," she said, continuing with their joke from the night they went to the cave.

He nodded. "Next time."

A small lump settled in her throat. She reached over and gave his hand a squeeze. "Thanks, Zac."

Taking a moment to gather their nerves, they eased across the dark room to a door on the far side. The door opened into the museum's broad foyer, where moonlight from the windows on the far wall glistened coldly from the marble floor and glass display cases. A thin mist seeped in from beneath the outside door, trailing across the floor in a thin veil. Neither of them felt the need to mention that they had never seen a mist do that before. It was enough to see the fear in each other's eyes.

"We need to do this fast," whispered Kenzie, to which Zac nodded.

"Yeah."

Far to their left was the opening to a hallway which led deep inside the mansion to where more exhibits were housed, and to their right was a staircase which swept up to the second floor. Beyond the staircase, on the far right side of the foyer, was the dark opening to the room where the cave's exhibit was housed.

They crept quickly across the foyer to the opening to the cave's exhibit, and once inside the room, Kenzie felt her stomach tense.

The glass display case which had housed the Cup was empty.

"Shit. Oh, shit," she cursed, hurrying over to the empty case. She swept her flashlight across the floor and around the room.

"That's where the Cup was?" Zac said, nodding to the empty display case.

"Yeah. I need to call Emma and let her know."

"You think Calvin has it?"

"Him, or those guys from Stanzos. But they would need a place to hide it, and that's at Calvin's."

She quickly dialed Emma's number, then waited several rings before Emma picked up.

"Kenzie?" came Emma's voice from the other end, sounding surprisingly awake and alert.

"Yeah. It's me. Did you talk to Maya?"

"She's here with me right now. What's wrong?"

"The Cup's gone. I'm at the museum right now, and it's not here."

There was a moment's pause before Emma spoke again. "Calvin took it, didn't he?"

"I think so," said Kenzie. "Do you know where he would put it?"

Another pause as Emma thought about it. "Maybe," she said. "He has a safe in his study, but I'll need to get the key."

"Do you know where it is?"

"He hides it in his dresser."

Kenzie swallowed. "Be careful, Emma. Did Maya tell you who that priest we met thinks Calvin is?"

"She did. We're both packing to leave tonight while he's asleep. I'll call you as soon as I find anything."

"Call me either way."

"I will. And you do the same."

"Okay."

Kenzie hung up and joined Zac, who was keeping watch near the room's entrance.

"Any luck?" he asked.

"She's gonna check his safe. Cross your fingers."

"Are we almost to the part where this gets easy?"

"Not until after the commercial break."

"Oh, yeah."

Kenzie peeked around the corner into the large, moonlit foyer, where the mist was now up to their knees.

"Kenzie," Zac whispered, tapping her on the shoulder.

She turned and found him shining his flashlight at the floor. Barely visible through the mist were dark blood smears trailing across the floor to a closed door near the staircase.

"They go in there," said Zac, nodding to the closed door. "Should we check?"

They exchanged an uneasy look with each. "I think we should," she finally said. "But be ready to run."

"I am."

They eased over to the door, and Kenzie gripped the knob. She slowly opened the door and shined her light inside. The room was a small maintenance closet with shelves of cleaning supplies, brooms, mops, and buckets. She angled her light down on the floor, then gasped, recoiling several steps back.

Two bodies lay there, drenched in blood. They wore the shirts Kenzie had seen before on the museum's staff, with the name 'Ruben' embroidered on one, and 'Stewart' on the other.

Kenzie swallowed and took a nervous step back. "We need to call the sheriff."

Zac stepped past her and into the closet. He knelt beside the bodies and felt each of their necks for a pulse. He looked back at Kenzie and shook his head.

"He'll need to bring the coroner too," Zac said, rising to his feet.

Kenzie joined him near the bodies and swept her light around the rest of the room. It shined across two knives on the floor near the bodies, both caked in blood, with long bloody smears trailing across the floor to the wall on her left. She followed the trails up the wall, then stopped halfway to the ceiling.

The Latin phrase 'In Aeternum Regnabit' — the last words Daryl uttered — was written in blood. Above the words, also drawn in blood, was the eight-pointed star with the eye in the center.

"Is that Latin?" said Zac, staring at the words.

Kenzie nodded. "Yeah. It means, forever he shall reign. It's what Daryl said in the cave before he caught on fire. We need to get out of here."

They backed into the foyer and turned to run, when Kenzie came to a sudden stop. Silhouetted against the moonlit windows were twelve dark ghostly shapes, drifting towards them through the knee-high mist. They were the same shadow-like wraiths Kenzie saw in the cave on the night Daryl died.

The specters of the long dead priests of Acheron.

"What?" Zac said, seeing the terrified look in Kenzie's eyes. "What is it?"

"There's twelve ghosts in here with us," she whispered, her eyes quickly searching for a way past the half-circle the specters formed around them.

"Where?"

"Twelve feet away."

Looking to her left, she saw only one way out. The stairs.

"Get up the stairs!"

Kenzie sprang for the staircase, with Zac close behind, and quickly bounded up them to the second-floor hallway. At the far end was an open door, through which firelight crackled from inside the room. Having once been used by Ethan and Elinor Crawford as their family's mansion, the museum had seven fireplaces in various rooms, including the room where the cave's exhibit was housed.

Kenzie and Zac raced down the hallway and ducked inside the room. Zac slammed the door shut and locked it, then backed over to where Kenzie stood.

"That's not gonna keep them out, is it?" he said.

She shook her head. "No. Maybe we can get out the window."

They turned to face the room, where moonlight streamed in through a large window on the far wall. The room was once used as a study used by Ethan Crawford, then after its dedication to the town, was converted to an office now used by Madelyn and prior curators. A fire crackled in the fireplace on the wall to their left, and on their right were shelves lined with books, statues, and artifacts. A heavy oak desk sat near the window across the room, and as they looked closer at it, both Kenzie and Zac felt their blood turn to ice.

A figure sat behind the desk in silhouette against the window, but Kenzie could tell from the figure's wide girth that it was Madelyn. And she wasn't moving.

"Madelyn?" Kenzie said unsteadily as she slowly approached the figure.

"Wait," said Zac, taking her arm. He shined his flashlight on the figure's face, and Kenzie let out a shriek.

Madelyn's face and body were burned beyond recognition, but her clothes and the desk remained untouched. It was exactly like what happened to Daryl that night in the cave.

"Oh, shit. Oh, shit," Kenzie gasped, holding her hands to her face.

"Let's try the window," Zac said, taking her gently by the hand. They hurried over to the window, doing their best to avoid looking at the corpse seated at the nearby desk.

They looked out the window. It faced the museum's front yard, with at least a twenty foot drop to the grass below.

"We can do this," Zac said, turning to look around the room for something heavy to break it with. On one shelf was a bronze statue of a man, presumably one of the town's founding fathers, and at two feet tall, it looked heavy enough to do it. He hurried over to grab it while Kenzie remained at the window, studying the grass below for an area that looked the softest to land in.

Neither of them saw the tall, dark figure of a man as it stepped out from the shadows near the door and stalked across the room toward Kenzie.

Zac hoisted the statue from the shelf, finding it weighed a good twenty pounds, and turned back to Kenzie in time to see the figure nearing her. In the crackling firelight as the figure walked past, there was no mistaking the severely charred skin.

"Kenzie, look out!" Zac shouted.

She spun just in time to dodge a swipe of Daryl's charred hand as he grabbed at her. She scrambled several feet to her right and found herself cornered behind Madelyn's desk.

Zac charged at the figure from behind, raising the statue above his head and swinging it down hard on the back of the corpse's head.

The corpse spun surprisingly fast, knocking the statue from Zac's hands before he could take another swing. It crashed to the floor, and the corpse stepped past it, all attention focused now on Zac.

Kenzie raced out from behind the desk. With the corpse's back to her, she lifted the statue from the floor and bashed it into the creature's back, sending it stumbling past Zac and into the wall.

"Here. Let me have it," Zac said.

Kenzie handed him the statue, and before the corpse could recover, Zac swung the statue hard at the creature's skull. The corpse stumbled forward into the wall, and Zac quickly nailed it again with the statue. The heavy bronze met bone with a sickening crunch and the creature dropped to the floor. But Zac was taking no chances. He swung the statue down three more times at the corpse's skull until it pulverized into a jigsaw puzzle of shattered bones. And the body lay still.

Chapter Thirty-Two
The Thing in the Window

Flashing red and blue lights colored the night. Rick's squad car sat alongside the curb in front of the museum, with two large white vans parked behind it, and a third van from the forensics team Rick brought in from Arkham.

Kenzie, Zac, Trey, Brett, and Dillon stood alongside the sheriff's car, where for the past half hour, Rick and Drew had pulled each of them aside and grilled them over the night's events. The kids' stories matched, but that did nothing to reduce the potential charges they faced for trespassing, vandalism, and breaking and entering.

When it was Kenzie's turn to be interrogated, she left nothing out, including the twelve spectres she saw coming towards her and Zac in the foyer. Rick looked predictably irritated and skeptical over her story, but Drew seemed more receptive to it. Maybe her discussion with him in the diner sank in. Kenzie saw him look away several times during the interrogation and over to Madelyn's upstairs window, as if expecting to see Daryl's corpse staring down at them.

The corpse itself was something that neither Rick nor Drew could explain away, and its presence upstairs, along with the blow marks to its skull, lent credence to Kenzie's story, which Rick begrudgingly acknowledged.

When they arrived on scene, both Rick and Drew had conducted a thorough sweep of the entire museum before turning it over to the forensics team and coroners. That was nearly an hour ago, and since then, occasional updates had crackled across the radios hung from Rick's and Drew's belts.

Zac, Trey, Brett, and Dillon fidgeted nervously as they waited to find out whether Rick would book them in jail that night or let them go home. Kenzie was the only one who didn't seem anxious, mainly because she had faced jail too many times to let it worry her anymore. She also doubted that Rick would want to lock up a bunch of kids. Sure, they had trespassed, but that was the least of his concerns that night.

What did worry Kenzie, was a quiet, subtle intuition that something bad was about to happen.

It was nearing four in the morning when Kenzie felt the first stir that something was wrong. She looked at the upstairs window to Madelyn's office and was hit by a sudden premonition of horror. Something was happening in that room. Something unnatural and macabre. A moment later, she nearly jumped as Rick's radio crackled to life with a frantic call from the teams inside.

"Rick, Drew. We need you in here now," the voice pleaded urgently, before the sound from the radio turned to a dull static hiss.

Rick keyed the mic on his shoulder pocket. "Dan. Repeat the last message. You broke up." When he released the mic button, only static came from the radio.

Kenzie looked back at the upstairs window and froze, feeling the hairs stir on her neck. Something stood there looking down at them, something in the dark, featureless shape of a man. And then it was gone.

Kenzie looked at the two officers, who were exchanging curious looks with each other over the radio call. They hadn't seen what she saw in the window.

"Go check on them," Rick instructed Drew. "Radio back what's going on."

"You should have your gun ready," Kenzie said.

The officers gave her a questioning look, but the fear they saw in her eyes was enough to convince them to play it safe.

"Go ahead," Rick said.

Drew slid the pistol from his holster and hurried off into the museum. As she watched him go, a worried knot settled in Kenzie's stomach. She looked back at the window, hoping to see the flashlights from the teams she saw earlier, but she only saw darkness and the crackling red glow from the fireplace. It was all disquietingly still.

Rick tried once more to reach the teams inside on his radio, but again it returned only static. He turned to Kenzie.

"You're sure you didn't see anyone else in there?"

She shook her head. "Just the stuff I told you about."

Two rapid gunshots echoed from inside the museum. Rick and Kenzie spun around to look up at Madelyn's window, just as the flash of a third gunshot sparked inside the room. Rick snatched up his mic.

"Drew, report," Rick yelled into the radio. "What's going on?"

A fourth gunshot echoed from the upstairs room, and then only silence.

Kenzie stared in horror at the window, and the deafening silence coming from the room. She spun to Rick. "You need to get him out of there."

Ignoring Kenzie, Rick keyed his mic again. "Drew, report."

Kenzie lunged at Rick, and before he could react, she grabbed his mic and keyed it. "Drew! Get out of there!"

Rick shoved her away, causing her to stumble back several steps.

"They're gonna kill him!" she screamed.

"Who?"

"Daryl and those things!"

With a sudden explosion of glass and debris, Madelyn's window shattered outward as something large and heavy crashed through it. It bounced once from the eave and tumbled down onto the grass. It was Drew's body.

Rick and Kenzie rushed over and found him alive, but barely. Rick keyed his mic and screamed into it.

"Maggie, I need an ambulance at the museum now. I have an officer down."

"You're gonna need several," Kenzie said, removing her jacket and draping it across Drew.

"Send every ambulance you have over here," Rick screamed again into the mic. "We have multiple casualties."

Rick clicked off the mic and chambered a round in his pistol.

"Stay here," he said to Kenzie, then raced for the museum entrance.

"Wait," Kenzie said, catching up to him at the door. "Let me go with you."

"Not a chance. You're waiting out here for the ambulance."

"If you go in there alone, you're gonna die."

Rick stopped and did a double-take. "What're you talking about?"

"You don't know what's in there, but I do. And I can see them, but you can't."

"See what?"

"The things you always say I make up."

He frowned and eyed her for a moment, but in his eyes, she saw the hard wall of skepticism breaking down.

"You're staying right behind me the entire time," he said, and she nodded.

"Okay."

Rick led the way as they crossed the foyer toward the staircase, then slowed as they neared it. To their left, his flashlight swept across the charred, broken bodies of the men from the coroner's office.

"What on earth...?" Rick muttered, sweeping the rest of the area with his flashlight.

"You know what on earth," Kenzie said. "It was Daryl."

"How could it be Daryl?"

"Just stop it. You know I'm right." Even Kenzie was surprised by the anger and assertiveness in her tone, but she'd had enough of his nonsense.

Although he didn't say it, she could see in his eyes that he knew she was right. They bounded up the stairs, taking them two at a time, then hurried down the hallway to Madelyn's office, where firelight flickered through the open door.

"Wait," Kenzie said, grabbing his sleeve as they reached the door. "Let me check first."

She stepped around him and peered in through the doorway. The charred, broken bodies of the forensics team lay on the floor near the crackling fireplace, and Madelyn's corpse remained propped up at her desk. But there was no sign of Daryl's corpse, or the twelve dark specters of the Acheron priests.

"It's clear," she said, stepping aside for him to enter the room past her.

Rick swept into the room, clearing every corner until he finally reached the shattered window on the far wall.

"Do you see anything?" he said, taking a final look around the room as Kenzie joined him.

"It's just us."

"So how in the hell did a corpse just get up and walk off?"

"Are you ready to believe me if I tell you?"

"Is it about Acheron?" he said, but this time she sensed a desperate resignation in his tone. He sounded ready to believe just about anything.

"That's part of it. But there's a lot more going on, too."

"And you know what that is?"

"Most of it."

"Let's you and I talk about all of this tomorrow."

"All of it?"

He nodded. "All of it." He keyed his radio. "Maggie, I need you to issue a statewide APB on the suspect in a multiple homicide. His name is Daryl Corbet, and I need you to listen to me and write exactly what I say. The suspect is covered entirely in fourth, maybe fifth degree burns, and has a fractured skull. He is extremely dangerous. Do not try to apprehend him. If anyone sees him, shoot him on sight." Rick keyed off the mic and took a deep breath. He exchanged a brief, worried look with Kenzie, then keyed his mic again. "And even when he looks dead, tell them to keep shooting."

Chapter Thirty-Three
Wolves in the Night

Emma shoved the last of her belongings in her bag and took a quick look at her watch. It was shortly after four in the morning, over an hour since Kenzie called her from the museum, and Emma hadn't heard from her since.

"The sun will be up soon if we do not hurry," said Maya, hovering over her own bag near the door to the guest room where Emma had slept the past few nights. "Do you wish that I should get the key while you finish?"

Emma shook her head and nervously squeezed her hands into fists to keep them from shaking. "No. I'm ready. We'll do it together."

Emma had a pretty good idea where Calvin might have hidden the chalice, assuming he had anything to do with its theft. And that was a pretty safe assumption. Several months earlier, Maya found a safe hidden in the wall behind a painting in Calvin's private study. She also found a key to the safe, which Calvin kept hidden beneath his clothes in the bottom drawer of his dresser. Maya had told Emma about the safe and key, thinking that one day Emma might need whatever cash was in the safe to make a hasty escape from Calvin's increasingly volatile outbursts. Emma assured her at the time that she wouldn't, that Calvin's mood would return to normal as soon as the animal trials on his company's projects finished and they received FDA clearance to begin human trials. That was months ago, and since then, the human trials had begun; but Calvin's mood remained as volatile as ever.

Emma called her parents earlier that day while Maya and the others were in Honduras. It was the first time she talked to them since moving to America with Calvin, and she wasn't sure what to expect. To her surprise and relief, she found none of the judgment she had feared. Their excitement at hearing her voice warmed Emma's heart in ways she hadn't felt in years, and she cried for most of the call. She wanted to go home, and they let her know she was welcome to whenever she was ready.

Emma was more than ready, and she realized she had been for a long time now. There was no love in Calvin anymore. He had grown cold and distant, consumed with passion for this new technology he was pioneering. It was called transhumanism, and he saw it as the perfection of the human species; a way to transcend biological limitations and elevate mankind to undreamed realms of consciousness and existence. But Emma saw it as the creation of something soulless and godless.

Any hesitation Emma had over leaving evaporated the moment Maya returned from Honduras and told her what the priest said. Emma knew right then that she had to get out of there that night, and she was bringing Maya with her. Their plan was to get to Arkham's international airport, where they would pay cash for plane tickets to Hungary to avoid being tracked. She had saved enough money from the small spending allowance Calvin gave her to buy plane tickets for herself and Maya, and would have enough left over to help Maya through the immigration process once they arrived. Titus would drive them to the airport, which was about thirty miles away on the mainland, then drive back to pick up Kenzie and Fr. Sean for their flight to the Holy Land. Emma and Maya wouldn't be needed for that trip, so their final goodbyes with Titus would be at the airport when he dropped them off.

All of this changed when Kenzie called with the news that the chalice had been stolen from the museum. Emma still saw a way to salvage the night, but it now required her and Maya to first retrieve the key from Calvin's bedroom without waking him, and then for the chalice to actually be in the safe. If it wasn't there, Emma had no idea where to even begin looking. It could literally be anywhere on the massive property, or not there at all.

"We should do this now before he awakes," said Maya.

Emma took a deep breath to calm her nerves and nodded.

The two women stole quietly up the stairs to the second floor. As they stepped from the stairs into the hallway, the air felt suddenly cold and heavy, alive with a watchful presence that surrounded them like a vapor. Knowingly or unknowingly, it was a horror that Calvin had invited into the house, and it portended of the horrors to come on a global scale if Calvin consummated the covenant.

This thought strengthened the women's resolve to make sure that didn't happen. They stole quietly down the hallway to Calvin's bedroom door, ever aware of being watched from the darkness. Emma tested the knob and was relieved to find it unlocked. She slowly pressed the door open and looked in.

Moonlight from long windows bathed the room in a ghostly pall. Looking across the room, she saw Calvin sleeping soundly in his bed, with the dresser, where Maya had seen the key, less than ten feet from the bed.

Making no more sound than mice, the women quietly padded across the room to the dresser, trying their best to ignore the dark presence that encircled them.

It was in here with them, something cold, malignant, and ancient. An inaudible hiss in their minds of unimaginable horrors, and a putrid rot that stung their skin. It defiled them in ways that could never be cleaned, and forced Emma to choke back the bile building in her throat.

Maya knelt and quietly slid open the bottom drawer of the dresser. Pushing aside the clothes, she checked the bottom of the drawer where she last saw the key. It was gone. She looked at Emma, and without saying a word, Emma could see from the worried look in Maya's eyes that this was bad.

"It's not there?" Emma whispered as quietly as she could.

Maya nodded.

Emma thought for a moment. If Calvin had locked the chalice in the safe that day, the key might still be in his pocket. She looked over at a chair near his bed, where his slacks were folded neatly across the arm. She turned back to Maya and pointed to the slacks. Maya nodded her understanding, and together they eased over to the chair.

Emma lifted the slacks and reached into the front pocket. With a noisy jangle, the keys slid from the pocket and fell to the carpet. Emma froze, her heart nearly skipping a beat. From Calvin's bed came a muted groan as he sluggishly rolled over onto his side, dragging part of his blanket with him.

Emma and Maya watched him in complete silence. If Calvin awoke now, they had no way of explaining their being in his bedroom. But as the seconds passed with no further movement or sounds from him, Emma was confident that he hadn't awakened. She quietly picked up the keys and hurried from the room with Maya.

Calvin's study was on the ground floor, in a room facing the mansion's backyard. A large window in the dark mahogany paneled wall overlooked the mist-shrouded yard, allowing thin trails of moonlight to paint the room in deep shadows.

Emma and Maya hurried in and over to the wall on their right. Across it hung large paintings of generations of the Hawkins family, some dating as far back as colonial days.

Maya stopped at one painting and peeked behind it at the narrow gap between the painting and the wall.

"This is the one," Maya whispered, and together the women lifted the painting from its mount and set it on the floor.

Built into the wall behind where the painting had hung was a safe, its front flush with the wall. The safe was roughly two feet tall and eighteen inches wide, with a combination dial on its door and a keyhole in its handle.

Emma inserted the key into the keyhole and twisted it, feeling the lock open with a satisfying click. She turned the handle and pulled open the door. Something dull and metallic stood in the back of the safe, and leaning in closer, Emma saw it was the chalice. Her breath caught momentarily in her throat, as if staring up close at a snake.

"Is it there?" Maya whispered, trying to see past her into the dark opening.

Emma gave a slow nod. "It's there."

"Take it, and we can get Titus and leave."

Emma took a breath and slowly reached her hand into the safe, fearing to even touch the cursed relic. As she slowly closed her fingers around its long stem, Calvin's gruff voice came suddenly from across the room.

"You should have left it alone, Emma," he said in a flat, emotionless tone, which carried a note of resignation over what he must do next.

The women spun and saw him standing in the doorway, a dark outline against the hallway, and yet his eyes somehow reflected the moonlight.

"You don't need to do this, Calvin," Emma pleaded, hoping she might reason with him.

"Do what?" he said, stalking across the room toward them like a panther cornering its prey. "Did you read something you shouldn't have?"

Emma and Maya took several terrified steps back, circling around behind the heavy mahogany desk. Calvin ignored them and walked over to the safe. He locked it, then slid the key into his pocket and turned to the women.

"We know about the covenant," Emma said. "It's not too late to stop it."

"Is that what the old priest told you?" he said, taking a menacing step toward the desk they stood behind. "That you could bury the chalice, and this would all be over? What else did he tell you, Maya?"

"That you're the devil," Maya spat, her fiery Latina blood tending to the surface at the most inopportune times.

Calvin's face broke into a sly grin that could have been that of a wolf staring at a lamb. The room grew suddenly cold, and the women became aware of a new presence in the room with them. Something infinitely more terrifying than the murderer who stood in front of them. In the moonlit shadows of a far corner, there now stood the faint, ghostly figure of a woman in a long red dress.

"You know nothing of the devil," Calvin growled in response to Maya's assertion. With one hand, he grabbed the side of the heavy desk and flung it aside like it was cardboard.

Before he could make another move, Maya grabbed Emma by the hand and sprang across the room toward the open door. As they neared it, it suddenly slammed shut, and a powerful, unseen force hurled them back across the room. They came down hard on the floor near the desk, and looking up, saw Calvin stalking towards them. Objects around the room began to rattle and shake. Books fell from shelves and furniture toppled over.

Calvin dropped on top of Emma and grabbed her throat in an iron grip. His eyes reflected furiously in the moonlight, and in their depths, Emma saw nothing but blind rage. She kicked and squirmed and clawed at his hands, but it did nothing to loosen his grip as he slowly squeezed the life from her.

While this happened, Maya had scrambled to her feet and rushed over to the bookcase. She grabbed a heavy trophy from the shelf and raced at Calvin from behind, raising the statue to swing it at his head. Just as she neared him, he looked back over his shoulder at her, his face a mask of fury. Suddenly, as if propelled by a cannon, Maya flew across the room and slammed into the bookcase, sliding down it to the floor where she lay stunned.

Calvin turned back to Emma, a sadistic glee filling his eyes as he squeezed her throat tighter. But he wouldn't allow her to die quickly. He would take his time, prolonging her agony by allowing her to take short, gasping breaths before squeezing again.

With a sudden crash, the room's door kicked open, followed a second later by the loud crack of two gunshots. Calvin felt the two rounds strike his back like hot spikes, and momentarily stunned, he looked down at his chest. Two dark red stains were spreading across his shirt where the bullets exited through his chest. His grip loosened on Emma's throat as he sat up and swayed for a moment before toppling sideways onto the floor.

All at once, an ear-splitting wail of rage filled the room. With a violent jolt, the room rumbled and shook like an earthquake. Objects flew from shelves and across the room. Paintings and fixtures fell from walls, furniture splintered, and with a roaring crash, the large window shattered inward, spraying the room in jagged glass shards and splintered wood.

Emma struggled out from beneath Calvin's slumped body and panted heavily for breath. She looked across the room and saw Titus fumbling for balance as he hurried across the swaying room toward her, his pistol still aimed at Calvin's slumped body. When he saw the body wasn't moving, he slid the pistol into his waistband and helped Emma to her feet, steadying her as she took in deep breaths.

Maya staggered to her feet and stumbled over to them, feeling a brief wave of nausea as the room swayed like a boat in a storm.

"Are you two okay?" Titus asked, his eyes going from Emma to Maya and then back to Emma.

Both women gave panting nods.

"Let's get out of here," he said, having to yell to be heard above the ruckus.

"We need to get the chalice," shouted Maya. She knelt down and fished through Calvin's pockets for the keys, when suddenly two loud barks came from the doorway. They all looked over and saw Calvin's two massive black pit bulls standing in the doorway.

Titus slowly drew the pistol from his waistband, taking care not to spook the dogs. "Don't make any sudden moves," he whispered, aiming his gun at the first dog as it stalked into the room on heavily muscled legs, its eyes blazing in the moonlight. It veered around to their right, while the second dog stalked in and veered around to their left.

"Get out the window," Titus said evenly, sweeping his pistol back and forth between the two dogs. He didn't know if he had enough rounds left to take them both down. "But do it slowly."

"What about the chalice?" said Maya, slowly rising to her feet.

"Just leave it," Titus said. "These dogs aren't gonna let us take it."

Maya and Emma sensed he was right. They slowly eased over to the window and climbed through, dropping into the backyard.

When Titus saw they were gone, he slowly retreated backwards towards the window, keeping his pistol trained on the dogs the entire time. He could probably take one of them out if he emptied his entire magazine into its head, but the other one would drag him down a second later.

Reaching the window, he eased his legs up and over the sill and looked down at the yard seven feet below, where the women were waiting. He then glanced back in the room and what he saw caused his heart to nearly stop.

The dogs were gone, and Calvin now stood in the moonlight glaring at Titus, his eyes reflecting a cold malignancy. Other than the two blood spots on his shirt, Calvin showed no signs of being shot.

Titus leaped down from the window onto the lawn, landing in a crouch near the women in the thin mist.

"Calvin's alive," he panted, rising to his feet.

"How?" said Emma.

Titus shook his head. "I don't know. But we need to get out of here."

He and the women took off in a sprint across the yard toward the stairs on the far side. From behind them came sudden loud barks as the dogs piled out of the house and bounded across the lawn toward them.

"Go! Keep running!" Titus shouted to the women, slowing down as he spun around and aimed his pistol at the dog closest to his left. He had time to fire two shots before the dogs leaped and tackled him to the ground.

"Titus!" Emma screamed and started to race back to him, but Maya quickly grabbed her arm.

"No. You can't help him," Maya said, as one more gunshot echoed in the night, followed by Titus's cries and the dogs' ferocious snarls and growls.

Emma's heart sank, but she knew Maya was right. They bounded down the stairs to the shore, then took off running until they needed to slow down to catch their breaths. They looked back down the shore behind them, veiled thinly in mist, then up at the top of the cliff, and fear gripped them at what they saw.

Calvin watched them from the top of the cliff like a gargoyle, and beside him stood the ghostly figure of the woman in the red dress. Neither of them made any movement towards the stairs to chase after the women, but that came as little relief. It probably meant that something even more terrifying awaited them on the shore. But they had no choice but to continue on.

"Come. We need to hurry," said Maya, and taking Emma's hand, they raced off down the shore.

Maya and Emma had run for over ten minutes, their feet aching from the slick stones, when they finally slowed to catch their breath. They were still several miles from Capetown, where they hoped to find Kenzie and tell her what happened. With Calvin in possession of the chalice — which he surely hid in a new spot — they needed a new plan. And the likelihood of coming up with one seemed bleak.

After a brief rest, the women pressed on. To their right, the cliffs towered high into the night, narrowing the shore at several points to the width of a sidewalk, and drenching their feet in the Atlantic's icy waters.

A little further down, the cliff extended into the ocean for a stretch, forcing the women to wade through waist-deep water that stung like needles. Waves crashed above their heads, slamming them into the cliff, then threatening to tug them out to sea as the water receded back.

Finally reaching the other side of the outcrop, the women climbed from the water, drenched and chilled to the bone. They sloshed on down the shore like automatons, too exhausted to run or do anything other than put one foot in front of the other and hoping they didn't slip on the slimy rocks.

And that was when the wolves came.

Fifty yards ahead of them, a dozen black bulks slunk stealthily from the dark recesses along the cliff and stalked towards them. Even at this distance, they could see the moonlight reflected in their fierce, hungry eyes. It went without saying that no wolf had been sighted on the peninsula in over twenty years.

The women looked behind them, hoping they might be able to retreat around the outcrop, and were horrified to see more wolves emerging from water and coming toward them. With the Atlantic, and its icy undertow to their left, and wolves to their front and back, they saw only one possible way out, and that was up the cliff.

Moving as slowly as possible to keep the wolves from charging, the women eased over to the cliff, but their hopes were dashed as they stared up at its nearly vertical face of crumbling stones and dirt. Even with ropes, it would be difficult to climb, and impossible without gear.

With no hope of escape, the women slowly turned to face the wolves, close enough now to hear the low rumbles deep in their throats. They formed a half-circle in front of the women, pinning them against the cliff, with taut, muscled limbs ready to lunge at any moment. Emma reached over and took Maya's hand, and as she did this, a soft, subtle wind whispered across the shore.

All at once, the wolves came to an abrupt stop, as if they had met with an invisible barrier. The hunger still burned furiously in their eyes, and their lips remained curled back in snarls, but they seemed unable to advance any further.

As the women watched this sudden strange behavior, the half circle of wolves parted in the middle, and through the opening they saw two men standing on the far side of the wolves. They wore the dark woolen habits of monks, frayed from years of use, and coarse gray beards hung from their faces. But in their faces, etched deep with wrinkles and leathered skin from long days in the blistering sun, the women saw kindness. They looked exactly how Maya thought prophets of the Old Testament might have looked.

The monks passed through the wolves' ranks, showing no fear of the hulking black beasts on either side of them. The monk on the right extended his hand, and at the sound of his voice, a warmth fell over the women and all fear of the wolves faded.

"Fear not, friends," said the monk with the outstretched hand. "No harm will come to you from the wolves."

Emma took his hand, and Maya took the outstretched hand of the other one, and together they walked through the opening in the wolves' ranks.

"Who are you?" asked Maya, studying the monk beside her.

"We are mere travelers," said the monk, "who, as yourselves, seek to stop the covenant."

Chapter Thirty-Four
The Map

Knock, knock, knock.

Kenzie awoke to a soft knocking at her apartment door. With a tired groan, she lowered the blanket from her head and squinted her eyes open. The sun was up, but thankfully diffused behind a layer of clouds. She looked at the clock on her nightstand and saw that it was six thirty — less than three hours since they left the museum.

Knock, knock, knock.

"Yeah?" she groaned.

From the other side of the door came Rose's voice. "You have people here to see you."

Kenzie came down the stairs to the cafe's lobby, her hair matted beneath a baseball cap and flannel shirt thrown over her t-shirt. As she reached the lobby, she saw Fr. Sean, Emma, and Maya seated at a table, both women looking tattered and worn-out. Even from the stairs, Kenzie saw defeat in their eyes.

"Hey," Kenzie said as she hurried over and sat down at their table. "What's going on?"

Fr. Sean nodded to the women. "I'll let them explain, but there's been a few setbacks overnight."

Kenzie turned to Emma. "What happened?"

For the next five minutes, Emma and Maya filled Kenzie in on everything that happened the previous night, ending with the two mysterious men who saved them from the wolves.

"Who were they?" Kenzie asked.

"I don't know," said Emma. "They looked like they might be monks."

"They were prophets God send to help us," said Maya. "The wolves were of the devil, but these men were of God. This I could feel."

Emma looked at Maya for a moment before nodding. "I felt it too."

"It is why the wolves fear them," said Maya. "I could see it in the way they look at the men."

"You said they looked like monks?" said Kenzie, a distant thought stirring in her memory.

"That's how they were dressed," said Emma. "You know, they were in those dark habits monks wear."

"I think I saw them at the cave the day the Stanzos guys were there," said Kenzie. "But I think I saw them before that, too."

Fr. Sean looked at her. "The prophets Chad mentioned?"

Kenzie gave a slow nod. "I think so. He said when they came, the shadow people fled. It's the only reason I'm still alive."

"It is the same way with the wolves, and how they leave us alone," said Maya.

"What happened to the men?" said Kenzie.

"They took us to the rectory where we met with Fr. Sean," said Emma. "When we looked back, they were gone."

"They know about the covenant," said Maya, "and give us a map to find where it will happen."

"Where?" said Kenzie.

Emma and Maya exchanged a look with each other.

"Acheron," said Emma. She reached into her purse and pulled out a folded sheet of parchment, and spread it across the table. "They said it will rise tomorrow night as the moon crests."

"Tomorrow's the night of the festival," Kenzie said, looking at Fr. Sean.

He nodded. "The sanguine."

Kenzie leaned in for a closer look at the map, feeling her pulse pound as she stared at the aged document. It appeared to be an ancient mariner's map, showing in faded drawing a rough approximation of the New England coastline. Emma pointed to a spot at the back of a wide inlet wedged between cliffs. Beside her finger was the word *'Acheron.'*

"Where'd they get this?" said Kenzie.

"They said it's from a ship that wrecked there long ago," said Emma. "The Alighieri."

Kenzie looked at her and then at Fr. Sean. "That's the ship that had the chest on it."

He nodded. "I remember the name from the first story you wrote on Acheron."

"They say we will need a boat to get there," said Maya. "Do you know where it is we can get one?"

Kenzie looked back at the map and studied it for a moment. "Can't we take this road?" she said, pointing to a line on the map drawn through a valley to the west of Acheron.

Emma shook her head. "It's all buried beneath marshes now. The only way in is through that inlet."

Kenzie thought about it for a moment. "My friend's parents have a boat we might be able to use."

"You're going to need a distraction to get close to the chalice," said Fr. Sean. "I'm sure they'll have security everywhere."

Kenzie leaned back and thought about it for a moment. "Would an explosion work?"

"If you had explosives."

"I think I know where we can get some." She then turned to Emma. "I hope you don't mind signing some autographs."

Chapter Thirty-Five
Allies

"Fuck, yeah, we're in," said Trey. Zac, Dillon, and Brett nodded in eager agreement.

Kenzie could have kissed them. She, Fr. Sean, Emma, Maya, and the boys were in the basement of Brett's parents' house — the infamous 'bat cave' — where she and the women briefed the boys on what happened, and Fr. Sean laid out a strategy for recovering the chalice.

Kenzie had called Zac before leaving the cafe, and by the time they arrived at Brett's house, he had rounded up the other Lone Gunmen. Letting them know Emma would be there went a long way towards rousing them from four hours of sleep, and Kenzie saw with amusement that they even combed their hair. That was a first.

Despite the worn-out clothes and lack of sleep, Emma's effortless beauty shined through. She was still the cover girl who had adorned thousands of boys' school lockers and bedroom walls. She signed the boys' copies of her swimsuit issue and posed for selfies with them, then joined Maya in telling them about their escape.

"What do you need us to do?" said Zac.

"We need some explosives to use as a distraction," said Fr. Sean. "Kenzie said you can get your hands on some."

"How big do they need to be?" said Brett.

"As big and loud as you can make them," said Fr. Sean.

"In case you guys were wondering," said Kenzie, "he used to be a Marine before he became a priest."

"Oh, cool," said Trey. "So it's okay if we cuss?"

Fr. Sean smiled. "Feel free."

"How many explosives are we talking about?" said Brett.

"Ideally, we'll need a dozen," said Fr. Sean. "Calvin's team will need to come on yachts, so if we pack the explosives in waterproof crates, we can float them out on inner tubes and place them near the propulsion jets."

"And blow up their yachts?" said Trey.

"You probably won't have enough explosives to breach the hull," said Fr. Sean, "but you'll be able to disable them from following you. But their main purpose is to be a distraction so you can get the chalice."

"Copy that," said Trey. "Let's do it."

"We'll need to pick up some supplies when the stores open," said Brett.

"Make me a list and I'll get them," said Zac.

"Pick up some walkie talkies, too," said Dillon. "We can use them as remote detonators."

"Done," said Zac.

"You really know how to do all of this?" said Emma, who appeared both stunned and impressed.

"Most of it's stuff we've done before," said Dillon. "Just never on this scale."

"You name the seditious activity, and we've probably done it," said Trey, before catching himself. "Is that okay to say in front of a priest?"

Again, Fr. Sean smiled. "You're fine."

"Cool. Just checking."

"I'm impressed," said Emma. "Kenzie was right about all of you."

"Did she mention I'm really mature for my age?" said Trey.

"Me too," said Brett. "Don't let my boyish good looks fool you."

"Did she tell you about the spider array I designed that got us into the museum?" said Dillon.

Kenzie groaned and rolled her eyes. "Guys. Focus."

Emma smiled. "She said there's no one she trusts more to have her back than the four of you."

The boys all turned to Kenzie. "You said that, Kenz?" said Trey.

"I told her to keep her pepper spray handy," Kenzie said.

Zac chuckled. "She has our backs, too. So, what else do we need?"

"We still need a boat to get there," Kenzie said, then turned to Brett. "Any chance you can get your parents' one?"

Brett shifted uneasily. "How long will we be gone?"

"If everything works out, two days."

"And if it doesn't work out?"

"Then you won't be around to get grounded," said Dillon. "See, either way, it's win, win."

Brett looked at Kenzie. "We're not gonna blow it up or anything, are we?"

"We better not," she said, "'cause it's a long swim home."

Brett thought about it for a moment. "I guess I can do it. But you guys need to hide me if my parents go ballistic."

"You can crash on my floor," said Zac, then turning to Kenzie. "Is that everything?"

"I think so," said Kenzie. "We can meet at the boat at six A.M. tomorrow to get everything loaded and catch the tide out."

Fr. Sean drove them back to the cafe, where they dropped off Emma and Maya to get some much-needed rest, then he and Kenzie drove to the hospital to check in on Drew. The last time she saw him, he was still unconscious, but alive when the ambulance arrived.

As they walked through the sliding glass doors into the emergency room lobby, they spotted Rick on the far side near the check-in counter.

"Hey, Rick," said Fr. Sean as he and Kenzie walked over.

Rick turned and nodded in acknowledgment. "Morning, Father. So, she's got you roped into this nuttiness?"

"I've been roped for a while. I hear you might be too."

"It's beginning to look that way."

"Any news on Drew?" Kenzie said.

"He made it through surgery," Rick said. "They said he has a concussion, and a fractured right arm and leg."

"But he's going to be alright?"

Rick nodded. "They think so."

Kenzie breathed a deep sigh of relief. "Thank God for that. I mean that literally."

He nodded in agreement. "You deserve thanks, too, Kenzie. I might be in there too if you hadn't insisted on coming into the museum with me."

"You didn't know what you were up against."

"But you did."

"I had a pretty good idea. Especially when the forensics team radioed down, and then we heard Drew's gunshots."

"You still think it was Daryl?"

She nodded. "I'm positive. I think you do too."

He took a deep breath before nodding. "Why don't you tell me everything you know about all of this."

"Everything?"

Again, he nodded. "Everything."

And so she did. Beginning with the night she saw Chad's ghost, she told him about everything that had happened and would happen. She told him about Acheron's covenant with the devil, and how its evil infested the land. She told him about Calvin's ancestral ties to Acheron, and let him read the journal entries she kept as photos on her phone. She told him about her ability to see the unseen world and sense things beyond the five ordinary senses. She told him about her trip to Honduras, and the priest's warnings; and about the Stigmatist girl and her visions of the Virgin Mary, and the dire message she had for the world. Humanity stood on the precipice of its doom. Finally, she told him about the map, and how the covenant would be renewed on the site where Acheron once stood. And would soon stand again in unholy triumph.

When she finished, she was relieved to see him following along attentively.

"Was it as crazy as you expected?" she said.

He gave a slow nod. "I'm not sure what I expected, but that was a lot. You believe all of it?"

"I've seen most of it, so I really can't not believe it."

He turned to Fr. Sean. "What about you, father?"

"I'm a believer. What about you? I'm sensing less skepticism than before."

Rick fidgeted with his Styrofoam coffee cup for a moment before nodding. "I'm getting there. So, what happens now?"

"I'm going to Acheron with some friends tomorrow to try to stop it," said Kenzie. "How's that for crazy?"

"It tops the list," said Rick. He turned to Fr. Sean. "You're not going, father?"

Fr. Sean shook his head. "Kenzie asked me to stay down here in case something happens at the festival. I'm under strict orders to get Rose and her dog out of town if hell breaks loose."

"At the festival?"

"Didn't Drew tell you about that?" said Kenzie.

"Is this about the writing you found on the wall in Floyd's cellar?"

"It was this," Kenzie said, opening the photos app on her phone and showing him the photos of the words 'libertas' and 'sanguine' on the wall.

"It's hard to see, but the words are libertas and sanguine," Kenzie said. "That literally means bloodbath."

Rick shifted uneasily. "And you think this is going to happen at the festival?"

She nodded. "I think whoever wrote that thinks so, too."

"I could use your help tomorrow, Rick, if you're game," said Fr. Sean.

"I don't see how I have a choice."

PART THREE

When Gods Walk the Earth

Chapter Thirty-Six
Final Farewells

A light rain misted down on the dock early that morning, and the smells of salt water and fish hung heavy in the air. Rick crossed the damp wooden planks to the far end, where Kenzie, her Lone Gunmen friends, and Fr. Sean were loading crates, rope, and large black inner tubes onto a twenty-foot trawler. Two inflatable dinghies, with outboard motors, were tied behind it.

The events over the past two days, and his talk with Kenzie at the hospital, brought a drastic change to how he saw the world. He had known for a while that unique problems plagued Capetown, but he never allowed the possibility that they were supernatural in origin. He slept better that way. But last night he slept like a wreck. The truth was, Capetown was diseased, infested with horrors too grisly and obscene to imagine. And he had allowed their gestation, filing those investigations into the infamous 'unsolved' case files, and doing his best to put them out of his mind.

But the proverbial chickens were now coming home to roost, and he no longer had the luxury of looking the other way. For better or worse, today would be decisive.

Kenzie looked up from a crate she was strapping down near the boat's cabin and saw Rick approaching down the dock. She walked over to the rail.

"Hey," she called down. "You here to join us?"

He shook his head. "I prefer my enemies to be flesh and blood."

"You're in the wrong town for that."

"So, I've heard."

Fr. Sean walked over and joined Kenzie at the rail. "Morning, Rick. How'd you sleep last night?"

"I doubt I'll ever sleep again," said Rick. "I put in a call to Arkham's PD to see if they can spare a couple officers to help us out with the festival."

"What'd you tell them?"

"Gang violence."

Fr. Sean chuckled. "I guess that's easier to believe than demons."

"They would have laughed me out of town. I'll let you know when I hear something."

"I appreciate that."

Rick turned back to Kenzie. "I'm guessing there's no talking you out of going."

She shook her head. "I'm pretty stubborn."

"I'm seeing that." He hesitated a moment before continuing. "Look, Kenzie, I owe you an apology. If I'd taken you seriously sooner, maybe none of this would have happened."

She nodded in acknowledgment of the apology.

"Can I ask you something without you getting pissed?" she said.

"Fire away."

"Did you know about this stuff?"

He took a deep breath before answering. "I knew something was happening. But I didn't know the extent of it."

"Why didn't you say something?"

"I couldn't."

"Why not?"

"Because your newsletter was drawing attention to things a lot of people wanted to keep hidden. A lot of the wrong people."

"The town council?"

He shook his head. "Bigger than them."

"Who are they?"

He took a cautious look around before turning back to her. "It's not something we should talk about here. But we'll do it when you get back."

She shifted uneasily at his worried tone. "Is this gonna be an Acheron File?"

"You won't want to write about this. These people are dangerous."

"I'd like to be in on that conversation too, if you don't mind," said Fr. Sean.

"Assuming you and I get through tonight in one piece, you're welcome to join us."

"I'm glad you said *when* I come back, and not *if*," Kenzie said.

"Just trying to keep it optimistic. I brought you something, in case things go south up there." He reached up and handed her a rectangular box.

"What is it?" she said, taking the box and flipping open its lid. Inside it was a pistol and box of 9mm ammunition.

"Hopefully something to get you home in one piece. It's Drew's, so I'll need it back."

She took the pistol and held it in her hands, getting a feel for its heft.

"No silver bullets?" she said.

"Couldn't find any, so I got you some hollow points. I trust you still remember how to use it?"

"I better. I spent enough time at the shooting range with you and dad."

"Just checking. This one holds seventeen rounds in the magazine, and one in the chamber. You pull back on the slide to chamber the round."

"I remember," she said. "Then you pull the trigger, and it goes bang."

"You got it. Only use it if you absolutely have to."

"I will," she said, sliding the pistol into the waistband of her jeans and the ammo box into her jacket pocket. "Thank you."

He nodded. "Try not to shoot Zac and your friends."

She smiled. "No promises."

"At least bury their bodies at sea, so I don't have to fill out the paperwork."

Again, she smiled. "That, I can promise."

"I probably don't need to hear any of this," Fr. Sean said with a smile.

"You'll hear all about it in confession when I get back."

"Just make it back," he said, giving her a friendly pat on the back before turning to Rick. "I need to finish helping these guys get everything strapped down, but I'll stop by your office this afternoon."

"I'll see you then," said Rick.

Fr. Sean headed off to join Zac and the others, while Kenzie turned back to Rick.

"Thanks for helping him with the festival," she said.

"Let's hope it's not needed."

"Fingers crossed," she said, holding up her hand with two fingers crossed.

He smiled. "Mine are too. See you tomorrow?" A tint of sadness showed through the smile. He couldn't help feeling they were saying their final farewells.

"See you then," she said, feeling a tint of sadness as well.

He turned to head off when she stopped him. "Hey, sheriff."

He turned back. "Yeah?"

"I'm glad I was wrong about you."

"Me too, Kenzie."

Rick arrived back at the sheriff's office a little after nine that morning. Across the street in the park, work crews were setting up booths and stands for the festival, which would kick-off in a few hours. Several workers unhitched a merry-go-round from the back of a truck and placed blocks beneath its corners to stabilize it. Others draped lights across the gazebo and adjusted the sound equipment.

Rick paused to watch them for a moment, looking for anything that might suggest danger. But as far as he could tell, everything appeared normal. Just as it had every year since the festival's inception.

And yet, something felt terribly off; something he couldn't point to or explain. It was just there, in his gut, a growing sense of anticipation and dread.

Even before entering the office, Rick heard the barks coming from the yard behind the building. He dashed through the reception area, past the empty desk where his assistant, Maggie, should have been, and out the back exit into the fenced-in yard they used as a kennel for the department's canine.

On the far side of the yard, a large German shepherd tugged furiously at his chain, barking and growling at Maggie and Randy, the dog's part-time handler.

"What's going on with him?" Rick said.

"Beats the hell outta me," Randy said, taking a wary step back from the dog. "He's been doing this since I got here."

"I called Randy when I couldn't get him to calm down," said Maggie.

Rick turned to the dog and took a slow, cautious step toward it, holding his hands out in a non-threatening gesture.

"Hey, Spike," Rick said, calling the dog by its name, "what's wrong, buddy? You're scaring these people."

The dog made a sudden, snarling lunge toward him, before being stopped by the chain.

Rick leaped back. "Jeez! What in the hell?" He turned to Maggie. "Can you call the vet and see if he'll make a house call?"

"Yeah. Do you think it's something he ate?"

Rick shook his head. "I honestly have no idea. But we'd better find out fast. I'm still down one deputy, so this guy was supposed to be my backup."

"I'll call him right now," Maggie said, then turned and headed inside.

Randy walked over to Rick, who continued watching the dog.

"Any idea what's got him so mad?" Rick said.

Randy watched the dog for a moment as it paced back and forth, testing the limit of its chain.

"I'm not so sure he's mad," Randy said. "Look at his eyes."

Rick did. "What about them?"

"That's not how they look when they're angry. That's how they look when they're scared."

"What's he scared of?"

Randy shrugged. "Beats the hell outta me. But whatever it is, it's gotta be bad."

Chapter Thirty-Seven
The Dogs

It was late afternoon when Fr. Sean stopped by Rick's office. He found Rick at his desk, loading rounds into his pistol's magazine.

"Find any silver bullets yet?" Fr. Sean said, half in jest.

"Just hollow points," Rick said, sliding the pistol into his holster. "I have a spare one, if you want it."

"What is it?"

"Glock nineteen. I keep it as a backup." He slid open his desk drawer and pulled out the pistol. He handed it to Fr. Sean. "I trust a Marine knows how to use it."

"It's been a while," Fr. Sean said as he took the pistol. He checked the chamber to make sure it was unloaded, then racked the slide. He lowered the pistol to his belt, then quickly snapped it out in front of him, aimed at a point on the wall, and squeezed the trigger. It snapped with a crisp click. The draw was as fast as any Rick had seen. Everything from the grip to the trigger pull was precision perfect.

"Like riding a bike?" Rick said.

Fr. Sean nodded. "Something like that."

The band was warming up in the gazebo by the time Fr. Sean and Rick headed from the office and across the street to the park. A good-sized crowd was already there, with lines forming at concession stands, hot dogs and hamburgers sizzling on grills, and kids taking their turn at games.

"Any idea what we're looking for?" Rick asked.

Fr. Sean shook his head. "Something that doesn't feel right."

"Like animals acting strange?"

"That could be an indicator."

Rick stopped and nodded to a pair of dogs he had been watching. They paced restlessly near a concession stand, their eyes warily scanning the park and tails between their legs.

"Take a look at those dogs," Rick said. "Do they look scared to you?"

Fr. Sean watched them for a moment before nodding. "They do."

Rick nodded to another pair of dogs, both whining uneasily as they nervously scanned the park. "Those ones are acting the same way."

"Is it the crowd?"

Rick shook his head. "They never had a problem with the crowd before. Usually, they're bounding around, playing and causing mischief."

"They look like they sense a threat," Fr. Sean said, looking around to see if he could see what they did.

"It's been happening all day," said Rick, "but earlier they were aggressive. We had to have the vet come out to check on the department's canine. He nearly bit me and his handler."

"What did the vet say?"

"He couldn't explain it. But he said it was happening all over town."

"When did the aggression stop?"

"As far as I know, sometime late this afternoon."

Fr. Sean looked back at the dogs and watched them for a moment. "They sized up the threat. And it's too big for them."

Fr. Sean and Rick left the park and drove to Hallows Pointe, arriving shortly before sundown. Rick carried a small paper bag as they headed down the stairs and across the jetty to the cottage. He knocked on the door, and a moment later it opened, with Ken Baxter's bearded face looking out at them.

"'Sup, Rick? Father?" said the grisly fisherman. "Thought you all'd be at the festival."

"Couldn't let you starve out here," Rick said, handing Ken the bag. "You might go missing in action on me."

Ken dug into the bag and pulled out a hamburger, wrapped in greasy paper.

"You forgot the fries," Ken said, staring into the bag.

"Next time," Rick said. "So, how're you holding up out here?"

Ken shrugged. "Ain't so bad, once you get used to all the quiet. You all having any luck finding a new keeper yet?"

"We're working on it," Rick said. "I appreciate you holding down the fort until we find one."

Again, Ken shrugged. "Ain't no big deal. Was about to go turn on the light. You two wanna tag along?"

Rick checked his watch. "We've got a couple minutes. Let's go."

They walked down the short narrow path to the lighthouse tower, where Ken opened the door and let them in. They climbed the winding stairs to the lantern room at the top, where Ken turned on the switch for the massive light. As its motor groaned on, they both stepped outside onto the catwalk.

"I need you to do me a favor tonight, Ken," Rick said as he leaned against the rail. Beside him, Fr. Sean looked out across the ocean, to where dark storm clouds formed on the distance horizon. Beneath the clouds lay the faint haze of a fog bank.

"What's that?"

"Keep an eye out for anything unusual."

"What would you call unusual?"

Rick looked at Fr. Sean. "You wanna take this?"

"Something that doesn't feel right," said Fr. Sean. "You're gonna need to go with your gut a lot on this."

"This one of them supernatural things that girl's always writing about, father?"

Fr. Sean nodded. "If it happens, it will be."

"And you all got me hold up here in a haunted lighthouse."

"We're not saying it's definitely going to happen," said Rick. "We just need you to be on watch."

Fr. Sean looked back at the distant storm clouds and noticed something peculiar. While the storm was further away now, the fog appeared to be closer.

"What direction's the wind blowing, Ken?" said Fr. Sean.

Ken held up his finger for a moment. "I'd say it's blowing south-easterly."

Fr. Sean nodded. It was the same thing he thought. "You'll want to keep an eye on that fog bank tonight."

Ken and Rick both turned to look in that direction.

"What about it?" said Ken.

"It's moving against the wind."

Chapter Thirty-Eight
Legacy

Christopher Crawford, known simply around town as 'Chris,' awoke to an unsettling feeling that morning.

It was the day of the Libertas Festival, the day when the town gathered in the park bearing his family's name to celebrate the town's founding and liberation centuries ago. The celebration was always an exciting time for Chris. As the sole surviving descendant of Nathanial Crawford, who many hailed as the town's most influential founding father, Chris was always called upon to give a speech to the town's residents, reminding them of the proud heritage they all shared. It made him a celebrity of sorts, at least for the day, and boosted business at the small hardware store he owned along the Main Street. But this year, things felt different. And not in a good way.

It started yesterday when he went to the museum to talk to Madelyn about his speech. He found the museum sealed off with crime scene tape, and when he couldn't reach Madelyn on her phone, he called the sheriff's department to see what happened. They refused to comment, saying only that it was an ongoing investigation.

He also heard rumors that the town's deputy was in the hospital, but when he tried calling there, they refused to release any information, citing patient confidentiality.

And then, last night, he had the dream. Although he remembered little of it, what he remembered caused his skin to stir. He remembered a fog engulfing the town, and within that fog moved eerie, ghostlike shadows.

After breakfast, Chris headed to his hardware store. He stopped outside the door for a moment to watch the work crews setting up for the festival. Someone had decorated the large bronze statue of his great, great, great, great, great — he was never sure just how many 'greats' — grandfather, Nathanial Crawford, with flowers. From what he knew of his ancestor, a slab of beef and a yard of ale would have been more appropriate.

He closed the store early that afternoon, as did most of the stores along Main Street, and headed over to a tavern along the seaport. The drizzle from early that morning had passed, but the sky remained gray and lifeless. Looking up at the sky, he hoped with all his might that the rain would return, and they would cancel the festival.

The unnamed fear from earlier that morning persisted as he sat down at the bar and ordered a shot of whiskey. He quickly downed it and ordered another. And after that, another. It took five shots to finally quiet his nerves. But even then, the alcohol couldn't deaden the growing dread that something terrible was about to happen.

Chris had just ordered a sixth shot when he noticed something odd — a sharp chill filled the air, as if a sudden icy gust had blown in. But this was unlikely, since the June air outside was balmy from the storm.

It was then that something red caught his attention from the corner of his eye. Looking to his left, he saw a woman seated several bar stools down. She wore a red dress, slit high on the side to reveal a perfect thigh, and as his eyes drifted to her face, his breath slowed. She was stunning, with raven black hair the color of night, and piercing blue eyes that watched him with mild interest.

Her lips curled in a coy smile as she caught his eyes traveling up the length of her legs to her breasts and finally her eyes, where he froze in embarrassment. He spun back to the shot glass in front of him and downed his sixth shot.

When he turned back, he was startled to see her now seated on the stool next to his. He hadn't heard her walk over or slide out the stool, and yet there she was, barely two feet away. The most breathtaking woman he had ever seen.

Every ounce of courage fled him. He nervously looked away from her to a corner table where two fishermen filled their glasses with beer from a pitcher. It struck him as odd that neither of them seemed to notice the woman, nor did the bartender, tending to a patron at the far end of the bar. On a normal day, a beautiful woman would have caught the eye of every male in the pub.

"Don't be nervous, Chris," came her voice, as softly as a purr. He felt her hand touch his chin and turn his head back to face her. "I rarely bite."

Chris let out a nervous chuckle. "Hi. Sorry. It's just... I..."

She reached out and touched her finger to his lips. The message was obvious. *Shh.* "Don't talk, Chris. Just look at me."

He shifted nervously, unsure of what to do or say. He'd never had the attention of a beautiful woman like this before. "Okay..."

He mustered the nerve to bring his eyes back to hers, and in that moment, he felt something subtle twitch inside him. Her eyes were deep, glossy, and piercing. They held onto his, never blinking or revealing any emotion, and again he shifted nervously. But he could no longer look away. He felt the background sights and sounds slowly fading until his full awareness was on her eyes. They seemed to bore deep inside of him to where his innermost thoughts and secrets lay; to the darkest recesses of his soul where unspeakable lusts burned and desires tempted. He had the faint sensation of falling, and vast gulfs of darkness sweeping in around him. He felt the stir of strange arousals and curiosities; and the terror of vague, inexplicable fears.

And he continued falling...

Sometime later — Chris couldn't be sure of how long — he regained awareness of his surroundings. As his senses filled with the pub's sights and sounds, he found himself seated alone at the bar. The woman was gone, with no sign of her having been there.

Chris rose to his feet and looked around. Everything was exactly as it was just minutes ago, with the fishermen pouring beer into their glasses at the corner table and the bartender tending to patrons at the far end of the bar.

"Hey, Kip," Chris called over to the bartender. "Did you see which way that woman went?"

Kip walked over, wiping a shot glass as he went. "What woman are you talking about, Chris?"

"The hot one in the red dress."

Kip looked at him oddly. "When was this?"

"Just now."

Kip shook his head. "I haven't seen a woman in here all morning who fits that description."

Chris turned to the fishermen at the corner table, who had been eavesdropping on the conversation. "Did you guys see her?"

Both fishermen shook their heads. "Nope," said one of them. "And doesn't sound like someone I woulda missed."

"Maybe you oughta take it easy on the shots, Chris," said the other fisherman. "You got a speech to give in a couple hours."

A sudden, uneasy realization struck Chris at the reminder of his speech. He sat down on the bar stool, and for a moment, could only stare in bewilderment. When he came in earlier, he was still at a loss over what he would say at the festival. While he had some vague ideas for his speech, they felt uninspired and like rehashes of speeches he gave in previous years.

But now, as he scoured the dark recesses of his mind, he felt the speech was in there, locked deep in the corners of his subconscious where he couldn't access it. At least not yet. But in some obscure way, he knew it would come to him that night. And a chill brushed his arms when he thought of what that speech might be. And how it got there.

Chapter Thirty-Nine
The Lost Voyage

All afternoon and into the evening, the trawler chugged north across the Atlantic's choppy waters. They hugged the coastline, keeping its rolling cliffs and shoreline within sight and avoiding fishing lanes.

While Brett piloted the boat from inside its small cabin, Kenzie and the others spent most of the day on deck, watching the coast's inlets and waterways roll past in the hazy distance.

They had plotted and re-plotted their plans all afternoon. Under the cover of darkness, they would drop anchor just outside the inlet's opening to avoid detection. Kenzie and Zac would then take one of the two dinghies to shore to search for the chalice, while Trey and Dillon used the other dinghy to tow the explosive-filled crates, strapped down onto the large inner tubes, into the inlet and leave them near the yachts. Emma and Maya would stay on the boat with Brett to keep watch, and notify the others by radio if they saw any activity on the shore or yachts.

That was the plan, anyway, which was based on lots of assumptions. The aged mariner's map showed only a general sketch of the coast and location of the city at the back of the inlet. It also showed V-shaped sketches of what appeared to be cliffs along the inlet's northern and southern borders, then hills further inland, placing Acheron in the basin of a large valley. What it didn't show was a layout of Acheron itself, so Kenzie and Zac would be on their own to navigate its streets.

The storm blew in shortly after nightfall, and with it came a dense fog, covering the ocean like a cloud. Waves rose and fell, swaying the trawler like a toy. Kenzie stumbled across the soaked deck to the cabin, where she found Brett wiping the condensation from the window with his shirtsleeve.

"How's it looking?" she said.

"If I could see anything, I'd let you know."

He gave up on the window, which frosted over as quickly as he could wipe it, and nodded to the instrument panel.

"Check this out," he said.

She walked over and looked down at the GPS system, which showed a line of zeros across the display.

"I'm guessing it's not supposed to do that," she said.

"Nope. And neither is this." He nodded to the compass, whose needle spun around dizzily.

"How long's it been doing that?"

He shrugged. "Maybe twenty, thirty minutes."

"So, about the time we hit this fog?"

"Yeah."

She swallowed nervously and looked out the cabin door at the boat's port side. It faced the coast, hidden somewhere beyond a wall of fog.

"I think it means we're getting close," she said.

"You think so?" he said. Suddenly, all of this was becoming too real.

"Have you ever seen your instruments do that before?"

He shook his head. "Nope."

"I think it's because Acheron's an aberration of everything we know. So, things might not work the way they're supposed to."

As she said this, the dense fog began to thin and fall away from around them, leaving only hazy layers of mist trailing across the waters. Off the port side, they could now make out the dark outline of cliffs rolling past in the storm. Brett slowed the engine to a crawl as they neared the cliff's end at the inlet's opening, then shut it off.

Kenzie and Brett joined the others on deck at the rail. In the distance, through the driving rain, they saw the dark hulks of a dozen yachts anchored in the inlet's black waters.

Then, looking far across the inlet to its back, they saw the dark, brooding outline of Acheron.

Chapter Forty
They Came in the Fog

Night had fallen by the time Rick and Fr. Sean pulled up to Rose's cafe. All across town, streetlights and gas lamps cast their glow along lonely elm-lined streets.

As they came in the door, they spotted Rose behind the pastry counter across the lobby.

"Hey," Rick said as they walked over. "You wouldn't happen to have any of that famous coffee of yours back there, would you?"

She smiled. "I think I can squeeze out another cup. I can put on another pot if you want some too, father."

"I'm good, but thanks," said Fr. Sean.

"So what brings the two of you here?" Rose said, as she filled a cup with coffee and slid it across the counter to Rick. "And don't tell me it's just for my coffee."

Rick smiled as he took a small sip. "You know me too well, Rose."

"Since you were a young boy, Rick Channing," said Rose. "So, why aren't the two of you at the festival?"

Rick looked at Fr. Sean. "You should probably do the explaining."

"Did Kenzie mention anything about something happening at the festival?" Fr. Sean said.

Rose nodded. "She asked me not to go and to keep her dog inside."

"Is he upstairs?"

Again, Rose nodded. "She locked him in her apartment before leaving this morning. He's been barking all day until a couple hours ago. Is something going to happen tonight?"

Fr. Sean shook his head. "I don't know. But it would be a good idea to stay inside."

"Will it be one of those supernatural things Kenzie writes about?"

"If it happens, it will be."

Rose's face turned ashen. "Have you told the mayor?"

"I spoke with him yesterday after I talked to Kenzie," said Rick. "But there wasn't a whole lot I could tell him at this point. We just don't know what the actual danger is."

Rose eyed him for a moment. "I'm surprised to see you believing Kenzie now."

Rick gave a slow, guilty nod. "I'll be the first to admit it. I was wrong."

"What changed your mind?"

"Seeing too many things that I can't explain, but Kenzie can. She probably saved mine and Drew's lives the other night."

"Kenzie mentioned he's in the hospital. How's he doing?"

"They said he's stable. They're keeping him another day for observation, but he should be ready to leave by tomorrow."

"Assuming this thing you're worried about doesn't happen tonight."

Rick gave another slow nod. "Exactly."

At that moment, the cell phone in his pocket buzzed with an incoming call. He pulled it out and read the caller ID: *'Ken Baxter.'*

"I need to take this," he said to Rose, then swiped on the phone's display to answer the call. "Ken. Everything okay?"

From the other end came Ken's voice. "I think so. But you know that fog father was talking about earlier?"

"What about it?"

"It's outside my door right now, and covering the whole jetty."

Rick's expression grew tense. "But you're okay?"

"I'm fine. Just wanted to give you a heads up that this thing's here and it's heading your way."

"Is the wind still blowing east?"

"Sure is. I'm telling ya, Rick, it's the damnedest thing I ever seen."

"How fast is it moving?"

"Couple knots. Should reach town in about ten minutes or so."

"Thanks, Ken. You stay safe. Don't go outside for any reason."

"Wasn't planning on it. You know what's going on?"

"Not yet. But I'll let you know as soon as I find out."

Rick hung up and slid the phone back into his pocket. He turned to Rose.

"We need to get back to the park. But please, promise me you won't go out tonight."

She swallowed nervously and nodded. "Okay. Is it happening?"

"I think so."

Ken hung up from his phone call with Rick and looked out the cottage kitchen window. On a clear night, he could see the tower and light from there, but tonight the fog was too thick to see more than a couple feet out the window. It was like trying to see through a bowl of thick gray soup.

He grabbed a beer from the refrigerator and took it into the living room, where he plopped down in the reclining chair. If he was going to miss the festival, he planned to make the most of the night. He clicked on the TV and was annoyed to find static on every channel. How in the hell did Floyd make it two years in this place?

As he rose from his chair to see if he could adjust the TV's rabbit ears to pick up something, a sudden loud crash from outside caused him to startle. It sounded like the door to the outside storm cellar slamming shut. He walked over to the living room window and pressed his face against the glass, hoping to find an opening in the fog to see what caused the noise. But it cloaked everything outside in a gray shroud.

Just as he was turning back to the TV, something outside the window caught his attention. It was a faint glow, like a flashlight moving through the fog. He pressed his face back against the window and looked to his left and right. There were several more of these diffused glows moving through the fog. He watched them for a moment, then startled back, the breath catching in his throat.

People were out there, moving through the fog like ghostly gray shadows. He never would have seen them if the lights hadn't passed behind them, casting them in faint silhouettes.

Ken eased back from the window, swallowing a nervous lump in his throat. He definitely hadn't signed up for spooky stuff like this when he volunteered to be the interim lighthouse keeper until the town could find a permanent replacement. He planned to have a long talk with Rick about this in the morning.

Three sharp knocks came from the kitchen door and Ken nearly jumped. He looked across the room at the opening to the adjoining kitchen, debating for a moment over whether to check it out.

Two more knocks came.

Taking a deep breath to chill his nerves, Ken gripped the beer bottle tightly in his fist and crossed the room to the opening.

Through the window above the sink on his right, he saw those same ghostly lights drifting through the fog. He took a nervous breath and poked his head further around the corner until he could see the door on the far side of the kitchen.

A thick sheet of fog flowed in from beneath the door, covering the floor in a foot of dense gray cloud. As his eyes traveled up the door to its window, he saw even more of those eerie lights drifting deep within the fog. Then he froze.

Someone stood outside the door, a faint silhouette against the lights drifting behind it.

Two more knocks.

Ken ducked back behind the corner. Whoever was out there had to have seen him. He quietly crept back from the opening to the center of the room, making no more noise than a whisper.

A loud crash came from outside and the power snuffed out, plunging the room into almost complete darkness. What little light there was came from those eerie lights moving through the fog outside the living room window.

Ken kept his eye on the kitchen opening as he quietly ducked behind the reclining chair. The fog sifted in, flowing in through the opening and spreading across the living room. It pulsed from within with that strange luminescence, casting faint light across the floor as it deepened to knee height.

And then *they* were there.

In the opening stood the dark, shadowy form of a man, with two others standing near the hallway to his right. Like phantoms, the dark forms floated across the room toward him.

Chapter Forty-One
The Screaming Starts

Rick's car skidded up to the curb alongside the park, and he and Fr. Sean hopped out. Looking around, they saw the lawn packed with residents enjoying food and games. Colorful lights adorned the booths, while long strings of lights, strung across the park and wrapped around trees, gave it a festive holiday feel. Nothing about it felt menacing.

They looked over at the gazebo, where dozens of people listened as the band wound down. A town council member, Marty Cross, climbed the gazebo's steps and walked over to a microphone.

"How about we give a round of applause to Capetown's own Ferrymen," Marty said, to which the audience responded with claps and cheers. Marty looked back at the band members, who nodded their appreciation.

When the applause died down, Marty turned back to the microphone. "And now, as it's been every year since I've been on the town council, it's my great pleasure to introduce the descendant of one of our founding families, whose name happens to adorn the park we're in. Ladies and gentlemen, please join me in welcoming Chris Crawford."

More applause broke out as Chris walked over and joined Marty at the microphone. The two shook hands, and then Chris turned to the microphone while Marty headed back down the steps and over to a concession stand.

"Good evening, everyone," Chris said, "and thanks for coming out. I promise to keep it short this year, so try not to fall asleep while I share a few thoughts about what makes our home here in Capetown so special."

Some polite chuckles came from the audience at his self-deprecating humor.

As Chris resumed his speech, Rick and Fr. Sean eased through the crowd and over to Marty.

"Marty, we need to talk," Rick said as they walked up.

"Of course," Marty said, turning to Rick and Fr. Sean. "What is it?"

"You're not gonna like this, but I think we need to shut down the festival and send everyone home."

Marty nearly choked. He watched Rick for a moment, waiting to see if there was a punchline, but apparently there wasn't.

"You can't be serious," Marty said.

"I don't like it either, but I think they're in danger."

"From what?"

Rick took a deep breath. "I don't know yet, but father and I both think something bad's going to happen."

Marty looked around the park for any sign of danger, but all he saw were families enjoying themselves. On the gazebo, a short distance from them, Chris's speech continued.

"... and from the land, our founders carved a life for themselves, handing down to us the rich heritage we enjoy today..."

Marty turned back to Rick. "But you don't know what this danger is."

Rick shook his head. "No. Not yet."

"Well, come back when you do know."

Fr. Sean was the first to notice that Chris's speech had abruptly stopped. He looked over at the gazebo, and saw Chris standing completely still, his unblinking eyes fixed on something in the crowd.

What Fr. Sean couldn't see, and neither could anyone in the crowd, was what Chris saw — the woman in the red dress from the bar, watching him from just beyond the people gathered at the gazebo.

"Rick," Fr. Sean said. "Look at Chris."

Rick and Marty both turned and fell silent as they watched Chris's frozen expression.

"I'd better check on him," said Marty. But before he could, Chris blinked away whatever it was and appeared to recompose himself. He turned back to the microphone to resume his speech, but it was apparent from his manner that something was off. Something had changed.

At that moment, just as Chris resumed his speech, the barking began.

"You've been lied to," Chris said into the microphone, his tone somber and ominous. "Nothing about our heritage was rich or great. Our ancestor were slaves to an oppressive God, who subjugated them to his tyrannical will..."

The barks spread across the park as dog owners frantically tried to calm their pets.

"... It was our neighbors to the north, the people of Acheron, who knew the true god," Chris continued. "A god who brought wealth and carnal pleasures beyond imagination. Who fed their unquenchable desires and insatiable lusts..."

"What the hell's he doing?" Marty muttered, eying Chris curiously.

Fr. Sean looked around as several dogs tore loose from their leashes and raced off. "It's starting," he said, turning back to Marty. "You need to get everyone out of here."

A sudden, distant scream came from down the street, causing everyone to fall silent. The crowd looked over and saw a girl racing toward the park. Behind her came a dense wall of fog, rolling past buildings like a tidal wave.

"There's something in the fog!" the girl screamed, just seconds before the fog swept around her. And then she was gone.

On the gazebo, a strange, detached gleam shimmered in Chris's eyes as he watched the girl disappear into the fog. He turned back to the microphone.

"Your past comes for you, Capetown," Chris said to the crowd. "Tonight, the world meets the god of Acheron."

Fr. Sean, Rick, and Marty looked back at the gazebo, in time to see Chris spread his arms wide and stare up at the sky.

"In aeternum regnabit," Chris bellowed into the night, then rose into the air until his feet dangled eight feet above the deck. With a sudden whoosh, his entire body erupted in flames.

Screams and chaos burst from the crowd as people scrambled in every direction, tripping and shoving others out of their way.

On the street, the fog rolled relentlessly toward the park, like a giant, formless creature. Streetlights exploded, windows shattered, and car alarms blared as it swept past.

"Everyone, out!" Rick hollered as he sprang into action. "Get out!"

Rick and Fr. Sean raced off into the frantic crowd, while Marty stood frozen near the concession stand, watching in stunned horror as Chris's charred body fell to the deck.

The fog reached the park, sweeping over the curb and across the lawn. Strings of overhead lights burst in blinding flashes as it rolled past.

As the park and neighboring streets plunged into darkness, Fr. Sean saw that the fog glowed from within with a faint, ghostly light.

"Go! Everybody, get out!" Fr. Sean shouted, picking up his pace as he and Rick raced through the crowd. Everywhere he looked was complete pandemonium as people knocked others over in their frantic dash from the park.

Terrifying, mournful howls split the night, and looking over his shoulder, Fr. Sean saw the dim outlines of wolves stalking through the fog.

"Rick!" he shouted, pulling the pistol from his jacket pocket. "There's wolves."

Rick slowed and looked back at the fog. Then he saw Marty standing by the concession stand where they left him, his body rigid with shock.

"Marty! Get out of there!" Rick shouted, but it was already too late as the fog swept in around him.

"Come on, Rick!" Fr. Sean said, looking at the far side of the park where the fog was drifting toward the squad car. "We need to get to the car."

They sprinted across the park to the car, reaching it just as the fog rolled in around it. Rick dove into the driver's side and opened the passenger door for Fr. Sean. As he started to climb in, a girl's faint, distressed voice called to him from the fog.

"Help me, father," came the frantic plea.

"Someone's out there," Fr. Sean said to Rick through the open door, before racing back into the fog.

Fr. Sean swept the pistol ahead of him as he probed deeper into the fog. It towered around him, keeping his visibility to less than fifteen feet in every direction.

"Where are you?" he hollered into the dense, eerily glowing cloud.

"Over here, father," the voice called.

Fr. Sean crept in that direction, then slowed as he saw the faint outline of the girl approaching him. Alongside her were two bulky shapes.

Wolves.

The girl emerged from the fog, fifteen feet ahead of him, and he felt his blood go cold.

Her clothes were drenched in blood from her torn throat, face, and arms. Black, empty cavities watched him from where her eyes had been. On either side of her, the large black wolves glared at him, their lips curled back in snarls.

"Your God is gone now, father," the dead girl croaked from her torn throat. "The world gets a new god tonight."

Fr. Sean fired three quick shots, their loud cracks echoing above the screams elsewhere in the park. He had no idea whether they hit their targets as he spun and plunged back through the fog to the car.

Rick had the car started by the time Fr. Sean reached it and dove in.

"Where'd you go?" Rick said.

Fr. Sean shook his head, his hands shaking at the memory of the girl. "I'll tell you on the way. Just go."

Rick hit the gas and squealed off.

Chapter Forty-Two
Acheron

After dropping anchor just outside the inlet, Kenzie and her friends pulled the two dinghies alongside the boat. Zac slung on a backpack, then he and Kenzie climbed down into a dinghy. He watched as she pulled a black ski mask over her head, completely covering her face.

"How do I look?" she said.

"Like the IRA."

Beneath her mask, she smiled at this. "Don't mess with the Irish."

"I'll remember that."

He pulled on his ski mask, then they sped off across the choppy waves toward the dark city, looming so ominously on the far end of the inlet.

Trey, Dillon, and Brett hauled the large inner tubes over to the side, then lowered them into the water. They used carabiners to attach the inner tubes to a long rope, which would allow them to be quickly unfastened as they pulled alongside the yachts. Also attached to the inner tubes were short leashes with powerful magnets attached to the ends. They would use these to affix them to the yachts' hulls.

Once the inner tubes were fastened to the rope, and the rope tied to the back of the remaining dinghy, the boys carefully lowered the wooden crates onto the inner tubes and squeezed them into the tubes' openings. The crates were about the size of an ice chest and lined with water-proof plastic. Inside them were pressure cookers, packed with enough ammonium nitrate to blow up a large bus. Wired to each pressure cooker was a walkie talkie set to a specific channel. When keyed from a remote walkie talkie, they would activate the pressure cookers, triggering the explosion. While the explosives might not be powerful enough to blow a hole in the yachts' thick hulls, they could easily take out the propulsion jets, leaving the yachts stranded and unable to follow them. And equally important for their purpose, they would be loud and fiery, echoing across the inlet and city.

As soon as the crates were loaded, Trey and Dillon climbed down into the dinghy, pulled on their black ski masks, then trawled off across the inlet toward the yachts.

Towering black cliffs rose high along the inlet's southern border, their base lathered in foam from crashing waves. Kenzie and Zac's dinghy bounced across the inlet's choppy waters, keeping close enough to the cliffs to avoid being spotted, but far enough away to not get slammed against them.

Through the gusting rain, they stared ahead at the rapidly approaching city. Although too dark to see more than its black outline against the storm clouds, they could already sense its enormity. It stood atop a sea wall, with buildings spanning from one side of the inlet to the other and sloping up hills as they disappeared in the distance.

They saw no lights in the accursed city. It appeared black and dead; a grim mirage that once lured unwary mariners to blasphemies and unspeakable horrors. Horrors that would soon walk again.

"We can dock over there," Kenzie shouted above the storm. She pointed to a long outcrop along the cliff's base, several feet above the water. It appeared to stretch the remaining seventy yards to the seawall.

Zac steered the dinghy over to the outcrop, and as soon as they bumped against it, Kenzie hopped out onto the rocks. She held the leash while Zac climbed out, then together they drug the front half of the rubber dinghy onto the outcrop.

Clinging close to the cliff's face to avoid being swept away, Kenzie and Zac crept along the outcrop toward the seawall. Several feet below them, waves crashed against the rocks, dousing them in sheets of water.

At its end, the outcrop abutted with the seawall. Built of tight-fitting, moss-covered stone blocks, the wall towered twenty feet above Kenzie and Zac in the darkness. A flight of stone stairs, carved into its face, angled up from the water to the top.

Kenzie and Zac took the slick stairs to the top, where they stepped through the opening in a waist-high stone wall onto a long cobblestone promenade. Although the city lay in darkness, the storm's ambient light was enough to see by. And turning to face inland, they beheld Acheron.

The city was everything Kenzie had feared to imagine. Void of any semblance of beauty or warmth, Acheron was vile and baleful, brooding beneath a dark, unseen pall of horror and despair. Its very soul was as black as the stones that made up its masonry. Along narrow cobblestone streets, sloping steeply up hills in the distance, stood houses and shops, whose vacant windows stared watchfully into the night. Thin layers of mist trailed its deserted streets and allies, where wooden carts and wagons sat idly. As they had done for centuries.

Atop hills in the city's center stood massive temples and structures to ancient, horrific gods, their dark outlines and spires scraping the sky like talons and skeletal fingers.

Acheron was what became of a city abandoned by God.

Other than the distant crash of thunder, and heavy patter of rain across the cobblestone streets, there were no sounds or movement. Acheron appeared as dead and barren as the cold stones that formed it. But the fleet of yachts in the harbor told a different story. Calvin and the others were here somewhere.

"Next time we hang out, let's do something that doesn't include demon-haunted cities," Zac said, nervously wiping his hands on his pants. Like Kenzie, he used humor as a tension release when he was scared out of his mind.

"We should do a Universal monster movie marathon when we get back. It's been a while."

He nodded. "Who's turn is it to buy the pizza?"

"I think it's mine."

"I think it is, too."

She took his hand and gave it a nervous squeeze. "Thanks for doing this with me, Zac. This would really suck without you here."

"You need me to be dinner?"

She shook her head. "To be my friend."

He squeezed her hand back. "So, how do we find these people?"

She squinted back the rain as she continued watching something in the distance. "Did you bring the binoculars?"

"Right here," he said, fishing the binoculars from his backpack and handing them to her. She focused them on a dark temple, seated high atop a hill in the city's center. Faint candlelight flickered in its stained-glass windows.

"Check out that temple," she said, handing him the binoculars. "I think that's where they're at."

Zac studied the temple for a moment through the binoculars, then nodded in agreement. "I think you're right. It's the only light in the whole city."

"We should probably check it out," she said, feeling like doing anything but that.

He gave a nervous nod. "Or we could go back to the boat and get the hell out of here."

"What would Mulder do?"

He took a breath. "He'd argue with Scully, then check out the demon-haunted temple."

She gave his hand another squeeze. "Let's do this fast and get it over with."

"Okay. But if I get killed, I'm haunting you, Walsh."

"We'll haunt each other."

They bunched their raincoats around themselves, then hurried off down the street, taking care not to slip on the slick stones.

Keeping close to the buildings along the side, they ascended the winding streets towards the city's center. The streets wove past dark buildings and what had once been marketplaces, rising ever higher in the storm.

Several times, they were forced to backtrack and veer down dark allies as they lost sight of the steeple over the rooftops.

And the entire time, ever since climbing the seawall, they felt the baleful presence of unseen eyes watching them.

They finally rounded a corner and came out onto a street running past the front of the temple. And their blood ran cold. Of roughly Gothic structure, it towered high into black storm clouds, brooding with contempt for all around it. It sat atop an elevation, six feet above street level, with a series of cracked, stone steps leading to a gate in the wrought-iron fence surrounding its yard. Along its sides rose stone buttresses, angling up to the windows through which candlelight flickered.

"There. We saw it. Can we go now?" Zac whispered.

Kenzie squeezed his arm as they ducked behind a cart across the street from the temple. "Do you really want to?"

"Yes. And no."

"You can wait here, if you want. I'm gonna find a way to look inside."

"How are you gonna do that?"

Kenzie scanned the property. Going in through the open front gate would be too risky, but maybe there was an opening in the fence. Then she spotted one on the far left side, where several rusted bars had fallen away.

"Over there," she said, nodding to the opening. Then she looked over at the temple. "I think I can use one of those buttresses to climb up to the window. I'll be right back."

Zac shook his head. "I'll come."

"You sure?"

He gave a slow nod.

"Thank you."

They dashed across the street to the fence, then squeezed through the opening onto the temple's grounds. Keeping low, they crept over to a buttress along the temple's wall and climbed it till they reached a window.

Kenzie pressed her mask-clad face to the stained-glass window, cupping her hands around her eyes to shield them from the rain. It looked down on the temple's main sanctuary, and what she saw caused her breath to freeze.

At least a hundred people, all dressed in black hooded robes, filled the sanctuary.

"Oh, shit," Kenzie muttered, wiping the rain from her eyes.

"What?" Zac said, seeing the horrified look in her eyes. He squeezed in beside her to look through the window, and his expression fell flat.

"We are so screwed," he muttered, sinking back down on the buttress.

She nodded in agreement. "I didn't think there'd be so many of them."

"So, what now?"

"I don't know," she said, shaking her head as she sank back against the buttress. Their entire plan was based on distracting Calvin, and maybe a dozen people, long enough for them to sneak in and steal the chalice. But with that many people inside, the possibility of sneaking past them undetected was gone. For a long moment, she just stared into the storm, her hand picking idly at the stone buttress.

Then a small chunk broke off, about the size of a golf ball. She looked at it, then picked at the area around it. More chunks crumbled off. She looked over at the other two buttresses and remembered seeing three along each side of the temple. And an idea began to form.

She looked up the temple wall to the top, towering high above them, then along the wall.

"What if we blew it up?" she said.

Zac shot her a look like she was crazy. "We don't have enough explosives."

"I don't think it would take that many. See this?" She broke off another small chunk the size of a marble and showed it to him. "I think one explosive could take out each buttress, and we put the other six in the basement near the walls. We set the charges outside to go off first, and that leaves the walls without support. Then the ones in the basement finish it."

Zac thought about it for a moment. He broke off a small chunk from the buttress and ran his fingers across its gritty surface. "This stuff's really old."

"The bricks in the walls are too."

Zac looked along the walls, then up at the top. "So, we bring this whole thing down on them?"

Kenzie nodded. She had already considered the moral implications of this. "They'll kill us in a second, if they get the chance. Calvin already had his dogs kill Emma's driver, and he tried to kill her."

"It's like that question about whether you would kill Hitler as a kid to keep the Holocaust from happening."

She nodded. "That's what we're doing. If we don't stop those people in there, the whole world's screwed."

Zac gave a slow nod. "I think we need to do this."

"I do too. I'll call Trey and Dillon and have them bring the explosives."

Chapter Forty-Three
Prophets

Rick's squad car sped down the dark street, past houses and shops, finally skidding to a stop at the small hospital on the town's northern edge. An ambulance idled out front, with several technicians loading patients in back. Beyond them, the hospital loomed dark, as did every house, street, and business in town.

Rick grabbed his flashlight from the glove compartment, then he and Fr. Sean climbed out and walked over to a technician.

"Where are you taking them?" said Rick.

"Arkham General. We lost power here about an hour ago, and the generator's not working."

"Is this everyone?"

"Drew's still inside. We'll need to take him in one of our cars."

"Don't worry about Drew. I got him. You need to get everyone out here, fast."

"Do you know what's going on?"

Rick wasn't sure what to say, but there was no time to mince words. "Do you read the Acheron Files newsletter?"

"All the time."

"It's one of those things. And it's bad. Get everyone over to Arkham General and don't go near the fog."

Rick clicked on his flashlight, then he and Fr. Sean headed inside the dark lobby, passing a nurse on her way out.

"What room's Drew in?" Rick asked.

"Eight. I was about to pull my car around to pick him up."

"I got Drew. You and everyone else needs to get out of here. And keep away from the fog, if you see it."

She saw from his expression that this was serious. "Okay," she said, and hurried off.

Rick swept his flashlight ahead of them as they hurried down the hallway to room eight. From outside came the sounds of engines starting and cars driving off.

They entered the dark room, lit only by faint moonlight from a window on the far wall. Drew watched them from the bed, his head bandaged, and right arm and leg in casts.

"Rick?" Drew said groggily, sitting up in bed.

"Hey, buddy," Rick said as he and Fr. Sean hurried over. "We need to get you out of here."

"What's going on?"

"I'll tell you about it in the car. But we need to hurry."

"What's in the IV?" Fr. Sean said, looking at the tube running from Drew's arm to a bag hung from a metal stand.

"Just pain meds."

"You gonna be okay if we unhook you?"

"Go for it. So, where are we going?"

"Rose's," said Rick. "We need to get her and Kenzie's dog and get the hell out of town."

"Where's Kenzie?"

"That's another long story I'll tell you in the car. But the short version is, she's been right about these things all along, and I've been an idiot."

"This should be good," Drew said.

"It is," said Fr. Sean as he removed the IV needle from Drew's forearm. He and Rick draped Drew's arms over their shoulders and helped him to his feet. He wobbled for balance for a moment on his leg cast, then they helped him over to the hallway door and opened it.

A faint, eerie glow lit the hallway like a night light. Looking toward the lobby in the glow's direction, they saw the fog filling the hallway from floor to ceiling as it flowed their way.

And deep within it were the faint outlines of wolves, their eyes reflecting red from the fog's glow.

"Go! Get back in the room," Rick said, hurrying everyone back into the room and slamming the door shut.

"Were those wolves?" Drew said.

Rick nodded. "They're all over town. We need to find another way out."

"I'll check the window," Fr. Sean said. He slid out from beneath Drew's arm and raced over to it. Looking out, he saw no sign of the fog, and only a short drop to the ground below.

"We're clear over here," he said, turning back to Drew and Rick. "It's a short drop, but I think Drew can manage."

"Beats getting eaten," said Drew.

Fr. Sean grabbed a nearby chair and swung it against the window, shattering it into dozens of glass shards. He knocked away the few remaining pieces from the base, then helped Rick lug Drew over to it.

"I'll go first," said Fr. Sean, "and help him down from outside."

Fr. Sean climbed out and dropped onto the lawn, then looked up at the window.

"Your turn, Drew," he called up. "Come out legs first."

Rick helped Drew bring his cast leg up and over the windowsill and then the other, slowly sliding him through.

A sudden, heavy crash came against the door on the far side of the room, followed by furious scratching and growls.

"Gotta move faster, buddy," Rick said, "that door's not gonna hold."

Drew did, sliding the rest of the way through. Fr. Sean caught his legs outside and helped him down. "Your turn, Rick," Fr. Sean called up.

More heavy crashes came at the door, as Rick scrambled through the window and dropped to the ground. They draped Drew's arms over their shoulders, then hurried down the side of the building and around the corner.

Up ahead, near the entrance, the squad car sat nearly encased in fog.

"Take Drew," Rick said, sliding out from beneath Drew's arm and drawing his pistol. "I'll cover us."

They scrambled as quickly as they could toward the car as the fog folded in around them, cutting their visibility to only a dozen feet in every direction.

From the hospital's entrance came howls and snarls as the wolves barreled out the door after them. Rick fired several shots blindly into the fog, but the growls and howls now came from all around them. They caught only faint, fleeting glimpses of the dark, hulking outlines as the wolves circled and closed in. Rick fired two more shots, but it was like shooting smoke, the wolves fading into the fog as quickly as they appeared.

As they neared the car, Drew's cast snagged on a rock, and he and Fr. Sean tumbled forward onto the ground. Rick backed over to them and knelt down to help Fr. Sean pick him up. When he looked up, the wolves had them completely encircled. Over a dozen gray, hulking shadows stalked towards them from every direction.

Then something subtle shifted in the surrounding air, like a warm rush of wind. The wolves stopped in their tracks, sniffed the air as they looked anxiously around, then slowly retreated.

As Rick, Fr. Sean, and Drew watched in stunned silence, the fog receded ever so slightly, and two men emerged. They had the worn, leathered look of hermits from many years in the sun; long, unkempt beards of coarse, gray hair; and the weathered habits of monks. The men approached them, then one reached his hand down to Drew. Drew shied back slightly.

"I mean you no harm, Drew," the monk said in a calm, gentle voice. "Please, take my hand."

Drew did, and as the monk and Fr. Sean helped him to his feet, he felt a subtle warmth spread through his limbs. He swayed for a moment on his cast leg, feeling the pain drain from his leg, arm, and head until it was gone.

"What's wrong?" said Rick, seeing the perplexed expression on Drew's face.

"I'm not sure," Drew said, "but the pain's gone."

"God has healed you of your injuries this night," said the monk. "You will have no further need of your casts."

As far as Drew could tell, the monk was right. He shifted his leg and arm to test them, and felt none of the sheering pain he felt just moments ago. He exchanged looks with Rick and Fr. Sean.

"I think he's right," Drew said.

"Who are you?" Rick said, eying them suspiciously.

"We are mere messengers, sheriff," said the second monk, "who were sent to bear witness to the end."

"The end of what?"

"Of all," said the monk, who then turned to look at Fr. Sean. "You, father, I see in your eyes that you already know much of the truth."

"You saved Emma and Maya from the wolves on the shore," said Fr. Sean.

The monks nodded. "As we have done for you this night," said the second monk.

"You also saved Kenzie," said Fr. Sean.

"We did indeed, father," said the first monk, who helped Drew to his feet. "Our regret is that we couldn't also save her brother."

"The girl and her friends are quite brave," said the second monk, "and I wish it were so that we could do more to help them, but our role is limited. We are here only to call to those who would listen."

"Are they still alive?" said Fr. Sean.

"For now, they are. But the dangers they face are grave, for the demon would not allow its plans of dominion to be easily thwarted."

"There has been much death tonight," said the second monk, watching the fog slowly recede down the street. "Go now to Rose, and there you will be safe until morning."

Chapter Forty-Four
When Gods Walk the Earth

Kenzie and Zac sloshed through the rain back to the seawall, where they met Trey and Dillon and helped them lug the crates up the steps to the promenade on top. They loaded the crates into the back of a cart they found along the street and hauled it back through the drenched streets to the temple.

"Holy shit," Trey whispered, catching his first sight of the dark temple brooding high in the night. "Could they pick something less creepy?"

They hauled the crates up the street and squeezed them through the fence's opening onto the temple's grounds. They carried them over to the temple and slid them up against the buttresses, placing three on each side. Dillon switched the channels on the walkie talkies to channel six.

"We'll use channel six for the walkie talkies out here," Dillon said, replacing the lids on the crates, "and channel seven for the ones in the basement. We'll keep channel eight open for communications."

"Copy that," Kenzie said. "So, I call you on channel seven when you're in the basement."

"Only if you want us to haunt you."

The boys walked over to a basement window along the wall, positioned about a foot above ground level. Trey kicked it, shattering the glass into dozens of mean shards, then crawled through. Holding tightly to the frame, he probed with his foot in the darkness until it hit something firm on his left, then lowered himself onto what turned out to be a desk. He hopped from it onto the floor, then scooted the desk over to center it beneath the window. He climbed back onto the desk, and one-by-one, Zac and Dillon slid him the crates which he set on the floor. Zac and Dillon then climbed through and joined Trey in the basement.

The room stank of rot and death, and things buried in the ground for centuries. Turning on their cell phone flashlights, they found the basement cluttered with furniture, statues, and aged paintings. The ceiling towered twelve feet above them, supported by thick wooden crossbeams, blackened in mold and mildew. Along each wall were three columns of stone masonry, which seemed to be placed at intervals opposite the buttresses.

Outside the temple, Kenzie climbed the buttress back up to the window and peered in. Calvin stood in front of the altar now, with the three Stanzos partners along his right. To his left stood a woman in a red dress who Kenzie didn't recall seeing her earlier; and being the only one in the room not wearing a black hooded robe, she was hard to miss.

Something was happening. The followers, who Kenzie came to think of as acolytes, had formed a line down the main aisle to the altar. One by one, they stepped up to Calvin, who held the chalice out to them. Using a knife, they sliced their palm and let the blood drip into the chalice. When they finished, they returned to their pew while the next acolyte repeated the action until they were all seated again.

Calvin returned to his spot behind the altar and set the chalice down. From somewhere in the sanctuary's rear, came a terrified scream. Kenzie tensed as four acolytes dragged a naked woman over to the altar and laid her across it. Each acolyte held a limb as the woman twisted and squirmed to break free, but to no avail. Calvin raised the knife above the woman, and Kenzie's heart nearly froze.

Kenzie snatched up the walkie talkie, and tuning it to channel eight, shrieked, "Guys! They're killing someone."

Silence came from the other end, as Kenzie slid the pistol from her waistband and aimed it through the window. At this distance, and with her hands shaking like crazy, there was no chance of making the shot.

"Kenzie?" Zac's voice crackled from the other end. "Repeat."

Kenzie's heart and stomach sank as she slowly lowered the pistol and picked up the walkie talkie. "They're going to kill a girl, Zac, and there's nothing I can do."

"Then look away."

But she couldn't. She watched in helpless horror as Calvin sliced the knife across the girl's throat. Within a few seconds, the girl's thrashing stopped.

Bile filled Kenzie's throat as she tore her eyes away from the horror happening in the sanctuary and stared numbly at the ground.

"Kenzie?" Zac's voice crackled again from the speaker. "What's happening?"

Kenzie's hand trembled and her teeth clenched as she picked up the walkie talkie. "Blow this place to the ground, Zac."

"We're almost finished."

"Just hurry."

She turned back to the window. Calvin and the four acolytes had the dead girl's body turned on its side on the altar, letting her blood drain into the chalice. When they finished, they laid her on the floor and Calvin raised the chalice in an unholy benediction. The entire congregation knelt, as Calvin said something Kenzie couldn't hear above the storm. Then he lowered the chalice and drank from it.

Kenzie's stomach lurched. She lifted the bottom of her ski mask just as bile heaved across the buttress. She wiped her mouth with her sleeve, then pulled the mask back down and picked up the walkie talkie.

"He did it, Zac. Calvin just drank from the chalice."

After a brief pause, Zac's voice crackled back, "We're on our way out."

Kenzie peered back through the window, and saw a new line formed down the aisle, with each acolyte taking their turn drinking from the chalice.

"Kenzie," came Zac's hushed voice from the ground below her.

She looked down and saw the boys standing beside the basement window. She scooted down the buttress and joined them.

"This better work," she said, "because they're all drinking from it."

"Let's go," said Trey.

They raced from the temple's grounds and across the street, ducking behind the cart they hauled the explosives in. Dillon switched the walkie talkie channel to six — the channel for the outside explosives — then turned to Kenzie.

"You wanna do this?" he said.

"Yeah."

He handed it to her. "Send them to hell, Kenz."

And she did. She pressed the 'talk' button, and twenty seconds later, the crates alongside the buttresses exploded in fiery concussions. The bottom third of them blew out in massive stone chunks, while the upper parts crumbled and fell, leaving the walls to sway drunkenly.

"Now use channel seven for the basement ones," Dillon said.

Kenzie quickly switched the channel, then pressed the 'talk' button again. Moments later, massive concussions swept through the basement, blowing out large chunks of the walls.

The temple teetered for a few seconds, then its towering walls crashed down in a thunderous wave. Dirt, stones, and debris filled the air in dense clouds before the rain washed them to the ground.

Then, an ear-shattering bellow tore through the night, like the roar of hundreds of jet engines. The ground shook and up-heaved in giant slabs. Fissures split the streets, crumbling down into bottomless depths.

From the temple's ruins, Kenzie watched a great column of thick black smoke rise miles into the sky. It writhed and twisted furiously, like an enormous tornado. Or a serpent.

As it rose ever higher, the clouds parted ahead of it, revealing a crimson blood moon against the black sky.

Kenzie held frozen, watching the towering, dark column coil and sway in the ghastly moonlight; and growing more certain by the minute that it wasn't smoke. At least a hundred yards wide, it moved with purpose, defying the storm. Then its top half arched down from the sky, and within it burned fires like a serpent's eyes. Massive, bat-like wings of black smoke unfurled from its sides as it surveyed the city. Its domain.

Acheron's god had come.

Kenzie could barely breathe. "We need to get out of here," she squeaked out, "but do it slowly."

"What is it?" Trey whispered.

Kenzie watched as he and the others looked nervously around, and realized none of them could see it. "It's Acheron's demon," she whispered. "And it's huge."

"Where?"

"Above the temple."

Kenzie crept over to a nearby alley and ducked down it, while the others followed. She stopped just inside the corner and looked back at the street. The demon's focus was on the far side of the city, sweeping its great neck from left to right, but not on them.

"Did it see us?" Zac whispered.

Kenzie shook her head. "Not yet."

With a thunderous flap of its massive wings, rattling buildings and carts, the demon swept off into the sky and disappeared into the storm.

"What the hell was that?" said Dillon.

"That was the demon," said Kenzie.

"Is it gone?"

"I don't know. Maybe," Kenzie said, then paused. Something was happening at the temple.

As they watched, a mist settled over the temple like a cloud; and through its milky haze, they watched the temple's massive walls form and rebuild in a blurred mirage of rising stone blocks and grouping debris. Angles met neatly in corners, buttresses assembled in great arches, and holes filled, until the temple once again stood as it did before the explosions.

Up and down the streets, gas lamps glowed on in eerie yellow orbs and fissures mended and sealed. Acheron was awaking.

"Oh, shit," Trey muttered. "I think this place is waking up."

"I think so, too," said Dillon.

"Wait. Quiet," Zac said, nervously looking around. "You guys hear that?"

The others quieted and listened. Over the rain's patter on the cobblestones rose a new sound that sent chills through them. It was moaning.

"We need to get out of here," said Kenzie.

They hurried down the alley to the far end where it met with a street, then crept to the corner and peeked around it.

All along that street and the adjoining streets, doors opened and Acheron's gruesome inhabitants poured out. They were loathsome, ghoulish abominations, made even more terrifying in the gas lamps' sickly glow. Moldy, mildewed clothes hung from diseased, translucent skin, shriveled and bloated from centuries beneath the ground, but never dying.

"There's no way we're gonna get past them," Dillon whispered. "There's too many of them."

"Maybe we can," said Zac, watching the inhabitants shamble about as if awaking from a dream. "But we need to do it now, before they figure it out."

With that, they took off in a sprint down the street, racing past the inhabitants who shambled and clawed after them. Reaching a corner, they rounded it and found more inhabitants shambling into the street.

"Cut across the park," Trey shouted, and they veered across the street to a park.

As they raced across it, dodging past long decayed trees whose branches twisted and reformed with ghastly semblances of life, more ghouls poured in from surrounding streets, coming faster now as their musculature returned.

"Watch the ground," said Dillon, taking a quick glance down at the hundreds of serpents slithering after them.

They raced from the park and across a bordering street to the corner. As they rounded it, the promenade and seaport came into view at the far end.

"We're almost there," Kenzie shouted as they sprinted down the slick cobblestones.

"Go faster!" Zac shouted. "They're running."

Kenzie stole a quick glance back and saw the horde of inhabitants swarming from the park and across the street after them.

They reached the seaport and raced across its cobblestones to the seawall. Beyond it, the ocean churned like a boiling pot.

"What the hell?" Trey said, stopping to watch the ocean.

"Don't stop!" Kenzie shouted. "They're coming."

They squeezed through the opening in the wall and took the steps down two at a time to the bottom, where Trey's dinghy was tied to a rock. Trey untied it and shoved it away from the rocks, then they all splashed through the water and clambered aboard.

Trey tugged on the engine's cord. It sputtered briefly, then died.

"Shit. Shit, shit, shit." He tugged on it again and again until it finally sputtered to life.

Kenzie looked back at the seawall as the dinghy splashed across the churning waters. The inhabitants had stopped at the top of the seawall, forming a line along it, but none of them came down the steps after them.

"Brett, we're on our way," Dillon hollered into his walkie talkie over the ruckus. "Get the engine started and be ready to leave when we get there."

"What's going on?" crackled Brett's voice after a few seconds.

"We stirred up hell."

Kenzie continued watching the wall as they sped across the inlet, and something was happening. Although too distant to be sure, the line of inhabitants looked like it was parting in the middle.

"Zac, can I see the binoculars?" she said.

He handed them to her, and she zoomed in on the top of the wall. Even magnified, it was still hard to be sure at this distance, but it looked like new people now stood amongst the horde of inhabitants, distinguished by their dark ceremonial robes. But Kenzie knew; she felt it in the tightening knot in her stomach.

Somehow, Calvin and the others survived the temple's collapse.

"Trey, can we go any faster?" Kenzie said, the breath catching in her lungs.

"I'm trying," Trey said, cranking the throttle on the already taxed engine. "Why? What is it?"

"I think I see them. Here, take a look." She handed the binoculars to Zac.

He trained the binoculars on the seawall and watched it for a moment. "I think she's right."

"So, you mean it's not over?" said Dillon.

Kenzie shook her head. "I think it's just starting."

The Author

Thank you so much for reading my book, and I hope you enjoyed it! If you're in the mood for more horror reading, please flip to the next pages for info on my other books.

If you liked the book and have a moment, please consider posting a review on Amazon at this link. They're a huge help to us authors.

Click here if you would like to receive free advance copies of new books for review, including the sequel to The Covenant I'm working on right now. I'll also be sending out free stories featuring Kenzie and her gang.

I have a more creative bio on my website at this link, but in thirty words or less, I'm an entertainment attorney, former Marine, and writer who scares the hell out of himself by writing scary books at night.

Thanks again!
Tom Lewis

THE NECROMANCER

"If this book doesn't scare you, I'm not sure anything can."

As a wave of grisly, ritualistic killings sweeps across Los Angeles, the only lead is a mysterious girl caught at one of the crime scenes. A girl with a terrifying secret — the power to raise the dead. A #1 best-seller in Amazon's 'Horror Fiction,' it's available on Amazon at this link.

HELL

The Possession and Exorcism of Cassie Stevens

"I never thought any book would come close to 'The Exorcist,' but this book surpassed it."

The survivor of a near-death experience is haunted by a shadowy figure she sees from the corner of her eye — something that followed her back from the other side of death. Read the story of the Exorcism Fr. Sean performed, a #1 bestseller in Amazon's 'Horror Fiction.' It's available on Amazon at this link.

AFTERMATH

In the wake of an alien invasion, a group of teens struggles for survival in the hostile ruins of Los Angeles. It's available on Amazon at this link.

Printed in Great Britain
by Amazon